Jad Adams

CAFE EUROPA

MELES MELES MARKS BOOKS

For Julie

Published by Independent Publishing Network for Meles Meles Marks

All rights reserved. No part of this book may be reproduced in any form or by any electronic or mechanical means, including information storage and retrieval systems, without permission except where legally permitted for reviewing and academic use. This is a work of fiction, any relation to actual people or events is entirely coincidental.

www.jadadams.co.uk

Copyright @ Jad Adams 2023

The moral right of the author is asserted.

Printed in England by Mixam UK, Watford

ISBN 978-1-80068-966-4

'Até, that hurts all, perfects all: her feet are soft, and move
Not on the earth; they bear her still aloft men's heads, and there
She hurtful harms them.'
Homer *The Iliad* (trans. Chapman)

Chapter 1

The three did not see the morning sky of Greece until the tiny plane shuddered, spluttered and took off over the hill of the Acropolis and on to the sea. In less than an hour they had crossed the grey-green water flecked with foam, dotted with tiny yachts and larger ferries. The island of Doxos came into view as the sun rose over the rocky green and brown mass, 'It's just how I thought it would be,' said Sarah excitedly, 'if I had ever thought of it at all.'

Anne craned round Sarah's head at the window to see, 'It's such a picture,' she said of the foam-fringed island, 'it's so perfect.' She clutched Anton's hand, 'See how blue that water is? Can we go to the little bay where there is that blue water?'

'Will there be swimming, and fires on the beach and Greek weddings and…lashings of retsina?' asked Sarah.

'There will be all those things,' said Anton, as usual failing to catch the jocular tone.

'I love it that we're going there, but I still haven't got much idea what we do when we get there,' said Sarah. Sarah was popular, rounded and friendly, she was twenty but still referred to herself as a girl.

It was May 2015. Sarah and Anne had been recruited for this adventure only a few weeks earlier on the green meadowland of the university campus, in front of the library where they were drinking wine out of plastic cups. Anton had approached them and asked if they wanted to come to a Greek island in the summer holidays. Afterwards they talked of going to Anton's island as if it were in his very ownership, a paradise in the Aegean for which he had the deeds in his pocket. Sarah had spent a good deal of time in Anton's company, but did not consider she knew him. Anton was dark haired, medium height, slight, quick-witted but sometimes so slow to grasp the most obvious things, that you wondered if he was really listening. Sarah's boyfriend Sven was always with Anton, he would be joining them on the island. Sarah smiled inwardly at the thought of spending so much time in the sunshine with sexy Sven, nothing could be better for their relationship.

Now on a juddering twenty-seater plane on the last leg of the journey Anton spoke with his usual precision, 'What we are going to do, first of all is get the place fixed up, my sister's got the builders in. Then waiting on tables, and...just doing all the things you need to do to keep a restaurant going.'

'Before Thursday I didn't even know you *had* a sister,' said Anne, Sarah judged she was a little irritated that she had not been the first to learn about this trip. Anne was Anton's girlfriend: inquisitive, pointy in features and skinny but perennially fretting about her weight and the security of her relationships.

'Hester, she's just come out of a divorce,' Anton said, 'she's bought this house and a restaurant on Doxos but needs help. We are answering the call.'

They made a steep descent over a large area of what seemed to be abandoned building works, down to a crude landing strip. As the three students walked down the steps, Sarah felt the slight pressure on her skin of the heat, smelling the scent of wild kuri plants, seeing the Greek flag flapping limply against the blue sky. When the plane's engines finally died she could hear the tinkling of goat bells, a hollow, tinny sound from the hills behind.

Outside the ramshackle building that served as a terminal, Hester stood waiting. Her lean figure showed no spare flesh, she was as tall as Sarah who was usually the tallest girl in a group. Anton had said she was over 30 but she had definitely worn well, Sarah thought. Hester had grey-blue eyes, a little crinkly round the edges but a friendly face, with light brown hair which was frizzy and unstyled. Olive skinned, she wore the minimum of makeup, just eyeliner. She embraced Anton warmly, Sarah felt she noticed some reserve on his part, maybe a lack of genuine affection in the hug. They gathered the luggage and piled it into Hester's battered black jeep.

'We will go for breakfast in the harbour, Agios Nicholas,' said Hester.

'Sounds good,' said Anne. Sarah could see Anne wanted to say something to establish her presence, presumably because she was closest to Anton and wanted to be liked by his family, 'in Athens we were told we had to wait on the runway for morning because there weren't any lights in Doxos airport.' She was amused by the quaintness of the experience.

'That,' Hester indicated a site with trucks and construction machines standing idle and a large signboard with the blue European Union flag on it, 'is our new airport, or was going to be our new airport. Our mayor was supposed to develop tourism by bringing in package tours. He got elected on the basis of all the business he could attract for hotels and restaurants. He got European Union money for it but, you know, money comes, money goes.'

Soon they were passing gnarled olive groves and flowering shrubs, prickly bushes and solitary, dusty trees springing from the parched earth. 'Not many trees' said Anton.

Anne, sitting in the back said, 'Ooops trouble in paradise – this sun's too hot on my head, I need a hat.'

'You wimps get out of England and you complain, look at my Italian skin, said Sarah.

'You're not Italian,' said Anne.

'Not totally, my skin is, my mum's Italian. So *va al' diavalo,*' she said merrily, and Sarah undid her buttons and pulled her blouse down as far as decency would allow, to have the blazing sun warm her chest.

They pulled round the bay and parked in the harbour among a tangle of cars, scooters, motor-bikes and taxis. They sat on plastic chairs at a café on the harbour front; water slapped against the quay walls where little fishing boats were moored and fishermen were selling the remains of the morning's catch from wooden boxes. They took in the smells of salt water, fresh fish and grilled meat where the café was firing up the spit. Hester went off looking for a menu as the three students watched men on motor scooters collecting vegetables; the baker's green three-wheeler piled with loaves and the fishermen sitting on the ground mending their yellow nets, using their bare feet to hold and stretch the fabric. Tourists in bikini tops were looking over the clothes outside the trinket shops; further down were the chairs and canvas umbrellas of a pizza bar and an ice cream parlour.

As they watched, two boys walked past and embraced each other naturally, both Anne and Sarah saw them and grinned to each other, at how incongruous such a scene would have been in their own country.

'They are so warm,' Sarah, said to Anne, 'Everyone is so friendly. Why can't everyone be so welcoming, why can't the whole of Europe be like this?'

'The isle is full of noises, sounds and sweet airs, that give delight, and hurt not,' said Anne, not without a little labour.

'The Tempest, yeah?' said Anton.

'Hey, why can't you just be good at your own subject, why do you have to be good at mine too?'

'You're so lucky to live here,' said Sarah to Hester who had returned, having located a lethargic waiter who took their order.

'There was some hard work,' Hester replied, 'the luck is what I'll need to make it succeed.'

Sarah was watching the boats bobbing about in the harbour, making wavelets of flotsam collect along the sea line, 'What's the eye for, the one drawn on the boat?' She pointed to a blue eye painted prominently on the prow of a boat, a black dot with a blue circle surrounding it, with a white circle around that.

It's apotropaic,' said Anton, 'To ward off the evil eye. It sends the evil gaze back to its begetter.

'What's Plan B? How do you ward off evil if you haven't got a talisman?' said Sarah

'Perhaps by doing a bit of good,' Anne mused.

After breakfast they piled back in the jeep and started off, past the shops with their wares displayed out front and the little whitewashed lanes running up the steep hill. They encountered what passed for an island traffic jam in the narrow street outside the police station and the group gazed at the sweet shop opposite with its squares of chocolate in silver foil; pyramids in lilac; discs in gold; pastry cones filled with cream; multi-layered gateaux and piles of little white pillows dusted with sugar.

Out of the town with the wind pulling at their hair, they swiftly left the built-up part of the island and buildings became more sparse or even abandoned and decayed along the coast road, with nothing but bushes scattered along the rocky lands and occasionally a lone donkey in a field.

They passed shallow bays scooped out of the main one, each with their own feature – a red and white church, a scuba diving club, then the gracefully curving bay of the small resort of Zeste with tourist supermarkets with lurid plastic beach items outside and a rack of foreign newspapers. The route took them on a wide sweep around the bay, opposite the harbour town of Agios Nicholas. They now saw it as a white cluster of square buildings topped by the grand Crusader castle. They were startled by the beauty of it, looking over the sparkling water to see the mountain encrusted with white and ochre houses and the domes and towers of churches, surmounted by the thick castle walls.

Past Zeste they drove down a little ribbon of tarmac with the beach and the sea on their right. There was one restaurant on the left, then more rocky road and finally Hester's restaurant stood directly in front of the sea, divided from the beach by the road that had by now narrowed to a dirt track. A patch of land beside it served as a car park. Fifty metres up, a track behind the restaurant led to a green and yellow house in traditional style, with a vine veranda outside the front door.

'*To spiti mas*' said Hester, 'our house. Or *to spiti sas*, really – your house, because I live above the restaurant.'

'It's wonderful,' said Sarah, 'it's paradise,

however did you manage to get it?

'I bought it before the Italians came and started buying everything up and raising the prices.' Hester said, 'the last owner renovated the restaurant. That and my flat weren't bad when I moved in and it doesn't need a lot now. It's the cottage where you'll live that I've been trying to get sorted out.'

They walked up the incline to the old house, feeling the prickly heat for the first time as they carried their luggage up the steep track. Hester kept talking nervously, 'I've done some basic sweeping and cleaning, but I was waiting for the plumber to finish before we got down to other stuff. The builder needs to fix the holes in the walls outside.'

From the bottom of the incline the house looked perfect, picturesque, a traditional one-storey structure with four shuttered windows on top with a balcony, two windows and a door at the bottom. 'It really is a Wendy House,' said Sarah as they staggered up the hill, becoming increasingly anxious as to exactly how broken down it was.

The old family house had roasted in the sun for a hundred years with scarcely a job of maintenance until it was way past necessary. Paint had scorched off the woodwork leaving it bare and open to the winter rains that had warped and distorted it. Close up, outside they could see the holes in the walls and shutters off their hinges with broken panes in the windows.

The house itself was sound, it was built to withstand earthquakes and had stone walls a yard thick. Cedar beams held up a roof lined with rushes and seaweed in traditional fashion. There was a large downstairs room and an enclosed courtyard in Middle Eastern style with a little spare bedroom off it.

Upstairs was a huge room divided into two bedrooms, both leading on to the balcony. In front of the house on a large forecourt, vines gave shade from the sun.

Inside, the floors had been swept, the double beds were new, the bed linen was fresh, but there was no mistaking the musty smell of mothballs. Vile patterned stuff covering the floors, the bulges in the walls indicated further degradation beneath layers of paint. Not a single door or shutter fitted properly, most held together with a nail banged in and bent over to form a makeshift fixing. Salt sea air had ravaged the building through the broken windows, the plaster inside was crumbling as if the walls were made of biscuit. Some holes, presumably filled when rags were not to hand, were stuffed with newspaper.

'What needs doing is...everything,' said Hester as they stood in the low-beamed bathroom, 'I planned to have it all done, it should have been finished weeks ago, and now it's a mess. I've expected the local workmen to have finished by now but they've just let me down time and again.'

Of all the disappointments the Wendy House presented on that first day, the worst was the bathroom. When the old house was inhabited by a fishing family, the toilet was situated in an alcove off the kitchen. That kitchen was now bare, stripped of cooking implements and gas stove, ready to be converted into a bathroom. A single cold tap sticking out of the wall over a soapstone sink was a reminder of the room's previous use. The stained toilet had water but no flush mechanism so it had to be sluiced after use with a bowl of water that rarely did the job fully, and waste came merrily bobbing back after each libation.

'Hmm, olde worlde,' said Sarah.

'Of course, you can shower at my place above the restaurant until we get one here,' said Hester, 'I know that's far from ideal....'

They stood on the balcony looking out, impressed by the spectacle of the castle and the town, the sunlight flashing on the sea and the passing yachts. The students were all a little travel weary, and swept with conflicting feelings, the beauty of the environment contrasting with the awfulness of their living conditions.

They sympathised with Hester as she detailed her battles to get Greek builders on site. She complained about the plumbers' lies, the plumbers' dissimulations, the plumbers' other jobs, the wholesale domestic disaster that is Greek plumbing. They tried to be positive but all were thinking they could not live like this for the whole summer. This was bad. They looked disconsolately at the broken windows, the peeling paint, they thought about the days they would spend here, the lack of showers, the truly awful toilet.

'Where do you start with all this?' said Anton, he pulled at the splintering, rotten door-step that gave a sigh and breathed out a scent of must as it flaked away. There was a grim silence.

'We divide up the jobs,' said Anne quietly. 'Don't look at it as one big problem, but lots of little ones.' They turned to her, she was not usually the most forthright speaker. 'The plumbing's really important, and an amateur can't do it,' she said, her pointed little face earnest, 'so Hester you should put all your efforts into getting that done. We can do all the repairs to do with wood, glass, painting, I am sure we can get tools and materials here – it's not a desert island after all.'

'So when did you become Bob the Builder?' said Sarah.

'I worked in Homebase all through my gap year' said Anne, 'I know what to do. And when Sven comes we've got *two* strapping boys who will apply themselves, we will get this place smartened up in a week. Good enough to live here, at least for the summer.'

Anton was pleased Anne had made an impression but faced the prospect of house restoration with perturbation: with no plans to show him the right way to do it or what materials to use and with no one else already doing it for him to follow, he felt confused and out of place, as if too many thoughts were rushing into his mind to be able to process them. 'All this building material, shouldn't the holes in the walls be done first?' he asked. Outside the house were sacks of cement, piles of sand and gravel and plastic bags of what looked like white blancmange. The house was pitted with holes, some of them deep

'Yup,' said Hester, 'the builders delivered that stuff in return for a down payment, but never came back. But if we are waiting for *two* lots of Greek tradesmen, nothing will ever get done. Anne's right, we'll do what we can, I'll get back to the plumber. I will tell him my pregnant sister-in-law is coming and it will harm her health to live in a place without sanitation, that's the sort of thing that impresses them.'

Hester would have preferred it if her brother had taken the lead rather than Anne, but any dynamism was better than none. Hester fretted about the size of the task, in fixing up the house and launching a restaurant. What had she let herself in for – and everyone else? She was determined to be a good hostess, they mustn't find her too despondent.

She left them to sort themselves into their bedrooms, rather less high-spirited than they had been, now they had seen the wretched condition of the house. Sarah took one bedroom where she would stay with Sven who come the next day. In the next room Anne was standing opposite Anton while he unpacked his black computer, as shiny as a beetle's carapace.

'It will be OK, won't it?' she said.

He looked at the white, slightly pointed face of the small girl, standing in front of the cracked window through which he could see the brilliant Greek sky. He had no answer but kissed her on the head, something he had found to work in the past in times of discord. She snuggled into his embrace.

Her relationship with him enhanced Anne's view of herself. That such an unusual person as Anton favoured her was evidence of her arrival as someone who fitted in to this university world of good-looking, clever people who said and did such interesting things, and she went to lengths to please him.

'I didn't know anything about Hester,' she said, for her ignorance of any intimate knowledge of Anton had been troubling her, 'tell me about her.'

'Hester's my half-sister, same mum, different dads,' he said, 'She was more like an aunt to me – fifteen years older and mainly out of the house by the time I was growing up. Her dad was Greek, they met when my mum was living on a commune on Skyros. Then mum came back to England and met *my* dad, then Hester lived with us but sometimes went off to Greece.'

Sarah appeared at their door. 'We'll make it work, it's Europe after all,' said Anne in response to her friend's disconsolate look, 'it's not the Third World or something.'

'Only just,' said Anton unhelpfully, 'this is the restaurant at the end of Europe, the outer edge of the continent. After us, it's Turkey out there.' He motioned towards the misty distance where the sky met the sea in a grey band, 'Asia the Romans called it, the province of Asia.'

'There be dragons,' said Sarah, gazing at the horizon.

Chapter 2

In his panelled office overlooking the town square, unadorned by any statue of a hero, the Mayor of Doxos was feeling a chill in his stomach. What a burden high office was, the stewardship of his people, herding them towards their best interests, protecting them from outside predators, mediating with the powerful.

This morning the Germans were coming. They had come before and been welcome; now matters were not so friendly. Through the Mayor's ingenuity, his good intentions and his generosity, he had arrived at a situation where the Germans were angry with him.

The Mayor had proposed a new airport for Doxos and utilised the expertise of the island's intellectuals to write a proposal stressing the under-development of this part of Europe, the potential of a modern airport in stimulating the local economy, international amity and other benefits expatiated by clever people in too many paragraphs to bother to read.

The European Commission sent a bespectacled, Finnish civil engineer to assess the project, he returned to his glass box of an office in the snow and soon they sent money all the way from Brussels, from the flat lands in the north where they had lots of money, piles of it that they kept along with their cows and their bicycles in big new buildings where there was so much of everything they wouldn't miss the small amount Doxos took.

The Mayor went through a proper tender process with such unknowns as specifications and sealed bids. Of three civil engineering companies, a German firm won the contract. The Germans had started with every good wish, lunches with salad and retsina, dinners going on into the starry night, starting with ouzo and finishing with Metaxa brandy, the spirit of friendship between Greece and Germany toasted countless times.

But soon the joy of light-headed lunches and soaked dinners wore thin with the practical demands of the construction project. First came the news that the ground was not right, was subject to slippage, would need to be expensively reinforced engaging new equipment, materials and expenses.

The Mayor had fought for the airport to be located on that land. Other land, he argued, was too expensive, or would disturb the culture of bee-keeping or the wild fowl so beloved of the environmentalists. Even as the ground began to slip under the weight of the hardcore and concrete the Mayor reassured himself, 'But it was my cousin's land. It was the most excellent land on the island.' The suggestion that there was any problem with the land was bordering on an insult to his family. This land matter was the first to sour relations with the Germans.

Then the money dried up. It had always been a problem, this money, from the Germans' point of view. It had been paid late to them, something they did not understand: they had done the work, the European Union had pledged the money to the Doxos authorities. The usual way of things was that then the money should be paid over by the contracting body, the council of Doxos. Why were they not being paid? It was, they supposed, a Greek thing, like the bad plumbing that meant toilet paper couldn't be flushed. They had to get used to it. *Siga, siga* said the Greeks, *slowly, slowly.*

It was always someone else's fault – the European Union had not sent the money, or the bank had made a mistake with the codes and put it in the wrong account so it had to be withdrawn and resubmitted, or it was a public holiday and thus reserved for general rejoicing, not financial dealings. Eventually the money did come in those early months, occasioning more celebrations and back slapping reassurances, though perhaps each time with a little less brio than previously.

A soon as the Germans had got used to the bad land decisions, and the late payment problems, the next stage of disillusion was non-payment. They had fallen foul of Até the deceiver of men, ancient goddess of the island with her glossy locks and fast feet. Months stretched past the previous point of late payment: still no cash. This was harder for the Mayor to assuage. At one time he had been to the site to cut the first piece of turf with a ceremonial spade and have his picture taken to an accompaniment of cheers, but now he hadn't been to the site for months, for fear of angry workers causing a scene or even taking him hostage. The Germans felt they had waited long enough, they were very insistent and had long since abandoned most of the niceties of civic diplomacy. They had stopped work. More than half of the workers had gone home. Others stayed, they wanted payment and they wanted it now.

The Mayor was well-fed rather than overweight, and on the tall side for a Greek so his bearing generally dominated a room, but the two Germans who were shown in were broader and taller: huge white, red and blond creatures like beings from another planet. The Mayor knew them well: Heinz the site manager and Kurt the chief engineer. Heinz was a man big in every way, even his fingers were plump like sausages. His eyes were slanted orientally by the rolls of fat on his face, but blue and piercing.

The site engineer was also a big fellow but older, and encumbered by the clipboard and file of schedules he carried as if to add weight to his doomed case. They made no motion to shake hands and sat down without waiting to be asked. 'The last of the men have left,' Heinz said blankly in his almost perfect English,, 'they have not been paid and they are sick of waiting. We are staying to close up, in a week we leave.'

'This is just a small local problem with the bank,' said the Mayor, his English was less than perfect but good enough for this meeting, when he knew what was going to be said, and he did not want an interpreter witnessing the scene, 'I told you, the man who has the combination of the vault was off sick,' he smiled and his hands fluttered to indicate the inconsequentiality of the problem they faced.

The big German did not smile, he had heard all the excuses and enough charm to tease out a whole coven of witches. It was the end: Até stood naked.

'When our men go back home,' said Kurt, 'they will claim money from the company that they have a right to. We must claim the total sum lost from you, for all equipment and all work to date, with damages for injury to our reputation. When we go, we send a report direct to Brussels telling them to investigate the airport contract. You have a week then everyone is off-site.'

Their words were measured because, apart from the sense of outrage the Germans felt, they did not in fact hold all the cards. They knew that if they told the European Union the job was compromised by missing money, the plug would be pulled, they would never get their money from that quarter, they would have to sue the island for it. Who knows, the company might go under for lack of funds before that, might be bought out, the island could go bankrupt, the Euro might plummet in value.

Certainly, the Mayor would lose his position, and would perhaps be arraigned, might even be imprisoned, but it would be the German civil engineers who would be associated with the failed venture in the eyes of the engineering community. They should have kept control of the project. They should not have been beguiled by a provincial mayor. They had come to the island of Doxos as independent contractors and had somehow been contracted in. They had been duped. The tipping point had been reached and passed beyond which blame for cheating them had trickled over to the engineers and become blame for having been cheated. For the goddess Até her work was complete – total deception had now been achieved, so that the deceived were moved to deceive others to lessen their shame.

So the Germans' interests and the Mayor's interests were linked in a way which, if not so convivial as in those balmy days when Teuto-Hellenic amity was toasted so warmly, had the added piquancy of shared misery, like unripe olives.

Still, breaking point was not yet reached, the Germans had come to deliver an ultimatum, the Mayor did not doubt it. They left with bad grace.

'One week,' were Heinz's last words as he walked through the door.

There was another factor in the Mayor's torment, he reflected glumly. It was really rather important that someone stayed doing some work, because the Mayor had his own constituency, his flock: he had to please the businessmen of Doxos. His opponents criticised him that his predecessor, their honest mayor from the party of the people, had taken only 10 per cent in graft on government contracts, a perfectly proper, even a patriotic share for a senior official of his standing. Now, the Mayor's detractors said, he was taking 25 per cent of public contracts and that was a liberty, they said. It was hard to cover up, it was just asking to be found out, and that was not right.

This was the Mayor's problem, he mused, his fatal heroic weakness, like the heel of Achilles or the pride of Oedipus: his fault was that he was just too generous. He could never resist the many calls on his good nature. Where had the money gone? Whenever he tried to think of it – a shiny new motor bike for his nephew, an extension to his house for his wife, jewellery for his mistress, gifts of money for colleagues whose loyalty rightly should be rewarded, a certain amount of gambling, but very little. The money had been spent and spent as if it would never end. His generous nature meant the European Union had bought treats for everyone on the island in the Mayor's immediate circle, whether he liked them or not – there had been no favouritism; whatever else the Mayor was, he was fair.

The altercation with the Germans upset the Mayor. He liked to be liked, he was filled with pleasure at seeing people enjoy the hospitality of the island. Allegations of incompetence or misappropriation of funds were the mark of a bad guest, a rejection of hospitality and that was hurtful, and those who behaved that way, after all, deserved to be relieved of their money.

Still, he had a problem here. The Mayor was not the holiest man but he was no more immune to the call of the church than any other son of the Orthodox faith and when he looked at the icon on his wall and breathed 'Oh Mother of God what am I to do?' it was more than an irreverent exhortation. His moment of prayer was interrupted by the appearance of a solidly built, square-headed man barging in past the Mayor's secretary and through the door as if he needed no appointment. He was swarthy with brilliant, sparkling black eyes; around his wrist was a chunky chain bracelet of what was, indeed, real gold. A mat of virile hair exposed itself in the V made by his open top shirt buttons. 'Vasilios, my cousin,' said the Mayor with his arms open in the excessive gesture of welcome customary for someone he would rather not see.

'I have brought you a gift,' Vasilios said, plonking down a bottle of whisky on the Mayor's desk. Oh, dire portent – a criminal bearing gifts did not bode well. He wanted something. The Mayor therefore got his own plea in early, 'Cousin, brother... how did you know I was in trouble, to come to me at this time? You have the gift of foresight.'

'Anything I can do to help,' Vasilios said. His gold incisor glinted in the sun from the window. 'Your island is my island too, my friend.' They embraced, each attempting to outdo the other in the strength of their hug. 'What problem do you have, my friend?' asked Vasilios.

'The Germans want their money for the airport,

the next stage of building, and, well, we haven't got it, Doxos is a poor island...' The Mayor spoke of the greedy foreigners taking advantage of poor Doxos, and tried to beguile his guest with talk of the profit to be made from the expanded airport.

'Save that for your shopkeepers,' Vasilios said. He was markedly unenthusiastic about the airport expansion and increased tourist revenue. Sure, there would be more opportunities, but more attention too. For him the fewer the number of people who knew what business took place on the island, the better. 'I like Doxos small, no one pays us any attention,' he said, 'that's good. But your problem: how much do you need?'

'Well, 800,000 Euros would do it, for now. That would keep things going, then I get more money through from the Europeans, and then I am over this problem.' Both knew payment would only postpone the exposure of a gaping deficiency in the airport project's finances, but that would be for another day; the Mayor wanted to stay focussed on patching up today's hole.

'I will loan you this money,' said Vasilios without hesitating to consider the amount, 'not a problem, I know you will return it when the Europeans pay you again. Think nothing of it. Here, take my hand...'

The Mayor gripped Vasilios's hand warily, 'One small favour I need in return,' he said, pulling the Mayor close to his pitted face, he could smell the coffee on Vasilios's breath, 'I want you to do a little something for me, a very simple thing.'

Vasilios looked troubled, the Mayor feigned concern, 'I too have a problem,' said Vasilios, 'There are many more coastguard patrols because of people smuggling – refugees coming in from Turkey – this is a hideous trade,' Vasilios felt people smuggling was a waste of resources that could be used transporting other things, on work of real value. 'Still, these smugglers do not bother me, it is the coastguards who disrupt trade.'

'So what is your problem now?' asked the Mayor, his hand to his closely-shaved chin, feigning concern.

'I need to pick up something from the sea. A consignment, a cargo, it will be left for me attached to buoys. There have been problems across the water and the supply was stopped, now there is a lot of stuff to pick up, we can't fail to do it. No one wants to lose merchandise but sometimes some is lost. This consignment I can't lose. I owe people in Athens, serious people.'

It was not exactly a closely kept secret that the supply of heroin from Afghanistan through Turkey was slipping into Europe via the island of Doxos and other rocky outposts of the continent. With farmers having taken the trouble to grow and harvest opium, dirt-shack chemists to refine its product into heroin, transporters to pack it on mules to cross borders, smugglers to set it afloat in the Mediterranean – it would be a waste not to salute this endeavour by picking up the consignment, dividing it up and sending it on its way. It would be a failing of Vasilios's honour not to do so, it would be a stain on the character of the island. What was more, it would cost him a great deal of money.

The Mayor was guardedly sympathetic to Vasilios not only because he was his cousin (second cousin, in fact) but because he shared certain values, the best kind – for family, for property, for personal enrichment. If Vasilios had released drugs on Doxos, the Mayor would have been angry, would have called him to account, but he did not need to. The Mayor always thought it one of the achievements of his stewardship of the island to keep drugs out – that is, what drugs were on the island, were resting there, they were in transit, they were not sold on Doxos, they were passing through, ready to be sold elsewhere.

In this he had the support of Vasilios who did not want to pollute his own island with drugs, nor attract outside attention to his business with a flourishing Doxos retail outlet. That these drugs were sold to the next island did not trouble him, people there would have to take responsibility for their own kids. Similarly, the sale of heroin in Piraeus or Thessalonica or anywhere else in Europe was someone else's concern; not that he actually thought much of anywhere else in Europe. This was in accord with the Mayor who was responsible for this island and not any others, he was not their mayor, after all.

'You know I am ignorant of all these matters my friend,' said the Mayor, 'what are you asking me?'

'I need you to make the Coastguard look the other way, when I pick up a consignment.'

The Mayor's heart sank. Behind his smiling lips his teeth clenched; the Coastguard was a man of steely intent. 'Have you approached him?' he asked.

'Yes, he doesn't want to know me but you, my cousin, you are a different matter. When you make a request, it is answered. You represent the people, you command respect.'

'I wouldn't be so sure,' said the Mayor, 'the Coastguard can be a hard man, unsympathetic.'

'Your skills my cousin, my Mayor, your skills will bring him round to do what is best for the island. How we all rely on you to lead us. Oh, and I forgot,' said Vasilios, approaching the door and about to leave,

'I need this favour over one of just three days this month, any of these three days will do – sixteenth, seventeenth, eighteenth, when the moon is in our favour.' The Mayor looked aghast, Vasilios explained: 'There is devilish activity, you know with satellites, watching us all the time, we need to go out when there is no moon, when it is dark and we can't be seen.'

The Mayor smiled weakly as his guest left. He was careful how he handled Vasilios, certainly the man was dangerous and in earlier life had killed people, but they were only people who needed to be killed, people who deserved killing, they were *fair* killings. The Mayor was not frightened, but he was wary. If he did not handle this carefully, it could turn out very badly indeed.

The Mayor left his office even more troubled than when he had arrived and drove out from the town square to the harbour of Agios Nicholas, then along the coast road around to Zeste where his childhood home had been, and on around to Aspasia's taverna, halfway around the bay.

The patroness came out of the restaurant, down the path past the tables to welcome him, walking confidently on her heels, her proud mane of black hair gathered up behind her ears, offset as usual by a red flower and a pair of large, round earrings. She gripped his arms in her manicured hands, the nails a perfect shade of coral pink, and kissed him on both cheeks. As he embraced her the Mayor said, '*agapoula mou*' – my little love,' in her ear, a remark that for all its familiarity still made her heart jump.

They went through to the large back room with heavy curtains at the windows and the open fire where in the winter they burned wood. Now the grand fire seemed redundant, as if it would never be used again. At the beginning of the season it always felt as if summer would last for ever. The tables had been put together to make a large square around which the owners of all the restaurants and bars on the island had gathered for their start-of-season meeting.

The meeting was presided over by the Mayor because, after all, a cartel has to be seen to be fair. They all welcomed the Mayor as if he were their long-lost friend and saviour of the island, his enemies greeting him most warmly. He sat at the top of the table with Aspasia at his right hand and Aspasia's nephew Kostas serving drinks and looked at these people whom he had known all his life, the canny business folk of Doxos.

'Got some competition now on this end of the island, Aspasia?' said Andres, one of the most successful owners in the busy resort of Zeste and therefore one of the most successful on the island.

'Not that I know,' said Aspasia, used to being needled by her wealthy rival.

'That Greek foreigner opening up the old place at the end, got some nice young girls living there, I expect they will pull in some trade...'

'Can't say I've noticed,' said Aspasia.

To the locals Hester and her guests were the *xenie* – foreigners. Doxonians knew Hester was half-Greek but she was not from the island so she was called the Greek foreigner, with no apparent contradiction. Even Greeks who had been born on the island, gone away to Australia or some other outpost of the Hellenic diaspora and then returned were also called xenie; and the Athenian professionals who were scattered through the top level of island society were likewise called xenie – though not to their faces.

'How's the airport going?' asked Yiorgos, who owned a bar in Agios Nicholas where the political opposition to the Mayor met and licked their electoral wounds, plotting revenge.

'On schedule' said the Mayor with more cheerfulness than he felt.

'I thought it was supposed to be finished for the beginning of this season.'

'Oh, that was the old schedule,' said the Mayor, 'the new schedule says up and running before the beginning of next season.' Amid resentful murmurings about this, he called the meeting to such order as these meetings ever reached and they got down to business.

Some of the restaurant owners were his supporters, some were not. For most he was the local power and they wanted to stay in with him. The Mayor was the fount of all favours so the opposition muted their criticism and got the best out of him, while watching hungrily for him to falter so they could move in for the kill. First the meeting took the form of a general, meandering talk: tourist numbers had been down last year, maybe thirty per cent on the year before. Projected numbers were not good, based on advanced bookings for hotels and apartment lets.

'People are going to Croatia and Bulgaria,' one owner lamented, 'there are just fewer people coming to Greece, and Doxos is no better or worse than the rest of the country.'

The others assented gloomily. It was a national problem. 'So what do we do?' said the Mayor.

'We have to keep the profit margins,' said Andres who was always the one for bold moves, 'let's say a ten per cent rise in prices.'

They discussed the value of a ten or seven and a

half per cent rise on prices, it was only right that the available tourists should pay more to compensate for their low numbers.

Eventually the Mayor called the meeting to a close and the business folk left with a profusion of warm salutations to go back and enjoy the quiet of the *mesimeri*, the sleepy afternoon. The restaurant owners and bar keepers of Doxos were the public face of the island's hospitality and they liked foreigners: tourist xenie who came, spent money and went away again. Hester, showing every sign of staying put, was less easy to categorise. They had been polite to the newcomer if they had encountered her, but the notion of inviting her to their price-fixing meeting had never entered the head of any of them. If anyone thought much of her it was to take bets on how long she'd survive.

The Mayor stayed at the table as Aspasia stood at the door bidding her rivals a safe journey, young Kostas finished clearing up the glasses and was also dismissed. The Mayor stood before Aspasia and took her manicured hands in his. He had known her a long time, she had been the mistress of his political mentor who had taught him the dark arts of public life on the island and she had been, so to speak, passed on as one of the fruits of high office.

Aspasia was always there for him, always available. A man in his position ought to get passionate sex, not dutiful wife sex. Aspasia either wanted to be penetrated deeply with her legs in the air or her bum towards him, or she acted as if she did which was quite sufficient for the operation at hand. Now the lines from which no amount of mascara could detract made a spiders' web of traceries around her sparkling eyes; when she pursed her lips the wrinkles appeared around her proud mouth, but she had a fine skin and an erect bearing, Aspasia walked as if she had been born to wear high heels. She led him by the hand to the bedroom at the back, a bedroom of many memories of sex on heated afternoons.

Aspasia now tended to have sex in the semi-darkness so she drew the curtains before slipping off her chiffon dress and opening herself up to him. Despite the loose skin around her neck, the flabby thighs, dimpled with cellulite, the breasts sagging, her pelvic thrust could still make him feel virile. She mounted him in reverse style, facing his feet so he could see the whole of her engorged pudenda as she rode him and he watched himself slip in and out of her.

With her looks in retreat, now it was technique and guile that kept Aspasia's edge. She worked hard on her craft, thinking always of times past when she was blonde and her tits defied gravity and she had men queuing up for her. She used to have a timetable, 'I'm sorry dahling, you can't call on me on Tuesdays, they are reserved for a very important person, a man of high birth....' Now anyone could see her, any day, though the work of the café had long supplanted sex work as her primary source of income. There was a time when she had pleased the most important men on the island; now there were fewer. In fact, the visitors to the back room were just some of the aged men that she saw for old time's sake, the retired lawyer and the architect whose mental faculties were no longer what they were, and who came out of a sense of habit, often forgetting why he was there, sitting on the edge of the bed in confusion. The only really important person she saw now was the Mayor.

It had been a good living so far, all of it earned by

Aspasia herself, with her charm, her grooming, her ability to be penetrated in every orifice, sometimes several times a day, taking pleasure from the accumulation of money from this hard physical labour. Aspasia had bought the café with the money she had earned that way, and from the sale of presents she had been given by her richer clients in the glory days. Every day she remembered that she had started off sitting in a bar waiting for custom; now she owned a bar. She never forgot that what she had, she had worked hard for, and must be defended just as hard.

After the vigorous sex they lay naked, the air conditioner cooling their sweating bodies. 'It's nothing to me,' said Aspasia, who had obviously been pondering it, 'that foreign bitch that's started up down the road, she's nothing to me...'

'I thought you weren't bothered,' said the Mayor, mildly amused.

'It *does* concern me.' She stopped trying to conceal the worry lines above her nose, 'I wasn't interested in disputing with that wanker Andres but I'm not happy some xenie has set up down the road, as if we don't have enough problems of our own...coming over here and taking our business....If we let one get away with it, we'll be flooded with them, xenie from all over Europe will come to take our trade.'

The mayor took her in his hairy, masculine arms, 'Are you my doll?' He asked, 'would I let anything happen to you? You need only ask.'

'It won't work, she'll be out of business in a month, she knows nothing,' Aspasia went on.

'Don't worry my sweet,' said the Mayor, 'you will see off any competition, tell me what I can do to help. She'll go down.'

He dressed, gave her bum a parting squeeze and went off into the warm afternoon, the *mesimeri* when the island slept, the quiet warmth enveloping him, back to the gnawing misery of his troubles.

Chapter 3

The students settled down to make a nest out of the ramshackle building. The house seemed to generate detritus; they swept it thoroughly but it was as if the place were constructed of dust that waited for movement and all that happened when they swept was that new dust floated down to fill the vacancy. At every stage a malevolent spirit replaced the dust and debris behind them so after having finished sweeping, it was time to sweep again. They cleaned the grime of ages from the escutcheons around the light switches and sent the bugs away with wide open shutters and a liberal sprinkling of bleach.

'I have always respected woodlice for their antiquity' said Anton, watching a scurrying crowd of the little creatures, 'the only surviving relatives of the trilobites.' In the afternoon the island slept, Anton and Anne took the opportunity to have sex for the first time on the fresh sheets in the dilapidated house, with the windows wide open and no one in front of the building, nothing there but the air and the sea and their nakedness.

Sarah listened to music on the earpieces of her ipod so she could not hear Anne's restrained squeaks of pleasure. She lay and wondered if she would have been invited here at all, had she not been Sven's girlfriend and Sven was Anton's best friend. Smelling the musty odour of the place, she wondered if it was such a good thing to have been so eager. Did Hester even need four people to help in the restaurant? She alone of the students knew something about the hospitality industry, her parents owned a hotel and restaurant in Surrey, with a pool, Jacuzzi and gym - ideal for conferences, mini breaks and clandestine assignations between work colleagues.

Sarah of the gleeful smile found her way through challenges. She had got on well at a middle range private school and had a gap year in Australia and New Zealand where she had thrown herself into every recreation – swimming, wind surfing, snorkling and romance. Greece was just another adventure. Sven would be here soon and everything would be fine, she consoled herself. He was coming by plane from Stockholm to a neighbouring island, then would be over on the hydrofoil.

Things worked out for Sarah, she had learned, she felt she was one of the blessed. She felt it so appropriate that she should be attractive and popular and good natured and comfortably-off; and to have a boyfriend like Sven. Sven, who was so morally righteous and so beautiful, so beautiful the touch of his hand alone would make her melt, the sight of his cheek as he slept would make her think of small children, the gaze of his blue eyes made her want to stay locked there, staring in forever. He was twenty-three, two or three years older than the undergraduates like Sarah and Anton.

'I believe we should tell the truth, even if it is painful,' he said, in their first real conversation in the student union bar. He was softly spoken but with the definite pronunciation of the Scandinavians. She looked into his eyes, this was the angel she had been waiting for all her life, he was beautiful and clever and spoke to her of the truth, what more was there?

'Don't people believe what they want to

believe, so it becomes true for them?' Sarah said, not really thinking about the words, but that here was this beautiful creature talking to her about truth, to *her*, about *truth*.

He was a considerate, if somewhat distracted lover. He made sure she came, even if it took time. She used to fantasise during sex that he was a Viking with his strong limbs and Nordic bone structure, and made the mistake of telling him, a mistake because he was not flattered, 'The Vikings were marauders and rapists,' he said, 'we are Europeans.'

The day after they arrived they set off to pick him up, back down to the harbour past the tables of old men playing backgammon and pouty Greek girls sitting in front of their Nescafés. They stood waiting in the crowd on the jetty. The people around them began to move as one, looking out towards the sea, as the yellow hydrofoil appeared first as a speck, then larger, swerving round and blowing up plumes of water.

The friends approached as the boat began disgorging passengers

'There he is,' said Sarah, waving, 'the tall blond one.'

'Good choice,' said Hester.

Sven had light skin and blue eyes, he scarcely shaved, but his chin showed bright bristles in the sun, like tiny spikes of bronze. He looked a little worn from the journey, that made him if anything seem more vulnerable and attractive. He embraced Sarah with vigour, shook hands with Hester and gave a light hug to Anne who reached up to pack him on the cheek. He was four years older than Anne and she thought of him as a leader.

He clapped Anton on the back in a vigorous

gesture of masculinity. Sven considered Anton the cleverest student at the university, or at least the cleverest he knew. He thought of this friendship as the beginning of a lifelong relationship where they would be close until they died, and he thanked providence that he had met Anton so early in his life, so they had the longest time possible together.

'Evcharisto poli, kalo taxithi' he said to the boatman who has handing over his baggage, a simple, 'Thank you very much, have a good journey' but Sarah thought him incomparably clever.

'Where did you learn that?' she asked.

'I learned some ancient Greek at school, so I could pick up a little when I looked at a phrase book. But I think maybe I talk to them in ancient language, like the prophet Jeremiah or something: *Hail ye ungodly denizens of the isle.*'

The jeep was now loaded with five people plus Sven's luggage, and Anne sat on Anton's knee to make room. They were becoming familiar with the sights of the island, the Greek lettering on shop signs, the backless tops of tourists gliding past on scooters. Then there was a new sight, in front of the police station where they slowed for the narrow street, Anne glanced over and saw what seemed to be a makeshift cage of people, a barred enclave with a clump of listless brown bodies, scarcely shielded from the sun by a canvas canopy. They were dark-skinned but not black, only as dark as some of the Greeks, perhaps twenty of them. Some were standing looking out to sea, others were sitting on the concrete floor, they were dressed in shorts, mostly in shirts, almost all barefoot. One, sitting on the ground, caught Anne's stare and looked quizzically at her.

'Who are they?' said Anne sharply

'They are refugees,' said Hester, not looking at them. 'We get a lot of them, smuggled in from Turkey. They come by the boatload, that would be the night's catch. They are held in a camp on the other side of the island, across the mountain from where we are, so the authorities can decide whether to let them stay or send them back...or whatever they do with them.' Anne was quiet, thinking about the refugees, their scrawny arms and resigned faces, until she was distracted by a crisis: they almost ran over a red tortoise, lumbering across the road. She squealed and they stopped just in time, and Anton jumped out to pick it up gently and put it in the brush to continue its way.

Sven was of a practical nature, as he examined the dilapidated house he was confident he could contribute to fix it up, and that raised all their spirits. In the early evening they gathered in front of the restaurant at the table on the beach for the full island experience, watching the lights of the town come on over the bay. They started nibbling pitta bread with black, local olives that were just slightly bitter.

'This is the taste Socrates had in his mouth,' said Sven, 'the same taste, the same climate and scenery, the rocks and the sea.' Hester tested her menu on the four: yoghurt dips and cheese and spinach pies, rice balls wrapped in vine leaves; traditional moussaka for the meat eaters and briam with courgettes, aubergines, tomatoes and peppers for the vegetarians; rounded off with honey and yoghurt and sweet prune syrup.

The four were intoxicated by the warm air of the night, the sight of the town with its white houses bathed in pink as the sun died, seeing the twinkling of lights in the calm water of the bay, the unfamiliar smells and tastes and the sharp, young local wine served in metal litre jugs. They now were excited by the challenge of the old house and eager to begin work in earnest. Hester confided in them that she had to make a success of the restaurant, it was her last chance, she had sunk all her savings and all the money she got from the sale of the house in her second divorce.

As the light of the sun died, suddenly the mosquitoes descended on them like supernatural sprites and Hester brought out green coils of repellent that stood on little metal structures and were lit to smoulder and smoke their way around the spiral to keep the bugs at bay. They talked by the light of candles in shades against the light wind, relishing every moment.

Hester drank more than usual; at last she wasn't carrying the whole project alone, it was such a relief having the four here. She told them the story of bringing the jeep in from England by freight. 'They called to tell me it was at the docks so I went along and they kept opening and closing this account book; then they opened a drawer and looked into it and it was empty.' Her bony hands mimed opening a book and pulling out a drawer, 'Then they opened the drawer again, and I looked into it, and yes, it was still empty, and suddenly I realised, "Oh, you want a bribe!" I said. They looked very grim because of course people pretend they don't take bribes. But I sorted out fifty Euros and put it into the account book and put it into the drawer. That released the car.'

'But they don't take bribes..?' said Anton.

'No, it was a present. Apparently the rule is that anything under 75,000 Euros is a present, then it becomes a bribe. They are still arguing that the car ought to be taxed in Greece when it's already taxed in the UK, I don't know whose cock to suck to get out of that one.'

'Does that work as well?' asked Sarah.

'If anything it works better. I wish I had bigger tits. With what I've got I can open my blouse all the way down and not make an impression.' Hester wanted to make the students like her, to treat her as one of them, but she was uncertain whether to be vulgar or maternal.

Later, in her bedroom above the restaurant Hester was lying down in the dark with the horned moon framed in the window. Suddenly there was a patter, a smattering of noise like big drops falling down like they had when she had first arrived at the beginning of the year. It was rain. Rain! And she had the bags of concrete outside. It had been hard enough to get the stuff there, she must get up to the house and protect the building materials. She threw a dressing gown over her damp body and rushed out of the door but obviously it was not raining. She was now overwhelmed at the realisation of her stupidity. The noise she had heard was the wooden beads of the fly screen beating on the door. This was absurd, there had not been rain for months. She stood outside staring out, wet with sweat, listening to the roll of the sea on the pebbles. What had she become?

Hester was a cross between a bird of paradise and a lame duck, always off on another adventure then needing to be bailed out. Once Anton had helped her to do a moonlight flit from an apartment. She had more of a gift for gathering people around her than for catching and keeping a particular one. She had sought the stability she craved in matrimony. There was a starter marriage that lasted eighteen months before she came home from work and found he had run off, taking the furniture; he had even taken the cats. She had many relationships, each time setting up a new home and hoping this time it would work. She had awful taste in men, the ones that weren't spongers were dreamers who would never amount to anything. Then there was another marriage; if the first was a starter, this was a finisher. At least the rise in property prices had left her with a decent sum to bring to Doxos to start anew. She had cousins on Skyros but didn't want to move there, she wanted a fresh start. This, she thought, staring out at the sea, is my last chance. Hester was far from religious, but a prayer crept out.

As if in answer, the morning of the next day, before the four were up, they heard noises in the rooms downstairs. Throwing on a T-shirt, Anton rushed to the balcony and looked out to see a sweating plumber heaving a ceramic shower base and leading the customary half-witted plumbers' mate. They called out 'good morning,' *kalimera*. The plumbers had come, as cheerfully as if they had never previously failed to come, never raised hopes, never left anxious customers clawing at the air in desperation.

Having delayed for months, they got to work with amazing rapidity and within a day the house had a flush lavatory, a hand basin, and the students would be able to have showers the following day when the mortar set on the base. The hot tank was also working now – though the time was fast approaching when hot running water would be a curse to the inhabitants of the little stone cottage who would yearn for anything cold.

Hester confronted the plumber, tentatively, for fear he would disappear like gossamer if handled roughly. The round-faced man said, 'I didn't come before because I thought you did not need the shower till your guests came.'

Hester tried to say, 'I don't need a plumber to think, I need a plumber to...plumb,' but her Greek failed her and after wrestling with the language she managed only a grudging, 'thank you.'

For the students this was to be the start of days of sanding, repairing and painting; going to the glazier for glass for windows; the ship's chandler for nails; the carpenter, who doubled as the island's undertaker, for wood beading for the windows. A gender separation began to assert itself as repairs began, with Anton and Sven working with wood to repair doors, sills and window frames while Sarah and Anne did the cleaning, sanding and preparing.

'What is this vinyl covering on the floor?' said Sarah, wrenching at the black stuff that tore off in irregular patches.

'Not vinyl but lino,' said Anne, 'I've read about it in history books. Look, there are lots of little bugs under there,' she squatted to watch them.

Sarah recoiled, 'Now you have introduced yourself to them would you like to say goodbye?'

Anne rolled up the lino pieces and threw them out along with whatever rotten wood could be removed, 'Goodbye little bugs,' she said as they went scurrying out of the debris to find a new home.

Anne organised the work according to a plan: with three bedrooms, they could use two and all work on the remaining one. They ripped up all the floor covering to expose ancient floorboards, took flaking plaster off the walls, sanded the windows and repaired them, splashed every surface with carcinogenic woodworm killer, ripped down loose plaster and covered the walls with a paint called plastico that acted as a latex covering, varnished the floor, primed and painted the wood. They painted the walls white and the woodwork blue, in deference to the colours of the Greek flag.

One night, after dinner under the stars on the beach, aching with unaccustomed physical labour, Anne and Anton walked up to the house. Sarah and Sven lingered. On the beach, she said to Sven 'come with me.' They stepped into the enveloping warmth of the darkness, walking out along the shore lit only by the crescent moon, leaving the restaurant behind them, hand in hand, hearing the sound of the sea suck and kiss the shingle. When they were far along the shore and the sand was coming to an end they sat down. Sarah said, 'close your eyes and lie back.' He did so, 'now open your eyes.'

Here, far from the lights of the town and away from those of the restaurant, was revealed in glory another gift of the island – the huge canopy of stars, the Milky Way like a continuous stream of light stretching above them.

They kissed deeply in the warm darkness. 'Days of hope,' he said.

Chapter 4

Outside Bodrum, the Halicarnassus of the ancients, site of that wonder of the world the Mausoleum, birthplace of Herodotus the father of journalism, some thirty miles across the wine-dark sea from Hester's café, Malik woke in an abandoned farm drenched in sweat.

Malik saw again, as if it were before him now, the door of his family home near Kabul open and the sights of disaster crashing in. Later when he thought about it he knew there had to have been noise outside, had to have been shouting, screaming, calls for help, a beloved voice in agony. Somehow he remembered it happening all at once: the screaming and wailing, the door opening, the sight of the blood in heart-stopping display.

Three or four men were carrying his brother Hamid. His legs were shredded, the flesh of his limbs and fabric of his jeans hanging together in gory tatters. His mouth was an open wail of pain, the air full of the noise, as one of the men cleared Malik's books with a sweep of his hand and they lay the screaming mass of his brother on the kitchen table.

Malik needed no explanation for this, Hamid had shared the fate of many: he was running an errand, took a short cut, and hit a land mine in a place where they were believed to have been cleared. Field workers tied up his smashed legs as best they could and brought him in, themselves covered in blood when they reached the town, shouting for help.

They lumbered in through the heavy, wooden door, Malik's mother and sister Farishta behind them. 'Get the doctor' his mother shouted at Malik and he ran out, through their small, walled compound, up the dusty street in the brilliant sunshine, not stopping to speak to a neighbour who tried to ask what was happening.

He ran down past the enclosed houses and the few shops to the doctor's house, up the path and battered on the door, gasped out his request to the doctor's manservant who retreated into the dark interior. Dr Ahmid rushed out grimly, carrying his leather bag. The doctor was not elderly by world standards, perhaps fifty, but his straggly grey beard and shuffling gait showed him to be an old man, in a place where few men lived out their natural span.

Malik pulled at the doctor's sleeve to make him go faster though he was moving as fast as he could, he knew more than anyone how rapidly blood is pumped out of an open wound. When they arrived, the field workers and Malik's mother had staunched the blood with makeshift tourniquets of torn rags.

The doctor, sometimes a guest at his father's table, now set down his leather bag filled with instruments, extracted a brown apron from the bag, quickly took off his coat and began to examine the writhing boy, snipping off the remains of his prized jeans. Men held Hamid down while Dr Ahmid made quick and accurate decisions based on a fund of experience, amputating one leg above the knee and trying to reconstruct the shattered fragments of the other. Malik was sent to help boil water on the bottled gas cooker.

Malik prayed for Hamid to live. Hamid was eighteen, only two years older than himself, but he worshipped his elder brother. Hamid wore what they called American clothes, he had a small goatee beard like his hero the singer Habib Qaderi, he taught Malik soccer and how to use a slingshot to hurl stones at targets which were supposedly marauding wolves. Real wolves were in short supply by the time Malik was growing up, the wars had not been easy on wolves – too many well-armed men looking for target practice.

The jeans were dropped in a bloody heap on the floor. Forever afterwards that bloodied mess of ripped up denim was a recurring image of catastrophe for Malik, he shied away from seeing blood, he was disconcerted even by seeing clothes thrown on the floor. Treatment was fast for the pain, many things were hard to come by in Afghanistan, but pain medication was always to be had. The next weeks were spent anxiously on Hamid's convalescence. First he drifted in and out of consciousness, being visited daily by Dr Ahmid and roused from stupor only to eat.

Hamid grew hollow eyed, hobbled with two makeshift crutches, one leg bent below him, some semblance of it had been saved, but twisted and misshapen, the foot no longer at right angles to the shin. The other was horribly absent, the gap under his thigh always a reminder of what he was not. Malik spent time with him, trying to talk, but the drug dulled his senses and he spoke as if he had heard, but from a long way off. He became increasingly bad-tempered and withdrew into his addiction. He retained his love of music, but played monotonous songs again and again, songs of loss, desertion and yearning.

He used to sit on a bench in front of the house,

swinging his bent, crippled leg slightly, perhaps because it gave him some relief from pain, maybe because it was a demonstration of what he could still do with his legs: the hinge of the knee at least still worked. It was a double tragedy, for Hamid was not only the eldest, but the brightest and the best, the chosen one who would save the family. It was Hamid's mission to reach out beyond the boundaries of their country, to seek the family's fortune in the world beyond.

For this the family had sunk their savings, had begged (in the most dignified way) for money from relatives, had called in favours, had raised cash from a money lender. Finally, funded by 10,000 hard-gained dollars for the smuggling operation, Hamid would be taking their hopes through the mountains and across the valleys and plains of Asia to a new life in Europe. There he would work hard, find fortune and send money back, might eventually send for his family to come and join him – there was no limit to the possibilities once Hamid had broken through the boundaries of the old continent and into the world of promise.

Malik knew little of this until Hamid's injury, just overheard remarks. Now attention turned to him, and he was quickly made the centre of preparations to travel out of Afghanistan before he too was injured, or unemployed and opium addicted, or conscripted into the national army or pressed into service by the Taliban.

'It was not God's will that Hamid should go abroad,' said his father, drawing Malik to his chest so his beard touched his son's face, 'you will go, you will make a life in the west.' Malik respected his father as a boy must, but they were not close. He was rarely hugged, so this moment had a meaning but quite what meaning was unclear. He later had much time to ponder whether his father was sad to be sacrificing his beloved son, or sad that it had come to this, having to pin the family's hopes on the second favourite.

Malik was unprepared for a journey, he was altogether less worldly than Hamid who knew about places and things – foreign music and films – and at the house of a friend whose father worked for the military, Hamid had learned to use a computer. Malik's world revolved around home and school and was only occasionally in town seeing strong men wrestling in a circle made in the red earth by animated spectators; or the mounted riders preparing for the goat-grabbing game. His experience had mainly been play and lessons interspersed with wedding and birthday feasts with cloths on tables in the garden. The butcher slaughtered sheep and goats, skinned and roasted them for the feast; travelling singers and dancers entertained them with old Persian stories, the beat of the tabla and melody of the harmonium.

He used to play football with other boys in the street and with toy cars; then his parents said it had got too dangerous and he couldn't play outside anymore and they went inside their walled compound. He never thought it was very dangerous. Sometimes armoured personnel carriers passed through, or he saw the black smoke rising from distant fires, heard the dull boom of far-off explosions, but Malik gave little thought to the state of the country. In a place where people talked of the crushing invasions of Genghis Khan, Tamburlaine and Babur as if they were recent history, a boy felt he had little to contribute. Malik did not even remember clearly the time of the Taliban – the fact that his mother could no longer go out to work was not something that concerned him as a child, nor the disappearance of an uncle who had criticised the regime in terms of mild jocularity and had not lived to laugh any more. Then a new war started and he and the other children were told to stay near the house, they saw the flashes of bombs and heard the bangs and sometimes saw planes overhead, but the war was not ferocious in their area.

If anything, the rule of the Taliban and then the war just meant his mother was with the children more and they could enjoy her daily tuition. There was less money and they were less well fed, but they were better educated. Mother knew classical Persian and taught English and French. Malik was slow at classical languages, had poor Arabic and Persian, but excelled at English, he licked up every morsel of the language that came his way, like food by a starving man. He loved the songs and films in English to which they now had some access, but foreign discs with music or film were expensive, as was the equipment to play them, and mainly he had to rely on what foreign books were still in the country, those that had been hidden from the Taliban or overlooked.

A missionary teacher who had worked at his mother's school in the 1970s had left some copies of old English books. They were tattered and yellow and dog-eared and spoke of England in a bygone age in language that was more than archaic. Malik's mother saved as many as she could carry without detection on her last visit to the school, she secreted them under the chador which she was obliged to wear outside the house. These formed the core curriculum of Malik's studies of English

In Pashto, he spoke like a normal boy, but when he was speaking English he used phrases from his books in his everyday speech – 'top-hole' 'spiffing', 'ripping' 'monstrous' ' brace up and be sporty' 'turn off the waterworks' 'not fair play' 'a rum thing' 'good egg' 'fathead' 'consummate ass' 'cheerio' 'absolutely' 'hop it' 'like the dickens' 'he was a pal' 'beastly' 'off his onion.' He kept up an interior monologue of English, talking to himself and refining his speech in that infinitely flexible language. In recent years he had been able to go to school, and was working towards a scholarship to a government college, but that hope had died in the familial kitchen where his brother's blood dripped on Malik's school books.

When the day came for him to leave he took a few things in his red school rucksack: a red and blue check shirt and a spare pair of jeans, some food, a plastic bottle for water, and a copy of a sacred text (though the family was not very religious, at testing times divine reassurance was welcome). He had a mobile phone in a leather pouch around his neck, to keep in contact, so long as he could keep it charged.

His mother embraced him with tears in her eyes, his sister, her pretty face convulsed with sadness, turned away rather than see him leave. Hamid waved wanly from his bench in front of the house. They walked the dusty street to the crossroads that formed the semblance of a town square in their community. Several of the men waved and shouted a blessing for his journey, they all knew Malik was off to seek his fortune in the world, as had so many others.

Malik sat in a Landover, his father beside him staring ahead at the turbaned head of the driver, as if unwilling to look at the son he might not see again. They bounced across poorly made local roads to the A76 and south to Kabul. They were passed by high-sided trucks filled with turbanned men like berries on a tree. The road into the city was a strange mixture of piles of rubble, the broken fragments of smashed buildings, and of newly built architecture, sharp-edged concrete structures of government and military installations. There were beggars, and the poor near-beggars who were selling wretched assortments of goods by the side of the road, but there were also signs of development: trucks with farm produce trundling past and men in palak hats doing building work. He saw women in blue chadors and women with only a headscarf. They passed army checkpoints and military vehicles filled with glum soldiers. Malik was excited at everything.

Further into town they stopped at a busy street with shops selling spices, carpets, leather bags and copper kitchen goods. He smelled concrete dust, wood cooking fires and perfume. He looked around at the cross-legged bread seller, surrounded by his round, flat wares; little girls in silver necklaces and dresses of warm ochre; the flashing fingers and long scissors of the rug makers. There was tinny music coming from the CD shop's radio next to the rows of skeletal machines of the Kabul bike shop.

The driver took them to a meeting-point where they changed to a people taxi. Here his father was to leave him to return to their home in the Landrover. He had already paid the transporters, there was little to do but put Malik into the bus for the first leg of the journey. 'Take care of my boy,' he said to the driver, with a catch in the throat that moved Malik, for his father was not a man readily given to the expression of emotion. His father hugged him and Malik stepped into the seven-seater people carrier that was soon filled, with twenty crushed in. Malik looked through the window, but the vehicle was so crowded he could not even turn to wave as the overloaded bus slowly started the journey and his father stood watching it disappear down the dusty road, towards the military checkpoint and out of Kabul.

Soon they were on the open road, and Malik saw the rocky high walls of passes, the panorama from mountain tops that looked as if they would never end. Who would have thought there was so much space, so many mountains and ravines in a country? Sometimes, off the road, they saw the rusting hulks of military vehicles smashed in conflict, or, down a ravine, the wreck of a van alarmingly like their own. In daytime Malik could see the road snaking off to the distance, snow-capped mountains rising from the plain in front of them, towns and single roads clearly defined drawing through the landscape.

They went through Hirat in the dark, hearing the low wail of the devout at prayer, then up to join the ancient road, the silk route across Iran. They stopped short of the border with Iran and, led by the co-driver, the company scrambled up the mountain and along a narrow but well-trodden goat path, up and around the checkpoint and across the poorly defined border, then down to join the road again. The minibus crossed into Iran empty; they met it a few miles down the road.

Outside of Afghanistan they were supposed to be fed by the transporters, but a state of perpetual hunger with one meal a day was to be Malik's lot for the coming weeks. All stayed in a house that night, Malik's first time on foreign soil, with the familiar, homely smell of kerosene. They were given wonderful flavoured Iranian rice with cool, fresh water kept in plastic bottles in a fridge. It felt like the best food Malik had ever eaten. Despite the Afghan tendency to exaggerate, Malik never overstated the discomfort of that journey; if anything, he tried to block it out, to experience it and forget it. The overcrowded minibus with its poor suspension seemed the lowest form of travel until, to cross the border into Turkey, they were put into a lorry with four or five other people so there were more than twenty altogether. The smell of body odour was already strong when he climbed in. When they drove the wind whistled through and gave some respite from that, but it made him cold. Malik was tired with the strain of holding his position, holding to the seams of the truck so he did not sway too much. He could get used to the people crowded in, could even feel it comforting that he was not alone, but he hated the feel of metal on his hands and the smell of diesel fumes in his nostrils. He kept thinking it would be over, one more day and they would be there, on the borders of Europe, but another day came and went with the reek of diesel and the jogging metal.

All were now hungry, Malik's own supply of food was exhausted. He eked out the plastic bag of sultanas given him by his mother, that when he opened had the dusty, homey small of the larder at the back of the house. First he ate ten a day, then five, then two, then as the supply diminished only one until the last precious fruit of home was gone. Sometimes in a town he heard the cries of street vendors selling walnuts or roasted corn on the cob, and smelled the cooking of street food mixed with the smoke of hookah pipes that must be smouldering just a few feet away in a pavement café.

The first lorry in which he was transported must have been used to carry building materials because the floor was covered in bits of broken brick and metal that dug in as they sat down, all squeezed in so there was little space for movement. Sometimes they heard the muezzin; one particularly devout traveller was anxious to know which way Mecca was so he could attempt to observe procedure and pray in the direction of the holy city.

Across Iran they were hidden in cheap hotels or warehouses until new transportation became available, when they would go to collection points where they met up with other migrants. Up to now all the other passengers were Afghans who knew each other's reserves and courtesies; now unfamiliar people were included in the mix: Kurds, Iraqis and, later, a scattering of others, Somalis and Eritreans. At stopping points when the group got out to sleep in a barn or a house a guide would tell some to remain there when the transport moved on and would give their places to others who had been waiting. This caused unrest, but as the carriers were the ones with the guns slung over their shoulders, the disagreements never became overheated.

When the roads were bumpy, it was too noisy to speak, but Malik began to talk, when it was possible, to another boy, an Iranian Kurd called Samir who had joined them. They sought a common language: Malik and the Afghans talked in Pashto, he could communicate with Samir in Persian but they reverted to English, the common language of the refugees. Soon they were, as Malik put it, 'getting along famously.'

Samir was a little taller than Malik with jet-black curly hair, worn longer than was common, and bright, flashing eyes with a cloth coat that flowed around him as if he were a magician. Malik's English may have been better, but Samir's was more suited to the twenty-first century, he made a point of understanding the difference between English English and American English, 'I will use a lift and not an elevator,' he taught Malik, though Malik had never seen one of any description, 'see films and not movies; wear trousers not pants; talk on a mobile not a cell phone.'

Samir was only a year older than Malik but he was more worldly-wise. Perhaps through his greater access to television and films, or perhaps simply from a naturally sharp wit, he knew things Malik had never considered before. 'We had it easy crossing Iran,' he said, 'now comes the hard part.'

'Why is that, we are just passing through Turkey, why should they care?'

'These guys that have taken control of the lorry,' said Samir, 'they are Kurdish nationalists, doing the smuggling to raise money for the Kurdistan Workers' Party. Now we'll have the political police looking for us too.'

'What will the political police do if they catch us?'

'Just send us back,' said Samir, 'Maybe they'll torture us to see if we are with the rebels, if we can tell them anything.'

'Can we? Are you with the Kurdistan Workers' Party?'

Samir smiled, posed as if he were thinking for a moment and shook his head, 'no, I'm with me. I told them I was going abroad to study to be a doctor, to come back and help them in the fight.'

'But you are not?'

'No.'

'Good egg,' said Malik. 'I thought they just ran it like a bus,' he added, confused and miserable in this complex new world, with capture and torture an accompaniment to travel, but pleased he had a wise friend to guide him through. Samir said the nearer they went to the European border, the more the danger of being caught and sent back – what shame that would be, to return to the family with nothing! Malik could not even imagine such disgrace and the thought of it haunted him.

They finally crossed the border into Turkey, it was easier than Samir had predicted: they sped through the checkpoint late on a Friday night – presumably the wheels were greased with bribes. They went on to a village near Agri and stayed there a while, regrouping with other travellers.

'Where are we?' asked Malik.

The devout man who had been trying to position himself towards Mecca in the truck, indicated across the plain a snow-capped peak. 'That,' he said into the crisp air, 'is Agri mountain, where the prophet Noah's boat came to rest after the flood. Truly God's world is wonderful,' he said, pleased to see the truth of scripture confirmed in so substantial a form as a mountain.

'Spiffing', said Malik, whose use of English expressions increased as he moved closer to the place itself.

'I can't see much,' said Samir, 'just a blur. I'm short sighted,' he said, 'in Europe I'll get glasses.'

'In Europe I will get new eyes,' said Malik, in a continuation of a game between them of topping each other's expectations – one would say 'when I'm in Europe I'll have a car' and the next would say 'when I'm in Europe I'll have a Volvo' and the other would say 'when I'm in Europe I'll have a Ferrari' – trying to outdo each other both in their English language and in their knowledge of western goods.

They talked endlessly about what they should say to the authorities when they got to Europe, 'I will say I am Palestinian,' said Samir, 'if you are Iraqi, and the Greeks get you, they can return you to Turkey.'

'How do you know all this?' said Malik.

'I met a few guys back home who returned, they told me,' said Samir

'People who had gone back – they got plenty of the old dosh and they went back to see their family?'

'No,' Samir laughed, 'they got caught and sent back.'

This fed the growing realisation in Malik, that had not been apparent at the start of his journey: that his mission could fail, that he might seek but not find his fortune, he might be returned to perpetual shame.

'It's got to be the government that made you run away or they won't let you stay,' continued Malik, 'A friend of my cousin got as far as Copenhagen – Denmark, right? – and they sent him back because he told the truth, said they were poor and had no work, so they sent him back. He should have said he was being attacked by the police because he was a nationalist.'

'And was he?' asked Malik, trying to comprehend the notion of a complete lie encompassing every bit of the past.

'No, he wasn't a nationalist and he wasn't being attacked by the police, but you've got to say that. You got to give them what they want. It's got to be politics, it's got to be clever. The truth is not our friend, my Malik, in the continent of Europe.'

'That's a rum thing,' said Malik, 'I don't know what to say.'

'Well, think of something – say the Taliban killed your brother and you were frightened for your life.'

'He's not dead' said Malik, 'he ran over a mine, I don't remember the Taliban being in control, not really, I was a kid when they went. They are still fighting, but not near my family.' Malik did not even know whose mine it was, whether it was the Taliban, Russians or Americans who had mined the area and left it uncleared and unmarked. Afghanistan had no shortage of foreign visitors. No empire, it appeared, ever felt fully virile until it had entered Afghanistan. Malik had done the history in his brown-covered schoolbooks: the British alone had invaded four times, one in each of the most recent centuries and twice in the nineteenth. As far as Malik was concerned, it could have been an English mine, but he hoped it wasn't, a mine was such an unsporting weapon.

Malik refined the story as he travelled further and further from home, so he no longer had to think of his brother, who should have been there in his place, but instead was sitting on the bench looking at the clear mountains, swinging his useless leg. Now Malik said his brother was killed, that way he wasn't there any more as a suffering, broken figure. The main contribution to his education of the journey across Asia was the discovery that a lot of existence was story-telling. Life was what he made it, and he made it up.

As they progressed close to the coast the daytime stops ceased, they parked only at night for the toilet. In some places they could see the stars and, nothing else, it was just dark. Sometimes he could peek out through a chink in the side of the lorry and see a Turkish street, a bazaar filled with people, men in American, not eastern dress, some women with headscarves but mainly both men and women bareheaded and men clean-shaven in this strange country, half-way between Europe and Arabia.

Eventually they had crossed Asia Minor and disembarked on the Ionian coast. It was a few days ride from Ephesus, famed as the site of the Temple of Artemis, a gruelling hard ride from that to Ilium, home of the horse-taming Trojans. Beyond that were the blistering wonders of Byzantium. Now it was the funnel for the desperate of the east, the huddled hopeful, forlornly staring across the sea, embracing their knees as they sat in the dust waiting for their precarious transport across the Aegean.

It was the first time Malik had seen the sea in real life. He was transfixed at the sight of it, how big and cold it was, how flat and all-expansive, how it went on and on and on. He stood enraptured by the motion of the waves, captivated by the sight of boats. Each one he saw sail past – the yachts, the ferries the tankers – he wondered if that would be the boat that would take him to Europe. It was warm now down on the coast, and out at sea they could see holiday-makers, Malik would describe them to Samir whose myopia meant he could not make out the men wearing nothing but bathing trunks and women in bikinis. Malik had never seen such things, even in pictures, and looked at them as a kind of exotic species, too strange even to be considered indecent, more like the fabulous beasts of Persian tales than real people.

Aside from their wonderment at the sea, at this stage of their journey Malik and Samir had few pleasures. They were housed in an abandoned pig farm, it had been left to decay since a new regime in Turkey had closed pig farms and restricted the sale of pork. The refugees, most of whom were Muslims, took strong exception to the fact that pigs had once been bred there, but the smugglers explained the place had been thoroughly cleaned and its previous incarnation meant they were safe there, as few law officers would want to investigate. They would not be there long, and it was all the accommodation they were going to get, so they could shut up and endure it for a while or get to Europe on their own. The smugglers were supposedly also Muslims but Malik thought of them as a godless bunch of ruffians

Anxieties crowded into the conversations between the boys – maybe the police will find us. Maybe the smugglers will get caught and give us to the police as a present, in return for letting them go. Maybe. Maybe the smugglers will just get in their vehicle and drive off, and leave us here. Some of the travellers they talked with had made previous attempts to leave and had been caught by the Turkish police or returned by the Greek coastguards. One man told of being dropped in the woods to wait for a boat which never came, and he waited three days without food and water before walking to the nearest town where he was picked up by the police.

Moves by the authorities to disrupt the drugs trade had an effect on people smuggling, many more piled up waiting for a chance to cross. The only positive thing was that the long wait gave Malik the opportunity to compose himself and regain his good humour. He had sent a text home to say they had reached the coast and would soon be in Europe. He was careful with the use of the phone, not to exhaust it until he had good news and a means to replenish the battery. Days passed and no transport, though they were daily brought food which was mainly olives, bread and tomatoes. Water was, mercifully, available from a nearby well.

Every day or so more people came in than left, they were joined by Somalis, Eritreans, Palestinians as well as more Iraqis, Iranians and Afghans. Perhaps once a week the pickers came with a khaki transit van. It was not obvious who was to be picked, but who had been there longest was definitely an issue. How they chose was a constant topic of conversation; was it nationality, or were some people paying them more? Did Christians or women get preferential treatment? Several times they had been there for the picker and had not been chosen, Malik was growing desperate – would he ever leave this place? Last time the picker had come he had paused then passed over Malik and Samir and Malik had a definite feeling, not justified by anything that was actually said, that he would be doing better alone. The thought gnawed at him, like a rat scuttling round a cage, like the thought that he must not fail, the anxiety of the family's fortunes resting on him. Then there was the irritation of being with the same person day and night; they were friends but Samir's superior attitude began to grate on Malik, whose qualities were less urbane but still valuable.

They used to go to a hill near the farm, where they could see the big hotels of Bodrum, and at night could see the lights of restaurants and hear the pumping techno music from the nightclubs. In the third week of waiting, Malik and Samir were playing five-stones in the dust on a hillside overlooking the sea and the road to the farm. They chatted in English and, having exhausted the talk of the things they would do when they were in Europe, Malik told Samir the story of Mr Smith and his five donkeys from his English lessons. He counted his donkeys but forgot to count the one he was riding on. Where does Mr Smith live? Samir said Liverpool. Malik declared Mr Smith was a good egg and supported Liverpool City football team.

In the distance Malik saw the khaki truck trundling up the road towards the farm. He was about to shout to Samir they had to get back to the farm when a thought stopped him: Malik was here for his family, for his own journey, this was his decision. Here he could tip the balance slightly in his favour. He knew Samir couldn't see that far.

'Your turn to get water,' he said to Samir, handing him their two plastic bottles. Samir acceded without demur. He too was bored and irritated.

As soon as Samir had gone out of sight, dipping down on the path towards the well, Malik ran as fast as he could towards the farm where the transit was arriving. One thing that was certain – you had to be there when the pickers turned up, they did not go looking for travellers, they had to be there waiting.

It was an unusual time of day for them to come and travellers were scattered but by the time Malik arrived the van was already filling. There was almost no space, he had been right to come alone. He presented himself before the picker, a man with a Kalashnikov across his shoulder. 'Yes,' he said, in there.' Malik got in, carrying his bag. 'Leave that' the picker said, 'no room' Malik wanted to argue but knew there was no point, he had seen travellers before divested of everything so more people could be piled in. The satchel has little enough in it now, anyway, but he had cherished it as a link with home, he dropped it on the dusty ground.

When Malik was pushed in by the picker he joined twelve people packed crouching in the back. The writhing mass of humanity groaned as another body squeezed in. As Malik edged in, Samir ran up, out of breath and with a pained expression. 'I called for you,' said Malik, 'when I saw the van. I waited for you, then there was just one space. Sorry.'

'I thought we were together' said Samir in dismay.

'We were together, we will be,' implored the younger boy, 'we will be together again my brother. We will meet again in Europe.' He took the mobile phone from around his neck in its leather pouch and gave it to his friend. Samir's tears made Malik cry too. 'We can keep in touch,' Malik said, and reached his arms out of the back of the van to place the cord around Samir's neck.

One side of the van was closed and Malik was saying his goodbyes with the pressure of the crowd behind him and in front the picker forcing back the disappointed travellers. With the van driving away, his face pressed against the tiny window in the van's door, Malik could see Samir disappear into the crowd of brown bodies, shouting in their disappointment.

Malik felt what he had done as a pain in his chest, he promised silently that in Europe, he would get Samir spectacles, he would get him a car. Soon he would be in Europe, would be able to find a job, would be sending money back to his family, Samir and he would live together in a flat, not an apartment, and they would look back on this day and laugh.

His mind was wrenched from these musings by physical discomfort, it was the most crowded journey he had taken, with almost no space even to breathe. The van bumped on a dirt track down to a secluded bay but in twenty minutes it was over. They jolted to a stop at which their transporters sprang open the doors and the travellers spilled out. Malik was glad to get his breath, and to look around at the blue skies and the bay with the sea slapping against the rocks where there was moored a little rubber dinghy. Malik gasped in horror as he saw it. The others exploded in disgust, where was the yacht, the fishing boat that would glide them safely to Italy?

A general moan of woe went up then everyone shouted together, 'What is this?' 'We have been robbed' 'You have tricked us.' They gathered around the man with a Kalashnikov and the other, the driver with a pistol visible in his waistband, the crowd edging in on them, but Kalashnikov man stood his ground.

'Believe me before God, this is easier' he said, 'a bigger boat would be stopped, would be detected way before you reached land. This way you have a chance. We were getting raided, every day losing boats and men, travellers getting captured, that is why we have to move you in this, but it's still safe.'

They looked at the dinghy with its oars and small outboard motor. Neither Malik nor most of the others could swim. None had any seamanship.

'What do we do,' someone said, 'we don't know how to sail a boat.'

'Point it west,' said Kalashnikov man, 'sail towards the setting sun, only thirty miles you will hit land.'

'Italy?' Someone said, for already there were fears that they were far from Italy.

'Italian islands' said the smuggler, which was only historically accurate, it had been more than fifty years since the Dodecanese were Italian.

'We paid for a boat with a crew,' said Malik, 'no one knows how to run this thing.'

'You want your own cabin?' asked Kalashnikov man, 'it is hard to get you all across. If you were in a big boat you would be caught.' He adopted a different tone, trying to be reasonable, 'This is all we can do – or you can stay on the farm, but we are in danger of raids all the time. We bribe one lot of police to look the other way and then another crowd come.' Mr Kalashnikov raised his hands in open gesture as if to demonstrate his powerlessness, an invitation for sympathy for his situation, but none came. Malik was reminded of Samir's wise advice: the travellers were a lucrative side-line in a terrorist operation, by now they were expendable.

Finally the twelve squeezed into the eight-seater boat, still grumbling but resigned. The man with the pistol showed then how to operate the outboard motor. 'Plenty of fuel to get you across, God willing,' he said.

As the boat was in the sea, stabalised with the oars, he said, 'OK, you have to remember this: if you get to shore, good, you are safe, this is what you want to do. Avoid all shipping, but the coastguard will be looking for you, for boats with travellers. If you are stopped by the coastguards, they will try to push you back into Turkish waters. You have to stick with them. They must rescue you if you are in trouble. They *must*, you understand, so if you are caught by the coastguards, take this knife,' he handed a long-bladed carving knife to a healthy looking young man, perhaps a Palestinian, 'and you stab the boat to make it sink. Wreck the boat while you are in European waters and they have to take you in. They won't let you drown.'

'Why,' said one man, the oldest among them and the most reluctant to get in the boat in the first place, 'why sink the boat?'

'Because the coastguards would just haul your boat back to Turkey and leave you in Turkish waters. You want to be in Europe, in Italy. And don't drink sea water – too much salt.' As the motor jerked into action and the boat shuddered out of the bay towards the open sea, Kalashnikov man called, '*Allah ma'aakum* - God protect you.'

The little boat set off from Anatolia, land of the sunrise, towards the wealth of Europe, with little fuel, no food or water or protection from the sun, weighed down with its cargo of people. Malik looked at his companions, an Iraqi man and his wife, a couple of Afghan young men, a Somali girl who looked sad, Malik imagined she had started the journey with someone else but they had died or fallen ill by the wayside. He had never been introduced and so had never spoken to her. The rest were men with whom he had travelled or had seen around the farm.

They talked little, only about the boats they saw on the horizon; they had been worn down with anxious travel and all knew this was the most dangerous time. One man who had been across by boat before and had been taken back by the coastguard confirmed the ploy with the knife – 'Boat OK, they take us to Turkey. No boat, they take us back with them.'

They saw other craft in the distance, but thought it best not to attract attention to themselves. They tried to control the movement of the boat but much of it was drift, or fighting against currents. A squall came upon them, buffeting and tossing the boat as if the ocean kept opening up, swallowing the boat and spitting it out again. After several hours the motor cut out, a wave came and covered the boat, everyone was shouting with water pouring in. When it stopped they had no idea what direction they were going in or where they had come from. Then the engine started again, they took their bearings, as best they could, and sailed on west.

Almost everyone was sick, but soon they had nothing left to be sick with and settled to a wretched, permanent nausea. One was worse than the others, the Somali girl, her skin as black as velvet but her legs and arms skinny, her frame no more rounded than a boy's. All through the hours of tumult on the boat she was sick, her claw-like hand digging into the rubber side, then it wasn't a vomiting noise she made but a harsh gargle, then the gargling stopped and, if she made a noise, it was whimpering. At some time, in maybe the sixth hour after they had left Turkey, the claw grip on the side of the boat slackened.

After a time, all realised wordlessly what had happened, the man next to her touched her shoulder, she did not move or resist. He moved her face to see the staring eyes. After one glimpse Malik looked down, to his wet shoes, the legs and water on the bottom of the rubber boat. This was not happening, the girl's skinny, black limbs were not being thrust over the edge of the boat like a spider shooed out of a window, the limp body was not being taken by the ocean, sinking beneath the waves, the men who had done it were not mumbling half remembered fragments of prayers for the dead.

The Coastguard, a man of meticulous habits, stood in his white uniform in the cabin. His patrol boat scoured the sea, a machine gun conspicuously mounted in the prow. The Greek coastguards ran a fleet of grey and white Italian Lambro vessels that were acquired with European Union funds to monitor fish stocks. Night was falling by the time they spotted the overloaded dinghy and changed course to head straight for it. When close enough they fixed the dinghy with a searchlight and kept it in vision while they swung to and fro before it to create a swell to drive it back. The dinghy decked and heaved to the screams of the travellers but the Coastguard's manoeuvre was not effective, the motor was still running. The Coastguard's boat went in closer to generate stronger waves. The crew, standing two by two in the tinted windows, watched dispassionately as their colleagues wrestled with the overcrowded boat.

The Coastguard ordered his boat alongside the dinghy and had his men throw a rope down. The travellers reached for it, thinking it was intended as a lifeline but it was yanked back and thrown again, not at the travellers but the motor, they were trying to foul the propeller and cut the motor.

'They want to pull us back to Turkey,' shouted Malik, realising if they cut the motor the coastguards could take the dinghy where they wished.

The man with the knife held it as if it were going to turn round and attack him of its own accord. 'Go on' shouted some of the other passengers, while others screamed and prayed. The man stuck the knife in the rubber rim of the dinghy and stared in horror as the wound opened and hissed, the air blowing bubbles.

He looked at the knife, at the hole, and his mouth opened, his body frozen with fear. For a moment they were transfixed amid the shouts of the passengers, the snarls of the coastguard's men, with the rope whipping past and the fumes from the engines, the white sea churned up in the motors of both boats.

'I am not going back,' screamed Malik, and he seized the knife from the petrified man and stabbed savagely, five or six times in a second, deep into the side of the rubber boat. The passengers recoiled in horror, a movement that tipped the boat up on one side. One man slithered off and into the water but clung on to the boat, sobbing and praying. Malik continued to slash the boat as the coastguard's crew shouted and the water pulled at the weakening dinghy, lurching beneath them.

The boat, already waterlogged, swayed and tipped and eleven pairs of flailing arms and legs gripped at the diminishing sides or reached for the ropes around the Coastguard's vessel. Malik let go the knife as he felt the water engulfing him, taking a hard mouthful of salty water as he struggled and grabbed at the tattered remains of the boat.

'Heave to, stabalise the immigrants, signal the search and rescue,' the Coastguard said without haste.

The Coastguard's men threw lifebuoys to the drowning travellers but made no attempt to pick them up. A blue and orange vessel drew up, a boat with low sides with easy access to side decks. The crew of the search and rescue craft reached out to the travellers with long, hooked sticks to draw them in.

They grabbed the drowning travellers, keeping some stable with a stick while they pulled in others. One by one they were pulled aboard and thrown behind the men like landed fish, ending in a heap of humanity gasping for breath. Thrown on the deck with a thud, it was only now, spluttering and gulping, that Malik saw the four lines of lettering on the side of the cabin, lines that were not in the Latin alphabet but in Greek. They were not going to land in Italy, but Greece.

The search and rescue boat drew a clean line through the water where previously the dinghy had been pushed by currents and buffeted by waves, now they headed straight to the home port of Agios Nicholas on the island of Doxos. This was it, this was paradise, the lights of the port grew larger as they approached and when they docked Malik could hear Greek music, could smell roast meats and frying potatoes; he could see, in the distance, the tables around restaurants where animated people sat, leaning into the light.

The travellers were first decanted to the Coastguard's station. The Coastguard's brief was to intercept boats carrying illegal migrants and get them to return voluntarily, or to drive them back if they would not go, and only in the last resort to take them back to Greece. Rescuing refugees alone gained no kudos, in fact neither the police nor the mayor and town authorities nor the civil authorities under whom the Coastguard operated were in the least bit happy about another bedraggled bunch of Asians being pulled from the ocean and delivered into Greece. In contrast, the apprehension of criminals at sea was a man's business. The Coastguard liked to capture the smugglers and take them to port, put them ashore for his men to organise them in single file with the smugglers first, their hands bound at the wrist with white plastic ties, with the train of refugees walking behind. In front of this procession the Coastguard walked to the police station, with his clipboard, like a roman general at a triumph holding a baton.

It was therefore helpful to put some pressure on the people fished from the sea to encourage them to confess to being the captain, in charge of the smuggling operation. Malik was shoved harshly and was thrown down on the boat but he was spared the roughing up process as no one considered the scrawny sixteen-year-old was in charge. The man who had originally been given the knife had been clearly seen, while Malik's rather more determined effort had been overlooked because he had been much closer to the coastguard's prow. Anyway, masculine credibility said it was the men who should confess, not the boys.

When questioned Malik kept quiet, merely saying when asked that there was no captain.

Eventually, with no confessions forthcoming, they were transported to the police station on the other side of the port, given water and some bread and left to sleep on hessian matting as best they could.

The next morning Captain Papadopoulos rearranged his gun belt under his stomach and strode in his splay-footed way into the interview room. Someone brought him a tiny cup of coffee and a glass of water. He sat down next to a civilian clerk to whom he gave curt orders in Greek throughout the interviews. He spoke to the refugees in English. After some five or six of them had been brought in it was Malik's turn.

'Good afternoon. The Taliban killed my brother,' volunteered Malik, pleased to be able to use his long-prepared introductory sentence.

Papadopoulos ignored him, 'What is your name, where did you come from what did you pay to get here?' he asked in a monotone. It was necessary to get through the questioning and registration of these people, it happened once a week at least, it was not necessary to listen to them except in so far as the forms had to be filled in.

Malik gave his name and home country. 'My father paid, my family paid, I do not know, I am a fathead where money is concerned,' he said, 'sorry.'

Papadopoulos looked up, Malik's English was better than his. 'How did you get here, what route did you take from Afghanistan?'

Malik explained he came across Iran and Turkey, he was in a truck so could not give an exact route. 'I imagine it was the usual way,' he said, trying to be helpful.

'Why did you leave your country?' asked Papadopoulos. Malik could see the coffee grounds in his little cup, and the coffee stain his lips had made on the clean rim of the water glass.

'Because there is no civil war in this country,' Malik said, and added a remark he had thought would endear him to the interviewer: 'People are not selfish,' and to show he was willing to work: 'and I want to learn computers.'

'Write this,' the policeman said to the clerk in Greek: '*It is obvious he abandoned his country in order to find a job and improve his living conditions.*'

Malik now had a choice between a red card and a white paper, both of which were written in Greek and Malik could understand the significance of neither. Captain Papadopoulos made the decision for him: 'Here is a deportation order, and a detention order. You must leave the country in thirty days.' The process was as mystifying to Malik as a conjuring trick, and later weeks of pondering it and discussing it with other detainees did not improve his comprehension.

'Very good, sir,' Malik said, still trying to put a positive face on this bewildering experience. 'What do you want me to do now?'

'Now,' said the police captain in his gravelly voice, 'enjoy your holiday.'

If he was pleased to see me he concealed it like a diplomat Malik remembered from his studies. The interview had taken perhaps three minutes. Malik went off with his inscrutable pieces of paper to join the other perplexed travellers who had already been interrogated, who waited outside the police station in a large, barred cage with the sea on one side, and on the other the police courtyard and the road. There they could watch the Greeks going about their business and the tourists chugging past on mopeds or walking slowly past the sweet shop, the pavement cafes and the supermarket, taking their time to enjoy the warmth and colour of the day.

Chapter 5

Sarah woke to an unfamiliar smell of old wood, staring at the cedar beams of the ceiling with the brilliant sunshine piercing through gaps in the shutters. She listened to the sound of the screeching cockerels, one after another calling out over the island, then the sound of dogs barking, one woken by the sound of a distant motor-scooter then others responding; the bells of the goats, the cooing of doves on the roof and the fluttering of tiny birds in the vine outside the window, seeking the early insects on the jasmine flowers.

She did not know what time it was, Sarah had stopped wearing her watch, to be free from time in this magical place. By contrast Sven had felt there was so much to do he must keep a work chart and a job list, and much of the time he was dead tired. She left him sleeping, his head on his arm, the body of Adonis under a single cotton sheet. She threw on a red sun dress that stopped halfway up her thighs that were now tanning to a Mediterranean hue; she revelled in the feeling of being free to meet the day almost naked, without the tightness of underwear in this clinging climate. Going out of the door to the balcony she felt the full force of the morning sun on her face, looking out to sea, across to the misty foreign shore, experiencing the incredible clarity of the air.

In the courtyard, shielded from the sun by the sharp shadows of the walls, Anton was sitting at the table making gentle clattering noises at his glossy black computer. He studied maths with philosophy and showed such a marked reluctance to talk about his subject that it made the others speculate that he was involved in a secret plan to construct a machine that would produce the theory of everything. Sarah's relationship with Anton was never very warm for he had a (perfectly accurate) notion that she was the sort of girl who would probably not sleep with him – had she been available, that is, and not with his best friend. Or if she did it would be on the off-chance and she would regret it the next day and not have the grace to conceal it from him. It was not that he was trying to have sex with her, but if he did, it would be a fruitless effort, so she was never at the top of his favour list.

Sarah walked gingerly down the steps beside the balcony, crumbling and bending under her weight, showing the steel skeleton that should support it, and went down to the bathroom that finally was blissfully clean and functional. Now the house was remarkably bug-free, but in the kitchen Anne was cleaning and sweeping out the bodies of the creatures that had crawled in during the hours of darkness and died from an inhalation of the toxic fumes of the spray they used on the floor at night. 'Sorry' she said, flinging them over the veranda wall where a semi-feral cat sniffed and turned his nose up at them as a potential breakfast.

Both girls had developed a frizzy-haired, crumpled and somewhat carefree air as the water from the tap was treated saline that did hair no good at all, despite all the libations of conditioner. Sarah's soft, chestnut hair had bodied out, giving her a wild, leonine look. Anne's shoulder-length, light brown hair had resisted attempts at management and she often now had it tied back in a pony tail, giving her pointed features an even sharper appearance, but was more revealing of the dimples at either side of her smile. Anne looked up to Sarah for her worldly wisdom, her foreign travel, languages and personal experience. Anne had hardly travelled out of the UK and had had sex with only two boys, Anton being one of them. Sarah was distinctly more experienced.

'Let's do the gender-specific thing and make breakfast for the boys,' said Sarah. They spread the table under the vine veranda with new bread; boiled eggs bought from Grandma Poppy, a neighbour who kept chickens; island-produced honey that tasted slightly of the trees that served as hives; and freshly ground coffee. Anne watched Anton eat, eager to please him; Sarah kept up a stream of chat, enjoying the sunshine and the fresh food, wondering when the tiny bunches of grapes would be ready to eat.

The house still looked a wreck from the outside but with bright spots of repair and paint; inside it was fully functional, but the big tasks remained. The team had come to the end of the line on house renovations. The house was made of stones that were covered with mortar to make them solid; outside staircases and balconies had been added on. Though the students had replaced window glass and ripped out rotten wood, the concrete skin of the place was derelict; the weather had torn holes in it that exposed the large, irregular stones of the house's construction; one balcony and the toilet roof were broken with the rusting supports exposed.

As the four finished breakfast, Hester came up to the house intent on remedying this last building problem accompanied by Alekos. He was a schoolmaster with excellent English that he had improved by working in other countries from which he had returned with the conviction of the relative excellence of Greece in every respect. Largely bald with a little black spade beard, Alekos had met Hester at the town hall where he was often present, translating or helping with documents. Though he had no official position, he liked to bask in the light reflected from the local power. He had been helpful for Hester in the more complex situations, had been with her to the tax office and the water board, through long waits and some complicated Greek bureaucracy. He had also arranged for the builders to come and work on the house, for which, unknown to Hester, he charged the builders a fee that was added to her bill.

Alekos sat down and had a coffee. He was always pleased to talk with the students, telling them it was an honour to meet such intellectuals; he also felt it his duty to educate them in his knowledge of the gifts of the Greeks whose DNA, he believed, encoded the means for the Greek to originate everything in creation worth the trouble. 'We invented philosophy and mathematics and drama, we invented dance,' he said, listing the achievements on his fingers.

'I think even primitive people danced,' said Sven.

'I mean real dance, classical dance.'

'Greek dance?'

'Yes, Greek dance.'

'I can't deny the Greeks invented Greek dance,' Sven conceded.

Alekos revelled in his role as an authentic Greek, charming the four with stories of the island and its people. He told them the patron of the island was Até, goddess of delusion, banished here by Zeus for her part in tricking even the king of heaven. He explained the Greek Orthodox church was the one true church and the Catholics were a breakaway from it. He pointed out that Doxos was crime-free because its people all respected one another like one family, not always in complete harmony, but in an orderly way.

The students were pleased to show him the progress they had made on the house, in which he was interested as if it were his own project, stroking the new paint and woodwork, testing to see if any nails protruded. Upstairs they displayed the wooden floor that they had spent a week cleaning, sanding, woodworm treating and varnishing. 'Have to replace this,' said Alekos, 'no good, old.' Far from finding it insulting, the students found his directness entertainingly foreign. It became a standing joke between themselves when anyone had completed a laborious task, the others would stand back and say 'No good – old.'

Still the building materials languished outside the house, the bags of cement, steel frames, huge piles of sand, grit and stones. Hester had brought Alekos along to ponder the perennial topic, the non-appearance of the builders. She now said firmly that she needed the work to be done, or would he ask other builders? He gave every assurance that the builders would come but he clearly had no control over them. Hester restrained her irritation with Alekos, she thought of his arranging the builders for her as a gesture of welcome and a hope of future friendship.

'They are not reliable,' Hester was saying, 'When will they come back? If they come back and do the job we agreed they would do, they can do it, but they need to be here now or there won't be a job to do.'

'What do you mean, they brought all this material,' he indicated the piles of sand and gravel.

'They have had a down payment to buy materials and start work. They did the first bit, they bought materials but then didn't start work. The building stuff is all mine. I will get someone else to do the work.'

Alekos started at this – it was hardly conceivable that anyone should relinquish an agreement with a builder, on Doxos you just waited for the builder. 'What do you mean?' he said, 'the builders won't be...' he looked for the word, 'pleased that you have had someone else do the work.'

'Greek workmen always have to have something to complain about,' said Hester. 'If they want the work they must do the work. If they don't contact me by the end of today, tell them I will get someone else to do it.' He went off promising to get the builders on site, muttering to himself about impatient foreigners.

Hester, Anne and Anton went down the short track from the house to the restaurant with its huge, purple bougainvillea flowering around the walls. The restaurant and her flat above it were very much Hester's place while up the hill, the house where the students lived was theirs, a house to whose material fabric they had contributed so much they fancied they had built it. Anton moved effortlessly between these domains.

Anton started to arrange pans in the kitchen, Anne joined Hester in the restaurant, organising the plates and glasses, napkin holders, cruet sets, dishes and cutlery that had been delivered in brown cardboard boxes but not unpacked.

'I didn't know Anton could cook,' said Anne.

'Anton can do anything that has a pattern,' said Hester, 'show him anything once and he can do it.' Hester took the naturally superior attitude of an elder sister – her brother was always hers, even if his corporeal self might be loaned to girlfriends.

Anne smiled sweetly, mildly irritated at Hester affecting to know more than she did about her boyfriend, but she tended to defer to Hester partly because it was her house and she was paying them, but also because Anne always thought of herself as the baby of the group. At nineteen she was a year younger than Anton and Sarah; and almost half Hester's age. Anne felt how remarkable a person she was to have such a special boyfriend as Anton, and excused his solitary behaviour as a symptom of his peculiar genius.

Exuding an air of complete mastery, Anton chopped vegetables and prepared dishes. He worked with meticulous ease on the kitchen's stainless steel surfaces, as if programmed to do it, keeping a range of pans sizzling or boiling at different rates.

They were running through the menu in preparation for the opening, making a different selection of dishes every evening on which the students dined and made comments. He made moussaka, lemon chicken, stifado, grilled meats: simple dishes that could be produced in bulk. Hester was not interested in the market for fish and lobster, the dishes served by the restaurants in Zeste to tourists. Over-fishing had reduced the supply and increased the price of fish; simple food was a better bet.

Hester watched Anton with a proprietorial air, more maternal than sisterly, as if she had made him herself. He had always been unusual; as an underdeveloped child he had been silent and withdrawn but all the while he was working hard at separating people out and understanding them. He had realised that people were different. First he used to see them just as people, they were tall or not tall, giving him an idea of the differences in the world: tall would be grown up, not tall would be his age or below. For a long time, for years, the child Anton maintained these simple distinctions, and when too much information came in, when one of the tall people tried to communicate, it was like water rushing in his head, and he became frightened and withdrew into himself.

It was trees that were the key to his understanding; first he had seen them all as trees, with no distinction between them. Slowly at first, and then with lightening rapidity, he realised that trees were distinct: tall and white, green and springy, spreading and five-pointed. His entry into the world was his realisation that he was not the first person to have done this. Seeing him gazing intently at a tree through the kitchen window Hester, then in her late teens, placed a book in front of him that happened to be around, The Observer's Book of Trees. She did not try to engage him with it, fearing the usual furious rejection, but he turned the pages and saw that the distinction he had made between trees had already been made. In what was the first complete sentence he spoke, he said 'I want to read.' This was astonishing as he had never expressed desire before except by reaching for things, it had not been apparent that he even knew what reading was. He had obviously been picking up information from his surroundings without interacting. Now he took to gathering knowledge with a passion. He learned to read within a week, he never needed to be told anything twice, and was exasperated when Hester paused or repeated herself. He tore through primary then advanced textbooks as fast as they could be obtained for him in order to reach his goal of fully understanding the tree book: silver birch, yew, plane. He read about the bark, the clusters, the shoots, the trunks, the spreading yellow twigs; he could identify the multiple suckers and long catkins of the caucasian wingnut, the pale underside of the silver leaf lime in the wind.

Hester and their mother found the odd little boy suddenly engaging not gradually or individually but wholesale, with everything, all at the same time. He wanted to know music, mathematics, words and nature; he wanted to know where food came from, then about methods of agriculture, then botany and biology to understand animals and plants, then organic chemistry to understand the processes taking place within the animals and plants, then physics to understand the workings of the elements of the chemistry. Everything connected to everything else, it was all just a matter of knowing enough. He read ferociously and was never without a book: at the table or bathroom or travelling or just standing still.

As a child at school Anton used to think of himself as an alien, noting the habits of the locals; in his first year at Sussex University he rediscovered this ability, that helped him to cope in an environment where there was too much input, the crashing waves of too many thoughts coming in. He liked to keep his surroundings ordered. Violence and uncertainty reminded him of the time he was bullied at school: a time of fear and pain.

Time slips and things change and that was hard to deal with, Anton liked things that did not change, the quadratic equation, the heroic couplet, the ordinary girl who was the same yesterday as today and tomorrow.

Cooking was bliss: the same ingredients, the olive oil, lemon juice and balsamic vinegar, oregano and garlic. The same operation of heat in the same pan, the same result, pleasing to all, a good use of time and a contribution to the community, a place where he fitted in. The thing he did not want to be was odd, unusual, a misfit.

Sven and Sarah joined them, she sat at one of the restaurant tables in front of the building with a teach-yourself-Greek book. Sarah was a natural communicator, had Italian from her mother and had picked up French and German from school, had enough Spanish to get by, and assumed she would therefore learn Greek fast, but it was a language as prickly as a gorse bush. She found it surprisingly hard even to master the alphabet, finding it difficult to overcome the tendency to give Greek letters their Latin values where they looked similar. She was frustrated that she would confuse even simple Greek words, like ticket, *esitirio*, with restaurant, *estiatorio*, presumably because she had learned them both at the same time; not to mention the difficulty of identical words for different things: *trapeza* for both bank and table, just with the accent in a different place. The usual challenge of tenses, plurals and genders was compounded because almost all the words in a sentence could be modified by the case it was in, so the comfort of familiarity was lost even with quite simple sentences. Accusative, dative and genitive: a little thicket of grammar in which to get inextricably tangled. Sven could help with his school-taught classical Greek, but if she were to communicate with Greek customers as a waitress when the restaurant opened, she must at least have the basics at her command.

Around midday Hester welcomed a small open-backed van of drinks: bottles of water, half-litre bottles of retsina with a beer-bottle top; squat bottles of orange juice; Greek Mythos beer with a laurel on the label and Heineken, locally called green beer because it came in a green bottle.

A young, good looking Greek man talked with Hester and began unloading crates. Sarah watched his strong arms heaving the heavy boxes, saw the muscles bulge, stretching the arms of his white T shirt. He caught her gaze and smiled with a perfect set of teeth and deep brown eyes.

'I'm Kostas,' he said.

'Sarah, pleased to meet you' she said as if being introduced to a boy at a midsummer ball.

'Are you here for long?'

'The whole summer.'

'Great, you like Doxos?'

'I love it,' she said, and flashed her most radiant smile.

'What are you doing,' he said redundantly, looking at her Greek language notes, 'soon you will speak Greek like us.'

Anton who had emerged from the kitchen, looked over but did not say anything, he knew the islanders spoke a form of demotic Greek so heavily accented it was like a dialect. Anton hardly spoke any Greek but could read a lot of the language and usually understood the basics of sentences.

'You will do it,' said Kostas, looking at her phrase book. 'Five letters can make the i sound,' he said, 'sometimes two letters go together to make a new sound: gg makes ng.'

Sarah knew this but gratefully acknowledged his advice. She thought it would be the Greek thing to do to invite him to lunch and, indeed, he seemed to expect hospitality. When she bent over to put her books in her bag he could see the start of the butterfly wind wisp tattoo on her lower back, just above the strap of her red thong.

They ate a simple meal of Greek salad, tiny fried fishes and cheese pies.

'What have you seen of the island?' he asked, 'have you seen the castle and the chapel, the monastery, the church of Our Lady of the Oysters?'

In truth, the students had seen little of the island, tied as they were to the restaurant and to restoring the house. Kostas explained that his uncle Vasilios delivered to all the restaurants. His family had the concession for distributing drinks on the island, drinks for the restaurant trade could be imported only through them. Kostas was just helping out, he did not want the foreigners to think he was a full time van driver or a hired hand.

'So what do you normally do?' asked Anne.

'I am island boy,' said Kostas with one of his glorious smiles, 'I do some of everything, some fishing, some driving, help my uncle with his business.' He asked what they did back home.

'We are all just undergraduate students at university except Sven, he is doing a master's degree,' said Sarah.

'A master,' said Kostas, 'like a boat-master. What are you a master of?'

Rather reluctantly, Sven explained that he worked on the theories of suicide of Camus and of Mao in relation to conversations in suicide chat rooms. Kostas understood the internet but what was a suicide chat room? Sven tried to explain but Kostas didn't really get it. In truth, Greek youngsters rarely made an impression on the virtual sofas of the suicide chat rooms, a fact that Sven took as a sign of the inferiority of their civilisation, an inability to dwell on the profound, as could northern European teenagers, from Lisbon to the Urals.

They cheerfully tried to explain this cultural disparity, 'Bulletin boards looking for other young people to share their last moments,' Anne said.

'Places where people talk about dying,' said Sarah,

'Come die with me' Anton said, 'what happened to good old fashioned cyber-sex?' another reference alien to Kostas but he laughed along with the others.

'It is the north,' said Kostas, 'the long winters you have. In spring they wake up, go out, see it is sunny, and jump about and fall off a cliff.' His fingers danced on the table. Sarah thought the silliness of it cripplingly funny, and Kostas played on the humour by having his finger dance on the table representing a suddenly lively northerner, then jump off like a person leaping to their doom.

Sven thought him a ridiculous youth, Anton found him not worth thinking about, but Anne was pleased at his help with simple Greek phrases of greeting, and Sarah found his smile embraced all the charm of the island, the spontaneous laughter and openness of the Greek spirit. She waved cheerfully to him. After he had left Sven said, trying to be positive, 'Young men like him without much prospects would be involved in drugs or crime back home, but here they are just hanging about and having a good time.'

'He does work,' says Sarah, a little irritated at Sven's patronising attitude, 'he looked like he was working when he came here.'

'Yes,' said Sven, 'I guess.'

Kostas went off in the little green truck, he was one of the princes of the island: good looking, well-built and well connected. He did not have to make any effort to retain his position, he just had to be. Greek boys did not have to do anything, they were adored by their mothers merely for being what they were, no extra effort was required, and none generally was vouchsafed. If they reached maturity sound of wind and limb, mothers expected nothing more of them by way of work or educational achievement. It was said they were breastfed till the age of thirty. This was the source of Kostas' confidence and his expectation that everyone would love him, at least on the island. Kostas did not think much about other people or other places. If he thought at all about what these northern visitors did in their own lands it was an idea of big white beings, trekking about to each other's houses in the frozen landscape like polar bears, or sitting outside on the metal chairs of chilly cafes, drinking their lager beers wrapped up in anoraks and mittens while the slush lapped around their feet. Whatever Kostas' limitations as to the world outside, however, he knew his familial obligations. On his way back to town he called in on his aunt Aspasia to apprise her of progress on the rival restaurant. She praised him and petted him, tried to get him to eat sweets and sucked in all his information about the new arrivals.

Back at the house after lunch, Sven and Sarah, enlivened by the wine and hilarity, and not enervated by the light labours of the day, began to make love. Sven had come slow to sex in his life. He had no special girlfriends, then arrived at the age of eighteen and found himself the object of female attention. Then, after his first degree in Uppsala, he came to Sussex to do his masters' and the magical effect just of being Sven continued to work its effect as it had in

Sweden, but with the added attraction of a glamorous foreign background. 'Isn't he gorgeous?' girls would say behind his back. And Sven was indeed an attractive man: tall, well-built with a cool demeanour that did not leap into conversations but presented itself with measured precision. He was funny, highly articulate, knowledgeable...Sarah checked off the list of all the things he was and how he was just right for her and she had taken him as her prize, her right as she felt it, as the most attractive girl in the European Studies common room to have the most attractive boy. '*This one mine*' she had said to herself.

He caressed her generous breasts and thighs that she raised as she gripped his white arms with their coating of blond hair. Sarah couldn't help but think of Kostas, she imagined the sex of a boy like him: not disciplined and considerate of her having an orgasm first, but dominating her as he swept over her with a crashing wave of uncontrollable male passion. The thought did it for her and she came in a flush that drenched her in sweat.

Sven was thinking of Anton: *this is how I would like Anton to penetrate me*, but he thought it in Swedish that made the sentiment more secret because even if she could read his mind, Sarah would still not know what he was thinking: *Såhär skulle jag vilja att Anton trängde in i mig.*

When the day was a little cooler Anne and Hester went down in the jeep to the vegetable market in the island's largest town of Megalo Limani on the other side of Doxos. As they drove around the high road Anne saw the magnificent spectacle of the castle, the string of windmills on the mountain below it, then the fishing town with its little red-domed church and the white blocks of houses scattered down the slope to the glittering sea. As they approached the town they passed the rubbish strewn by the side of the road and heard the incessant noise of the motor scooters taking over from the country sounds. Megalo Limani was relatively recently built, most of the buildings were from the 1930s, in contrast to the mediaeval town by the harbour. The roads were wide, houses had generous gardens set before them.

Outside the market a farmer was squatting by the gutter, washing his carrots with water from a hose before he took them in to sell. The market was a series of huge piles of tomatoes, purple onions, lemons, green peppers and potatoes, yellow plastic bowls full of garlic or cherries. Anne was struck by the aroma of fresh vegetables – celery, cucumbers and peppers at absurdly low prices, most things a Euro a kilo, as if the owner had got bored with individual pricing and just stuck the same tag on everything.

Among the green and leafy vegetables inside the market, Hester stopped to talk to an apple-shaped young woman with long dark hair who carried a huge basket of nectarines, almost too big for her. Hester introduced her to Anne as Jess, 'The island's about eight miles square, you'll probably meet everyone here,' she said.

'Many times,' said Jess, who had a London accent, 'you can't help meeting us unless you become a hermit, you'll meet us all so many times you will be sick of us and scream for variety. I sort of live here,' Jess said, 'well, we still live in London but come here as often as we can.'

Jess was in her late twenties, younger than most of the expats.

'You've got quite an appetite for fruit,' said Anne, 'are you making jam?'

'I do voluntary work with the refugees I am taking them some fresh fruit, they don't get any in the diet they get in the compound.'

'I saw the refugees in a cage on the harbour when I arrived,' said Anne, 'they looked in a terrible state.'

'That would be some of them, there's a new lot every week, sometimes every day, they are held in a camp on the other side of the mountain. I take things once a week, for the new arrivals and see what people need by way of clothes, most of them come with nothing, the smugglers make them leave everything behind to make room for more people.'

Anne showed such interest Jess offered to take her; Anne was game for a new experience. She told Hester and Anne left with Jess who squeezed her figure into her dusty blue Ford. Jess had plumply rounded breasts, arms and thighs and her feet hardly touched the pedals. She kept up an incessant stream of chatter. She explained she had bought an old house five years before and was steadily improving it. She started on another tale of procrastinating builders, then stopped herself, 'Everyone here, is a building bore, sorry about that.' Her husband or boyfriend or partner, Pete, whom she always referred to as 'my man' worked for one of the big trade unions in Britain. Jess worked for a housing charity, 'I just can't get enough of the poor, you see, here I am on holiday and I am off with the refugees. It's called a busman's holiday but I don't know why, maybe in the olden days busmen were known to go to bus stations in holiday resorts and have a tootle around the town in someone else's motor. I'd get bored if I didn't do something in the community.'

'I would too,' Anne said, 'I'd like to have something to do. I'm going to have loads of time here, otherwise I'd just spend it on self-indulgent things like going to the beach.'

'That's what a lot of people go on holiday for,' said Jess. She caught the suggestion of the non-conformist conscience. 'Have you done anything like this before?' she asked.

'Sure, my dad's a minster and homeless people are always calling at our house for a handout. I give them food – you know, Angry Tramp and Baseball Cap Tramp and Polite Tramp, you have to be able to identify them or you will keep giving things to the same person. Where do you get your stuff?'

'The Red Cross and some Greek charities donate things and volunteers give them out: clothes, soap, toothbrushes, that sort of thing. There are people on the island who keep culture going – humanitarian efforts like this, and plays and music. I call them the Olympians. There's a committee of them that co-ordinates this refugee work but I don't deal much with them, haven't got the language, see, not at that level.'

'Who are they, church people?'

'No, not here, the Greek Orthodox church thinks that charity begins at home, and it stays there. The committee is more like more like professionals, you know the solicitor, a doctor...some individual priests are very good, and a few of the churchgoing women are involved.'

They were bouncing over a poorly made road, approaching a forbidding building of three storeys surrounded by a high wall. A manually operated gate which was open, led to an asphalt drive in front of the building. The rows of identical windows on the rust-coloured building had thick iron wire rather than bars. There was only one bored guard sitting in a cubicle at the entrance.

'Not exactly high security is it?' said Anne, 'Escape from Doxos wouldn't be much of an epic.'

'They don't need much guarding, they are not imprisoned, actually,' said Jess, 'but there's nowhere else for them to go, and if they left here they couldn't come back, so they stay where at least they are getting fed.

'What are they here for, what are they waiting for?'

'To become Europeans.'

'Are many accepted?'

'Not in Greece. The best they can hope for is to avoid arrest and make their way into a more friendly country.' Jess shouted something in Greek to the guard who waved her through.

The compound was originally an orphanage, built during the civil war of the 1940s. Children would be kept there and taught a trade, like boot-making for boys and laundry work for girls. The children who had originally been detained there were not, in fact, orphans, they were the children of communists who were imprisoned or had fled to Russia. Some, but not all parents had been killed in the political pogroms of those challenging times but the children were all treated as orphans anyway, because, it was reasoned, what sort of a parent was a communist? A child may as well have no parents. The authorities reassured themselves the children would be better off without such parents, so orphans they were.

This meant, in more enlightened times, past the civil war, past the junta and past Greece's entry to the EU as a democracy, the structure of the orphanage remained as an abandoned building. In the wake of the refugee crisis, a cousin of the mayor generously took the old orphanage off the hands of the island's council for a small consideration and had it set up to receive the hopefuls who had begun to wash in on the waves of eastern destitution to the shores of European prosperity.

Dotted around the asphalt courtyard were low walls surrounding what would once have been flower beds but were now dusty voids. Small groups of men were sitting on the walls, thin-limbed characters, some African but mostly of Middle Eastern appearance, all with black hair, most dressed in jeans or trousers and shirts with baseball shoes or flip-flops on their feet.

Anne thought they would be swamped when they entered as Jess had told her there were around two hundred in the compound, but only about twenty came up to exchange greetings. They were more listless, less grabbing than Anne had imagined they would be, like a crowd at a bus station waiting from a broken-down bus to be repaired so they could get on their way.

As word came of their arrival more came up to see the visitors, almost all men; women and children stayed behind bars in a separate barracks, most not coming out to the courtyard. Anne passed fruit out to the outstretched brown hands. 'All gone,' said Jess as they distributed the last of the fruit. 'We'll go to the store to get some toiletries and other stuff.'

Jess said it would be a good idea to take someone with them to help them carry the boxes, and would Anne like to choose someone – which Anne correctly surmised was a test, a way of assessing how she related personally to the refugees.

Most of those who had come around were now off eating their fruit or sharing it with others. There was a boy who was hanging around, perhaps wishing to engage in conversation; his positive attributes were that he was smiling, and small, she didn't want someone bigger or older than her.

'Hello,' she said to him, 'I'm Anne, who are you?'

'I am Malik, at your service,' he said.

'Would you like to help us?'

'I can give top notch services.'

'Well,' said Anne, startled by his turn of phrase, 'I imagine that is what we want.'

The three of them drove to the store, some distance from the compound, with Malik looking around animatedly as if it were his first view of everything.

When Anne asked what it was like in the compound he was not expressive, 'Not bad, it isn't for long,' he said.

The store was little more than a couple of lock-up garages that opened to exude a smell of soap and disinfectant and the sight of racks of metal shelving. Jess climbed a ladder and handed down boxes of toiletries and clothes that she had Malik pile into the car until there was almost no space for the people. 'Top hole,' said Malik when they had finished.

'How do you talk like that?' asked Anne.

'Good English?'

'Yes, good indeed, but old...upper class English.' There had been no mention of class in his reading matter, so Malik assumed she meant his spoken English was of a high standard. 'There were books at the school where my mother taught,' he said, 'left by a foreign teacher, my mother saved some from the burning, brought them home.'

'The what?'

'The book-burning, you know, when they burn books.'

'We don't do a lot of that in Sussex. So what were

the books she saved?'

'The Inimitable Jeeves, Stiff Upper Lip Jeeves, other Jeeves and Wooster books. by PG Wodehouse,' Malik pronounced the author's name wrongly but Anne did not have the heart to tell him, she said she had not read them but knew of them. She tried to engage Malik on the journey he had undertaken from Afghanistan but he was not forthcoming. 'I don't mind saying it rattled me,' was all he would come out with.

Jess said she would take Anne back first or they would be zigzagging from one side of the island to the other. 'Malik will help me distribute this stuff, I'll stop off at Hester's to drop you off.'

Anne invited Jess to come and meet her companions so when the car pulled up they all got out. When they arrived at Hester's their host was in despair, talking to a builder on a mobile phone, '*Ella thoulevete, tora* – come, work, now.' The builder put the phone down on her. The other students were with her but, in truth, to commiserate rather than make any contribution.

'This is Malik from Afghanistan, he came over on one of the refugee boats,' said Anne.

'What ho,' said Malik.

'*Salaam alaikum*' said Sven, and Malik responded in kind.

'Welcome to fortress Europe,' said Anton.

'Sporting of you to say so,' said Malik, 'are you from England?'

'The four of us study in England,' said Anton.

'I love England,' Malik said, 'everything about England – your Dickens your Shakespeare, your Spice Girls – once five, then four.' Samir had encouraged him to put more contemporary references in his speech, but this one evoked general hilarity.

'Getting a bit retro there, Malik' said Sarah, he laughed merrily with them. Now he was really getting on in European society.

Hester was too distracted to engage with the visitor, she was explaining her building nightmare to Jess who was giving what sympathy she could and making suggestions of alternative builders who, she conceded, were probably no more reliable than the ones whose current non-appearance was generating grief.

'We can't get the house properly fixed up, the builders won't come' Anne explained to Malik who regarded her with his alert expression. Standing together they were about the same height and perhaps the same weight though while Anne looked slender, Malik was scrawny.

Malik said, 'you are badly up against it.' Anton mused on this curious character Anne had brought in, who now went to the piles of building materials, the grit, the big sharp stones, the sand, the bags of cement, plaster and limewash. Dog-like, he sniffed and pawed at each one.

Anton moved from the group surrounding Hester and giving audience to her lamentation to watch what Malik was doing, conscious that here he was witnessing someone who understood the nature of things.

'Big holes,' said Malik, 'two of these' he picked up one of the larger, sharp stones, 'one cement. Cement makes it stick.' Like most things Anton learned, this was so obvious once he had run it through his mind that he incorporated the knowledge as if he had never not known it: the cement is sticky, the large grade gravel gives the mix body.

'Next, this,' Malik took a handful of the coarse sand and let it trickle through his fingers, 'Sand and cement, four to one,' he went round pointing at the piles

'That's the mixing ratio?' said Anton. He watched the little brown boy darting between the piles like an imp.

'My father is a builder,' said Malik, I have watched his work many times, since I was small. I know how to mix. But I am not strong like my father and my brother, I am better at books.

'Lots of need for building work in Afghanistan in recent years, eh?' said Anton.

'Spot on' said Malik nodding vigorously. Anton may have had his deficiencies in the empathy department, but in his favour, he had a truly egalitarian ability to see through the background noise of personality to value genuine ability. Malik knew how to build. He knew how to reinforce concrete with the steel cages, making a wooden box in which the concrete could set. As soon as he had described it, Anton, looking at the remains of the existing structure with its rusting, exposed ribs, realised he was right. What Malik did not understand, he could work out by touching the materials, feeling their qualities of grittiness or stickiness.

'You have what you need here,' Malik said, 'tip-top.'

'We have a builder,' said Anton, 'Malik. He knows what to do, we've got the materials.' The others looked dubiously at this apparition, a teenage illegal immigrant claiming to be a builder just when they needed one. 'It's only a repair,' said Anton, 'we aren't building a new house. We are filling holes, we can make it work.'

No one said anything so Anton continued, 'Sven – are you in?'

Sven was, as usual, willing to do anything Anton suggested, and had been emboldened by the work they had already done, 'How hard can it be?' he said.

'I'd happily muck in, but I don't know if I would be much use, I'm not built like a labourer,' said Anne. Sarah did not contribute, she did not want to be negative, but this was not the holiday she had expected, or had signed up for.

Jess was ecstatic, 'Brilliant,' she said, hopping about like a boxer, 'bypass the pigging builders.'

'That's heavy work,' said Hester.

They discussed how they could repair the house: not as well or as fast as professionals, but they could get it done bit by bit. Malik was beaming around him, unable to keep up with the verbal dexterity of the students, but delighted to be in their company.

'I don't know if they'll let Malik out every day,' said Anne.

'Bribe the guards,' said Jess, 'it will be worth it. Tell them you will always be with him and you will bring him back. They don't care.'

Hester nodded, seeing how this could work, 'We'll try them at ten Euros a trip. Malik,' she addressed him 'we have to talk about payment for you.' She worked out a daily rate on the basis of a Greek builder's wage for a four-hour day. Malik was overjoyed.

Jess took Malik back to the compound and left him at the gate, waving and cheerful. The following day Anne and Hester went to make an arrangement with the guard, who was quite indifferent, so long as he could account for all of the residents at the end of the day.

Malik did not tell anyone what help he was giving, or that he was getting paid. Some of the refugees were as dangerous as the smugglers, and Malik was only just scenting his way around. Bullying and conflict between the national groups was a constant feature of the compound. 'Some of the characters are hard-boiled' as Malik put it. Generally people stayed in their national communities and spoke their own language.

Anne picked up Malik the next day in the jeep. At the house the boys were waiting in working gear that showed their physique: Sven was tall and broad-shouldered, not muscular but toned; wearing a faded red shirt and long shorts; Anton was back in his black jeans and a black T shirt, looking more wiry and alert than physically strong. They were working on the front, the side of the house which was in shadow from the sun, assembling their tools – the cold chisels, buckets, hammers, shovels, thick plastic bags for debris.

They took a small section of wall first, to see if they could do it, hacking out two square metres of loose rendering around one of the big holes and replacing it. Malik taught them the alchemy of building materials, making a thick slurry of stones, sand and cement to the right consistency so that when the boys threw it into the holes and spaces they had exposed, it did not slide down the wall but stuck there. They cut out and filled larger spaces, using ladders, the balcony and a primitive scaffold to reach the first floor. Soon the house was a patchwork of old and new, practically filled holes and partially rendered walls, but every day it was more solid, more completely theirs. Those nights the students slept with the smell of drying cement in their nostrils, refreshingly cool and clean after the must of the old house.

Malik mainly mixed mortar and the two boys shovelled it into buckets, quickly discovering the limits of their strength and filling them only half full. Anne chatted to Malik and did light work, helped with filling bags with debris and keeping control of the water hose for the mixes. They were putting in only three or four hours, for the glare of the sun prevented longer shifts, so long as they had made some progress every day they were happy.

They had not expected it, but there was a shift in attitude of the locals towards them. When they called in at the hardware store for tools, clearly soiled from some hours of labour, the men working there praised them with 'bravo,' impressed in a way that surprised Sven and Anton, who thought they were just doing a do-it-yourself job as anyone did at home. When he saw their work Alekos was moved to tell them he respected them for it, with a clear implication that he hadn't had much respect previously.

The building of reinforced slabs of concrete for the side balcony and the toilet roof were harder challenges than filling holes had been, but ingenuity and effort overcame their failures, along with Malik's knowledge, until they were walking up the ladders with buckets of cement to pour into moulds. Their arms ached with the strain and sweat drenched them but Sven and Anton felt like pioneers, when they had bashed and bruised themselves with the unfamiliar weights and pulled their tendons for a building, they had a stake in it, a stake in this land. Anton found it surprisingly satisfying to do physical work. Thinking of sex kept him happy with this laborious task: sex sex sex in his head like a persistent song as he smacked the mortar mix into place, his mind finding its own rhythm and shutting out the confusion of all the images of the world. Anton had found he could pretty much do without close interaction with other people except for the sex, and had not thought that would be such a problem, but he had had a troubled first year at university. Sex had been easier at home – mainly with a schoolmate's sister, a younger girl who for some unfathomable reason was obsessed with him. He imagined university would throw similar opportunities his way, but he was faced with the paradox that the smaller catchment area of home was an easier seduction ground than the large one of university.

The opportunities were there and he took them but he was introduced to a world of feminine neurosis: women who banged on his door in a panic in the early hours of the morning, overwhelmed by some personal obsession; or who would say they would meet him and did not; or the former drug addict who morphed into an alcoholic. He called them the train-crash girlfriends – not to their faces, of course. There was a personal commentary running in his mind to interpret the world, remembering the definitions of the past and feeding him information. He felt mentally endangered: if he was going with all these weird girls, then he must be weird himself, and that was something he refused to be. That was when ordinary girls became a project for his exquisitely tuned mind.

First he had to tackle what ordinary people did and he didn't. He had no small talk, Anton never knew what to say in casual conversation, and would say what occurred to him, which from the girl's reaction he realised would come across as weird. So he dawdled in bars and common rooms where students met and eavesdropped conversations, picking up phrases and nuances of speech – always sound positive, don't project yourself, draw the other person out by asking questions, use humour which is the combination of disparate elements to render the ordinary absurd.

Then he met the princess of ordinary, Anne. When he first saw her Anne had been dressed in a blue denim skirt, tan coloured knee-length boots and a little top with lace detail. Five foot five, shoulder length mousey brown hair, blue-grey eyes. She was recently arrived at the university, he was in his second year. She was a Methodist minister's daughter, from Biggleswade, not London or Cambridge, but Biggleswade, not even the most boring town in England, which would have been a distinction in itself, but in the right division to be so. Anton fell for her immediately. He was filled with the familiar desire, for her average height, the silhouette of her body with its simple lines, clearly but lightly defined hips and breasts.

Her conversation was, 'How did they make cheesecake before there were digestive biscuits to crumble, to make the base? Or was there no cheesecake before there were digestive biscuits? It's one of those questions, you know, like: Are there paperclips in heaven? If there are, does that mean there is office work in heaven, where for a lot of people office work is hell...or if there are no paper clips, doesn't that mean heaven is deficient in some element, and it can't be, because it is perfect...'

'They are to hold the angels' lists together,' Anton said, 'the lists of good deeds, on their celestial clipboards.' Anne judged that the right answer.

Sven watched Anton in their building work,

enjoying being with him in this shared task. He noticed the glistening of his friend's arms as he carried mortar or chipped with a chisel, noticed the smell of his sweat. For Sven there was a supreme rightness about being together, the feeling of being males in a manly occupation, the dirt of labour on their brows. Their muscles developed and biceps visibly increased after only a few days of heavy work. Sven was more interested in noting the changes in Anton's body than his own. Sven also enjoyed working with Malik, his sense of purpose and his optimism impressed the gloomy Swede and he made a point of talking to Malik at lunch.

He asked Malik why he wanted to go to England. He said, 'Good country, peoples are kind, they give you a passport and a place to live.'

Sven tried to disabuse him of this benign notion but it was stuck in his mind. 'Why not aim for Sweden?' said Sven with a touch of national pride, 'lots of fresh air, lakes and forests. Why England all the time?'

Malik was engaged, fancying there was competition to take in refugees in Europe. His vista opened up, from one green country to more than twenty, their uneven map colours and jagged boundaries fitting in to each other as a continental jigsaw.

Sven talked with Anton about the refugees' faith in the welcome they were going to receive in Europe. Anton said if people had sacrificed a great deal to a belief, it became more and more necessary to keep the faith, they convinced themselves of its truth despite all the evidence to the contrary. Anton said, 'Like people who give up their jobs and sell all their possessions because a cult leader has prophesied the end of the world. When it doesn't come, they convince themselves their calculations of the day were imprecise, or their faith has put off the apocalypse, anything except that they were wrong from the start.' Sven saw the wisdom of this, and it appealed to his bleak sensibilities, a little piece of cold northern logic in these sunny climes.

Not everything was uncomplicated between the students and Malik. When Anne first picked up Malik in the jeep from the compound on her own she was wearing shorts. He had never been this close to a woman who was not a family member, and never been so close to any woman in such a state of undress. He knew it was not unusual in this country, but seeing half naked women at a distance on a boat or a beach was different from sitting next to them, and for a time he was silent. Anne was quite aware of his discomfort and had considered being more covered up when she dressed that morning, but reasoned with herself that he was in her continent and it was he who must adjust. If she went to Arabia she would dress accordingly. This coincided with what Malik's father had told him, he must not be moved by unusual sights but must keep the faith. Malik therefore followed that good advice and acted as if there was nothing at all unusual in talking with a girl in such immodest attire, while they organised the hose pipe and counted out the ratios.

Once Hester had given him some money, Malik asked Anne to take him to a mobile phone shop and he bought a tiny, inexpensive phone that he used to send a text message to his parents that he was in Europe and had work. Later that evening, sitting in the courtyard of the compound, he sent a text to Samir to wish him well and tell him that they would soon be together again, God willing. Samir replied, almost immediately, as if he had been looking at the phone waiting for the call: 'In Europe I will buy you a jet plane.' Malik was reassured, it was the same old Samir. They did not correspond for long, as Samir's credit was limited, but Malik was able to tell him about his new friends and the building work and look forward to seeing him. Hope flourished. One of the other refugees came up to Malik and asked if he could send a text on his mobile. Malik, quick to grasp an opportunity, said he could, for the price of one Euro, thus commencing his business career.

After more than a week of working on the house they slapped white limewash on the walls of the courtyard in the morning and were disappointed at the grey and streaky appearance. The tawny concrete was now white, but it was a dirty white. They went down to the restaurant for lunch, unhappy at their failure. When they returned to the house for the afternoon rest it was like an icing-sugar palace. Once the sun had hit the limewash it gleamed brilliantly, like the snowy slopes of a high mountain lit by solar rays from a clear sky. It was enough to give the four snow-blindness if they looked for too long, as they marvelled at the transformation.

During these days of work at the house Hester was mainly in the kitchen, Sarah helped or learned Greek, sometimes assisted by Kostas who came round on his shiny motorcycle, to talk about the island and beguile Sarah with his wonderful smile.

The conduct for life together evolved until it was finally codified by Anne and Anton, printed out and stuck on the back of the front door:

'Rules of the Wendy House

1) Use tap water for all purposes except drinking. Drinking water bottles can be filled from the

restaurant's supply but then it has to be carried up the hill to the house, so use it carefully. If you are going to drink from the bottle, label it as yours before you put it in the fridge.

2) No objects are ever to be placed on the steps of the narrow internal staircase – anyone coming down backwards will slip on them. This warning is from dire experience.

3) All food must be put away in the fridge or sealed containers. No food should be kept in bedrooms – food should be defined widely, not just food for you but food for bugs as well, who find tissues filled with bodily fluids a proteinageous treat (yeuch).

4) The drains won't take toilet paper. Once used it has to be placed in the poo bins (double yeuch). The last person out of the house every morning has to take the poo bin liner and any other rubbish out to the rubbish bins by the restaurant.

5) Spray each room in the house once a week with the green bug spray to discourage roaches. This should make them feel unwelcome so they should stay away. If you see one, a direct hit with the green bug spray will ensure he gets the message.'

They later added a rule about transport which found its way to the end, in default of any other place to put it: '6) The jeep and two scooters can be used by anyone but check with Hester when you take the jeep out. If one person is going out alone, take a scooter rather than the jeep to keep fuel costs down.'

On the days of building they sat around in the evenings, exhausted but satisfied with their labours, enjoying the tart local wine and Hester's dish of the day. These big dinners all together on the beach were to be the times they remembered as the best of Doxos.

They were tired but were still planning the work they were going to do; with the tables on the beach lit up in the moonlight like a theatre set.

'Have you decided what you are going to call the place?' Sven asked Hester.

'I call it the café. The restaurant if I'm feeling posh,' she said, 'Hester's, I thought, though it doesn't sound great in Greek.'

'No aspirated H,' said Anton, 'Esters – not so good.'

'Shouldn't you call it something European?' asked Sarah, 'Treaty of Rome Inn?'

'Maybe something with a little more zing – Strasbourg by the Sea,' said Sven.

Anne said, 'In my home town we had a place called Burger Le Caff, the "Le" was like a concession to our continental partners.'

'Something that sounds like a European language but isn't?' said Sven.

'How about Café Europa?' someone said, and there was later disagreement on who it was, but by universal accord that was it, and the next day they went to the ships' chandler's in the harbour and bought pots of glossy, coloured paints that yacht owners used to paint markings on their boats, and the four painted a sign to Sarah's design on the outer wall, that was visible to boats in the bay, so as the yachties cruised into the harbour in the afternoon to berth for the night, they passed the sign that proclaimed 'Café Europa' with a welcoming 'OPEN' underneath.

Chapter 6

In the third week of labour at the bottom of the mountain, work had ceased on the house and their attention was transferred to the restaurant. Café Europa opened in stages, first selling just drinks and snacks while Hester worked towards a grand opening of the place as a fully functioning restaurant.

In the early days there was a surprising number of visitors. The café was well placed for tourists exploring Doxos who had run through the limited number of activities to pursue on an eight-mile-long island. The natural inclination once a tourist had rented a motor scooter, and had not yet injured themselves coming off it, was to drive all around, taking each road as far as it went. A trip around the bay had to culminate at Café Europa, after they had cycled past the pride of the island's restaurants in Zeste.

Inquisitive parties from the Greek population also visited to look around, some were even customers. Hester had set herself the task of having at least one conversation in Greek a day, to improve her language. She was still struggling, but valued the challenge of a character like Grandma Poppy who had no word of English.

Grandma Poppy was a tiny, cheerful woman like concentrated sunshine, who blessed the Virgin for every day she survived without her abusive husband who had died thirty years previously, occasioning the usual widespread lamentations that the island had lost such a good man. Grandma Poppy was wrinkled as a walnut and burned as brown from the sun. She came all smiles, bringing the customary present, without which a visit to a new home would be incomplete. This was a plate of little delicacies she had made of filo pastry folded over to make triangles filled with the wild spinach that formed part of the diet of the poor and dolmades made of rice and herbs rolled into balls and wrapped in vine leaves.

Hester sat Grandma down and gave her a coffee, nibbling on the gifts. The students' food preferences had made her think about variations on the menu to accommodate modern tastes. Anne was vegetarian and Sven was largely so, but he would compromise on fish.

She questioned Grandma Poppy about the contents of her snacks. '*Oxi crio*,' Hester said, no meat?

'No, no meat,' the old lady said sadly, and looked away, shamed by her poverty.

'No' said Hester, '*oxi crio kalos, xortaphagos*...it is good to have no meat, vegetarians....'

'*Xortophagos?*' said Grandma, as if it were the first time she had heard the word, which it may well have been, vegetable eating being the habit of the poor of necessity, not choice.

'*Xortophagos t'aressi xortariko*' Hester got out, 'vegetarians love vegetables.'

Old Grandma's face erupted into smiles, she had no idea what a vegetable eater was, excepting the obvious, that they appreciated her preparations.

Hester made a deal for Grandma Poppy to deliver a tray of her snacks every day at an absurdly low rate which nevertheless delighted Grandma. She went off overjoyed at the deal, as much for the recognition of her efforts as for the money. That haughty bitch Aspasia had disdained Grandma's poor contribution to island cuisine in favour of meats imported in a refrigerated van, but with Hester she had found a new friend.

Inevitably, Aspasia arrived in the early days to welcome the newcomers with a gift, her black hair piled up, trademark red flower behind her ear. Aspasia wore stilettoes, a mustard dress trimmed with black, and carried a black handbag as if she were making a social call.

Despite herself, Hester was flustered, wiped her hands on the apron she was wearing, quickly took it off and threw it aside. She had not met Aspasia but had seen her peering out from the window of her restaurant as Hester drove past.

Aspasia's dress contrasted with Hester's jeans and T shirt. Physically, despite her glamorous appearance, beside the lean figure of Hester, Aspasia seemed middle-aged, well-groomed but bulging around the midriff and arms.

'Neighbour' said Aspasia in Greek, throwing open her arms, 'welcome.'

She handed over the pot plant she was carrying, a red poinsettia, as if a visual representation of Aspasia herself, Hester gave it an admiring glance for as brief a time as propriety demanded and set it aside.

Hester touched the arms of the older woman as she kissed the air on either side of her face, a gesture that Sarah, witnessing the event, was later to imitate, acting it out with Anne to the amusement of the others, to indicate the minimum level of contact with the maximum disdain.

Hester offered her guest a drink, Aspasia asked for 'only water', which Hester sent Sarah to fetch. Aspasia accepted the glass gracefully, looking at Sarah with the venomous discernment of the older courtesan observing young beauty, put the glass to her lips but did not drink, and put it down.

'You have such lovely young people with you,' said Aspasia.

'My brother's friends are staying here,' said Hester.

'I did not want to bother you when you so busy getting ready but, how fine your restaurant looks now. You will do so well.'

'Please, look around,' said Hester, welcoming her guest to do what she was already engaged in doing, pausing in front of pictures and running her finger along the edge of tables. Followed by Hester with her face frozen into a smile, Aspasia went into the kitchen and turned, looking round at the hanging pots and the implements laid out with Anton's usual precision. She peered in the toilet, out the back door at the rubbish bins and to the forecourt where the tables spilled out onto the beach.

'Wonderful,' she said, 'How much did you pay for it?' Hester gave a figure 20,000 Euros below the actual price. Aspasia knew the real price, and Hester was reasonably sure that she knew, the lying about these things was just another stitch in the rich tapestry of island dissimulation. Telling the truth to a neighbour about a property purchase would have been highly suspect, as if the speaker had something to hide.

'We are close to your restaurant Aspasia...' Hester said.

'There is sunshine for everyone,' she said.

Aspasia drove back to her restaurant around the bay, her lipstick melting slightly into the lines around her mouth as she grimaced. She reassured herself that, though the place looked clean and efficient, the xenie would fail, they had no idea about the business, couldn't speak Greek, were in a bad position – people don't want to go that far for a restaurant, hers was as far as anyone wanted to go.

She called the Mayor who was at his desk, with more on his mind than Aspasia's entreaties. It was a week before the deadline set by Vasilios for the nocturnal expedition that he did not want observed by the Coastguard. The Mayor had received a loan from Vasilios to pay off the Germans who had accepted with bad grace and resumed work until their next payment which would be, they anticipated, deferred. Now, the Mayor contemplated, he had replaced one problem with another, perhaps a worse one. Vasilios would want his money back, he could only have it when the EU paid another instalment. However, if they didn't pay up, Vasilios couldn't have his money and instead of the danger of losing his position and possible criminal arraignment, the Mayor would be facing a rather stronger penalty from Vasilios. The only possibility he could see was carrying out Vasilios's mission and getting the Coastguard to eschew his job while Vasilios picked up his drugs. Then Vasilios would be happy and prepared to wait for his money, might even let the Mayor off some of the debt. The worse case was if he failed to repay Vasilios and failed to secure the conditions for Vasilios to pick up his package. That way Vasilios would lose out twice, and Vasilios was not a good loser.

Such were his thoughts when he picked up the phone to receive Aspasia's call, 'Light of my eyes, what can I do to make your day wonderful?'

Aspasia complained the foreigner must be stopped. The Mayor held the phone a little way from his ear as Aspasia explained: 'She may talk like a Cypriot but... It looks beautiful in there – clean, new paint, new dishes....all those young people working for her...'

'I will do what I can,' said the Mayor. To her protestation that she wanted a fuller commitment he said firmly, 'If it is within my power, I will do it.' As both he and Aspasia knew, this was a matter of propriety: a girlfriend could make only so many demands on him, not more, that was the prerogative of a wife. If Aspasia wanted someone to nag, she had better get a husband.

The Mayor asked if Alekos was about in the building and called him in, 'What's happening with your xenie friends who have the restaurant at Lands End?'

'They have worked hard,' the schoolteacher said, 'they are going to have a big opening night, they've invited all the xenie from the island and some of us.'

'They can't just open a restaurant,' said the Mayor, 'we need to have an inspection. I will get Theophilus to do it, and would you be there to translate? He has no English.'

The Café Europa team had invited to their opening party all the expatriates that they knew, and any guests staying with them, and such Greeks as they knew well. By 11am on opening day the restaurant already hummed with activity. Anton was putting the shining kitchen in order for making food that could be served easily to a large number. Anne and Sven were decking the entrance and the uprights of the awning with bunting and blowing up blue and white balloons. Sarah was hand-writing decorative menus.

Alekos called, looking official and rather sheepish, apologetically leading a little chap in a tie and shirtsleeves, with a toothbrush moustache, who entered as if he had a right to do so and woe betide anyone who stopped him, though there was no apparent impediment. 'I represent the council of Doxos' said Mr Theophilus in Greek, not extending a hand of greeting, 'I have to check that you comply with the regulations for restaurants.'

'No one has mentioned anything about a regulations check,' said Hester dryly, and I have often been to visit the council and the tax office. Everything here is in order.'

'I will decide that. You must comply with the regulations,' said Theophilus with no further explanation. He had a thick book which may or may not have been regulations for the operation of restaurants. It did not, anyway, have the appearance of a well-thumbed volume.

In fact Mr Theophilus was a surveyor who acted as a buildings inspector; the island had no environmental health inspector. Mr Theophilus was a fervent nationalist and pillar of the Orthodox Church. His most cherished beliefs were that Macedonia was Greek, the Elgin Marbles should be returned and that Turkey should always be referred to as Asia Minor. He had never been off the island, except to Rhodes to study, and he was not sympathetic towards foreign settlers.

He peered into cupboards and refrigerators, examined the light switches, checked the controls on the cooker, the water supply, looked into the dustbins. Hester watched impassively as the little man opened cupboards and made notes on a clipboard. The students sat at a table, anxious and restive amid the uninflated balloons and fancy menu cards and the big 'Welcome' sign they were going to erect.

He looked at his clipboard. 'This is not good,' he said, 'It is not hygienic – the bathroom must be tiled, not just behind the basin, but all over. To the top. This is not acceptable, you must do it.'

'When do you want us to do this?' asked Hester, hoping for the usual Greek laxity with time, where tomorrow was as good as the next day or the next week.

'Before anyone comes in, no member of the public can enter or we will close the place. Immediate, all very serious...' Alekos was not relishing his position as interpreter here, and was interpolating words such as, 'Excuse me...' and 'I am sorry but...' which were not part of Mr Theophilus' usual vocabulary.

Hester nodded and said, 'Is that all? Then you may leave now.'

She watched them leave then sat down, almost weeping with rage and frustration. 'Bastards. So they take it for granted that there is a poo bin full of shitty toilet paper on the floor, because that is what they expect, but they then complain about the lack of tiles.'

'The poo bin as a cultural norm,' murmured Anton. The students gathered around her, not sure whether to continue their tasks or commiserate.

'They are just trying to stop us opening,' said Hester

'They have to follow the regulations, said Sven earnestly, everyone has to.'

Sven had worked as hard as anybody to make the house and café work, but for Sven if there were a rule it was his to obey. He could not conceive of a law that was operated selectively. Back home sometimes laws were relaxed a little or made easier because of age or cultural difficulties, but the idea of applying a law only in order to persecute people was so alien it was not conceivable. The rules were there to help, to make things safer and better for everyone.

Hester rounded on him, 'Do you think so? In their restaurants they make them up as they go along. This is sabotage.'

'We just can't postpone the opening, we have invited everyone,' said Sarah

'It would be too humiliating,' said Hester, 'I can't bear it.'

'We could say we are just having people round for drinks,' said Sarah, 'how could they stop that? The guests aren't going to be charged anyway.'

'It's been advertised as a working restaurant, we can't pretend it isn't.

Anne said 'Let's just tile the place. It's six square metres of plain white tiles at most. I've put bathroom tiles up before, let's just do it.'

'My first thought,' said Hester, 'but it would take too long,

'You have to leave a day for the cement to dry before you use the place,' said Sven, 'or all the tiles fall off.'

'In the north probably,' said Anne, 'but even at home you can decrease the setting time by applying heat. Here we have heat.'

'We've got lots of that,' said Hester. Her face, flushed with anger in the ambient temperature, was testament to the fact.

'Plus what were these regulations?' said Anne, 'not that we believe in them, but, look, let's follow it through – the man said the toilet must be tiled, we can tile the toilet, it doesn't have to be grouted. We can do that tomorrow.'

'Can you tile it in a day – well, the rest of today?' Hester asked Anne.

It's a day's job, said Anne, yes, I can do it. we've got seven hours before the opening, just time to get to the tile shop before they close for the afternoon.

Hester left the others to continue preparations for the opening party and set off with Anne in the jeep immediately. They were at the tile shop just before they closed, meeting the owner as he was about to lock the door, and had to cajole him, eager as he was to get out to the beach, to let them buy immediately. They did not want to browse and choose and change their minds, as he feared they would, but just asked for six metres of plain white tiles, a cutter, a bag of cement and one of grout, which he supplied as if he were doing an enormous favour.

That afternoon Anne worked in the heat, in the small room, wearing shorts and a vest, kneeling on a towel that was soon soaked in sweat, measuring and placing tiles on the toilet walls while Sven behind her mixed mortar and cut the measured tiles with a satisfying click. Row after row, the tiles rose up the walls until the room was solidly panelled with gleaming porcelain. They were clearing away the fragments of tiles when the first guests arrived to step under the bunting.

Anne and Sven went to get cleaned up, Anne was first in and out of the shower. She put on a small blue sun dress and, sitting on the edge of the bed and holding the mirror up, put on as much make-up as she ever wore: eyeliner, a dash of blue eye shadow, '*for party lashes use an extra volume black mascara*' she remembered. She regretted that her fingernails were broken and her hands were red and lacerated with the sharp edges of cut tiles, but determined nevertheless to have a good time. She walked down to the restaurant and looked in at the open kitchen door where Anton was organising trays of dishes to hand out that Hester and he had made, with some contribution from

Grandma Poppy – plates of cheese pies, spinach pies, tiny fishes, grilled squid, fried cheese, tuna salad, fried aubergine slices and wild spinach.

She stroked his shoulders to reassure him she was there, but not interfering. He acknowledged her cheerfully, knowing this was what was expected of him, but when Anton was in meticulous planning mode he liked to be alone, in complete control of his world, of the sizzling, warming and browning of food.

Outside Sarah was resplendent amid the tables with her flowing locks of chestnut hair, serving bottled beer and local wine in bright aluminium jugs. Hester had invited the Greeks she had got to know such as the tradesmen and suppliers, and a few had come – though none of the professionals such as the architect or her solicitor turned up. Kostas had come early, on his shiny motorcycle, and chatted to Sarah, but left when the place started to get busy. Seeing him go off on the red Yamaha, Sven said, 'There aren't roads on the island for that thing to get to full speed, it is status only.' Alekos did not come, though he had said he would, and when they saw him later he apologised for his part in the inspectors' visit, saying he was just asked by the Mayor to translate.

However, almost all the expats came for what was a significant event in their community. Many businesses had been set up by Doxonians who had gone abroad and returned or had family on the island, Café Europa was the first that was set up by expatriates with no previous connection to the island.

The expatriates were a disparate bunch, mainly older than Hester, some retired or close to retirement. One of the younger ones was Toby, a stocky, prematurely balding man from Britain, and his copper-haired Austrian wife Renata who came to find paradise and raise a family. They were the only ones among the expatriates with a small child, a boy born on Doxos the previous year. Toby worked as a consultant, writing computer programmes for big companies. He had realised that, as his work was mainly with organisations in Canada, there was no particular advantage in staying with the drizzle, dirt and crime of London. His international clients had no interest where he worked, so long as he could deliver. He might as well be sitting at his computer overlooking the Aegean as the North Circular.

Bountiful Jess came with her intense, sharp-eyed man Pete. They were ever faithful and supportive of Café Europa in its troubles; they acted out of a general feeling that the people were good and the government was the enemy in every case. If defined at all, then 'the people' were those who had no political power. This had been their upbringing in politically active families, schooled in radical movements in the UK, and here on Doxos it was no different, they applied the lessons of engagement and direct action.

Richard and Ilva also appeared, bringing gifts of flowers. He was a somewhat dissolute former television executive, and his younger Swedish girlfriend was eager to be his wife. She sometimes chatted a little to Sven, both finding it welcome to speak in their native language.

Others came from industrial areas of the north of Britain, Scandinavia or Holland. A typical couple had worked hard all their lives in driving trucks or assembling parts on a factory line. In order to leave the north they would put together their two small pensions, when that was added to their pensions from the state and whatever savings they had, it afforded them a very comfortable lifestyle under the sun of

Doxos, and an attractive place for children and grandchildren to visit. They gathered in the town square to grumble about the exchange rate, swap tips on travel to and from the island, and reflect on the cheapness of life here.

One of the more unusual expats was Freddie who habitually wore long shorts and a T shirt, and always looked crumpled, like a boy who had come in from playing. He lived up and over on the hill behind them; he would make a point of coming over to see the students, down a poorly navigable track. In his previous life he used to do up flats for rent and made a modest fortune when property values were spiralling upwards. Now he lived on investments, rarely having to return to England for business.

He was a cockney and had a pretty, quiet Greek wife perhaps twenty years younger than he. Apart from the obvious attributes of youth and physical attractiveness, her primary quality seemed to be that she was largely without family attachments. Freddie volunteered when he first came over the hill, in one of his many outflowings of intimacy that she was, 'the best kind of Greek girl. The Greeks are lovely, best people in the world, salt of the earth, it's their families that are murder. If you want a Greek, have an orphan, that's what I say...' Recalling this in later days, Sarah would sometimes pause, stop what she was doing and say philosophically, 'ave an orphan, that's what I always say,' which invariably evoked a smile from whoever in the team was nearby.

Hester told the company about the difficulties she had with the Greek authorities, making Anne the hero of the hour and provoking a stream of similar stories. Ex-patriot meetings tended to resemble the Canterbury Tales or the Decameron, where each in the company attempted to out-do each other in 'Stories Where a Hopeful Expatriate is Thwarted by Greek Avarice.' There was the tale of a French couple who bought a house from someone who did not own it; the Greek solicitor who put his name on the deeds of a house that foreigners for whom he was acting were buying and built another floor on top of it while they were away; the home locked in a seven-year dispute with distant relatives of the seller who appeared on the day after the purchase to claim their inheritance.

The company were laughing in shocked horror at these excesses when one of the island's two police cars drove up and disgorged Captain Papadopoulos and the building inspector, the latter was marching up to Hester even as the policeman was closing the car door. Hester knew of these raids: the police really did take people off to the police station, she had no doubt they had the power to have her accompany them.

'*Ella*' said Hester to Theophilus, who was red-faced and panting, 'come.'

She marched him into the restaurant building with the assembled company watching in shocked amazement. The CD playing tinkling Greek music fortuitously stopped now, adding silence to the drama.

Hester, dry-mouthed but in control, indicated the toilet and let Theophilus walk in to see the gleaming display. '*Plakakia*,' said Hester, indicating the toilet walls, 'tiles.'

Mr Theophilus, perfectly aware of his situation, of the audience, and of the displeasure of Captain Papadopoulos peering in behind him (who made no secret that he felt this was a petty errand, undeserving of his authority) gave a slight nod, turned on his heel and got back into the police car. Captain

Papadopoulos said a curt 'good evening' before joining him and driving off. The entire scene had taken less than two minutes.

'Quiet, everyone, please quiet,' said Hester in the doorway of the restaurant, struggling to restrain her hilarity. They watched as the car rolled off down the road back towards Zeste. Once it was out of sight past the bend, the company burst into laughter.

The local Greeks who had come all joined in with glee: the greengrocer and his family of little boys; the plumber and his young wife and plump child; the suppliers in their white shirts and fresh jeans. The students had wondered how a battle with Greek officialdom would play with their Greek friends and acquaintances: would they be seen as foreign trouble-makers? Hester, living between two worlds, had caught on her antennae the contrary feelings of the locals and the way they read the situation: they hated the taxes, the town hall bureaucracy, the arrogant behaviour of the police; the everyday corruption. They would not stand up against their own authorities, they had too many conflicting loyalties for that, and the system could be made to work in their favour, so they did not tamper with it. But if someone else bested the authorities, that was another matter, and they would cheer from the sidelines.

Thus stimulated, the evening was a success to cherish. Who could forget the image of Sarah, confidently striding between the tables in a purple dress with tiny shoulder straps, with a mobile telephone held to hear ear by one hand and an order pad in the other...Anne after completing her marathon on the tiles, coming to the beach all smiles to join Jess and Pete's table and talk animatedly about her refugees...Anton, a white T-shirt on top but still with his black jeans, emerging from the kitchen to the communal tables with a fresh dish of his own creation...Sven, as handsome as Adonis in a collarless muslin shirt trimmed with gold, turning his troubled countenance towards the sea, but smiling on the company and getting up to dance with Sarah to Greek music...Hester presiding over the company like a lioness over her brood, surveying her hard-won territory.

The party went on into the night, its noise drifting in the soft darkness to where Aspasia sat on her veranda, seething with indignation. When the guests finally left Café Europa the students and Hester sat, exhausted, watching the darkness envelop the magical island as the house lights went off across the bay and Doxos went to sleep. This was a good day.

Shortly after the opening Sarah and Anne had been dropped off in town when Hester went on somewhere, and they took a taxi back. Sarah asked the driver to take them to Land's End which was the unofficial name of the location of Café Europa, though it also referred to the whole stretch of road. The taxi driver rolled around the bay, holding his silver worry beads in his free left hand that he held out of the window in the cooling breeze while a Greek singer crooned on the radio.

He stopped outside Aspasia's restaurant, 'End' he said simply.

'No,' Sarah said, communicating partly in Greek with some English and added gestures and, 'go on.'

'No more restaurants, this is the end,' he said.

'Drive to the end of this road, I'll show you.' Sarah said.

'Ah,' he said, as if just realising the source of the

confusion, 'that restaurant. Closed.'

'No,' Sarah said, 'open. You drive.'

He took them around the bend, a mile or so on and reluctantly pulled up at the forecourt of Café Europa. Sarah paid him and he went off grumpily. He's lost face,' Sarah said, 'he was wrong and a woman was right.'

'No wonder we're not getting much custom if the taxi drivers are refusing to bring people here,' said Hester when they explained to her.

'It could have been a genuine mistake' said Anne, always eager to believe the best in people, 'maybe he didn't know the restaurant was re-opened.' Hester gave her a glance of pitying scorn for her naivety.

That afternoon, to Sarah's design, working on Anton's computer, they produced leaflets with a little map of the bay and 'road ends' in Greek. In English it said: 'Café Europa – the restaurant at the end of Europe.' Sarah and Anne went out to the newsagents in town, a shop that supplied the community's stationery needs, and photocopied a pile of them. On the way back and they drove the jeep to the taxi station in Plakia. 'OK I'll do this' Sarah said to Anne, fluffed her hair up and undid her top two buttons so she presented a bulging cleavage, with a visible bra. She jumped out of the jeep and strode over to engage the grizzled taxi controller with the usual hello, how are you. She told him she was from Café Europa. Anne watched as the man's eyes rested on Sarah's bust. Sarah gave him some leaflets and explained they were out at Land's End and once she had told this powerful man, she knew all the taxi drivers would know the location in future. The taxi controller thanked her more profusely than was absolutely necessary and watched her bronzed thighs climb back into the jeep. Anne admired her more than ever.

The next move was obvious: if they could give the taxi drivers leaflets, why not the customers directly? After the initial success of the launch the place had few customers though by now visitors were flocking to the island by ferry, hydrofoil and plane, and Agios Nicholas was noticeably busier than it had been when they came. People had to want to visit Café Europa, there was no passing trade. This started a phase of outreach that attracted even more notice: at least once a day a couple of good-looking young people would be handing out leaflets on the main beaches and to passengers arriving on the ferry and hydrofoil. The leaflets gave directions and offered a free drink to new customers.

The other restaurant owners looked with distaste on this activity which did not fit in with their usual practice. The traditional method was men in tight trousers standing outside restaurants at dinner time endeavouring to hook in passers-by. Having young women inviting diners to join them at all hours of the day seemed to be taking an unfair advantage. The students plotted variations: Hester thought it was better to have Sven go out sometimes, 'It's more often women who decide where to eat,' she said, 'so let's not advertise ourselves with two pretty girls, let's have Sven and one of the girls.'

So Sarah and Sven spent more time together on these forays to the harbour and the beaches. Here Sarah began to find some of Sven's qualities a little grating. Sven always thought there was a right way to do everything, even, as they had discovered during the renovations, painting a door – first do the panels, then the horizontals then the verticals, even if it were a rustic panelled door of basic design like those in the

Wendy House. Sven had many principles around the pillars of honesty, diligence and saving the planet. He thought even drinking from a polystyrene cup was an offence against the environment. Sven was ever conscious of his place in the universe and the necessity of using time purposefully. This was admirable in its way, but being saintly and meticulous did not chime so well with the holiday spirit. Sven was thoughtful on these journeys out leafleting, making evident the contrast between the easy-going atmosphere of the island and his contemplative personality.

Out here they were assailed by the sounds of the island: the sirens and horns honking to announce a Greek wedding; the call of the gypsies selling carpets from a truck; the church bells of the island ringing out on Sunday from 7am, or any day at all to announce a death. 'For whom does the bell toll?' asked Sven.

'For some dead guy, not for me,' said Sarah.

On one of these excursions, seeing a raucous wedding procession pass by, Sarah exclaimed, 'It's the sense of community I love about it here, this must be how it used to be in Britain, in the fifties, when people knew each other and cared for each other, lived in families and were...friendly.' Sven was about to point out that the 1950s were not a golden age, and if anything were a more anxious time in Europe than the early twenty-first century, and in Greece they were murderous, but he thought better of it.

Sarah adored the sight of Sven but had trouble with his moods. He had a grounding in brutal realism that was difficult to break. She searched in their conversations for affirmations of his love for her. She loved the sense of their being a couple together, the appropriateness of it, they looked so right for each other, so beautiful and clever. She wanted him to say he didn't find anyone else attractive. He said he won't go with anyone else, but couldn't truthfully say he had no desire for them. 'What would it have been like if we had never met?' she once asked. Sven treated it as a factual question – they were the best partners each could meet at that time and place. If they had lived in another place or gone to another university, he would never have met her. 'We are popular people, we would have found someone else,' which had the merit of being accurate, but was not exactly what she wanted to hear.

Sven, however, wanted to hear only the absolute truth coming from his own mouth. He never explained where his adoration for the abstract principle of truth came from, but he had been, as it were, pre-betrayed by a lie. Sven was an unwanted child. His mother had not told his father that she was pregnant until it was too late to do anything about it. As an honourable man, he had to marry her, but he had always resented her for it and let Sven know as soon as he was old enough to understand. Sven consequently conceived that the world's ills all emanated from a disregard for the truth, and he endeavoured to be honest in all things. His ambition was a life without lies. In personal affairs he could be disappointingly abstract, and would say things like, 'The need for sex is like a disease. All we higher animals have got it, this incessant urge. You cannot cure, you can only treat it.'

'Thanks,' she said, 'so I am the treatment.'

'I wasn't talking about us,' he said, taking her in his arms, 'or I was, but all of us, everything, just that we are part of everything.'

'Not exactly a valentine card, but I think the best I'm going to get,' said Sarah.

Sometimes she wished he would just let go and let his feelings take him. Even when she tried to have an argument with him, he would set forth for and against and argue rationally from basic propositions until she wanted to scream. She used to love his display of principles – in many ways she still did, but sometimes she just thought: let it go, get a life.

Still, he had the charm of his beauty and brooding masculinity. The sight of his neck with its little curls of blond hair, his brilliant blue eyes and his strong arms always melted her and she thought, there is no end to the wonder of this man. He was everything a good man should be: handsome, clever, strong and full of character. She should be pleased.

The students and Hester had worked out a rota so each did some work supporting the café – cleaning, serving, leafleting, preparing food. Sven used his spare time in working on his dissertation. This left less time for Sarah who had some course work to do but whose primary task, both as a personal goal and of value to Café Europa, was getting to grips with the Greek language.

Only a certain amount could be achieved on paper, she just had to get out there and talk to people. She worked out that when they say something, there has to be a verb in there, if there's an 'o' at the end of a word it's what they are doing: *thiavaso* – I read. If there's a '*tha*' it's what they are going to do: *tha thiavaso* I am going to read. She did much by grabbing chance words and miming.

Her helpmeet in all this was Kostas who, in truth, did have great patience. He in fact had little to do except talk to this pretty girl, and she appreciated both a chance to practice the language, and his attention, his brown eyes constantly looking in hers.

For Sven this was not objectionable, there was no reason why Sarah should not have male as well as female friends, why should she not enjoy this Greek boy's company? Sven thought Kostas a foolish youth but would not have felt it part of his role to tell Sarah what friends she could have, it would be an imposition on her human rights.

For Kostas, the situation was incomprehensible: here he was stealing the girlfriend from this tall white boy and yet he made no objection. Kostas did not understand Sven, for he had seen him smack at a cold chisel with a club hammer like a man, but he had also seen him hanging out washing on a line like a big woman.

Sarah was always thanking Kostas for his attention, he was always looking into her eyes and saying there was nothing he would rather do than be with her which, unlike many things he said, at that particular moment was true.

For Anne and Anton too their duties at the restaurant and the minimal amount of housework they did left time for them to be together. They liked to explore the landscape round to the left, past the restaurant where there was no more road, just a little worn track, they could walk hand in hand with the scent of wild oregano in their nostrils. There they found a hollow, a socket in the bay, mischievous currents had scooped it out of a curve so it became a place of concealment, so no one within it could easily be seen, a viewer would have to be close to see that there was anyone there at all. They called it Pixie Hollow and would go down there to sit with the water lapping their feet.

Anne was the only girl with two elder brothers, she was used to being petted, but expected constant reassurance. She had her entrancing tricks. Out of apparently deep thought she would pop up with a question to Anton. 'Why when people are all different colours,' she would say, 'is dust always grey, when it is made of people?....Why does the moon look bigger when it is low on the horizon than when it is high in the sky, when it is the same moon, the same distance and the same person watching?' When he asked where all the questions came from she said, 'I've always done it, when I was ten I used to ask Why don't I remember what life was like when I was five? If animals believe in God, is it a god in their image? Does each animal have a different god? Why are stockings sexy and socks are silly?'

'That's a pretty profound question for a ten year old,' he said.

'No, that's me now, I just threw it in to see if you were listening.'

Anne was still preoccupied with the refugees. She had ceased to surprise Anton with her instant sympathy for any pitiable object – a sick pup or a long-incarcerated serial killer, or even a tumbled-down tree seemed to elicit a response. If Anton had a certain lack of empathy, Anne made up with a superabundance of it.

'Malik is like a character in a story book,' she said, 'he put his pack on his back and walked out to find his fortune in the world.' By now she was confident enough to enter the building where they were held and even the dormitory. She thought the refugees, with their limited contact with women, would be threatening but they were curious, shy and perhaps even frightened of her. The place smelled of urine and body odour, Anne brought mops and household cleaners so at least they could be partially occupied in something useful. Anton was somewhat squeamish so she did not tell him any details: the scabies, insufficient washing and toilet facilities, questionable water supplies, the inadequate diet of rice and pasta dishes. She could get on well enough with this as her project, Anton need not be involved.

The detainees protested when there were visits from officials, but most lived in a listless hope – this was better than their travelling conditions, maybe it would get better still, they could climb up the gameboard of European nations, dodging and sidestepping. Malik already felt himself to be a long way towards England in having English friends. Anne saw him every other day and he was often out with her, now gaining a position of superiority with other refugees for his ability to move in and out of the compound and his access to resources.

Anne was disconcerted at the state of the refugees as they arrived. 'They turn up with nothing, almost naked,' she said, 'what belief they must have to go through that. Some have been picked up after being put ashore on one of the uninhabited islands off the coast, and told they were in Italy, and they just wait there with no water until someone rescues them.'

'Yeah,' said Anton, thinking about the comparative uses of lemon zest and lemon juice in cooking, and not sure what he was supposed to say.

'Don't you care about them?' asked Anne, it was unusual for her to challenge him so directly.

'I think it's good that you care about them,' he said, 'there are just too many people for me to care about all of them.' He struggled internally for a better response and finally chose the practical: 'I hope it is better than where they came from, or their effort to get here will have been wasted.'

Activity became harder as the temperature rose. The heat increased day by day; just when it seemed it could not get hotter, a day would come that soaked them in a sheen of sweat, even as they dried off from the shower. It became so hot that for their afternoon sex Anton and Anne would arrange themselves so he was standing and she was lying on her back, not exactly comfortable but it made for coupling with the least physical contact between their sticky bodies, though they still emerged from the exercise dripping so much that sweat stung their eyes and soaked the sheet under Anne's slight back.

Anne thought what glorious opportunities she was being given here: learning the restaurant business; renovating an old house; working with the refugees; having sex every day with this boyfriend who wanted her all the time, who never tired of her and always made her come. Anton thought as he watched her modest breasts, scarcely moving with the controlled exertion, how easy this girl was to please, how simple and uncomplicated, how with Anne he gazed into the heart of beloved ordinariness, simplicity itself. While inside Anne, he was ordinary too, and that felt good.

Ever practical, Anton helped Hester to assess who was coming to the restaurant: explorers of the island would stop there, but this might be only once. Café Europa could attract newcomers with leafleting, but holiday-makers were there only a couple of weeks. Anton considered the expats were their key to success: it wasn't that they spent much, part of the point of having their own homes on Doxos was to eat at home, but all through the summer they had friends to stay and those friends wanted to eat out. To be sustainable, Café Europa needed to bring in the expats and their visitors, and the expats would still be there in winter when there were no tourists. The Doxos cartel's interest was in obtaining the maximum amount of money from tourists in the season. Hester was looking towards a long-term business.

One day Anton declared, 'We need broadband.'

'You mean you need broadband, do you know how much trouble it was getting dial-up?' Hester replied.

'Trust me, people will bring their computers, people live through their computers much more than they used to, you are living in the last century.'

Hester questioned whether people on holiday lived though their computers quite so much as Anton considered they did, but to intervene when he had decided he wanted to do something was more trouble than it was worth so they went off to Plakia. In the post office the sulky counter assistant tried to fob them off with a disc that was for an inappropriate item of software, and then with a number they had to phone to speak to technical assistance and finally, exasperated, sent them to the post office manager who sat in his office with his tie and neat moustache, clearly even less familiar with the technology than the counter assistant. In a last ploy to get rid of them, they introduced Hester and Anton to a back room where a boy sat humming to himself and rocking slightly amid the clutter of computers, keyboards, monitors and wires. They nodded at the boy, who looked warily at them. Anton said to Hester, 'Would you wait here for me?' without saying more, or any word to the boy, he opened his laptop and made a few key strokes swung it round and showed it to the boy. Delighted, the boy clapped his hands once and turned to his machine and began to input.

Within half an hour they had a connection at Café

Europa, organised remotely by Anton's new friend, they took away the equipment to connect it up.

'What language were you talking to him?' said Hester.

Anton resisted the implication, 'It's how he communicates, he said, 'he feels more comfortable with machines. As our American cousins say, he has issues with intimacy. The telecom people need him, they couldn't run the place without someone like him, but they keep him out of sight, I just had to find him.'

Leaving the post office they met a frustrated Toby who was up against a deadline with a project for a company and his connection had gone down, courtesy of the state monopoly telephone company. After a day and a half arguing with them, Toby was feeling hopeless, flustered and desperate in the heat.

He was as relieved as a man cured of toothache to be told there was broadband at Café Europa. Toby brought his computer and set up under a beach umbrella in front of Café Europa with the occasional water and coffee and in three long days he had completed a programme that saved his business career, and shipped it off to Canada. Stimulated by this success, Anton did up an old laptop computer that Hester had lying around and Café Europa offered the free use of it to customers wishing to check their emails. Even the more advanced cafes in Doxos who had installed computers charged by the quarter hour for their use. Hester's prices were also reasonable, increasing the comparative attractiveness of Café Europe. Bit by bit, the location, their relationship with the expatriates, the attractive young people serving, leafleting, low prices and free internet, meant Café Europa was edging forward and other restaurant owners started to notice.

One afternoon two pleasant young Danish men, who looked as if they were accountants in civilian life, drew their scooters up to the end of the road, had a snack and a beer at Café Europa and went off to explore the surrounding countryside on that deserted part of the island. They spied Pixie Hollow and scrambled down to enjoy this tiny unspoilt piece of beach, like a little private grotto, ideal for nude sunbathing, not an activity for which Doxos was renowned.

Unfortunately they were seen by Grandma Poppy, out on her hunt for wild herbs growing down the rocky slopes. She looked, then looked again, unable to believe her eyes that such a scene was taking place on her island, in her bay. Here were two fully grown men, not children or even boys, as naked as they day they were born, in plain daylight, in full view, obviously intimate with one another, putting sun cream on each other's bodies. Here was a vision of indecency as shocking as any she had seen, she let out an involuntary gasp and scrambled off to spread the word. Among the first of her eager listeners was Aspasia.

In truth the young men had gone out to the secluded bay, stripped off, swam, sat looking at the sea smoking cigarettes, then dressed, climbed up the cliff and went back to their hotel for a sleep. By the time the news of a sighting had passed from mouth to mouth to be reported to the Mayor, however, this had blossomed in the minds of the locals into an extravagant orgy – they had had sex in plain sight and encouraged local boys to join them in a fully functioning fairy ring, each pleasuring the next in a demonic circle.

Once again Captain Papadopoulos stood in the doorway of Café Europa.

'How may I help you today Captain?' said Hester.

'We have heard of perverties,' he said in serious tones.

'Tell me about perverties,' Hester said sweetly.

'Two men, tourists, they were here and then down, in the bay down there, with no clothes. Naked men, together. They are perverties. We do not have this on the island.'

Hester was nonplussed. Surely the nude sunbathing homosexuals had nothing to do with her. She did not know them. They were dressed when they were at the café. She did not own the bay and was not responsible for it.

'We take public morals very serious, here, I hear it from the mayor himself,' said Captain Papadopoulos, 'You must warn your customers not to do this.' Hester consented that if she saw any customers intent on nude sunbathing she would step in with an admonition.

Captain Papadopoulos considered his task incomplete. 'There is another thing,' he said, 'No tables on the beach – very bad for the environment.'

'I don't understand what you are saying,' said Hester, 'it's traditional to put tables on the beach.'

'The erosion of our beaches is serious, the European Union is very concerned about this,'

'You are going to try to stop all restaurants having tables and chairs on the beach?'

'New restaurants, new regulations.'

'So you are telling me restaurants all over Pantoni and Zeste are
  allowed to have tables and chairs on the beach, but we are forbidden?'

'They have the rights of history, they have been on the beach for a long time.'

'So you are telling me to take my tables off the beach, when everyone else on the island can do it?'

'No, only old people can do it, no new people.'

'This is not fair, we will see,' Hester said, but before Captain Papadopoulos had gone, she gave instructions for the chairs to be moved to the road and the restaurant's forecourt. She spent a morning of increasing heat and anger talking to the ministry of tourism branch in Rhodes and the ministry of culture in Athens, becoming more frustrated at every period on hold followed by official indifference.

Gathered at lunch, the table now beside the road and not on the beach, she explained, 'The authorities don't want to know, they say it's a local matter how the islands handle their rules. These are bylaws they can make at a whim.'

Sarah stayed silent, why was everything connected with the restaurant so difficult? The easy-going spirit of the island seemed exhausted by the time it reached Lands End.

'Could we put them on a structure, a wooden platform to protect the beach, wouldn't that satisfy them?' asked Anne.

'It's not about the beach,' said Hester with more than a touch of irritation, 'they are trying to put us out of business. They'd just tell us we needed permission for the structure.'

'Surely they have a point,' said Sven, wishing to give the authorities the benefit of the doubt, 'there is erosion of the coastline and human activity has to contribute to it.'

'You think?' said Hester, 'then they can start somewhere else, get one of the other dozen restaurants with tables on the beach.'

'They had said it was historic,' he said, 'they don't want to take away a right other people have enjoyed, but if they pass a new law to protect the environment, then we should accept it.'

'I don't believe there's any law, they are just making it up as they go along. It's not about being a new or an old restaurant, it's just because we are xenie.'

'Why can't they just be nice?' said Anne

'We are in their country,' said Sven, 'maybe we should keep our heads down and do what they ask and they'll stop bothering us.'

'No one in Britain tries to stop foreigners running a restaurant, they come from all over the world to do it,' said Hester. 'Anyway, they won't stop till we are closed.'

'This restaurant has been here a long time,' said Anton thoughtfully, 'under a different name and different ownership.'

'How does that help?' said Anne.

'Somewhere, there will be a record,' he said, 'didn't I read that there are albums of photographs of old Doxos, going back to the nineteenth century?'

Sven and Anton went off to the square where the smell of meat grilling for souflakis mixed with the exhaust of motor scooters, and entered the little-visited town archives. In the musty library they had the good fortune to find a young librarian who had been seconded to this remote island as part of her degree studies. Sometimes she sat in the archives all day without a caller, so was only too happy to see two attentive young men. They examined every flaking book that had photographs, seeing the tumble of buildings down the mountainside in sepia, the weather-beaten faces of fishermen long since dead, children dancing in the street at religious festivals, blessings from black-hatted Orthodox priests.

After the examination of many false leads, hopes raised and dashed, they finally found the winning picture. It showed two tables on the beach, three Greek fishermen gathered around them, looking gnarled and whiskered, drinking ouzo and playing backgammon, unmistakeably in front of what was now Café Europa and unmistakeably on the beach. The unchanged chimney and extant outhouse clearly identified the location, plus the description of the back that said Lands End.

They sought permission to borrow the dilapidated album with the picture from the library for half an hour and took it over the square past a couple of soft-haired Greek girls in shorts who were sitting in front of the fashion shop chewing gum and talking on mobile phones. In the multi-tasking stationers, photographer and print shop they had three laser copies made: one in a frame to hang in Café Europa. Another was mounted in the stationers where the owner, a cultured man, was pleased to have another picture of old Doxos. In his window he displayed a number of pictures of bygone days on the island, as well as new ones with the island resplendent under the moon or sunlight, and the customary board of plump brides in white dresses with matching flowers.

One they retained to give to Captain Papadopoulos should he return on the same mission, but the denizens of Café Europa had an idea that he would not return, that the presence of a picture establishing historic rights on display over the road from the town hall would deter further harassment on that score.

They felt relieved, but Hester's nerves were taut –

who knew when the next attack would come? She sat in her office sipping wine and looking grimly out to sea. How hard could it be?

Chapter 7

As the days passed the Mayor grew more troubled about his deal with Vasilios and the problem of the intractable Coastguard. He looked out of his office onto the square and saw the boys from Café Europa in high spirits as they crossed to the stationer's, how good it would be to be a tourist here with not a care in the world.

He reflected on his options. This would not be the Mayor's first engagement with the Coastguard, he had been watching him for more than a year. As soon as he arrived the Mayor made a point of getting to know him and making him welcome, as he always did with any new focus of power on the island, that was the Mayor's job. The taciturn coastguard made a point of not getting to know the Mayor, but at every function when they were together – Independence Day, October 28th, Easter celebrations and such events, the Mayor would always be prepared to say a few words. He would indicate a fine woman and see if the coastguard's nostrils flared; the Mayor looked for the knowing glance, the narrowing of the eyes that denoted a connoisseur. He would watch how fast the coastguard finished his drink, did he drink greedily and look for another? No, he put his glass down still half full, as if he had been merely making a gesture of accepting hospitality. The Mayor would say casually 'Such a good looking boy that Kostas…' to see if there was a response, but the coastguard didn't even look round, he simply said 'It's a healthy life for the young on the island,' as if in compliment to the Mayor's stewardship of the environment. So he wasn't moved by drink or by sex with girls or boys. What was his weakness, the flaw of a man who didn't even smoke cigarettes, let alone show an interest in drugs?

At the annual war memorial parade, the Mayor had continued his quest for the essential truth of the Coastguard, putting a trigger point into a casual conversation, in this case of how the island would be improved by tourist development once the new airport was built and big planes could come, 'there will be more bars, hotels, restaurants, maybe even new things, perhaps a casino.' Now, at last, the coastguard showed a flicker of interest, a twitch of the hand, a raising of the eyes to meet those of the Mayor. 'And where might you put that?' he asked, as if he couldn't care less, but the Mayor rejoiced internally, his heart was uplifted as if a choir of angels had given voice: Joyous News indeed! Now he knew something, he had an entry point. It might not be used now, it might never be used, but just as he knew how to control everyone else in a position of authority on the island, now the Mayor knew the lever he could touch to direct the Coastguard.

He reflected on this. Now at his time of need, he must bring his knowledge to bear calmly but with definite purpose. With some reluctance, for there was every possibility of such schemes going badly wrong, the Mayor engineered a meeting. To show willing, he went to the Coastguard's office in Megalo Limani. The coastguard service was, to the mayor's mind, very un-Greek, it was unresponsive to the ordinary niceties of gifts and familial obligations. Coastguards were posted away from their home region deliberately to subvert the natural order of preference and favour.

The coastguard wasn't anyone's cousin, no one on this island anyway. A Cretan, he kept to himself, his family were away on his own island. Still, he would learn, with the Mayor's wise counsel, what it was to have obligations.

On the pretext of signing some papers that both had to approve, the Mayor called in to see the Coastguard in his office where he was sitting in his white uniform with his gold-trimmed hat on a hook on the wall. The Coastguard thanked him for coming over and ordered coffee from one of his men who showed the Mayor in, without waiting to ask the Mayor what he would like: a man who called wanted coffee, the rules of hospitality demanded it. The Mayor said he was in the area anyway, was pleased to oblige. They had a short conversation about their business, which concerned parking restrictions on the harbour.

The Coastguard's man, in blue T-shirt and trousers, brought in a tray with a tiny cup of coffee on a saucer and a cool glass of water for each man and put them down wordlessly. 'Must be a lonely life for you out here,' said the Mayor, once he had left.

'I suppose, it's the job,' said the Coastguard, pleased that his staff saw the most important man on the island coming to bring papers to his office. That was prestige, that was what he had worked for all his life.

'I know what it's like,' said the Mayor, 'we have to be a bit careful about our recreations, can't mix too much with other people, everyone wants you to do something for them.'

The Coastguard agreed, loneliness was the price they paid for high office.

'We do a little gaming,' said the Mayor, as if

offering a solution to this problem, 'some cards, just friends, me some of the other men of influence on the island.'

'Why, thank you,' said the Coastguard, 'I'll bear that in mind.'

'Just some drinks, mezethes, and we play a few hands among friends. You know Aspasia's restaurant, around the Zeste bay towards Lands End? That's where we meet, we'll be there tonight, as it happens. You are very welcome. Do you want to come as my guest? You don't have to play, of course, just meet some people.'

The Coastguard was warmed by the conversation, the deference shown him by the Mayor, he could drive round to Aspasia's this evening, why shouldn't he have some time off, time for himself? Everything for him was work and the family, and his family were far away

'Yes,' he said, 'I'll come along.' In the Mayor's heart, the choir rejoiced.

'See you tonight, then,' he said.

The Coastguard sat looking at his hands, his clean hands with clean nails, unscratched and uncalloused. He had not gambled for seven, seven and a half years – but this was not gambling, this was just being in a place where there was gambling, and that was different. If he were strong enough to resist gambling for so many years, then he must be strong enough to be in a place where there were a few cards and not be tempted. If he could not do that, then he was not so strong as he thought he was. He should, he reasoned, test himself like this, it would be good for him, it would make him stronger to resist such temptation. The Mayor was right, he reasoned, he was lonely, and what harm could there be in watching?

He called his wife as he did every day at this time when the kids were safely home from school and she could tell him about her day. She was slight with black eyes and silky black hair, nervy and absolutely devoted to him with every fibre of her tiny being. She wanted to talk about their favourite subject, the new house he would build for them, she was thinking should they have a balcony at the front as well as the back, so they could keep an eye on the children playing in the garden while they sat out in the early evenings.

One of the students would sit at Café Europa reading a book in the slow afternoon, tending to the few visitors around at that time, while those who had been distributing fliers in the morning or doing other jobs took some time off. One day, about four weeks into their stay, Sarah and Sven had lunch in the afternoon and Sven dozed off then got up to work, irritated at the time he had lost. The island that eats time, he thought, rousing himself, with the drinking lunches, siestas and the need to see so many people. Everything you needed had to come from somewhere else, so you took a trip out to the town or to Agios Nicholas, and then every acquaintance had to be greeted – Hello, how are you going? Well, how are you? – taking up time with trivia. There was so little time left for his own work and he had a dissertation to submit by the end of summer. Looking round for his clothes he said, 'I hate this drinking at lunchtime and dossing about all day. We have things to do with the restaurant, the building, I am supposed to be working on my thesis...'

Sarah was awakened by his irritated movements, and did not respond well to his tetchiness. 'Isn't this holiday also about being with me?' she said, 'Do you hate being with me?'

'No, Sarah,' he said, 'not everything is about you, it's about trying to organise time to use it efficiently. We need a better timetable. *I* need a better timetable.

'Just enjoying it doesn't seem like such a bad use to me.'

'No, I suppose not to you,' he said, and went down to get a shower, unwilling to enter into an argument with her that would take up more time and achieve nothing.

Sarah was annoyed with his ways, with his precise speech, his order and exactness. Somehow today the gorgeous hunk had receded in her mind and had been replaced by the querulous pedant.

Sven lived in a force field of gloom where all his actions affected other actions, where the future was uncertainly predictable but had the sense of foreboding, as if you did something unpleasant today to ward off a worse horror tomorrow. Everything had to count for him. What if it didn't count, Sarah thought heretically, looking down at her painted toenails peeping out of the linen sheet, what if there was just now?

She went down and out of the front door, avoiding Sven who was now at the marble table in the courtyard with his books. Down at the restaurant Kostas was waiting for her, sitting astride his motor bike in his blue jeans and white T-shirt, making her think of the James Dean posters that they had in the pizza restaurant back home. Her heart was raised to see him. To Sarah, Kostas seemed so full of the spirit of the island, of the free wind blowing across the rocky landscape and the sea. His infectious smile and his confident gaze encompassed everything magical about the Mediterranean to her.

'Come with me round the island,' he said, just as hopeful and expectant of success as the first time he had said it.

'Don't give up, do you?' she said, 'yeah, alright.' She pulled her hair back in a scrunchie, slinging her Indian handbag over the back bar, getting up behind him on the bike, pulling her skirt up so her thighs grabbed the seat close to his body.

They zoomed round the bay, then instead of keeping on to Agios Nicholas, turned right up and over towards the other side of the island. At a high point he stopped, where they could see the sea on both sides of magical Doxos. They sped on, along a road dotted with little wayside shrines to accident victims until he stopped at one, 'This was my friend Panos,' he said, looking out to the sea over the cliffs down which Panos fell when he tried to take a bend at 120 K an hour and swerved to miss a vegetable truck. Kostas reached his hand to touch the pitched roof of the shrine, the little house of the dead, 'we will have the good times for you Panos.' She touched his shoulder in mute sympathy.

He took her round in the cooling breeze of speed on the open road to the western part of the island – rocky promontories, sheer drops, mountainsides known only to the goats, the monastery with eagles soaring above it and the oldest church ruin on the island. Back out towards the coast, they left the motorcycle on the road and clambered down the rocky path to the Church of the Our Lady of the Oysters, where the image of the Virgin had been miraculously found in an oyster shell and a tiny church nestling in the rocks commemorated this event. Sarah looked in the little, musty-smelling chapel at the hand painted icons, the tapering brown beeswax candles and brass incense burners.

There was no one but them, just the road, the sky and the scrubby rocks of the landscape rolling down to the sea. A lone motor scooter chugged past, slowed and phuttered off into the distance. Then there was silence but for the crashing waves. Nothing mattered but the hot landscape and the inexpressibly blue-green sea.

Kostas was always paying her compliments, a thing she missed in her relationship with Sven who considered chat-up lines coarse and dishonest.

'Your father must be a thief, because he stole the stars from the sky to put them in your eyes,' Kostas said, staring intently at her.

'Oh shut up with your awful corny lines,' she laughed, but she was pleased that he was talking her this way, just being chatted up was sexy, but she felt in control, Kostas would not do anything she couldn't handle.

Kostas looked into her eyes and told her he loved her from the moment he first saw her, for a moment she let the intoxicating pleasure of love enter her, feeling her skin bristling with the excitement, then she said: 'You're a sweet boy but I've got a boyfriend, and anything else would be too complicated,' adding: 'sorry,' then rather regretted the playground epithet.

'One kiss,' he said, moving towards her, his handsome face with his deep, dark eyes framed against the land with the blue, blue sky behind his black hair.

'One kiss,' she said and he took her in his arms and kissed her for a long, long time. He was good at it, but a kiss was enough.

'Time to go,' she said, and he acquiesced with grace, one thing island life taught was the value of time in bringing events around. Kostas felt no need to rush. Kostas told her she was the only girl for him, and he would always love her as they mounted the hill to returned to his motor bike.

As they climbed up and saw the red and chrome machine Sarah said, 'Where's my bag?' The strap of the orange and red bag had been wrapped around the back bar. Her bag was missing, the Indian bag in maroon and gold with embroidery and little mirrors that she had bought in Indonesia, that she had left on the back of the red motor bike, the bag that contained – ipod, phone, passport, credit cards – it contained her whole life.

'Omigod, I can't lose that,' she said, quickly becoming frantic.

'Did you drop it, on the road? We can go back and find it,' said Kostas.

'No, when we walked down to the chapel, I thought I'd take it, then I thought – no, no one is going to pass here, it will be safe. It was on the back of the bike just wrapped around there. Who could have come here? It must have been that motor scooter, I heard it pass – they must have slowed down and grabbed it.

'Yes,' Kostas said, suddenly focussed.

'We've got to go to the police,' she said

'No,' said Kostas, 'just stay here.'

'What are you going to do? They must have gone half and hour ago, you'll never catch them...' she was facing hysteria – how do you get a new passport if you are stuck in Doxos?

Kostas had assumed a determined stare, 'Stay,' he said as he mounted the bike and roared off, an enormous sound coming out of the powerful machine, raging across the mountains.

Sarah stood looking at the empty road trying not to cry. She knew she shouldn't have come – lost passport, driving licence, credit cards, money, European health insurance card....She was careful, always took passport out with her when abroad in case an official needed it, though none ever did. What did she have in the bag? Report credit cards stolen, but to whom? No phone anyway, out here. Return ticket home would be easy to replace, but passport? What else? University ID – was her driving licence in there?

As the minutes passed she began to be fearful – what if he didn't come back? How long should she leave it? She had no idea of the time anyway, she wasn't wearing her watch. Out here in the sun with no shade she could get heat stroke and die, end up a pile of bones by the roadside. Now, she had to get a grip, this was stupid. Doxos was not big, she was young and healthy, she could walk to another settlement – then what? She tried to remember the Greek for 'help'. Her little Greek dictionary was in the bag. The chattering of the cicadas increased from a murmur to a scream then suddenly cut out, giving way to an eerie silence: no vehicles, not even any animals, just the wash of the sea.

As time passed and Kostas did not return she began to doubt him, feared maybe he was in on it, maybe it was some scam – but what? What could possibly be done while she was here that couldn't be done at the restaurant? Was it an identity fraud where they would clone her data before she could get to complain about it? Why did she come out with him? she thought miserably.

It may have been only twenty minutes, but it seemed stretched longer. She was in despair and ready to walk off back down the road when she heard the welcoming sound of Kostas' motor bike in the distance. She felt such relief at his return that she almost forgot the bag that had caused all the misery, but there it was on the handlebars: the familiar red and orange handbag with the little mirrors, he screeched to a halt and handed it to her with a smile. She looked inside, the contents seemed rummaged but were there: ipod, phone, purse with credit cards, passport.

'What... how did you do that, where was it?' she asked, relief passing over her as a cool wave. She looked at him, standing grinning before her like a winner at a school sports day, only now noticing that the knuckles of his right hand were grazed and bloody.

She took the hand, 'You've been hitting someone haven't you?'

'There aren't so many people on the island who steal like that,' said Kostas, 'I know them all. I had to visit them.'

'What did they say?'

Kostas laughed, showing his excellent teeth, 'Say...they said they were sorry, they didn't know it was your bag or they'd have left it alone.'

For Sarah the release of tension and the pleasure at seeing him was ecstatic. She wanted to live in a perpetually brilliant now that would last forever, this moment of relief and joy at seeing him. How could she ever have doubted him?

'What of you, lovely girl, what do you want?' She put her arms around him and pressed him close, he pushed her chestnut hair back gently and breathed in her ear, 'I know somewhere we can be alone.' She felt the rush of emotion like a blow to the stomach. Now was the time she had to do it, there was no other. She did what she always did in these circumstances, and went with the emotion of the moment, forgetting the future in one incandescent present.

Close to the Virgin of the Oysters was a place where grass grew in the soft sand to tie it together as a natural mattress. Not a few Greek boys and maidens of various nationalities had made use of this natural feature.

She pulled her top off and unbuttoned her bra. He took off his white T-shirt showing his muscular torso. This was meant to be, thought Sarah. Both were excited, the foreplay was minimal, she ached to clutch his hairy thighs and pull him into her.

They both came quickly, excited in the pleasure of the moment. The black curls of his hair were dripping with sweat of the exertion and excitement and her face was flushed red. 'Are you OK?' he said afterwards, pulling his jeans on.

'Great, considering it's not long ago since I used to give Christmas presents to my teddies,' she said.

'What is teddies?'

'It's a girl thing, I won't bore you with it.' Kostas had passed over his urge to know all about her and did not press the enquiry.

'Do you really love me?' she asked, enjoying the novelty of being with someone on whose response she could rely.

'I love you more than anything in the world,' he said, and she snuggled closer into the comforting deceit of his embrace.

Five things Malik was learning about Europe:

One Not everyone speaks English. He always knew every country had its own language, but he had been told 'everyone speaks English'. In fact many of the Greeks who spoke English, spoke it worse than he did, and most of them on the island did not speak it at all. Malik realised this gave him a natural advantage that he prized. 'Top notch,' he said.

Two Not everyone is welcoming to travellers. The spirit of hospitality, universal in the east, stops somewhere in the middle of Turkey. Thereafter it reappears in patches and even in Greece there are flashes, but the welcome to travellers does not extend to sharing food and drink. It is replaced in some places by official provision, or organised charity, or nothing. In some places it is, according to Malik, a very bad show.

Three Not all European women are whores, even though they have no modesty. Not having modesty alone does not make a woman a whore. Anne was not a whore though she had no modesty. This was a troublesome concept and one to which Malik would return. Even the women who clearly were whores because of they way they showed their bodies, the way they spoke back to men, even some of *those* women, like the fat girl Jess, were nice whores, so much nicer than the respectable Greek women who would not even look at him, as if he did not even exist, or should not exist. This was all a very rum do, thought Malik, and required more exercise of the grey matter.

Four Another thing: friendship with women was almost as important as friendship between men in this continent, but friendship with women was temporary. Sven and Anton had had other wives before Sarah and Anne and would have other wives afterwards – he had asked and they had told him. That made sense to Malik, a chap could be a pal for life. Malik's friend

Samir would soon be in Doxos with him, and he would be a friend for life, when they were old and rich with their families around them they would talk about the perilous journey they had made when they were young friends.

Five Trade was the key to Europe. You had to have something to sell that people wanted to buy. His relationship with Anne meant he could go to shops and buy cigarettes and top-ups for his mobile phone. This made him a power in the camp where he could sell them on. He would let someone text on his mobile phone or he would buy vouchers for other people's phones and make ten per cent on the deal. Other detainees would ask him for medicines or foods, and he would ask Anne, who would often be able to supply them, from Red Cross or other resources. He would take a sum from the recipient, for his work in acting as an intermediary. These many small sums, these little deals meant Malik was in constant demand, always welcome and even popular with the guards as an intermediary and a free spirit, one of the inmates with a personality: a real person.

Malik was filling out, beginning to have flesh on his bones so he was more robust than the scrawny youth who had first appeared at Café Europa. He relished his status as a friend of the English and he worked on his friendships. Sarah, though not a natural friend of the poor, enjoyed his company for his curious mode of expression, talking of 'revelry and what not' and 'a spot of supper and dancing' in his accented English. Sarah tried to improve his store of present-day idioms but when he rendered 'fuck this for a game of soldiers' as 'bugger the military' she gave up in hilarity. Anton did not have much to say to him after he had found out that Malik knew little of the politics of his country, probably less than an informed outsider, but Anton was not unkind and he appreciated Malik's qualities. Anton used people like a book: flicked through them for the information they could give him, then returned them to their place. He used Malik no differently from others. Sven, however, took to Malik like a brother, joking with him, playing football, teasing him. With Sven, Malik felt like one of the Café Europa family, not a visitor, a refugee receiving aid, but a member of the band.

Even when Malik was 'the old merry self' as he put it, there was anxiety: he had no idea what would happen to him, whether he would stay in Greece or be deported back to Afghanistan or have the right to move to another country. Malik found it no more easy to get through the system, with the combined help of Jess and Anne. The three of them sat down at Café Europa one day to discuss it. Anne had discovered, in her labours on Malik's behalf, her own essential truth: the rules are always against you. With Jess's help she had tried to comprehend the Byzantine qualifications of entry, periods of residence, admissions and asylum policy, but had retreated in confusion and the conviction that there is no legitimate way into Europe.

'If they are caught,' said Jess, 'undocumented migrants are fingerprinted, held for a while in detention centres and then released with orders to leave the country within thirty days. There are deportation orders handed to them in Greek. But the deportation orders can only be enforced if the migrant's home country is willing to take him back.'

Anne looked blank, 'So what does that mean?' she said, 'Malik is an asylum seeker, isn't he? The Taliban killed his brother.'

'I don't know if that qualifies him. The Taliban killed a lot of people, and they're not the only ones. Look,' said Jess, her round, pretty face earnestly attempting to comprehend, 'if you don't understand the system, join the club. They do send genuine asylum seekers back, there's even a name for it – refoulement. As an illegal they get detained for a while – weeks or months – sent on, or given a deportation order and told to leave the country under their own steam. Asylum decisions are given in Greek. The applicant is not given the result of the application so they don't know whether to appeal. Basically it's a fucking nightmare, it's Kafka by the sea. I've stopped trying to understand it, that way madness lies.'

'Oh my giddy aunt,' said Malik, 'What is this aunt? Why should an aunt be giddy?'

Kostas drove Sarah back to Café Europa and they parted as friends with a chaste kiss. Walking towards the café, she saw everything was the same: the tables set for service, the Greek pop music playing softly in the background.

Hester was out at the front, 'You'd better see Sven,' she said as soon as she saw Sarah.

'Why, what's happened?' she said, shocked. Had she been found out?

Just then the phone rang and Hester ran to get it, saying, 'He's up in the house.'

What was this? Did Sven know? Was he angry she had gone off with Kostas? Sarah went up the hill to the house, thinking she must get in the shower to wash off the smell of Kostas before she came into close contact with Sven.

She found him upstairs packing a small rucksack on

the bed, 'I must return to Stockholm,' he said.

'Why, what has happened?' she said, her own transgression looming in her mind.

'My grandfather died this morning, my father's father. My parents will want me at the funeral. I want to be there, of course, he was my grandfather...'

That's alright, thought Sarah, *only death.* 'Poor Sven,' she said, 'when are you leaving, you can't get out tonight.'

'No, I'm on the next plane out, to Athens, tomorrow morning, and get the connection to Stockholm. If you will take me to the airport...'

'Of course I will. Let me take a shower and we'll talk.' The water was running and Sarah was soaping herself when Sven came into the bathroom, he was wandering around listlessly, not settling to anything

'Is your grandmother alive?' asked Sarah.

'No,' he said, 'there's a wife, his third, 30 years younger than him.'

Sarah was drying herself, but Sven was oblivious to her perfect nakedness. 'My mother and father lived with him, with my grandfather, when they were first married. Until he had an affair with my mother and they left.'

'Wow, that's a lot of baggage.'

Sven nodded glumly, as if that was only a part of it. He was unwilling to talk further, and as Sarah was working that night, she went down to the café.

Sven was sitting up with a book propped on his knees when she returned to the bedroom. He wanted to make love so they did, somewhat mechanically; neither of them was fully engaged in the act. Sarah was also still a little tender down there as a result of the afternoon's exertions. She had a sense of obligation, she felt responsible for Sven, and guilty, but she was not used to guilt and found it difficult to handle so was also resentful, annoyed with him for making her feel guilty. She faked an orgasm so she could get it over with, not something she did often, or ever before with Sven. He was too preoccupied to notice.

The next morning Sarah woke to a familiar soreness and was about to smile in recognition of a naughty deed when she remembered Sven and his grandfather. She reached over to find his place empty. She opened her eyes to the brilliant sunshine reflecting on white walls, pulled on a dressing gown and went on to the veranda where Sven was sitting watching the sun rise across the bay. She knelt and took his hand, he seemed indifferent.

'How did he die?' she said, 'I didn't ask, I just assumed he was old, he died.'

'Felo de se,' said Sven, 'he died by his own hand.'

'I'd call that racial stereotyping'

'Yeah, yeah...suicide. It is a bit Scandinavian. But he was old, he felt it was time to go. He went. He took pills, nothing dramatic, left a note explaining.'

'What an awful thing for his family, for you.'

'There are enough people in the world,' said Sven. 'If he makes a decision it is time to go, that is sad for us, but it is his decision.'

'If everyone did that where would we be?'

'Everyone won't, and the world is not short of people anyway. He was that kind of man. I admired him most in the world, I used to, when I was a child. Then I admired him less.'

'Was he sick?'

'Life is a terminal illness.'

Sarah ignored this gloomy remark, it was probably not the time to tell Sven to lighten up.

'Were you close?' she asked, looking out over the sea to the town on the mountain and the Crusader castle above it.

'He was like me – or I am like him – or I was like him, but as I am alive and he is not, I suppose I should say he was like me, because he will always now be in the past tense. But it is the first time I have said this, the first time that I have thought of him in the past tense, so it is a bit confusing.'

Sarah fought a flash of irritation at his pedantry, which she concealed by taking his pink hand with its little golden hairs and smiled in a gesture that she hoped conveyed her inarticulate concern. The death of his grandfather seemed to have struck him deeply; Sarah was not insensitive and would have been sad at the death of her grandparents, of whom three remained alive, but why did he make such a big deal about it?

She drove him to the airport through the scent of coffee brewing in the houses along the way, and kuri plants from the open road.

'Look, there's been more work on the new airport,' she said as they drove past the site. The German crew with their hard hats and fluorescent jackets were back on the scaffolding.

Sarah hugged him and told him to be back soon. She spoke with genuine affection, but as soon as the little plane juddered off the runway she was driving back and wondering when she would see Kostas, now her time was more her own.

The Coastguard was in an open-necked blue shirt and trousers today, not his white uniform. This evening, unusually, he was doing something for himself, not for duty. As he eased his white BMW onto the flattened earth beside Aspasia's, he muttered a prayer to the Virgin. It went to that place where prayers go, but it was to be answered not by the Queen of Heaven but by the island's own Até.

Aspasia gave a warm welcome to the Coastguard and took him to the back room where her nephew Kostas was serving drinks. The back room was where some of the leading men of Doxos met: lawyers, politicians, civil engineers, to enjoy pursuits of a masculine nature. Today the patrons were Vasilios and the Mayor who were joined by Mr Theophilus and an architect, both of them people who owed favours to the Mayor and could be relied upon to keep quiet about what was going on – in as much as they knew, for the Mayor could be very circumspect. There was knowledge within knowledge: the Mayor and Vasilios knew what was happening and why; Theophilus and the architect knew the process but had no idea of the motive; Aspasia would see the mark's hand while she was bringing refreshments, and would signal the key cards to the Mayor. Her understanding was limited to this technical part of the operation. Kostas knew to keep quiet – anything he gleaned, he must forget.

The Coastguard looked around the room with the green baize table with five places. He felt the quickening pulse, the dryness of the mouth. The mayor introduced them as 'just a few friends' They were in the middle of a poker hand, playing five card draw for small sums, with piles of chips before each player and the pot in the middle.

The other participants nodded in a friendly but disinterested way, they weren't here to make friends. He knew this atmosphere, could hear the talk about hands, the familiar words, the chink of plastic chips, the cigarette smoke, the smells of tense sweat and the whiff of cellulose from the cards, stale alcohol in the air; the Coastguard could swim in it like a fish, how comforting to be in such control of himself and his tastes. He felt calm, what hurt could there be in watching?

Kostas served him a drink on a tray, he was, in fact, the only one in the room who was being served real alcohol, the rest had a dilution of tea poured from a Scotch bottle, the Mayor wanted them all to be clear-headed, he also wanted them to be constantly reminded of the purpose of this evening, so at every taste of the bitter liquid the conspirators were reminded that this was work, not pleasure; they were there with money provided by Vasilios that would return at the end of play.

The Coastguard wasn't expected to drink much, to think *they* were drinking was sufficient. The Mayor was not there to play his hand, but to play the man opposite him, now sitting on an adjoining table and watching the game, petted by Aspasia who stood and stroked his shoulder, and attentively serviced by Kostas.

The Mayor and the others affected the seriousness of the professional but played sloppily. They bet a round, the Coastguard's eyes fixed on details – the way they handled the chips, the way they looked at the cards, held the hands, touched their faces, how they sat. Only then did he attend to the plays they made: who was betting, by how much, who was checking and who was calling and raising. Finally, meticulous as a man dismantling an engine to see how it was working, after understanding the mechanics of the players, he turned his agile mind to the cards, a constant in all games and therefore the easiest aspect to comprehend: what were they discarding, what therefore remained in the pack?

The Coastguard was thrilled at the speed with which his quick mind reasserted itself in the game – he immediately understood these players, their motives and their plays. Theophilus and the architect had a tendency to fold early – real amateurs, they had no sense of the game. They were there to make up the numbers and, the Coastguard surmised, to bleed money. They were loose players, trying to bluff against the whole table with a pair of threes or betting on weak hands, holding on to aces when there was no strategic reason to do so, because aces symbolised success for them. They were talking about their hands, 'I may have something here,' 'What was the highest hand you can have again? I've forgotten' 'This is no good, I'll never be a millionaire this way.' The Coastguard did not take account of the words but the tone, listened for the sense behind the sense.

Vasilios played recklessly, betting strongly and raising at every play, and would easily force Theophilus and the architect to jettison improving hands by big bets, making them fold in fear when often he had nothing, just one high card. The Mayor played a tricky game; tended to bet weakly even with a strong hand; he bluffed frequently to get other players to call his legitimate bets.

People assessed the odds as percentages and created complicated formulae to determine actions, but if you were a master, if you were really into it, you just understood as the Coastguard did – assessing the game at every second. These players in Aspasia's back room would have been drawn and gutted like fish in the sort of casinos where the Coastguard had played.

The Coastguard had forgotten how good he was at

this game, how he was born to it. In playing mode he lost all contact with the world and entered the spiritual plane in which all that existed was the play. Surely he was strong enough now to withstand the challenge. His life had faced disaster eight years ago, but he had recovered. He was strong enough now to re-enter the arena, he had learned control, he could master himself. The last test of his resolve was this temptation, his certain ability to engage in just one hand and disengage.

'I'll join you for this hand if that is good for you,' he said.

'You're welcome' said the Mayor casually, 'the ante's twenty-five Euros,' Aspasia drew up a chair for him and the Coastguard asked for 500 Euros' worth of chips and entered the white light of being.

It was like the old days, the years of promises of abstinence washed away – why had he ever stopped doing this? This was what he was made for, his whole mind, every cell of his body was concentrated on the cards, his existence circumscribed by the green baize tablecloth. The Coastguard felt the pulse of the game flooding through him, better than orgasm, better than drugs. It was more potent than love, more than the first drink of wine. He casually took his turn, paying the blind and beginning to bet, 'I'll raise you,' he said.

He played easily and automatically, first dealing with Theophilus and the architect. They were checking – failing to bet or calling because they were frightened, only playing when they had strong hands, folding when anyone said 'boo' to them. The Coastguard let them win a little, just enough to keep them in the game so they thought they would get their stake back; the object at this stage of the game was to keep them in but losing money.

By midnight Theophilus and the architect were out. The Coastguard had their money. He was head to head with Vasilios. The type of play was not a charade, neither of them were good enough actors for that, everyone played as well as he could, according to his ability. Even aggressive players have good hands sometimes, and Vasilios sometimes won, thinking it was all a result of his strategy, which confirmed him in aggressive play. Vasilios's role was to raise the stakes, behaving as the sort of gambler who hated losing, and put more and more money into the pot as if the bigger the stakes the less likely he was to lose. The Coastguard was calling on more and more money to keep in the game. He was flush with winning against Vasilios, taking the pot that by now must have been worth E70,000, with Vasilios betting heavily and the Mayor doing his bit to swell the pot.

Finally, the pot odds in his favour, the Coastguard bet his pile of chips and Vasilios folded, leaving the Mayor in. The Coastguard was bluffing, playing with a single pair, two tens. The Mayor had three of a kind, the Mayor took the pot.

The Coastguard felt he had been playing brilliantly, but even great players can fall foul of bad luck. It was the game to him, not the money, the money was nothing, a token of winning. Wife and family, career, home all disappeared in the rush to the white light, nothing else existed, just travelling on that beam, adjusting the controls that allowed him to stay there was all the rational thought his mind had left. The fuel was money, he needed more. He had to borrow to keep in the game, but he had it, in a savings account, he was just putting the money into play to earn some interest, it would work in the game and it would come back doubled. He was great tonight, as great as he had ever been – whyever had he stopped doing this?

'You'll accept an IOU?' he asked the table. The Mayor looked as if for confirmation to the others and assented. The Coastguard wrote a marker on the headed notepaper for Aspasia's restaurant, and asked for chips for E100,000.

They had a break, in which the Mayor set up the sting: a substitute deck. Soon the Coastguard picked up his cards to inner rejoicing: he had been dealt two pairs, two nines two twos. He bet moderately, biding his time. He discarded the odd card and drew another. It was another two. He was in poker player's bliss. This was perhaps the happiest he had ever been. This was what the Mayor had been preparing for: at last the mark had a hand on which he would bet his life. He was right, the Coastguard was thinking: what could possibly beat him? Four of a kind or a straight flush. A straight flush, an almost impossible hand, you might not see it in a lifetime of regular playing.

The Mayor took his cards and leaned forward to bet giving a self-satisfied smile. He did this when he was bluffing, he couldn't help it, just at the corners of his mouth – a tell. The Coastguard recalled that earlier the Mayor had folded against his two sevens when he had a drawing hand and could have stayed in – the man was a pussy, he was a typical politician, all bluster. The Coastguard held politics and politicians in contempt, and had never himself attempted to comprehend the dark arts, which unbeknown to him left him in thrall to them. Aggressive betting now, he judged, would make the Mayor fold, but he would have to be drawn out first, would have to be coaxed to bet everything.

He bet by 10,000, modest for the current stakes. The Mayor raised that to fifty, so the Coastguard would have to match it at least, and then would have so much invested in the game he would not fold, not with the good hand the Mayor knew he had. At the next round the Mayor put in almost his entire stack, the chips in a pile in front of him so large he had to push them forward with both hands. The Coastguard did not hesitate. There must have been E200,000 in play on the table but he pushed it towards the centre. 'I'll see you,' he said quietly.

He placed his cards face up on the table, 'Full house,' he said quietly, and he laid his three twos and two nines out.

The Mayor nodded and turned over his cards: He had four of a kind, four queens. The Coastguard saw their stupid, mocking faces and the lifeblood drained from him as he guessed how he had been played: The Mayor was faking the tell. He was bluffing that he was bluffing.

The guilt struck like lightening into his heart, the thunderbolt of God apportioning blame on him and him alone.

The Coastguard, realising his body wanted him to scream, or cry, summoned the last remnants of his dignity and said, 'That's it for me, goodnight,' and quickly left. The others nodded and murmured, without jubilation or exclamations, taking their cue from the Mayor who wiped his brow with a napkin. It was a sombre thing to see a man lose so much.

The Coastguard stumbled towards his car, the night breezes cooling the sweat on his body, wanting to be alone with the unfolding realisation of what he had done. He had been proud, he had been brought down. Dust and ashes were to be his lot, his mind was spinning with the horror of it.

The men prepared to leave. The Mayor thanked them and said to Vasilios, 'We'll work on this tomorrow – well, later today.'

When they had left Aspasia put her arms around him, the strong man who would vanquish her foes for her. 'Did I play my part well?' she asked. Was everything to your liking?

'Yes, my sweet,' he said, 'yes you did.' The Mayor's mind was on other things, the unfolding process of his plan.

'Now you do something for me,' she said, in the morning light he could see the lipstick draining into the wrinkles round her mouth, 'Get rid of that xenie bitch down the road.'

Chapter 8

Sarah had not been sure she would have sex with Kostas again, or even go out with him again, but in the absence of Sven it seemed the thing to do. For this, she had to be deceptive, she did not want comment on her behaviour from the others – though it appeared they either did not know or care. Anton did not notice much, unless it was brought to his attention; Anne was busy with her refugees – 'Mother Theresa' as Sarah called her. Not much escaped Hester but she was not one of those for whom sexual fidelity had a high premium, in others or herself. It was of more concern to Hester that she suspected Sarah was trying to get away with doing as little work as possible, but in her favour she was attractive and that was an asset to Café Europa, she was associated with the place as that big girl with full breasts and thighs striding out over the beaches of the island to distribute fliers. Her sex life was not Hester's concern.

Kostas was not perturbed by the presence of a boyfriend who could return at any moment. In some ways it was preferable, for a level of discretion was ensured that way. No one wanted to make a big fuss when there was a boyfriend or even a husband involved, Kostas liked a quiet relationship.

When Sven left, he took veneration for the truth with him. Sarah did not in fact relish the truth. The truth was cold and harsh, hard facts like a handful of gravel. From childhood Sarah had learned that Lies R

Us. Oh, comforting little lie that would sit in the mind like a curved stone in the hand worn smooth and familiar with constant caressing. The maintenance of her status as one of the blessed relied upon certain reassurances that she must make to herself. She believed everything, ultimately, was for the best, that whatever the challenges, the good guys would win in the end, like they do in the films. She believed her parents had a good and faithful marriage, despite evidence to the contrary. She was a good and faithful girlfriend, she would not cheat on her man. On the other hand, how could you ever get a new boyfriend unless you were seeing him while you were with the old boyfriend? To be without a boyfriend altogether while looking for a new one was unthinkable; that was for unpopular girls, who weren't pretty or clever.

She deserved her thrills, and Kostas was there to provide them, his very presence excited her. She saw him the afternoon of the day Sven left and they went swimming. When they were still in a depth shallow enough to stand up, he swam underwater and grabbed her around the waist and they rolled over, laughing and spitting out salty water. She regained balance and floated on her back while he swam under and tickled her, they embraced, they could see the sea floor, the brilliant pebbles like jewels through the perfectly clear water.

They watched a fisherman smashing an octopus he had just caught on the concrete jetty to soften it up, Kostas waved and exchanged greetings with the man, he seemed to know everyone on the island. Kostas told her it had to be smacked sixty times to make sure it was pliable; first against the concrete, then with a hard stick, then threaded with string and thrown to right and left: flip-flop. The fisherman gave Kostas and Sarah two sea urchins, brown spiky balls. Kostas cut the hard shells open with a knife; he showed her how to scrape out the gooey orange meat. Sarah prepared to go for it, 'I think I would need to starve for a while on a desert island before I started to relish this stuff,' she said, but was surprised at the rich fishy taste of the roe. 'I so love this country,' she said, 'it is so…natural.' Kostas extended his arms and danced a few steps, clicking his fingers to make a beat of Greek traditional music.

'I feel so full of joy here,' said Sarah, 'Seid umschlungen Millionen,' she sang, translating for him: '"stand up you millions." This is what life is all about, hanging about with mates, having a good time, the sun, love: Diesen Kuss der ganzen Welt,' she said kissing him. '"This kiss is for the whole world."'

'What's that all about?' he said, he had never learned a word of German, he could communicate with German girls in English.

'Don't you know this, it's the European anthem,' she sang a few more bars, but clearly there was no recognition in his face.

'You are funny,' he said, and wrapped her in his musky embrace.

Sarah cultured a fantasy of living with Kostas on an island, a small island off the coast of Doxos, where he would fish for their food and she would prepare vegetables and do the washing, it would be a simple life with just each other. She would welcome him home from the sea and in the afternoons they would make love on a rustic bed. It was never anything but a reverie, but it gave her pleasure. She wondered if she should put a picture of Kostas on her social networking site profile, noting the break in her relationship with Sven, but it was courtesy to let Sven know that first. She had trouble explaining social networking to Kostas, who saw all his friends most days. She thought of his failure to understand as an aspect of his being an island boy, it was quite sweet really.

Having sex with Kostas was really engaging with Greece, Sarah mused that you could only truly understand a country if you were intimate with its inhabitants. It was after swimming that for the first time she took him in her mouth. Kostas liked being fellated but was not so eager for a reciprocal arrangement which he proffered once, early in the relationship, but inexpertly and without enthusiasm.

As she got to know Kostas and his ways, she thought of the contrasts between him and Sven. She had enjoyed Sven's open blonde nakedness, often seeing him walking from the bathroom with nothing on, unconcerned that Anne or Anton might come across him. By contrast Kostas seemed to want to hide his brawny body, his brown, muscular arms and hairy legs. He was more than happy to get naked to have sex, but not comfortable with his nakedness, he was quick to dress and not interested in sitting naked to talk. He enjoyed the sight of Sarah's generous body, but she had the feeling he wanted it concealed, to be seen only by him, and only during sexual encounters.

There were real differences between Kostas and Sven's sexual approach. Kostas would not touch spunk, as if contact with it would defile, whereas Sven sometimes used to finish her off even after he had come and she was full of him. Kostas would not even blow his nose on a tissue that had sperm on it, and cleaning up after sex was women's work. Sven always wanted to know everything, nothing was free from his probing and questioning. He always wanted to know what Sarah was thinking, why she had done this or that thing, what was her motive; how had she made life choices in the past? Apart from some loving talk and of course making love itself, Kostas didn't seem to care what Sarah thought or did. It was, in its own way, a blissful release.

Six hours after he had walked out of Aspasia's, too devastated to speak, the still unsleeping Coastguard restlessly fingered his amber kompoloi beads, looking at the blank wall ahead of him, the pain of tension in his guts like dysentery. This was bad, as bad as it gets. What had he done? What had possessed him to go there, to play, to put on those stakes? It was as if another person had done it. It was all they had in the world of years of work, of saving, and of inheritance from the family – from his wife's family – all thrown away in a night of madness. He could not let her down, not again. My little wifey: the thoughts of her seared into his mind, *psihoula mou* - my little soul. She thought him so powerful and romantic, the embodiment of heroic virtue, he could not let her down, he would truly rather die.

The last time this had happened, almost a decade ago, he remembered the tears and abject apologies. He had promised, solemnly promised on all the saints and the Virgin, many times, that he would never gamble again, but far from home a man had temptations. How could he keep a vow that had been made elsewhere under different circumstances? He had thought it was not binding but it was, it was always binding, everywhere.

He wondered if he had better just die, if the world would be better off without him, certainly his wife would. If he died in an accident related to work, if he could contrive such an event, then she would have enough insurance money to start over, to marry again and bring up the children free of him.

Now he was planning a death by accident. From his abject misery there gleamed this spark of hope: a direction to engage his industrious spirit. He could work out a way to die. Now, that would take his mind off his suffering, his sin. Maybe he could die from fumes – but it must not look like a suicide or there would be no occupational insurance payout from the coastguard service, it had to be an accident. He could be fatally injured by a propeller that came off its bearings but that would be grisly and he might just end up with a severed limb. How could he die accidentally at work when so much of his work was done at his desk? He needed to be so injured he would bleed to death fast, but how? Somewhere in the workshop, maybe, or in the machine room where the engines were serviced. He pondered the options each in turn.

A large ant crawled across the letter Hester was reading on a table in front of Café Europa. She flicked it off as she turned to Freddie who was toying with an Amstel beer, 'what is this,' she asked 'iota, kappa alpha?'

'Someone grassed you up,' said Freddie, 'it's IKA, as in "Eeek a mouse" like in the early sixties sitcoms, but with less laughs. It's social security for tradesmen. But they don't pay it, the employer pays it.'

'I've heard of it,' said Hester, 'but no one pays, do they?'

'Nope, especially if you do work on your own house. You are supposed to pay, even for do-it-yourself jobs, but of course people don't, it's one of those taxes made to be ignored. Unless someone grasses you up. Someone informed on you to the authorities, to say you'd had work done. Who might that be?'

'Who? Aspasia down the road, or the builders who didn't want to do the work but got pissed off when someone else did it. Or anyone, really. I'm the xenie, I'm an open target.'

'You'll never know, the best thing is to go to the IKA office and grovel. A little bit of grovel goes a long way here. Foreign grovel especially appreciated,' he made an expression of lip-smacking enjoyment.

Freddie was off to Megalo Limani so they went together in his green Toyota, Hester was fretting about how her store of money from the divorce was dwindling with every challenge to Café Europa. Hester liked Freddie, he had the easy-going attitude of the Greeks with a cockney liveliness. He had no great ambition, but he liked to make things work. His Greek language was awful, he made no effort with the accent and was always getting the endings of his verbs wrong, so he could not make it clear whether he was doing something or had done something or was asking them to do something, but the locals liked him for his willingness to speak Greek, however poorly.

Hester left him to go to the electrical shop and walked off past the fish market and the standing tap where people gathered with plastic containers to carry drinking water home. On her way to the IKA office she almost ran into Aspasia, coming out of the hairdresser's.

Hester gave the customary 'How are you' greeting to which Aspasia said 'good' but swallowed the 'and you?' which formality required. Instead she said,

'How's business?'

'Very good,' said Hester, where in England she would have responded 'not bad.' Here it was proper to self-promote and exaggerate, particularly with a rival. 'I'm just off to the bank to pay in the profits.'

'You make money, you get all those customers because you keep your prices below ours,' said Aspasia.

'I don't know about anyone else's prices, I don't eat at other restaurants,' Hester said, amused at the older woman's impotent anger. 'My prices are what they are because I look at what it costs to produce and add a profit. Welcome to the market economy Aspasia, so nice to see you.'

Hester could not hide a smirk as she went off in the direction of the IKA office. In an office piled with unfiled papers a weary IKA man consoled Hester by saying the fine would be small. He had been worn down by arguments and counterclaims in a life playing the part of the instrument of vengeance for neighbours informing on each other for petty sums. It was a welcome change to encounter someone like Hester who simply paid up. She handed over several hundred Euros. The IKA officer was pleased; he had no complaint about foreigners.

Waiting for Freddie to return, Hester sat in a café opposite the bakery, watching the stout baker bring out trays of warm bread before he sat and ate a bun himself. At a table in the same café she saw Vasilios, whose name she did not know, a big man with sleeves rolled back to show strong arms and expensive jewellery, with two Greek girls fussing around him, more like pets than women, one bleached blonde, the other redhead, wearing clinging clothes that exaggerated their skinny bodies: one with tiger-skin patterned slacks, the other with a skirt up to her thighs, both wearing tiny tube tops.

Freddie appeared and waved at Vasilios before sitting down opposite Hester. 'Who is that colourful character?' she asked.

'Vasilios, eldest son of one of the main business families here.'

'You mean criminal business,' Hester laughed, 'he looks like a gangster and they look like gangster's molls from a 1950s film.'

'Don't say that stuff too near them, don't assume they can't understand English, they watch a lot of movies.'

'American gangster stuff?'

'Yeah, and South American gangster stuff – they like that more – more violence and in those the drug dealers win.'

'Art imitating life, eh? Is that what he is into?'

Freddie looked more serious, 'Look at my face,' he said, she looked at him: his black curly hair, light brown skin, slightly flattened nose from his mixed-race inheritance. She wasn't sure what she was looking at until he said, 'No scars, see? I've been in some of the worst places in London and known some of the worst people, men who would cut you a new mouth soon as look at you. I haven't been hurt because I don't see anything, I don't know anything. It's not a bad way to be.' Hester reflected there was a good deal not to know.

The Mayor knew he had to clinch this deal quickly – the moonless nights were approaching and he worried about what the Coastguard would do if he had no way out. He gave him most of the day to consider his position than called upon his white-uniformed cardmate. He was shown into the Coastguard's office. As soon as the door closed he said to the dour Coastguard, 'My friend, things got out of hand. That wasn't supposed to be a high stakes game.'

'Well, it was,' said the Coastguard blankly.

The Mayor looked across the desk, clear except for an in and out tray, some pens on a desk calendar and a framed picture. He peered round to see a photograph of the Coastguard with an elfin woman and two bright looking children, a boy and a girl. He was going to pay a complimentary remark about the Coastguard's family but thought better of it. 'You owe a lot of money,' he said quietly, 'maybe we can come to an arrangement, I need a favour.'

The Coastguard looked at him with interest while the Mayor explained some businessmen needed to move a package, the contents were immaterial, from Turkey on some moonless night, they must not be intercepted. If the Coastguard could arrange this, his debt would be cancelled.

'If you had said this to me yesterday I would have had you arrested,' said the Coastguard quietly. The room was silent expect for the whirring of a fan.

'Such a difference in a day,' the Mayor said philosophically.

'I understand what this is about, said the Coastguard, that's what all this, the friendliness and the card game was for. The game was a set-up.'

'You didn't complain when you were winning,' said the mayor.

'I am not complaining now,' the Coastguard said, his dignity still intact, 'I just don't want you to think I am unaware of it.'

'Come, my friend, we are professionals together on

the island...' said the Mayor, appealing to the esprit de corps that was supposed to exist between professionals when they made deals to benefit themselves at the expense of the locals. The Coastguard did not consider the Mayor the equal of the professional class, he thought of him more like a well-connected chancer who had played the political game and won.

The Coastguard immediately understood the situation, the means and terms of his entrapment. So that was what it was all about, how foolish of him not to have seen it coming. All his work, the charts, the regulations, the examinations, all the training with weapons, the drills with the men, assuming the habit of command...it all came down to this – his only exit was to look the other way for these criminals and betray his oath to his country. He had been attentive and smart, he was an experienced player, how had he let himself be beaten? There was no point in asking, as the Mayor would say he won fairly. The goddess of folly had prepared a draught and he must drink it.

The Coastguard was a decisive man, he had been in danger at sea when there was no time to consider the options. This situation would not improve with delay. The Coastguard knew that his chief deluder must want the deal very badly, to have gone to such trouble to entrap him. He looked across the desk calmly at his adversary, now he fully understood. 'I think yours is the only deal on the table, Mr Mayor,' he said. 'I can die, or I can take it. But don't make it so hard for me that death would be preferable, do you understand?'

The Mayor was taken aback, he thought there would be some wheedling, some persuading to be done, before he became assertive and threatened his opponent into submission. 'My friend we are not talking about death....' he started to say.

'I am not your friend and I *am* talking about death.' The Coastguard, instinctive gambler that he was, had raised the stakes. He could not win, but he could get the best deal for himself. 'I have done something stupid and I must pay the price,' he said, 'but on my terms or I will take the other option. I will do what you want once. Your people have to be successful on one night. I can justify not going out one night by planning a big operation soon after. Don't ask for this favour twice or we both go down together. I will do this one thing, but I will not be your creature. I know what I have done, I have let myself be caught through my foolishness – no, don't talk, I'll talk to you. In return for wiping off this debt, I will cancel patrols on the sixteenth. Only that night, no other time. You understand? The most I can do is not schedule a patrol on that night. If we are called out by some fishing boat that's got into trouble I have to go, just no routine patrol. Boats are crewed by eight men, you can't order them all to keep quiet, half of them want my job, most are young, none have any connection to the island. I'll save the resources from one night to send all the boats out on another night. Don't ask again, don't see me again.' The Coastguard reflected on the honest life of which he had always been proud. He did not drink, didn't go with women, he was a steady man, always had a job, never a day off sick, now he had to betray his sacred trust. The cup that Até fed him was bitter indeed.

He had the Mayor shown out by an officer who took his opportunity to chatter to the great man about a house building project that his neighbour was trying to stop. The Mayor told him to come to the town hall, and entered the mercifully air-conditioned coolness of his car to drive to Aspasia's.

The Mayor crossed the island, his island, feeling the bristles on his chin, feeling the age in his bones. Time was when they would do this sort of game, when he could be up all night at cards, fuck a woman and still be ready for the morning's work. Well, now there were obligations. He still wanted to win, he wanted to be successful in this endeavour, but there was something missing – then he realised it, like a man having forgotten his own name day or his favourite drink, it was so obvious but he had forgotten: there was no fun in it, the fun had gone, it was all business, the money had killed it. They used to play this sort of trick for a million drachma, that would be...maybe two thousand Euros. They could afford it, it was good to win, the mark could afford to lose, the money went in no time, but now, Vasilios's deal was worth millions of Euros, the airport scam was worth millions...that was real money, it was the sort of money people died for, the sort of money people killed for. That wasn't fun, it was just more obligations.

He returned to Aspasia's where he had arranged to meet Vasilios who was engaged in a long conversation on his mobile phone when the Mayor arrived. Too much consorting with Vasilios was not good for a man in the Mayor's position, it was better not to be seen in public with a known criminal, but a gentleman could turn up to Aspasia's establishment with no questions asked or anticipated. Even if either were seen stopping at Aspasia's, it would be assumed that they had gone there to enjoy female companionship and this would not be a matter of comment, or interrogation, so it was a fine location for the conclusion of their business.

Vasilios's sleeves were rolled up showing the enormous watch nestling in the hairs on one of his arms and the gold chain on the other. The Mayor waited for Aspasia to leave and sat down next to Vasilios, talking in low tones. 'Right,' he said, 'you're on for the sixteenth. No patrol. But that's the only time I could get, he's going to cut up rough if we tried to push it. Said he'd rather die and I believe him, and that'd do none of us any good. Just a lot more questions.'

Vasilios accepted, 'I need only one night, I can do it.'

The Mayor said distantly, 'That was a difficult thing to do, the Coastguard was good, he was damned good. That was one of the toughest things I ever did and I did it for you my cousin, you take it from here.'

Vasilios left and the Mayor kissed Aspasia, noticing in the sun the age-spots on her cleavage. Again he walked through the heat to the cool of the car, the only place he could really be alone. The Mayor eased onto the road and back towards the town hall. Yes, more obligations. The Mayor was firmly in Aspasia's debt. Debts have to be paid, or they come back in a more dangerous form. That was the lesson he had endeavoured to explain to the Coastguard.

Sometimes a life of seeing Kostas every day was the island idyll for Sarah, sometimes she found she did not love everything about him. Among the things she did not like were that he had no more concern for the environment than most of his compatriots. Sarah noticed the way he threw his cigarette packet on the ground rather than taking the litter home. She picked it up and put it in her bag to throw away in a proper receptacle.   He thought she was keeping it, like a young girl, as a token of him, and smiled indulgently.

They used to go to the café at the start of the bay of Zeste where the trendy young of Doxos hung out, the boys with spiky haircuts, the girls in skin-tight jeans, amid tables covered with ashtrays, cigarette packets, lighters, mobile phones, sunglasses, water, beer, and fruit juice. Bored looking Greek girls sat in front of iced coffee in tall glasses, with a studied indifference to Sarah; foreign girlfriends were not popular with Greek girls. Sarah noticed how sometimes they sniggered at a shared joke. After initial attempts to be friendly, Sarah said to Kostas that she would rather not stop off at the Greek kids' café again. Kostas complied, in his way: he stopped the bike and let it idle while he exchanged greetings with his friends, with Sarah on the pillion behind him, but he didn't get off and go in.

Once he stopped by and talked to his friend Tassos with Sarah on the back.

'You like Greek boys?' Tassos asked Sarah in Greek.

'You make me think of the sailors who went with Ulysses,' she said in English, her Greek not up to a complex statement.

'She says we are like Greek gods to her,' said Kostas, in Greek. Tassos was delighted at this and clapped his hands in glee that set them all laughing. Sarah recognised the translation was not accurate, but let it all go in the mood of general hilarity.

Kostas' friends were uncomplicated, their favourite word was *malaka* which translates roughly as 'wanker.' They sometimes seemed to have conversations which consisted of little but the use of this word in various constructions.

It was not a secret from Sarah that Kostas was involved with some dubious characters. He did not introduce her, but Vasilios and the men who hung around a particular bar in Megalo Limani would acknowledge her when she passed, she was Kostas' girl so she was a friend. It made her feel part of the island life when she walked past with Anne, on their way to distribute leaflets to passengers coming off the ferry.

'How do you know them?' Anne asked.

'Oh, they are friends of Kostas, he knows everyone.'

'They look tough, what do they do?' asked Anne.

'Dodgy business,' said Sarah, 'some dodgy characters and some dodgy business. It's his family.'

'What, "Dodgy" is the family business? "Dodgy incorporated"? "Dodgy and Sons?"'

'I think so,' laughed Sarah, 'well dodgy.'

'Kostas didn't have second thoughts about going into the family business?'

'He's not really a man for second thoughts,' said Sarah, 'here they come...' and the girls were caught in the wave of holiday makers in the clutter of taxis, wheeled baggage and café tables.

For the week that Sven was away, Kostas came over a couple of times a day and Sarah went off with him. Once the initial thrill of sex on the beach or sex in a grassy hollow had worn off, Sarah became more aware of the drawbacks – sand in intimate places or bugs crawling out of the undergrowth, not to mention the odd curious child who might happen upon them. The sun was also high in the sky at the times she could get away, there was little cover on the island, the landscape was largely bracken, or prickly trees growing in sandy soil. This meant open-air amours, with the fierce sun burning them. It was urgently passionate the first couple of times to have sex standing up against a tree, but the thrill palled and Sarah longed for a more comfortable trysting place. Kostas did not himself have a location where they could have sex, he lived with his mother over in Kephali, he had never taken Sarah there and just mentioned that was where he lived when they passed the turning.

Early one afternoon with the sun blazing, Kostas came and met Sarah by the tables, his handsome face the way she loved it, against the background of the sea. She was wearing light cotton trousers and a lilac vest top. In the heat she had abjured underwear as too restricting and uncomfortable so he could see the shape of her body clearly through the thin fabric. 'There's no one in the house,' she whispered, 'we can go to my room, but I don't want anyone to know, can we drive around and park, and walk back from behind the house?'

Subterfuge appealed to Kostas. Sarah climbed on the back of the bike and they waved goodbye as they went off along the bay road but then turned right up a tiny road that weaved into the hills, serving isolated houses. They parked and scrambled down the track to arrive behind the empty house, feeling a delicious sense of the forbidden as they entered unobserved.

Upstairs in the bedroom Sven's clothes were still there in a neat pile, his books and notes rather less tidily spread on the desk. Sarah's clothes were hung on hooks behind the door, her shoes were in a jumble under the bed. ''Scuse the mess, I didn't know I was going to have a visitor,' she said.

The couple undressed quickly, giggling at their audacity, and fell to kissing and fondling, his firm body contrasting with her voluptuous curves.

Out at the restaurant tables, Anne felt cramps in her lower stomach. With the change in location and climate, and all the work, she had not been keeping track of her cycle. Her period had come on suddenly and she had to go back to the house for a tampon.

Going to her room she heard the feral sounds from the bedroom next door. She didn't think but pushed the unlocked and ill-fitting door to see Sarah with legs up and Kostas on top of her. Anne made an involuntary 'Oh' that distracted the lovers, and closed the door so she could not see them but said through the gap, 'Sorry. I didn't know what it was, what the noise was.'

'Well, now you do,' said Sarah with mock patience.

Flushed with embarrassment, Anne quickly went to her room, as if she were in the wrong and had to get out fast, then ran downstairs to the bathroom to attend to her tampon.

Sarah threw on a Chinese silk dressing gown (an item Anne had always rather admired) and went into the bathroom where Anne was washing her hands. She did not welcome the intrusion, she had been brought up to keep anything to do with menstruation private, including from other girls.

'That didn't take long did it?' said Anne, meaning the copulation, Sarah thought she was talking about the relationship.

'It's been going on for a long time, the feelings between Kostas and me,' she said, 'I can't help it.'

'I suppose it did look like watching pandas mating, waiting for you two to get it together,' Anne conceded.

Sarah took the humour as a sign that the floodgates of confidentiality had opened, 'What a lunch box,' she said, 'hugely hairy – more a lunch muff, balls like coconuts....'

'Stop,' said Anne, irritated at the intrusion on top of her feeling sticky and in pain in this heat, 'skip it. I'm not interested, I don't want to know, you're on your own in this.'

'Please yourself,' Sarah said, her wit having deserted her at this trying time. 'But please don't tell Sven. I mean, if he needs to be told anything I will tell him myself. But this is the wrong time for him, I can't just send him a text when he's at a funeral telling him I'm breaking up with him.'

Anne could see the logic in this, though she had not immediately realised the implications for Sven of Sarah's indiscretions with Kostas. She said, 'Well, I'm not a sneak, but I won't cover up for you either, I won't take sides. I mean, I don't want a lecture on the categorical imperative of the truth ....' Anne ran out of words and they looked at each other, and they laughed, because a verbal essay on veracity is exactly how Sven would treat any duplicity on Anne's part in the matter of Sarah's fidelity.

Anne wanted to get away from it, feeling prickly and irritated. She just left, shaking her head. Sarah returned to complete her coitus, somewhat less enthusiastically than before. She did her best to rekindle lust but she was angry. What was that little shrimp doing being judgemental over her? Anne with her geeky boyfriend couldn't tell her what to do. Just because Anne had only ever shagged two boys she couldn't expect everyone else to join a convent...

Anne went back to the restaurant, feeling uncomfortable inside and out, somehow ashamed at what she had seen, as if *she* had been dirtied by it. Shagging someone else in the Wendy House! How could she? Anne supposed the signs were there but she hadn't been watching carefully, just thought they were all friends together. She imagined that Kostas and Sarah might get it together but, really, it was just a flirtation, Sven was a *real boyfriend* with connections back home and a future, he was going to make something of himself. To throw that away for a holiday fling seemed to Anne unnatural.

She was still irritated when she took the jeep up to the refugee compound to see Malik that afternoon. This was their regular liaison. Gradually, by wheedling the authorities and making the best use of the available supplies, by using Malik as an intermediary, she had the refugees clean the detention centre thoroughly, including the latrines and showers, so it no longer smelled of urine and unwashed bodies, but was more like a Spartan youth hostel. This work relied on a constant supply of bleach, mops and disinfectant that Anne would provide from the store, using Malik to do the lifting.

She drove to the guard post where Malik was waiting and he jumped into the jeep all smiles and off they went down the bumpy road. She tried to reciprocate his cheerfulness but she had been biting her nails and looked pensive.

'Why are you down in the dumps?' he asked.

Too stressed to prevaricate she simply said, 'I just found Sarah and Kostas, you know, together. It made me upset.'

Malik went silent, adultery was a very serious offence as far as he was concerned. 'What happened?' he said, 'how?' Anne immediately regretted telling him, but wanted to talk.

'I just heard something and walked in on Sarah and Kostas doing, you know, doing it.'

For Malik the idyllic life of the students had just crashed and died. 'And Sven is away?' he said, 'He had to be with his family? A death? That is …bad form. Did they see you, do they know that you know?'

'Yes,' she said I just opened the door, I wasn't spying on them or anything.' For Malik, who had never had much privacy, even the notion of spying on people who lived in the same house was alien.

'Did you suspect nothing?' asked Malik.

'It wasn't up to me to suspect anything,' said Anne, 'they were friends, I suppose they were getting a bit close, but it wasn't my business.' Malik looked at her gravely, 'I am sorry to have mentioned it, I shouldn't have bothered you with this,' she said, now flustered, realising how seriously he took the matter. Because they had been laughing and doing chores together, Anne had underestimated the cultural distance between them and wondered how she could change the subject.

'Sven is my friend,' he said, feeling a debt of honour.

'Yes, me too, I shouldn't have said anything.'

'What will Sven do when he gets back?' Malik said, genuinely worried.

'I don't know, I suppose that is why I am upset. Sarah will have to deal with it, I won't say anything.'

'That's a rum thing. If she says nothing, then what happens, she keeps deceiving him?'

'I suppose so,' said Anne.

'What will happen to him, in this country?' said Malik.

Anne did not get the drift of this remark, and simply said, 'I don't know.'

Malik became quiet, the conversation clouded their

afternoon's work. Sven was an honourable man who had always taken time to talk to Malik, such a man could not be shamed in this way.

That night in the heat, lying on his iron bestead and listening to the snores and occasional cries of other residents, Malik lay awake considering his position. He pondered the dilemma, the question Anne had not understood: *What would happen to him in this country? What would happen to Sven when he killed her?*

Even more pertinent to his position: what would happen to Malik, if he told Sven and Sven killed her? Would they blame Malik? That would be her blood on his hands too, for telling Sven. Would they punish him? Send him back? But what if Sven was being shamed, and Malik did not tell him, then that would be Malik's fault. Nothing in previous life had prepared Malik for such a conundrum.

What would Jeeves do? Probably contrive a way for Sven to find out without Sven holding anyone responsible. The only honourable thing to do would be to let Sven find out: if he found out on his own he would believe it, and Malik would not be responsible.

That night on his way back, Sven took a flight to Kos, intending to get on a hydrofoil, but found himself stuck on the island with no ferry to Doxos that evening. Sven booked into a hotel and wandered through the old town watching the would-be blonde girls with their little tops, jeans and sandals with bulky costume jewellery, day-glo watches and sparkly belts with messages: SEXY or GIRL as if this were information that was not self-evident and had to be conveyed at all costs.

In the early evening there were still some Greek

families out for a meal. Couples glided past, precariously perched on bicycles made for one. Stout restaurant owners were checking their books; young men with svelte figures invited holidaying couples into their restaurants.

As the night wore on, nightclub-goers emerged in a riot of high heels, bleached hair and exposed flesh. Spiky haired boys in camouflage trousers walked past glowing signs for Mythos beer and nightclub names in purple and green fluorescent lights. Big screens at the bars showed pop videos; troubadours with guitars gathered audiences around them at restaurants. The island's squares and streets had been taken over by young people with skin in various stages of white to brown and the occasional black, but mainly the fair flesh of the north with the accents of Germany and Scandinavia.

Sven listened to the Babel of voices with the fizzy lager beer of Europe on his tongue. He chose to eat at a relatively quiet place on the edge of the ruins, where a few cats skirted around between the light and noise of the restaurant and the darkness of the ruins into which they could flit if a waiter, thinking the tourists were not looking, aimed a kick at them.

Sven considered what he should be doing. What was the right thing to do? In a world of climate change, ecological disaster, population growth, unending wars – what should one person do? It was easy now to think about the 1940s, what Sweden should have done to stop the holocaust, the carnage on the eastern front, the destruction of European cities. The path of righteousness for a nation was easier to decide than for an individual; particularly in retrospect. But what was one person to do *now*? Of the world's many evils, which should now be fought, and how?

He listened indifferently to the repetitive technobeat of Europop, watching the flashes of coloured light from the strobes of the discos. On his left, intermittently illuminated, was the dark of the ruins of the ancient agora. In the piles of stone stretching out into the darkness a few columns had been built up to give the impression of how high a Roman building would have been; there were some clearly Byzantine fragments of a fountain.

Shadows in the dark tugged his mind from thoughts of the individual man's moral position in the world, the line of thinking that in television game shows would be called his 'comfort zone.' The shadowy people flitted among the ruins of the ancient agora. When the breeze was in his direction he could hear they were making whistles to each other to let their location be known for an assignation. For a moment he could not understand what they were doing then he realised: it was a cruising spot for gays.

Sven was mildly amused that with the languages of Europe about him, the lights of the bars and discos to the right, to the left and within sight (had it been daylight) men were having sex in the open air. The thought of these men sucking each other's penises did not enthral, he was no more moved by it than a display of unwanted goods in a shop window – it was there, it didn't excite him, if it excited other people, that was their business, it did not concern him. Sven thought with fondness that if Anton were here he would have started a discourse on whether Hippocrates would have considered homosexuality a medical condition, a blessing from the gods or a sin. How much he missed Anton, with his well-stocked mind and his unflappable manner, you never knew what he was going to say, it was always different, and sometimes, brilliant.

As Sven sat there alone, thoughts of the men in the ancient agora filled him with loathing and fascination in equal proportions. He returned to it like a guilty secret. It was not that he wanted sex – or even wanted homosexual sex. He had never been oversexed and had never had difficulty in getting girls, they came to him. He did not just want sex, he wanted sex with one person. He forced himself to consider what these men did and whether it was attractive to him, but he did not yearn to go into the darkness, down into the ruins of the ancients and join them. It was not an aching for sex he felt, nor yet a desire for homosexuality, it was a yearning for Anton.

Chapter 9

Workers at the Café Europa became more tetchy as the heat increased and waiting on tables left them bathed in a sheen of sweat. The kitchen was a furnace even with doors open at both sides, until they bought a fan at least to move air through. A pen became slippery in the hand through nothing but the exertion of crossing the restaurant to take an order and the damp hand smeared the written word.

In the house the crossover point had come, where the water coming through the taps directly from the black tank on the roof outside was almost too hot to shower in. Water stored in the shaded tank of the indoor immersion heater was cooler. It was the arrival of the water paradox: the hot tap produced water that was significantly cooler than the cold tap.

The students needed so much drinking water at the house that they took to carting it up in large containers that they decanted into plastic bottles. Water flowed like liquid jewellery into the funnel in the brilliant sunlight. Anton and Anne plucked the first almonds from the tree growing near the house. Grapes hung so abundantly from the vine veranda they were in clusters on top of each other, though yet unripe.

The sun beat down day by day on the flattened earth and concrete of the Café Europa settlement, then at night the ground gave up the heat it had soaked in, so that warmth continued to envelop the hazy darkness which was enriched by the fierce mating calls of insects.

Sarah had a text from Sven saying he was coming back the following day or the next, depending on transport links. She pursed her lips and sent a cheery message back. She knew this day was going to come. Or maybe not – she had allowed herself to drift along in the pleasure of the moment.

Sarah went down to the harbour to pick up Sven in the jeep, remembering in a flash how different she had felt when she had waited expectantly, just a few weeks previously, for the same yellow hydrofoil to bring him. Now she had been celebrating vibrant life with Kostas and Sven was arriving from a house of death. Sven ought to be told – or not. What happened if she did nothing? Let matters come to a head as they would. Sarah was always hospitable, she did her best to make Sven feel welcome. She embraced him with what she hoped was felt to be eagerness, 'How was it?' she asked, unsure of the etiquette, never previously having had to approach the social task of welcoming someone back from a death.

'The funeral was…funereal,' he said, his blue eyes sparkling.

'I always marvel at your command of English' said Sarah, 'How were your parents about it all, your father?'

'They were OK, they didn't make a lot of it. What has happened while I was away?'

'Here… heat. The sun has happened, all day and most of the night. We are all wilting. But the restaurant's going great. More Greek people are coming and that's good to see, it's not just foreigners, Hester says it shows the locals never liked Aspasia and the restaurant owners' cartel. Hopefully she'll have customers after the summer.'

Sarah's skin had tanned so she was a glowing light brown colour. She was wearing a loose cotton blouse and skirt, with no makeup, for the sweat made it smudge and dribble.

'The sun's got to you,' Sven said, 'you look like a farm girl.'

'Oh, thanks,' she said.

'Not badly,' he laughed uneasily, 'I mean you look natural, nature's child.' He kissed her. He smelled of the lotion he used to prepare his sensitive skin for the ordeal of shaving. His tall blondness, uncorrupted by the sun, seemed more out of place on Doxos than ever. Dressed in a white shirt with the sleeves half rolled up, and a neatly pressed pair of jeans, he could have been relaxing in any capital in the world.

Sarah chatted on while she drove to Café Europa. The first of the team they met was Anne who was wiping tables down. She reached up to give Sven a kiss on the cheek, and the story of Judas in the Garden of Gethsemane occurred to her, as if *she* had betrayed Sven. This was silly, Sarah's behaviour really wasn't her responsibility, but she felt guilty, nevertheless.

Hester emerged from her office and hugged Sven, 'You didn't have to come back, if you are needed to support your parents,' she said, 'have you got a house to clear out, that sort of thing?'

'No,' said Sven, 'my grandfather had a widow, a third wife, much younger than him, not related to me. They do not need me to do those things. I said I would be here with you for the summer and I will be here.'

Hester felt no need to engage herself over Sarah and Sven. She mused she might have objected if her brother's girlfriend was running off with a delivery boy, but who was she to care about Sarah? Plus, if

Sven was going spare she wouldn't mind giving him a bit of comfort. Let nature take its course.

Anton emerged from the kitchen and took Sven's hand as if to shake it, Sven pulled him forward and hugged him so Anton hugged back, quite unable to judge which situations were satisfied with a handshake and which called out for a hug. Clearly this was a hug.

Sven said, 'I've missed...' he was going to say 'I've missed you,' but instead said, 'our conversations.'

'What are you reading now?' Anton asked, his small talk limited as usual.

'I've gone back to Durkheim,' said Sven, happy to get back to their life together, 'to the fin-de-siècle, the great Ur-text of suicide.'

'I thought that was The Sorrows of Young Werther...' said Anton, the others phased out and returned to their tasks.

Sarah invited him to have sex that afternoon, though it was an exercise of unwelcome exertion in the heat, she thought it was the thing to do. He tried to lose himself in the familiar moisture, fleshy thighs, the welcoming openness, but he was preoccupied, she didn't finish, and he did so only with an effort. 'It's the heat,' she said, 'it's sent my metabolism haywire.' She felt she was betraying Kostas by having sex with Sven; she recognised the absurdity of the notion but felt it just the same.

Sven lay awake beside Sarah's naked body, browned from the sun in contrast to his own whiteness. He watched the muslin curtains drifting gently in the slightest of breezes that came from the sea, hearing the seagulls and the low whir of insects.

To act with any honesty, he ought to tell Anton

how he felt – but to what avail? What would he be trying to get out of it? He wanted sex with Anton. But why should Anton agree to that? And even to ask might damage the relationship they already had. It would upset Anne who had never caused him any problem, it would outrage Sarah who would want to tell everyone how she had been treated. But balanced against the dangers, the probability that Anton would say no, there was what he could gain: the supreme sense of living in the light of honesty, of having told the truth to the person he cared about most. Was that not worth the risk?

In the Mayor's office, somewhat shielded from the heat by the spluttering air-conditioning, the Mayor sat at his broad desk with Alekos and Theophilus opposite him. Até of the glossy locks, the great deceiver, hovered over their heads.

'Give me a solution to this problem of the xenie,' said the Mayor. I'm getting pressure on this from our own restaurant owners, what can we do to make this go away?'

Alekos said 'Why not go easy, they have worked very hard, they won't just go away. Why do we need to make things so hard for them?'

Irritated at having to defend his position, the Mayor said, 'We can't have foreigners setting up here, they have different values, remember the outrage of the naked bathing.' The Mayor had the politician's happy knack of believing, as he said it, anything that came out of his own mouth with perfect conviction, 'We can't let Doxos become like Kos or Falaraki, with all that disgraceful behaviour....drinking too much, taking drugs, doing obscene things in public.' If it crossed the minds of anyone that these places were run by Greeks they were not moved to mention it, but nodded their heads in agreement that such curses should not afflict Doxos.

Alekos and Theophilus knew the only pressure the Mayor was suffering was from Aspasia but they were there to help. As he was not a council employee but just enjoyed being part of the machinery of government, Alekos had more freedom to question policy. The mayor liked having him in on this sort of job, for Theophilus was diligent but had no imagination, and the business with the xenie and her restaurant required imagination; leaning on her alone wouldn't do it.

Theophilus was, however, a master of regulation. The articles, clauses, bracketed numbers and subsections, the lovely little footnotes in their prickly nest at the bottom of the page, these to him had a beauty of their own, divorced from any application in the real world. To Theophilus, steeped in the lore of the ancients, it was the return of Byzantium, the empire so revered as to have almost passed into legend but it had once truly held dominion over these lands via the institutes, the digest and the codex. For Theophilus the charges and offices of the Eastern Roman Empire had a rich potency, like rising incense and crumpled velvet encrusted with shining braid. He luxuriated in thinking of the titles of the venerable ruler, the bearded ones, the doorkeepers and chamberlains of access, the one who sleeps near the emperor and the keeper, the very keeper of the inkstand. Theophilus was out of his time, he was born for rule by intrigue, plot and conspiracy, he was made for the empire of gold.

For him, embracing the European Union had been a private epiphany at the end of a long road, for he had been a fierce opponent. With the zeal of St Paul he had long resisted EU membership as an encroachment on Greek sovereignty. Later, after accession, he had fought with tactics of obstruction and delay its edicts over land registration and property ownership. Just recently, however, he had experienced a conversion, he had seen the flash of scarcely concealed jewels in EU documents that made his little moustache twitch. There were many things the Union did that bemused Greek administrators: concepts such as openness and impartiality – what was the point of having power at all, unless it was to benefit your family? Why enforce a law that only aided another nation? But the EU did have one delicious prize to offer: the Greek civil service fell, like the embrace around the neck of a long-lost family member returned to the hearth, upon European Union bureaucracy.

'I have found a regulation,' said Theophilus quietly.

They looked at him with interest. He said clearly, as if enunciating a passage from holy writ, 'Procedures for the approval of establishments…Chapter 12 section 3: compliance with any requirements of national law concerning training programmes for persons working in certain food sectors….Rules of hygiene for foodstuffs…verification of compliance with these rules…'. He looked up, 'We can locally impose a hygiene standard,' he said.

'And we can close them down if they haven't got it?' asked the Mayor, with his usual sharp grasp of policy.

'National law,' said Alekos, 'excuse me if I do not understand this entirely but have we got national laws for training programmes for restaurants?'

'There is a national training standard, but it is not compulsory. You can make it so, here. You, sir,' said Theophilus, addressing the Mayor, 'make the national law on any area where there is no national law already existing.'

'Good, this'll finish them,' said the Mayor, eager to get on, then thought, his active mind always eager to improve the working of a scheme, 'let's make it positive – let's send you along. Alekos, from me, to help them comply with hygiene requirements.'

'Special permissions,' murmured Theophilus with satisfaction, his eyes twinkling behind his spectacles. This was indeed inspired.

'If it is your wish sir,' Alekos said, 'though...' he was going to say: *Why not just let them run, it's only a business?* but thought better of it, the Mayor's mind was made up. 'What if she takes a test?' he said.

'The test is in Greek,' said Theophilus, with quiet triumph, 'and it is conducted on Rhodes.'

'She would have a right to have a Greek speaker with her,' said Alekos, 'her Greek's OK for everyday, but not good enough for exam conditions.'

'You could offer your services,' said Theophilus, and, exceeding his conspiratorial abilities, 'and you could get her answers wrong.'

Alekos gave him a sidelong glance, indicating this was not going to happen.

'Let's not make it too complicated,' said the Mayor, drawing the meeting to a close. 'She needs a Greek health certificate or she closes – simple as that. Thank you my friends.'

Malik had the measure of the guards at the front of the refugee compound. Some needed bribery, some just a few words and a joke, some would not let him out under any circumstances. This fine day he slipped out past one of the soft guards who never cared what he did and made his way over the hill in a cheery mood, slowly because of the heat, past the olive groves and the pastures where goats grazed, and picked up the path towards Café Europa. There was a figure ahead, standing at the brow of the hill. It was Kostas who was smoking a cigarette by his motorbike.

'What ho?' said Malik.

'What do you want?' said Kostas.

'Just passing the time of day, old chap,' said Malik,

Kostas had no high regard for refugees and had particular suspicion for one as educated as Malik. It was as if a donkey should have started to talk and perhaps even have the effrontery to comment on its conditions, this was not what beasts of burden were for. Refugees did not bother Kostas so long as they stayed in their place, and none of them pretended they could speak. He particularly resented this boy's acting as if there were some kind of equality between them. Kostas turned his back on Malik, he had other things to think about.

Malik shrugged and continued. With his short black hair, trainers, T-shirt and jeans, he looked like any other youth in any part of Europe. Malik's emotions would easily tip one way or another, like reeds in the wind. His unhappiness was a fleeting cloud before the sun. He was not without cares, for he was worried about his forward journey. Soon the Greek authorities would decide what to do with him, and this might mean they would deport him, send him back. That was the worst fear and had to be avoided at all costs. He was worried about seeing Samir again – two boats had come in since he had arrived and countless other travellers had ended up at the camp as individuals, coming over in smaller groups. Still no sign of his friend.

On the positive side, he had a thriving business going supplying phone cards, cigarettes, nappies, medicines, all the things the camp inmates needed to be brought in. The sun was shining, he at least was in Europe, he had food at the camp that was regularly supplied without effort on his part, he had friends in Café Europa, things were looking good.

As he approached the restaurant he passed Sarah, struggling along up the track on one of Café Europa's scooters. She held on one handlebar and waved cheerfully with the other had as she phutted past. He waved and felt shame – she was going to see her adulterous lover and he had given her a sign of goodwill. This was not how a man should behave. Fornication was an abomination and an evil thing. But the expectation of how people should behave was always confounded in this place, Malik's moral certainties were being bent by his practical needs: Anne wanted him to forget altogether that he knew anything about Sarah and Kostas. Anne was his link to the outside world, without her he would be stuck in the camp with the listless refugees, waiting for a decision, he needed the supplies he helped her distribute, giving him kudos in the camp, she was his passage out to go on buying trips, giving him local wealth and power.

As he passed the house and approached the restaurant he saw with dismay down there the familiar figure of Sven in shorts and a T-shirt, organising equipment on the beach side of the restaurant. Malik did not know Sven had returned until that moment. This made an abstract ethical dilemma about whether he should reveal information into a burning, immediate concern.

Malik sauntered up to Anne who was wrapping cutlery sets in paper napkins ready for the day's customers. He told her how he hoped he soon would be introducing her to his friend Samir; he told her of his latest text message with his friend across the water and she listened indulgently to a tale she had heard before. As she had work to do, he went over to see Sven, concealing his misgivings as he shook hands.

Sven was setting up a beach volleyball pitch as a further attraction for the café in the quiet morning and afternoon periods. Malik helped to sink posts for the net into the sand and support them with piles of stones. Sven told Malik the rules: how to tip the ball, what were permitted passes, how to keep score, and they played as much of a game as they could with just the two of them. Eventually they sat down exhausted. 'There,' said Sven, 'another skill for you, now you will be able to play volleyball with the best of them on the beaches of southern California.'

Malik was moved that Sven was thinking of his journeying on through the world picking up skills, it was just the way Malik saw himself. Sven was a pal, and he had just seen Sven's woman go off to meet a man and that was wrong, it shamed Sven and it shamed Malik if he did not tell him, and that weighed heavily on Malik.

In a secluded spot on the other side of the mountain, Sarah and Kostas had stopped their machines and faced each other in the dappled shadow of a clump of trees. He put his arms around her middle, down the waistband of her trousers and embraced the cheeks of her bum. She felt the trickle of sweat between her breasts, pushed her fingers through the hair on his muscular arms. This felt deliciously forbidden. It was even more exciting now there was a danger of exposure. She was ecstatic with the illicit delight of it, she was drenched in sweat and guilty pleasure, feeling thirteen years old again, venturing into the forbidden playground of sex for the first time.

She was underneath him, sitting on top with thighs around him, on all fours with him behind. She felt at one point that she was putting more passion into the engagement than he was, that he was going through the motions like a character in a pornographic film. But she overcame her reservations with a fresh effort to engulf herself in sensation.

Afterwards, she asked what they were going to do today, 'I could be out a couple of hours, are we going somewhere?'

'Not today,' he said, 'sorry, I have some things to do, I must work sometimes, it is not all pleasure, even on a beautiful Greek island.'

She pursed her lips but said nothing. He smiled apologetically, hugged and kissed her, and drove off without looking back.

Sarah gathered her clothes together and scooted off into town to do some errands and cover her tracks, feeling Kostas dribbling out of her. She met Jess and Pete there, buying fresh fish from the back of a van, and said a few friendly words. With the island's small number of focal points, meeting acquaintances was inevitable, often several times a day. It was no place for secret assignations.

Alekos drove up to Café Europa on his scooter and went straight in to see Hester. She had grown wary of him, he had not been pleased that she had not been prepared to wait for the builders that he had arranged and who showed no sign of turning up. Still, she received him gracefully.

'The Mayor wanted to welcome you to the island, he is sorry he has not had time to visit.'

'He is very welcome any time,' she said, wondering where this was leading.

'He has asked me to make sure you have the right certificates to comply with European law,' said Alekos, as if he were a salesman offering a product.

'What would that be, then?' asked Hester.

Alekos spoke of the national food hygiene standard, at which Hester told him to wait, went back to her office, brought out a large envelope and pulled out a certificate that said in not particularly elaborate script "Chartered Institute of Environmental Health. Level 4 Award in Managing Food Safety in Catering" with Hester's name and the date she competed the course. 'I have this one run by my local council in Britain. It's called an Advanced Food Hygiene Certificate.'

'Ah,' said Alekos, a little taken aback, then recovering himself said, 'then you will have no difficulty in complying and taking our certificate.'

'This certificate gives me the highest standards in Europe,' she said, 'I don't need to take another.'

He looked at the certificate with minute attention. 'This isn't transferrable, it isn't recognised, here, he said. Food safety is different here, hotter weather, different foods, often served outside.'

'If it is valid in England it is valid here,' she said, 'it's all Europe.' She tried a different approach, 'The other twenty restaurants on Doxos, what of them? So every restaurant on the island should have a certificate? Tell the Mayor he can't discriminate, the rules have to apply to everyone.'

'Why of course,' said Alekos, as if grievously insulted at the very thought of discrimination, 'All have certificates...or they have been established a long time and do not need permission.'

'I haven't seen any other restaurant with a certificate on display.'

'We shall have to look into that. You get the certificate by going to Rhodes and taking an exam, very straightforward, I am sure, for someone as accomplished as you.'

'I can't keep giving bribes to people, Alekos, I just want to run a business.'

Alekos was offended at the mention of bribery, it was an affront to citizenship. 'This is the national law,' he said, by now completely believing his own story, 'you have to take a food safety test or you must close down.'

'If you try to enforce this,' she said, with an air of determination, 'I will challenge it in the European Court.'

'You have a right to do that,' he said, conspicuously unmoved by the threat. Both knew that by the time a case got anywhere near being heard she would have run out of money, and even if she got that far, there would probably be a different mayor and everyone would have forgotten about the xenie and her restaurant.

She rounded on him, 'Why don't you enforce the regulations when it really matters? You've got dogs chained up all day long in the sun until they go mad; and ugly concrete buildings erected in front of beautiful views; and fridges and washing machines dumped on the seashore. You could make a difference doing something worthwhile.'

'I can't help you if you are going to be like this,'

said Alekos.

'You are not helping now, you are just trying to close us down because we are successful.'

Alekos said, 'Mr Theophilus says...' but she interrupted.

'You can tell Theophilus to piss off from me.' As he walked away shaking his head she shouted, 'You should be ashamed of yourself, you could do better.'

Anton emerged from the kitchen, 'I don't think that went so well,' he said, as Alekos walked to the rough ground used as a car park and drove off.

Sven and Malik had been attracted by the shouting, and came over to see if he could be of any use, they turned up in time to see Hester cursing after Alekos.

'Shouldn't you try to get along with the authorities,' said Sven, cradling his volleyball, 'or they will make things difficult for you.'

'How much more difficult can they make things, what can they do that they haven't already?' she asked, 'It's just more bollocks. They are trying to get rid of us, are they going to try any harder? What will they do, use a flame thrower? Well, everything I have is in this restaurant, they're not going to take my savings.'

She went off fuming to telephone the tourist authorities in Rhodes, 'We'll frame my hard-earned certificate and put it on the wall,' she said as a parting shot.

Anne had been observing this scene miserably, looking as if she were going to cry. Anton, fixated on cooking, did not notice and returned to the kitchen, but Sven put his arm around her, 'Don't let scenes like this affect you,' he said, 'it's just life.'

Sven returned to his seat on the other side of the restaurant with Malik, who had been pondering his dilemma. For Malik there was no inspiration from the resourceful Jeeves bringing into play the psychology of the individual, a pinch of the old magic to make everything turn out right. He ought to induce Sven by some plausible ruse to go to the place where he would see the adulteress and her partner in crime in their act of fornication but where were they, and what plan should be used?

His head was filled with the entanglement of morality versus practical considerations. No cunning ploy struck him to reveal but not reveal the adulteress; to reveal her in such a way that he was not thought guilty of the deed.

He thanked Sven for the volleyball lesson. 'When I get to England, I will go to country houses at the weekend, they have croquet and village sports, and teas with cucumber sandwiches, all the English do it, you know.'

'Not quite everyone, I think,' said Sven quietly. 'Sarah's family have a country house, but it's a hotel. They have a tennis court and a gym, but that's a business.'

'Tell me something old chap,' said Malik as if asking the sort of general question he often did, 'How does it go, with adultery in your country?'

'In the west,' Sven said, thinking he was giving a lesson in morals, 'if someone is unfaithful, partners might get divorced or split up, or if the one who was unfaithful is genuinely sorry they might get back together. Some people have open marriages, where either partner can go with whom they like....I don't think those are very successful. Mainly people think it is a betrayal, whether it's the man or woman who does it. We are not so concerned about sex as about the betrayal of a relationship.'

Malik was stuck by the word betrayal – this was

not a word to use lightly. As for the rest, it was too much information for him to take in at once. 'Doesn't a man kill his wife, or his daughter, if she, you know....does fornication?'

'It happens,' said Sven, 'but that is criminal, it is murder, the man is then punished by the state.....why do you ask?'

'I don't know, I just asked...' he said, his wit failing him.

Something in Malik's embarrassed and even fearful tone made Sven stop, 'Are you saying Sarah has been unfaithful?' he asked, immediately grasping the implications, 'with Kostas I suppose?' Malik put his head down, unwilling to say the shameful thing or see its effect.

'Why are you telling me this?' Sven really meant why *you*? Why not someone else? but the inflection was lost on Malik.

'It is your woman, you must know, it is a damned shame. I am very sorry. Anything I can do to lighten the load....'

Sven felt it as a blow, not of jealousy or anger, but weariness: it was just another thing to do, another thing to worry about. There was the emotional upheaval of his grandfather's death, his unexpressed feelings for Anton, anxiety over his dissertation and now this. There had been signs with Sarah, he supposed that things were not quite right, but he had passed over them, preoccupied with his own thoughts.

'Thank you for telling me that, I'd like to be alone now.'

Sven went out to look at the sea, sucking and washing at the pebbles. In the background he could hear Hester raging to Anton about the hygiene certificate thing, trying to raise the ministry of tourism in Athens, struggling on the telephone at the extent of her Greek language. Life was not getting any easier.

Malik went across uncomfortably to Anne who had just finished serving a German couple. 'What's up with Sven?' she said, already wary.

'I saw Sarah going to see that man, just now. I couldn't keep mum about it.'

'What did you say?' Anne asked miserably.

'I asked about adultery, he worked it out for himself.'

'He worked it out for himself? With some encouragement from you.'

He was surprised at how upset she was, but reassured her, 'Sven is not going to kill Sarah,' he said, 'it was an adultery, it had to be revealed. That Kostas is a cad.'

'Sven and Sarah aren't married, they are boyfriend and girlfriend, it's not adultery.'

'But they are...betrothed.'

'No, none of that stuff, none of that at all. They are just going out together. No, he's not going to kill her, no one's going to kill anyone. It just makes a mess of everything you getting involved.'

'What should I do?' he asked, feeling inexplicable cultural confusion.

'It wasn't your business, you should have let things find their own level.' She was beginning to feel that Anton's approach, of engaging as little as possible with the world, was the way to go for a less stressful life. She had brought Malik into Café Europa and he had messed up. It was her fault.

'Look,' she said, 'don't get involved in things you don't understand. Sex and relationships are very important to us but there's lots of other stuff: education, debt, careers, homes – we aren't like you, we have different values. There's not one thing that matters more than everything else, so much that you're going to have to kill someone for it. It's all a balance. You'd better go now.'

Malik made an unhappy journey on foot the four miles to the camp, wondering where it had gone wrong. He felt less concern for Anne's feelings than for Sven's. He was a pal. She was a woman and she was not the injured party in the adultery business, but on the other hand, Anne had been more use to him. How complicated it all was. His business, his income, his chance to build up capital from the other refugees – all depended on his relationship with Anne.

Anton and Anne were working down at the restaurant when Sarah returned to the house that afternoon. She opened the door, 'Hello honey I'm home,' she shouted, and went straight to the bathroom to wash off the smell of sex. Suitably refreshed, she climbed the stairs to the bedroom where Sven was sitting in a chair on the balcony, a book lying limply beside him.

'Where have you been?' he asked

'Just to town, shopping,' she said, wary of his flat tone and direct question.

'You've been with Kostas?' he said quietly, as if unwilling to use the name.

'I saw him, yes...' she said.

'When you said you were going away to get shopping from the town really you were going with him? You were lying to me?' She stood dumb, unwilling to tell an outright lie when he obviously knew so much. 'You could have told me, it's the deceit,' he said, miserably. 'No wonder you haven't been interested in sex, I thought it was me.'

'I didn't start seeing him – like that – until you had left,' she said, which was so close to the truth it counted as true, she felt.

'I suppose you could count yourself lucky if you've got away with just one of the more treatable STDs. I hope you haven't given me anything.'

She accepted the insult without wishing to engage with it, he had a right to be upset, she shook her head. 'I know it went too far,' she said, 'I wanted to get in touch with the locals, I didn't want to be like these people backpacking around Europe and talking only to other foreigners.' She was trying to elevate the conversation but knew it sounded specious.

'I think you have connected about as closely as could be expected,' said Sven quietly, 'the most cosmopolitan traveller couldn't fault you on that.'

She could see there was no way this conversation was going to get any better, 'Well I'm sorry but there it is. I have been with Kostas, I wish you hadn't found out this way.' She was near to tears. Sven shrugged, there was little more to say.

'Look Sven, I am sorry, and I do care about you, can't we be friends?'

'I'll have to move out,' he said

'Whatever you want to do,' said Sarah.

She went down to the kitchen, got a beer from the fridge and sat in the courtyard, listening to the tinny sound of goat bells in the distance and the whirring insects. She did not want to be the cause of Sven's leaving Café Europa, but she could hardly stop him. She did not exactly have favours that she could call in and beg him to stay. She heard the floorboards as Sven walked through the house, and left, closing the front door without saying goodbye to her.

Sarah felt guilty but also thought it right that she

had followed her heart. She told herself she would have reacted with more sympathy to him if he had been jealous, had raged at the misappropriation of her precious body to another man. His anger at the deceit was... so... *him*, so much about his priorities and not hers, all about the sacredness of truth. Well, fuck the truth, sometimes you just had to have fun.

She wanted to be out of the house, she texted Kostas, who didn't reply, and took her Greek primer out to a slope to a clearing in the gorse bushes where she sat down listening to music on her iPod and looking at a list of words. Her liaison with Kostas had not been so valuable as might be imagined in the field of language studies. They hadn't spent a deal of time smacking out some work on the nominative and the accusative or placing a list of adjectives in the appropriate case as the textbooks prescribed. She lowered her head and excluded everything from her mind but the experience of learning.

Walking down to the restaurant, Sven was miserable that he had to disentangle himself from Sarah and their sleeping arrangements; all this was very selfish of her, all a lot of trouble for him, it could have happened some other time. He went in to see Hester who was, unusually, sitting with a glass of wine. 'Do you know what's happening between Sarah and me?' he said.

'Not good, eh? You are breaking up? Sarah's been seeing a lot of that boy, it didn't surprise me, I'm sorry.'

For Hester a renewed attack by the Greek authorities was enough to worry about, the possible departure of Sven was too much. She couldn't let her team disperse, it felt as if the whole place was cracking up. She set on appealing to his well-developed sense of honour. 'How are you placed, now Sven? I was counting on you staying for the summer. If I could do without someone, it wouldn't be you.'

She was right, Sven had been wondering if he should just go, but he could not bear the thought of leaving Anton. Also, he had given his word he would be there for the summer and so he should, he should not let Hester down. No, it was unthinkable he should go.

'I can stay,' he said, 'but I have to move out of the room I have been sharing with Sarah.'

'Do you want to talk about that, about what happened?' she looked into his face with her blue eyes, like the bead-eyes on a tall, stringy doll.

'Not much, there's not much to talk about, Sarah and I aren't together anymore, but we're civilised we can still work together.'

'OK, I suppose not everyone has to consider their exes the embodiment of all that is stupid and evil...' she said, with mock cheerfulness, 'maybe that's just me.'

She smiled benignly at her own foibles, 'Make whatever arrangements are good for you, Sven. There are enough bed sheets, you do your own laundry up there, you don't have to ask me, I wouldn't know how many beds you were using at the house. I've no objection to whatever arrangement you want,' she was about to add 'you can sleep with me if you like,' but thought it was too early to make a pass. 'Anything I can do, you let me know,' she said, patting him on the arm, a pat that turned into a warm grip before she released him.

She watched his toned body turn and his tight buttocks as he walked up the hill. It would be a waste of a good man to leave him celibate. She could do very well with him, but the new threat from the council weighed heavily upon her. She was drinking more than usual and permanently in a foul mood.

Sven took his clothes, books and computer out of the room he had shared with Sarah, down the hall, and out to the spare room that led directly on to the courtyard, taking large armfuls so he would not have to make the short journey too many times.

The little side room with its baking concrete roof was hotter than the upstairs bedrooms. There was not much in it – a bed, a chair, a stone shelf on which sat a candle for power cuts and a stick of insect repellent. On one of the whitewashed walls there was a picture of the annunciation with Mary looking pale and rather vapid.

Sven lay on the bed feeling the heat of the late afternoon, thinking he must leave. What had induced him to stay? Through the glaze of sweat, he thought about his wanderings in the dark streets of Stockholm, the city of Strindberg: the stained old wood of little cafes with their warming liqueurs, the tall yellow houses and the fresh cool smell of the harbour, with his mind filled with ambitions for the pure motive, the unequivocal life.

Instead here he was on this island with the taste of disgust in his mouth, the lies and mistrust. After all he had said about truthfulness, still to be lied to. He had sailed the boat of self out into the stormy seas of life, to run aground on this hopeless island, lied to and unloved. He should have been working on his thesis but he was waiting at tables, for goodness sake, his girlfriend had gone off with another man, the only light in this darkness was Anton and he did not dare reveal his feelings for him.

Later, going to the fridge for some cold water Sven encountered Anne who was sitting at the marble table in the courtyard compiling a list of things she needed to collect for her refugees,

She looked up to see him emerge from the side room. 'I'm living here now,' he said, 'Sarah and I have broken up.'

'Oh, I'm sorry,' said Anne, 'what happened, do you want to talk?'

'Sarah was having an affair. She was, I don't know what you say, carrying on, with that Greek boy. Did you know?'

'Yes,' she said, 'I found out by accident.'

He was visibly upset by her admission, more than he had been when talking to Sarah, 'Did anyone not know but me?' he said, 'did Anton know?'

'No,' said Anne, instinctively aware that Anton's duplicity would hurt Sven most, 'no, I'm sure of it, I only didn't say anything because Sarah said she would tell you.' In fact, Anne did not know if this were precisely true, she could not exactly remember, but it was the sort of thing Sarah would say, so it was near enough.

Sven went off down to the restaurant while Anne climbed the stairs to talk to Anton in their bedroom.

Anton said, 'Did you know?'

She nodded, 'I'd walked in on Sarah and Kostas...in a clinch, you could say, so I knew, but I didn't want to talk about it.'

Anton nodded. For all his unusual ways, Anne welcomed his complete acceptance of life as it was – saying, 'I didn't feel like it' was a perfectly adequate explanation for Anton. It was his principal reason for taking or not taking any action.

Looking out of the window towards the restaurant,

Anne could see Sven sitting at a table on his own. She said, 'You must go down and speak to him.'

'Is there something I should say? Do I need to speak to him now especially? Why is that?'

'Duh – because you're his friend,' she emphasised the last word: frieeend.

'I'm not sure he does want to speak to me,' said Anton, wearily leaving his computer, 'maybe he wants to be alone, but I'll follow your judgement.'

Anton did like spending time with Sven, it underlined his position in the world: normal guys had best friends and were always with them, they went to the pub with them and talked about sport. Anton did not do that, he drank little and could not see the point of sport, but Sven *was* his best friend.

He found Sven sitting at one of the wooden tables with a glass of Metaxa brandy in front of him, spinning a two Euro coin showing the abduction of Europa by Zeus in the form of a bull. 'You know the Greek government lied about their currency deficits to get into the Euro zone in 2001?' he said, 'no one believed that a country's treasury officials and their ministers would lie so blatantly, so they were believed.'

'What was the consequence of such a wicked act?' asked Anton.

'Nothing, what can you do? Bring back the drachma? They were subject to a severe talking to.'

'In the headmaster's office, then they sniggered back home, having got away with it.'

'Exactly.'

Sven drank glass after glass of Metaxa brandy, demonstrating another difference between the Greeks and Scandinavians. Greek boys did not get so drunk they could hardly stand up. Anton helped Sven back up the hill to the house, up the stairs in the courtyard and onto his bed in the small, hot room. Anton washed and returned to Anne who was sitting up in bed reading a novel.

'What did he say?' she asked eagerly.

'Many things, we talked a lot – the banality of evil; functionalism versus intentionalism, you know, the usual stuff.'

'What about Sarah, didn't you talk about Sarah?'

'What was there to talk about?' asked Anton in genuine surprise, 'She's gone off with some bloke.'

'But how is Sven taking it?'

Anton raised his hands in a gesture of emptiness, 'He's taking it like a man, with resignation. What is he expected to do? Fight some Greek biker for her? She made her choice. Now I've had more than I wanted to drink and I'm tired so let me go to bed.'

After he had lain down Anne looked at the canopy of stars, like light shining through a fabric, and thought how fragile their relationships were.

The next day the brightness of the sun irritated Anton and his head hurt. He was annoyed at having drunk more than usual and resented Anne for urging him to comfort Sven. It was nothing against Sven, who accepted him unquestioningly and had interesting things to say, but he was upset that he had a hangover interfering with his thinking when he was trying to write. He went down and sat at the table in the courtyard.

Anne joined him. Sarah's infidelity had broken the fellowship, made Anne ill at ease in the home they had created. Her morning orange juice tasted too acid in her mouth. She wanted comforting.

'Pay me some attention.' Anton put his hands around her waist and moved them up to her breasts.

'No not that,' she said, 'tell me what you are doing. What are you working on?'

'The same thing I've been doing all the time we've been here.'

'Come on, talk to me, she said, all you are interested in is your work and I don't even know what it is, I think you love your computer more than me.'

'Now you know what we say,' said Anton, 'If you can't say it without a cliche....'

'Don't say it at all,' she echoed him in a sing-song voice. 'Yeah, I've got that.'

'This stuff I'm doing here' he said, indicating the gleaming black computer, pleased the conversation was turning towards something he understood, that did not cause the rushing in his mind, 'It's a neo-Malthusian thing, a calculation of how many people would die in a limited nuclear war in different scenarios – Indian sub-continent, Arabia.....the initial blasts with different warheads, the deaths from fallout – the consequences for public health, another wave of deaths from poor sanitation, from disease following the destruction of infrastructure, the polluted water, even riots have to be factored in. Then there are the refugees and mass migration from the affected areas.'

She listened with increasing horror, 'That's terrible, it's like Armageddon,' she said.

'It's not quite the end of the world,' he said, 'it's about the impact on us, in Europe, of other countries going to war. All of Asia and half the Middle East have nuclear weapons, what's the chance they won't use them? We need to know what happens next. I have to put in the data for various factors: likely targets, initial blast, radiation deaths, ...' he saw her expression, 'But this isn't a war game,' he said

'Oh that's alright then,' said Anne, still recoiling from the horror of it.

'War is just the start,' he said, warming to his subject, 'I am working on the effect of different scenarios on population, on migration. Basically, what would a nuclear war in Asia mean for the population of Europe? Of course, it's going to be bad for humanity, but there are winners and losers in every conflict. What would be the effect on resources, on migration?'

'That's so grisly, she said, 'Doesn't thinking about it make it more probable? Is that what you do all the time?'

'Right now it is. There are a lot of factors to work in, and each change affects all the others,' said Anton.

Anne said, 'I thought these were maths problems you were doing.'

'Sort of…applied maths'

'My mind can't take this,' she said.

He thought she meant she did not understand the principle and went to explain it, then realised it wasn't an intellectual incapacity she was expressing, but an emotional resistance.

'I'm sorry I asked,' she said, 'I've got to get down to the restaurant, see you later,' sometimes she felt she really didn't understand him at all.

She passed Sarah in the kitchen, preparing to go out and see Kostas. There was now no easy banter between the girls. There was no enmity, but they were formal with each other, as if they had just met, two strangers who were obliged to share a kitchen.

Sarah contacted Kostas by text and that afternoon they met by the tree where they had had sex before. She hadn't wanted to tell him by text, now she threw her arms around him. 'We can be together openly,' she breathed into his neck, 'Sven found out.'

'How did he find out? Who told him?' asked Kostas. It was an important part of his survival mechanism to know who would betray him.

'I don't know. Anne knew, of course, but she wouldn't say anything. Malik had seen us, he was walking over when we met, yesterday probably said something and Sven worked it out ...' she saw his angry expression, 'Oh who cares, he was going to have to be told anyway.'

Kostas questioned whether the cuckolded boyfriend did in fact need to be told, ever, but kept his reservations to himself.

'Now we can be together,' she said, looking into his face for reciprocal emotion.

'This is wonderful light of my eyes,' he said, a direct translation of the Greek phrase.

They had sex but it was without the passion of previous encounters. Sarah wondered if it was her fault, if she had become too clingy, expecting too much of him too early, and must back off a little. She had read about this sort of coldness in relationships in women's magazines but had not experienced it herself.

After his less than strenuous endeavours Kostas roared off on his bike. That night they were out, on the boat, the Spirit of the Island, Vasilios had a special job that they had to keep quiet. He was aware that he should be staying close to Vasilios in case he was needed for anything. Taking time off to fuck a foreigner was not part of the plan.

Late that night, a voice called for Anne outside the house. She went to the balcony and saw the small form of Malik, 'Come down, you've got to help me,' he whispered, trying to make his voice carry.

Anne was not asleep, or even very tired, the heat made her restless, she threw some clothes on and went downstairs, What are you doing here?' she asked.

'I bribed the guard,' he said thinking of his hard-earned ten Euros, 'Samir is coming tonight, he texted me.'

'So why are you here?'

'I want to welcome him. I know this is right.'

'Do you know where he will be?'

They will come into the harbour, they are trying to be caught, they know they will come to the camp here.

'But don't the Greek authorities want to discourage them?'

'Maybe the coastguard will try to make them go back, but if they have to pick refugees up, they will. The owner of the hostel, the Mayor's cousin, he gets thirteen Euros a day for each of us staying there from the government, they can hold us for thirty days, it's good business.'

'I'm not pretending I understand this, but then, I never have. So what, you want me to take you to the harbour and wait there with you for Samir to come in? Well, it will be an adventure, I suppose.'

Malik clapped his hands merrily, 'Good egg,' he said.

Alright, she said, 'I'll get my phone, I'll go and tell Anton and I'll join you, but just this once, if he doesn't come, don't expect me to do a midnight vigil night after night. It's a bit hot to sleep now, anyway,' she added, by way of superfluous explanation.

Anton was tapping away on his computer, catching up with work he hadn't done that morning. He could make do with very little sleep when he was working. He happily acknowledged she was going, as if he did not mind whether she were there or not, but he kissed her and patted her slight behind.

Down at the harbour Vasilios, Kostas and a few men of Vasilios's occasional employ mounted the gangplank of The Spirit of the Island and, without turning the ship's lights on, cast off into a black sea.

Chapter 10

Samir and eleven of his companions shuffled out of the farm. The traffickers had developed a higher level of organisation after an unfortunate incident where they had to shoot one of their customers down at the embarkation point. Now they had tighter control, people were picked in advance. Most still arrived at the seashore expecting to be in a boat with a captain, though Samir had disabused those to whom he had spoken of the notion that they were crossing the Aegean in anything but a life raft. Samir's advanced knowledge, gleaned from text messages with Malik, gave him an easy superiority that fitted with his naturally arrogant manner – Samir always knew what to do, could always interpret a situation when others dithered.

His group were packed into the tiny van and driven down to the water's edge where there ensued the usual argument about the size of the boat, the smuggler hoisting his gun on his shoulder, then the twelve cursing people crammed into the eight-man rubber dinghy. The boat went out fearful but in hope; Samir told them of his friend who had gone before, about Malik's rescue by the coastguards, a testament that the system worked, even if it did terrify in its mechanism.

In this case there was at least someone among the hopeful band who could pilot a boat and had a compass. They needed it, for the night came down like a black sail within minutes of putting out from the sheltering bay. They started the engine and chugged off under the stars, some uttering prayers, others looking at the lifeless sea, some just wedged in so tightly their eyes looked nowhere but at their neighbour opposite.

Anne and Malik went off in the jeep, around the bay where the water was dark and silent with only the lights of the town reflected in it, and the stars startlingly visible. They went slowly through the hot darkness, up and around the perimeter of the island, along the cliffs, flashing past the white-painted trees that were the only marker of the edge of the road, beyond which was a sharp drop.

Curving round the bay in the hot night, they entered through the oldest part of Agios Nicholas, jumbled with Italian villas whose fading colours were still visible, and the bare remains of Ottoman buildings that had been torn down after the departure of the Turkish heathens, then used as the foundation for traditional Greek houses. They left the jeep and walked down towards the harbour, past the closed tourist shops and around the empty tables and chairs of the pizzeria, shadowy in the moonless night.

'Are you nervous about Samir?' Anne asked.

'The natural anxiety for a childhood friend,' he replied.

'Your words crack me up,' she laughed. Malik was pleased to entertain, he worked on it, thinking alone of things to say to the students. He wondered what had happened to Sarah and Sven but as it had been a source of conflict, he did not raise the subject. Malik tried his best to charm Anne with stimulating conversation, but mainly they waited together in silence.

The Spirit of the Island had left the harbour without lights as the coastguards often did, the men keeping a lookout for tourist yachts moored in the bay – they couldn't afford the time and attention a collision would cause. They cast off and pulled the wet ropes aboard as the boat chugged out from the harbour. A mile out, they turned on only sufficient lights to allow the boat to be steered in a sea that was like oil, flat and dark.

Vasilios was in the cabin leaning over a chart, precisely plotting the course with the aid of a compass and a location finder. Kostas stood on the deck seeing the disappearing lights of the town behind them. He knew his way around a boat, he had lived his entire life within sight of the sea. This night was special, though: the darkness, secrecy and the male comradeship added to his sense of pride at being on this mission with its muffled engine and dimmed lights.

Once they were clear of land, alone on the untroubled sea, Vasilios ordered his men to tether sheets of orange plastic around the bows. Kostas, wary of asking too direct a question of Vasilios, looked at the sheeting and tipped his head up, giving the motion of questioning without verbalising it. Vasilios deigned to answer: 'It's a precaution, anyone sees us, they'll give the wrong description. Maybe from satellites, or just from a distance on the sea, they'll think we are that boat of the coastguard's.'

'And if the coastguard sees us...?' asked Kostas.

Vasilios smiled, 'Get on with your work,' he said.

Fifteen miles out Vasilios called for lights. He was looking at the hand-held direction finder that emitted a low bleep, then increased its frequency as they neared their target.

'Here,' said Vasilios. They held the boat, letting the engine idle. He scoured the vicinity with his increasingly excited direction finder then spotted a yellow buoy bobbing slightly above the surface. They chugged over with the engine little more than idling, then held the boat still. Tied to a buoy was a taut line, a man reached out and pulled at it with a boat hook. It resisted, but when three of them joined in hauling at it, a large corner rose out of the water. The string was tethered to a huge bale wrapped in plastic, heavy like a block of dough. Kostas hauled in the dripping package and thought that was it, but the line was still taut, another was pulled up, bashing against the side of the boat. They threw that too down behind them like a drowned sailor, then another until there were four plumped-up packages as fat as old women dripping on the deck, then eight, then twelve with hardly space to place them, and the men hauling up the last were falling over the earlier bales behind them with no space to put the new ones.

Finally the bales were all aboard, sixteen of them, lying on the deck in pools of water like overweight swimmers exhausted from their efforts. Kostas found himself standing next to Vasilios, looking at the precious cargo. 'That is one big load,' said Kostas, 'I can see why we had to come out like this – too much to hide.'

'Clever boy,' said Vasilios, who had a soft spot for his nephew. 'There have been interruptions in the supply, so now there's a lot coming through at once, but you don't have to think about that.'

On the quayside Malik was restive. 'Is that them? Look, can you see something out there?'

Anne strained and could see nothing moving, looking into the darkness until she saw swirling mirage shapes. 'Do you know how long he was going to take?' she asked.

Malik shrugged 'Don't have the foggiest,' he said, 'not long, the coast is near, the sea is calm. Not like when I came over. Maybe four or five hours.'

'So when did he leave?'

'It was going to be sundown this evening so, between eight and nine.'

After another hour, and they had run out of things to say, Anne said, 'I think it's time to give him a call.' Malik dialled what had been his own number, on the phone his parents had given him, that he had given to Samir on the fateful day when he had driven away without him.

In the dinghy Samir's heart jumped when the phone hanging round his neck rang. He fumbled with it and answered, 'Malik my Malik. I hear you, yes, we are close, I think, we are near. We have been moving towards a boat we saw that was resting. I can see a boat like you said – orange sides.'

'I long to see you my brother,' said Malik, dancing with joy on the quay, 'get close to the boat. First they'll try to push you back, only they won't let you drown.'

'God willing I will see you tonight, my Malik,' said Samir. 'There,' he whispered to the man who was steering the boat with its feeble rudder, 'make for there. Let's get close.' They steered the boat further towards the orange ship in the darkness.

Vasilios and Kostas looked out into the sea, still breathing heavily but calm after their exertions. Then from somewhere across the water came the tinkly, melodic sound of a mobile telephone ring, then the beginning of a conversation.

Kostas started as if he had seen a ghost. 'What the fuck was that?' said Vasilios. They peered out into the sea but now could hear nothing above the throb of the engine

They leaned over the side of the ship, straining their ears to hear the source, staring into the void. Suddenly there was a clamour of voices from behind making them spin around. 'Stick the holy cross up my arse it's a fucking invasion,' a crewmember cried, desperately manoeuvring the boathook to beat a man clinging to the side.

Kostas and the others clambered over and around the wet bales to get to the side where a raft of people were reaching out their arms and crying from the black sea. It was a whole boat full trying to board the Spirit, all screaming, some women wailing, a crowd of faces and hands rising from the water, the strongest clambering over the other and grabbing the side of the boat with desperate strength.

The first thought on the Spirit of the Island was to get out of there, just engage the engine and move, but the hands were grabbing and crawling up the sides of the ship, hands right to the edge, some pulling themselves up. The man with a boathook smashed at them, other crew members punched at faces and pushed hands away that seized and gripped even as they were being beaten. Still they were rising out of the sea like creatures in a horror film, some clinging grimly to the ropes by the side of the boat.

Every time one was smacked down another came clawing up, with the wailing and screaming as of souls in hell, clinging to the ropes and the orange sheeting round the boat. The sailors were calling on the divinity and suggesting that the Holy Virgin had forsaken them.

On the waterline the dinghy was rocking and folding in on itself with the scrambling people, four had already been tipped screaming into the water, others were holding on to the ropes or the orange sheeting People were falling back from the beating they were getting from Vasilios's men.

Samir knew he must take the bold step: he slid the knife from its scabbard and raised it. A woman grabbed him in terror and tried to wrest the knife from him, the men were already holding onto the ropes around the Spirit of the Island or were thrashing about in the water. Samir knew the only way forward was to be bold, like the Kurdish warriors of yore. He steadied himself as best he could, his long hair and his red coat flowing, raised the knife and slashed at the curved rubber side with all his strength, tearing a deep rent from which the air bellowed.

The rubber boat on which the people writhed shrivelled and its entire contents went sprawling into the water, each reaching out for the boat or clinging to the rubber remnant.

Vasilios, seeing the dinghy in distress, seized his moment and ordered full speed ahead. Kostas and the men bashed down on the desperate few who still struggled to board, the man with a boathook smashing and smashing at the head of a man still hanging on until he too joined his companions, struggling or drowned in the dark. Soon at that spot there was no more light, no more hand holds, nothing between them and the bottom of the ocean, the taste of salt water, struggle and despair. Samir had experienced his last deception.

'Fuck me, that was a shocker,' said Vasilios, the nearest anyone had ever seen to this strong man being shaken. 'No one hurt here?' The men were sweating and breathing heavily. 'Get the orange sheeting back in, roll it up.' They performed their tasks then were pensive, just sitting, waiting to get back, unload the cargo and go home. Kostas, for all his bravado, had never killed anyone before and was shaking. Not that he had killed anyone there, of course, they had sunk their own boat, it was their own fault, he reassured himself, they should never have been there and certainly shouldn't have tried to board, he was an innocent of any killing….it was an incident best forgotten, nevertheless.

Anne and Malik were still looking out, Malik excitedly pointing towards each imagined blip on the sea. A boat sweeping into view around the rocky edge of the harbour caught their attention. 'It's the right size,' said Malik, who had familiarised himself with boats since reaching the Aegean, though they had been alien to him from his upbringing.

Their hopes were high and Malik jumped excitedly but as the boat came closer, looming out of the night, it became clear this was just a fishing boat. They watched idly as the boat was moored, a truck drew up and the crew started unloading packages.

'Oh, look, it's Kostas,' said Anne, 'let's ask him if he's seen anything.'

They walked towards the boat where Anne called to him, Kostas tried to affect his usual easy disposition. He walked to them, and led them away from the boat.

What are you two doing out?' he asked Anne, holding a hand up as if to shut them out from the harbour, but trying to seem casual.

'Waiting for a refugee boat, one of Malik's friends is coming over,' said Anne. Kostas started, then hoped they did not notice in the darkness with only the street lamp to illuminate his momentary alarm. 'Do you see anything when you were out there, maybe the coastguard picking someone up?'

'No, not at all, no refugee boat,' said Kostas, 'we have to unload the catch, you had better go.'

Something about the urgency with which he said it compelled a further question, 'What are the conditions like out there? You are back early,' she said.

'Kostas' called Vasilios from the shadow between the truck and the boat.

'Bad weather,' Kostas said, turning to go, then he realised how ridiculous it sounded looking at the glassy sea and said, 'bad weather out at sea, not by the land. And we had trouble with the engine.'

'What happened?' asked Anne, instinctively going into questioning mode.

'Nothing happened, we were just out fishing, that's all, you shouldn't be here.'

'What happened?' echoed Malik, as much to himself as anyone else.

'Why are you here?' shouted Kostas at Malik, he would not have shouted at Anne but she jumped too, wary of his tone, his anger and fear, noticing the sweat reflecting the street light on his forehead. 'Go away, there's nothing for you here,' he directed his remarks at Malik but intended them to apply equally to Anne. He had never had much contact with the Afghan and wanted none.

'Kostas,' called Vasilios. He was not a man used to asking twice for anything.

'You haven't been here,' Kostas said as a parting

remark as he hurried back to the truck.

'So who the fuck were they?' asked Vasilios, looking at Kostas as if he were going to break him in two.

Kostas said, 'It's just a tourist,' feeling guilty for even knowing them, 'I told them to go away.' Kostas thought better of telling Vasilios that he knew the refugee by name and what their mission was, judging that wouldn't go down well with the boss.

'Stop messing with the xenie,' said Vasilios, 'they're trouble.'

Anne and Malik continued their vigil further down the harbour, out of sight of the men, uncertain of what to make of the meeting with Kostas. They waited, by no means certain that the appearance of the Spirit of the Island was in any way connected to the refugee craft, but feeling uneasy nevertheless. 'Look,' said Malik, and pointed: in their usual places were the coastguard's boat, the mounting for the coastguard's machine gun spikily reflecting the glow of the street lamp. Next to it was the Halmatic, the orange search and rescue vessel, in its dedicated mooring, showing no signs of having been out.

Malik tried again to raise Samir on the telephone.

'Maybe water got into it,' said Anne, feeling increasingly uncomfortable with everything about this night.

Malik felt a slight chill, he realised he had gone into a nervous sweat and a light wind had cooled him. What should he do? His strong brother Hamid would have known what to do, he would not have stood on the quay and let his friend down. What would he have done? Malik did not know, for he was not Hamid. He should have gone, Hamid should have come here, not Malik, he was the one who was chosen. Waves of shame swept over Malik. He had done everything wrong. 'I have to be back to the old homestead,' he said, trying to appear bright, 'the guard that let me out will be going off soon, I need to get back while he's there.'

'OK,' said Anne, they got into the jeep and drove off, past the place where Vasilios and his crew had been unloading their cargo, but they were long gone.

'Well, that was a night to remember,' said Anne, relieved to be back in the vehicle and in control. 'We just missed him,' she said, 'he will have put in at one of the little islands around Doxos, he will be picked up and brought along later today. Or maybe they went off course and they will have put in somewhere else, floated into a quiet bay.'

Malik was mumbling. Anne asked what he was saying. 'It is Fajr,' he said, 'the time of day for the beginning, for dawn, it's a prayer for morning.'

'It will be alright,' whispered Anne, without conviction.

Anne dropped off Malik and swooped round the deserted roads through the lengthening shadows of the island dawn, back to Café Europa.

In the quiet house she mounted the stairs and entered her bedroom where Anton was just waking up, a process accelerated by her entrance. He was a quick riser, not dogged by drowsiness, his tousled black hair and his white body emerged rapidly from the bed.

'Are you just coming in? You dirty stopout,' he said in mockery, for Anne never did anything naughty, 'what's up?' for she looked anxious.

'I waited with Malik, for his friend Samir to come,' she said, 'they didn't come, they didn't....I am sure something terrible has happened, they have capsized...' The night of tension and the ugly interaction with Kostas had disconcerted Anne. She began to cry, sitting on the edge of the bed and crumpled over. 'Kostas was there and he was horrid,' she said through her tears, 'he was unloading a boat. Told us to get lost.'

This time, the time when girls cried, was the most paralysing moment of not knowing for Anton, what did you do when someone cries? Where was the model to follow, the pattern, the template of action that could be adapted for every weeping incident? He sat beside her and held her rather stiffly round the waist in what he hoped was a caring gesture. He looked at the curve of her back, where her T-shirt exposed it, spots and freckles and tiny hairs. Her head was bowed and both hands held up to her face, now blotchy and streaked with her damp hair. He handed her a tissue. This was not what he had a girlfriend for.

'What can we do...?' she sobbed.

I don't know bubbled on his lips - but he always knew what to do. He couldn't acknowledge ignorance. Maybe it was OK not to know, maybe sometimes, but was this one of those times? Anton was waiting for someone to come in, someone who could deal with the emotional insistence of this sobbing girl. His eyes were fixed on the old wooden door, its rough surface covered with new paint, hoping to be rescued by someone who would know the answer; that was a bit unlikely so early in the morning.

Anne raised her head and pushed away hair sticking to her face. His mind rifled through his stock responses, 'How does it affect us?' or 'What happens if we do nothing?' wouldn't quite fit the bill here. He waited, the sweat becoming clammy on his brow, for something to break the moment.

'There must be something we can do' she said. He shook his head sadly.

'Nothing I can think of,' he said, wishing he were away from there.

Her frustration from the edgy night bubbled over, 'Come on, you're the boy genius, what should we *do*?' This disconcerted him even more. Now this girlfriend was turning into a monster of philanthropy and efficiency. He thought of the junky, the alcoholic, the psychotic girlfriends. Where did he go wrong? This was the crisis of ordinary.

He diverted attention, 'Sven's the one who's got all the morality, ask him.'

'That's not any help, it's not about morality, it's about doing something...or not. About doing the right thing.'

She pulled away from his clumsy embrace, 'I'll go and grab the bathroom while it's free,' she said, and left him in the upstairs room with the new light streaming through the windows.

Down at breakfast at the wholesome wooden tables in the light of the rising sun Anne explained to the team that she had been out waiting with Malik for a refugee boat and feared it had gone down.

'You haven't got any evidence of that,' said Anton.

Hester had regard, even affection for Malik, but it did not extend to his friends, fellow detainees or compatriots. She responded to Anne's need for some kind of response with, 'I don't know what you think could be done. If your worst fears are confirmed, what then? People set out on the sea in these overcrowded boats they use and they drown. It's surprising how many get through. Even in England a coroner would say it was misadventure.' This was not consoling for Anne.

'To die is a bloody big adventure,' said Sarah, without mirth. She had just joined them and was spreading fig jam on a piece of bread.

Anne said, 'We saw Kostas and his uncle, they had been out in a boat,' Sarah looked up but said nothing, 'they weren't particularly pleased to see us.'

'What were they out for?' asked Hester. Sarah did not fill the silence with an answer, though they expected her to know, if anyone did.

'My guess is they were moving drugs,' said Anton, oblivious to the idea that Sarah might be offended at her boyfriend being described as a criminal, 'or why do it at night? And why be concerned when they were seen?'

'Yeah,' agreed Sven, buttering his toast, 'because the policy now is to allow Afghans to harvest opium as a bribe for not supporting the Taliban. So you can have a war on drugs, and a war on terror, but not both at the same time.'

'Democracy triumphs again,' said Anton.

'You don't know that it was drugs,' said Sarah, 'you just want to think the worst of Kostas.'

'We don't need to think at all,' said Hester, asserting her authority over the conversation as the mother figure in this sensitive area, 'it doesn't need to concern us. We've got enough problems without worrying about drug deals.'

'Can we find out, can't we do something?' asked Anne, feeling the conversation was escaping from her. Sven shook his head, unwilling to disappoint. 'Is this showing leadership?' she said, referring to a conversation of some days earlier when Sven had talked about international morality.

'I was talking about the advanced countries taking a lead in Europe,' he said.

'Well we're from advanced countries, why don't we lead? What's the point of being moral if you never do anything?' she said, surprised at her own audacity.

Sven resented the tone. He said, 'You're very forthcoming now, you didn't bother telling me Sarah was shagging some Greek.'

'Charming,' said Sarah.

'I didn't think it was any of my business,' said Anne.

'Well I don't think this is any of my business,' said Sven.

Anton was confused by this exchange. He thought: what is the equivalence here? A boatful of people maybe die equals a shag with a local? Or is it more than one? More than one shag, or more than one death? The relationship of one thing to another, his touchstone, had been lost to Anton in this exchange in which both Sven and Anne seemed to know exactly where they were.

'Getting a bit hard-core here innit?' muttered Freddie, who had just appeared and had caught the tail end of the conversation. Everyone welcomed him, grateful for the diversion.

'What's this about you closing down?' he asked Hester.

The clatter of eating stopped, 'What was that?' she said.

'Town gossip,' he said, 'council are closing you down because of bad hygiene.'

'The fuck are they,' said Hester, who seemed to become even more feisty when Freddie was around. 'The bastards are saying they want me to have a Greek food hygiene certificate, they don't want to recognise my British one.'

'Yes, I thought it was something like that. What's that going to cost, then?'

'A visit to some functionary in Rhodes. Clearly I haven't bribed enough people, they want me to pay off the Greek national debt.'

'Didn't they say they wanted you to take a test?' said Sven. 'Why are they so much against you? We are guests here, we have to respect their ways of doing things, maybe we have offended them in some way we don't even understand.'

'We are not guests,' Hester said angrily, 'I've got as much right to be here as a Greek has to run a kebab shop in Tottenham. They just don't like the competition. Would you leaflet the ferry and the hydrofoils for us today, Sven, we're open and we are staying open.'

'Sure,' said Sven, who was always very dutiful – if he had an allotted job, he would do it diligently.

'I'll call the solicitor and get back to hanging on for the Ministry of Tourism,' she left for the office where Freddie joined her. The others finished breakfast and dispersed, leaving Anton and Anne. He realised none of them, including him, had dealt well with Anne's distress.

He had another try, 'So what should happen now?' he said to Anne, 'what do you want?'

'Someone has to have responsibility,' she said, 'someone has to know something. Can't we ask the coastguard?'

'I can't see how he could make anything happen. Why should the coastguard know or care?'

She shook her head, 'Because he has charge of all this, all this water and the traffic on it,' she felt hopeless, exhausted and miserable. Finally, in desperation at Anton's blank expression she blurted out, 'You've got to help me, I'm running to stand still here. You, you crowd, you're all more brainy than me and better looking than me and richer than me. I need some help to keep up.'

'I'd never considered we were richer than you,' said Anton, in genuine surprise, 'just hadn't thought about it.'

'Yeah,' she said, in exasperation, 'You're the cool kids and I'm just here, hanging on.'

'I didn't know I was one of the cool kids,' said Anton, 'I just get on with what I'm doing and don't care what people say about me.'

'That's what *makes* you one of the cool kids,' she said.

'I am sure my expectations were wrong,' he said, 'I didn't expect to see you turn into the Little Mother of the Refugees. I wanted you because you were normal, everyday.'

'But that's what people do,' she pleaded, 'they develop, they change, improve…hopefully.'

'Hmm, character development,' said Anton, 'like in the novel.'

'Yes,' she said, 'like in the novel.'

'I'd never considered that. I thought of you as my prize for not being weird. This saving the refugees isn't what I thought we would do here, it's not what I thought we were about.'

Anne paused, 'I never thought of myself as being a prize before' she said, 's'pose it's good to be considered a prize at all.'

'That's my girl,' he said. 'You were my anchor to the ordinary.'

'I like being an anchor,' she said in a small voice, 'I

don't like all this…bad feeling and argument.'

He held her with genuine affection and said in her hair, 'Nothing has to happen, we can just wait and see. This afternoon, let's go down to Pixie Hollow like we used to when we first came here, just like it always was. I've got to prepare the day's food but I'm not cooking till tonight. This afternoon, at twelve, we'll spend some time together. You go back and get some sleep,' he kissed her on the head and hugged her slight body and went off to the kitchen, feeling pleased with the way he had handled the situation.

Anne walked back up to the house and tried to sleep, but just lay back looking at the cedar wood roof beams. She was troubled by the confusion of the night, by having challenged Sven and been rebuffed, by being told she was a prize by Anton – exactly what did that mean? Was she a consolation prize? She went downstairs to the courtyard with a book she was supposed to read for next term and sat on the stone bench in front of the marble table. Finally giving up on the book, she started painting her toenails the way Sarah did, from a coral pink bottle with a tiny brush in the cap.

Sarah emerged from the kitchen eating a triangular baklava from a plate with a fork. 'Would you like some?' she asked. Sarah felt she had no allies now and was feeling isolated. She wanted to reintegrate herself into the group and was additionally relieved to have found that it wasn't Anne who had betrayed her to Sven.

'No thanks,' said Anne, 'though it looks good. Don't you worry about getting fat?' said Anne who was forever fretting about her weight.

'No, said Sarah, licking honey from her lips 'I'd just go out with boys who like big girls, there's enough of them.'

'Is it always about who you are going out with?'

'No, it isn't, it's about pleasing myself – myself first, then the boys I fancy, then girls. It's girls who are interested in weight. As long as you're not so fat your arms stick out at the sides, blokes don't care.'

'I wish I had your confidence.'

'Do you want me to do that for you?' She indicated Anne's straining to varnish her tiny toes.

'No, thanks, I'll manage,' she said.

'Have you ever pretended,' Sarah mused, 'you really knew something when you didn't, just to get someone to like you?'

'I thought people pretended to know things to get *you* to like them,' said Anne.

'Yeah, maybe,' said Sarah. 'My friend was really into this boy and she said she liked Guns and Roses and didn't really but had to listen to loads of it. Sarah imitated the boy: 'So you like Guns and Roses? Excellent: what's your favourite song?'

Anne joined in , 'Er....that one that begins with the long guitar riff.'

'Sweet Child of Mine? Excellent, oh, that's *my* favourite too!' So she ends up not having a relationship with him but having to talk all the time about music. When I was younger, about thirteen, I pretended to like horror films with this older friend and I had to see them, you know, all of them – Scream, Amityville Horror, Nightmare on Elm Street, Halloween Three: The Evil Never Ends...' Anne was politely amused, but not getting into the spirit of the conversation. 'You're still upset about last night aren't you?' asked Sarah.

'Well, I'm trying to be normal, I suppose I should give it a few days,' she said. 'What do you think about Kostas, doing the things he does, with that Vasilios, they really are criminals aren't they?'

Sarah was taken aback to hear the word said out loud, 'They do a bit of this and a bit of that, some of it not entirely within the law. It's the family business,' she said, 'it's traditional, you are born into it and get on with it, like any other trade, like being a shepherd or a fisherman round here. Anyway, he doesn't talk to me about business; he's very traditional, women and men inhabit separate spheres here and they don't overlap much.' Anne looked dubious, Sarah threw open her hands in an empty gesture and continued, 'Look, I don't know what he was up to, but I don't think of smuggling as real crime, it never really has been, you know, "Watch the wall my darling as the gentlemen go by."'

'I s'pose not,' said Anne, 'anyway, I don't care about him, I'm worried about Malik's friend and the refugees.'

'Why? What can you do?'

'Not a lot, I suppose, but if I do nothing, that makes a difference to me. I'd better go down and see Anton, we were going to walk along the coast like we used to.'

Anton laboured in the kitchen in the forest of pans and utensils hanging from the ceiling, practising the alchemy of food amid the smell of hot olive oil, crushed garlic and oregano. With concentration he chopped and fried the onions; topped and tailed and washed the green beans; de-pipped the sweet peppers and tomatoes; sliced the aubergines and marinated them in salted water. He ran the potatoes through a machine to clean and chip them, but himself created a sauce by reducing balsamic vinegar and adding brown sugar.

Anne watched silently for a while then he took her hand as they walked along the track with the hills to their left and the sea to the right, until at the end of the road the track that led along the coast petered out and they climbed along finding what stable ground they could.

'What do you want to do after, after uni, I mean?' Anne asked.

'I want,' said Anton, 'to be a sauce chef, a really good one.'

'You what? I thought you were going to be a macro-economist or an astro-physicist, finding the theory of everything and all that.'

'I suppose I could do that,' he mused, breathing in the salty air, 'but sauces are what interest me now.'

Around at Pixie Hollow where the currents cut a little cup in the coastline, eddying around and around with the swell of the sea, two travellers had arrived, bobbing and nudging against each other. Currents and eddies played with the sad floaters being tipped and lifted in the rocky bay, nibbled at by tiny fishes and little brown crabs, the poor flesh waxy, pearly eyes bulging and what wretched clothes they had on billowed out by the water, the gases already stealthily beginning to distend the stomachs of these voyagers.

The two students came over the cusp of the hill, Anton was chatting on when Anne blurted out, 'What is that, in the water?'

Anton looked down into the bay where they were heading, beside the tiny patch of sand. 'That's what you think it is, it's two people,' he said slowly, 'and they look dead. I'll go and take a closer look to see.'

He started to scramble down, then turned round to see her terrified face. 'Have you got your phone?' he said, 'I haven't brought mine.'

She fumbled about in her bag and he took the pink metallic mobile phone from her trembling hand. 'Be careful,' she whimpered.

'You look away,' he said, but she watched him scramble down the gentle incline, praying for his safety. She thought of his bravery in venturing down to the hollow of death. Anton did not think of danger or horror, he had just never seen a dead body before and was curious.

As soon as he was close he saw there was no chance life remained in the big, wet dolls that had been men. They lay together the same way, like lovers in a watery bed, one face up and one down, both had naked feet that the water had wrinkled.

They had been dark-skinned, or coffee coloured, but not black. The one face up had his lips, the lobes of the ears and eyelids nibbled away, leaving the eyes bulging and showing opaque corneas. Anton took a piece of driftwood and poked at the nearest body, it responded like a toy boat, with no agency of its own, just reacting to the force that had been exerted on it and the pressure of the waves.

He took a couple of pictures and, not knowing the police number, called the restaurant for Hester to tell the authorities. For all the heat of the day, Anne was shaking as he led her back to Café Europa.

In a short time Captain Papadopoulos came, in charge of a couple of men from the council who Hester had previously seen on the refuse disposal truck. They parked a van as near to the descent to Pixie Hollow as they could reasonably get, took a stretcher and ropes and scrambled down to recover the bodies.

Papadopoulos spoke to Anton and Anne, who was finding the situation surreal: sitting at a table of the restaurant talking to a policemen in uniform while stout-armed men behind him were hauling bodies up a cliff. There was little to say. Papadopoulos explained, 'Refugees, migrants, we see a lot of them. These ones did not make it.'

The students expected the scene to be as it was in television crime dramas, blocked off with police tape, scanned over by forensic officers in white suits, but Captain Papadopoulos and the two council labourers were what Doxos' finest could muster.

Amid the holiday snaps on Anne's phone was a picture of loathsome death that Anton emailed to his computer and deleted from the phone's memory. Back in their room, Anton studied the pictures in minute detail. At this stage, with a new experience, the investigative instinct took over in Anton: he had to know everything he could about death by drowning. He researched forensic sites to identify fine froth at the nostrils, florid patches around the face, bleached skin of the hands and feet.

He turned round to Anne who was lying motionlessly on the bed staring at the ceiling, looking small and frail as an injured animal. 'You can tell time of death by the degradation of the body,' he said, 'roughly – not exactly, no putrefaction or adipocere formation. They were recent, the bodies weren't bloated. Shouldn't you tell Malik?'

'What's the point?' she said, 'I can't even be sure the dead men came from his boat... the boat he was waiting for. I'd like to tell him something useful.' Wanting to acknowledge that she appreciated Anton's being helpful at last she added, 'It's not a good sign, though.'

'Well, think about it,' Anton mused, 'things get washed into Pixie Hollow by the sea all the time, the tide's diurnal, I think we're getting now what went into the sea last night. Sorry. Of course it might not be that boat, there could be lots of them out there finding land and sinking all the time.' He looked out of the window, across the sea, there were a couple of yachts and, in the distance, a ferry ploughing across the skyline a few miles out.

'But you think if a boat went down last night, the bodies would be washed ashore today?'

'Yes, I think that, but I'm no expert on the currents around this island.'

'I don't want to do nothing,' said Anne, 'I'll go to the coastguard myself.'

Anton resisted visiting the coastguard's office, as he resisted going into any situation where there were too many variables and he could not easily place himself. 'What do you expect to get out of this?' he said.

'An explanation? Peace of mind?'

'You don't want much do you?' Anton looked at the slight girl who had given him a great deal of pleasure and had caused him no problems up to now. He hugged her saying, 'I don't think seeing the coastguard with you, is going to achieve anything, but I'll do it, I'll go with you.'

'Thank you so much,' she said, 'I don't know why but it means a lot to me,' and she snuggled into his embrace. Anton looked forward to learning something about the tides around this island.

Anton and Anne drove round to coastguard's building which was set behind a garden of trees planted in bare earth; grass did not flourish in this climate. One of the advantages of the relaxed approach to life on Doxos was the ease with which one could see officials. There might be a wait, but waiting was Greek, the notion of an appointments system was foreign to the island.

It was unremarkable that people would want to see the Coastguard. People came to have their insurance documents certified in order to confirm that their yacht had crashed in bad weather; or they needed to get permission for a long mooring; or report a pollution incident; or inform against a neighbour with an illegal catch. There were always a couple of people waiting in the Coastguard's languid outer office on a bench on one side of a counter behind which were three or four of the Coastguard's men in their customary blue T-shirts, sitting behind their busy desks of papers and overflowing ashtrays.

Anton stood and looked at a maritime chart on the wall showing the island and the sea around it. Anne was not used to making approaches to authority, this was one of the most frightening things she had done in her life. She looked at her hands with their evidence that she had resumed a habit of biting her nails in these difficult days.

Eventually they were shown through the general office smelling of smoke to the air-conditioned, whiter box of the Coastguard's office. The students saw a handsome man with large brown eyes and a chiselled face in a white uniform shirt who sat with his arms on a blotter on his uncluttered desk. Behind him were his certificates from the Merchant Marine Academy and other institutions. He did not stand for their entry but stayed behind the broad desk containing two telephones, an empty in-tray on one side and an out-tray on the other containing a small, neat stack of papers; on one side sat a picture with its back towards the visitor, presumably of his family.

He motioned them to sit, and said in perfect English, 'You wanted to see me? How can I help?'

He addressed his question to Anton but Anne answered.

'We were wondering if you could tell us about a refugee boat. One was supposed to be coming yesterday...'

He smiled kindly at the young woman, 'These aren't scheduled journeys, they don't tell us when they are going to sail.'

'You often intercept them...' said Anton.

'We patrol what are called the southern maritime borders of Europe,' the Coastguard said as if teaching a class, 'it is an extremely challenging theatre from a border control point of view. Usually it is not policing the waters but a maritime search and rescue operation. We are picking people up all the time. Sometimes we don't catch them, they get through and enter illegally, we can't do everything. Why are you interested in this?'

'We were talking to a boat, last night, with a mobile phone, from the shore, me and one of the refugees we know, a friend that we see,' said Anne. 'Then we couldn't contact them anymore. Later we found some bodies in the bay near us, we were hoping you could help us to understand what happened to them.'

'You shouldn't encourage them, they are illegal immigrants,' he said. 'We don't run a ferry service for refugees. If we are there, if we find them, we will pick them up as a humanitarian duty and as part of our duty to patrol the southern European borders. We can't know everything that's on the water at any one time.'

'There was a boat that went out, the Spirit of the Island,' said Anne innocently.

'How do you know this?'

'I was there, at the harbour, with one of the refugees, I know him well, he thought one of his friends was coming over. I saw the Spirit of the Island come back.'

Despite the air conditioning, the Coastguard developed a sheen of sweat on his upper lip. 'OK, so a boat went out, boats go out all the time for fishing, for recreation, transport…we don't track each one.'

'Is it possible to say,' asked Anton, 'looking at the currents, to say where a refugee boat sank in order for the bodies to be washed up by the tide on the north east side of Doxos?'

The Coastguard asked for the question to be repeated to give himself time to think, 'No, he said, the currents are all too uncertain, the weather and temperature would change them, the time of year…'

'Surely you could take those factors into account,' said Anton, 'you can count on the phases of the moon, judge an average wind speed.'

'We could, but there are too many things to work out, too many things to do. Now I cannot help you further. There are, you understand, things I must do.' He looked towards the door, inviting them to leave, 'Why don't you just enjoy your holiday? Why do you want to get involved in all of this? What are these people to you?'

Anton took this as a factual remark; Anne noted the tone of condescension. As they were leaving, she turned and summoned the courage to say, 'Why didn't your patrol boat go out last night?'

The Coastguard felt he had been struck a blow. 'That…' he said, 'that's operational, it's classified. I must get on with my work. He looked down at his empty desk.

'I don't think we got much out of that' said Anne

outside the building.

'We tried,' Anton said. He was uncomfortable with conversations where he did not already know the answers, or at least the region where the answer lay. When something was being concealed, it was a microcosm of his whole life – something was hidden from him and all he could do was accumulate knowledge until he reached a stage when all was understood.

'He didn't say he would make enquiries,' said Anne, 'maybe he already knows.'

They returned to their duties at the restaurant. When news about the bodies circulated on the island, far from diminishing interest in Café Europa, it increased attention among the ghoulish and the merely curious, who went out to the cliffs to experience a thrilling proximity to death, though the bodies were long gone. On the other hand, those people who had never favoured Café Europa felt the incident confirmed their opinion that there must be something wrong with the place: the police were always there for something.

As soon as the young people left his office, the Coastguard dragged a handkerchief over his brow, reached for a telephone and called the Mayor.

'The other night, Mr Mayor, what happened? I've just had people in asking about it. I thought you were going out for – I don't know – but I didn't think it had anything to do with refugees.'

'It didn't. What refugees?'

'I've got xenie talking about missing a boat of refugees and about seeing the Spirit of the Island come back. They'd been in contact with a refugee boat, then it went silent.'

'It was quiet, no one knew anything about it,' said the Mayor, 'what you say, it's new to me.'

'Well now the xenie know about it and they're keeping one of the refugees as a pet!' He whispered urgently so his men in the next door office would not hear, 'So who the fucking Mother of God else knows about it?' The Coastguard rarely swore and never blasphemed, but after days of unrelieved tension had finally lost his equilibrium and cast aside his air of self-control. His shame had been drowned but now it was rising from the deep, it was a kraken awakened to emerge from the sea and seize him. 'So what are you going to do about it?'

'I shall,' said the Mayor quietly, feeling the ground crack beneath him as if it were going to open up, 'I shall attend to this.'

He called Vasilios, not on the town hall line but from his personal mobile telephone, and said urgently, 'We must meet. Now.'

'Aspasia's?'

'No, at the chapel of St Sabbas.'

'See you,' Vasilios was low on social graces, he found he could get by very well without them. He did not take orders from anyone, and he was busy with his consignment, but when a man of the Mayor's standing said he wanted an immediate meeting, he got it.

Vasilios's life was circumscribed by his physical form: most important were food and drink, next that he should get sex, the needs of his family obtruded to some extent, the needs of his extended family a little less; the needs of the island were important to him only so much as they had to be satisfied in order to ensure his own comfort. He liked the prestige he gained from being born in the right family, a prestige that he had built up by his own efforts. Everyone respected him, he had no interest in whether they liked him or not. He could understand favours: indeed, his business economy operated as much on favours as it did on hard cash, but a gesture of altruism would leave him bewildered, wondering what the angle was. He was essentially a conservative, he would not tolerate disorder. He left his men dealing with the consignment and tore across the island on his four-wheel drive.

The Mayor drove in his blue Mercedes to a high point, and waited outside a tiny white chapel with a red door. Soon Vasilios appeared in his Range Rover. They faced each other on the pebble drive with the sea visible on all sides, where what winds there were teased across their sweating faces.

'Well?' said Vasilios.

'What happened out there last night?' asked the Mayor

Vasilios was used to meeting official challenges with a blank stare, but even his heart jumped at this. 'Nothing happened,' he said, 'we did the business we needed to do, nothing happened. Why do you ask? What's up?' Vasilios was not indifferent to the truth, but found many more valuable qualities to cultivate such as consistency and self-interest.

The Mayor looked sceptically at him, 'The Coastguard is getting questions, from some xenie, from some xenie who have already been giving me problems, the ones from Café Europa.'

'Yeah, I know them. What have they got to say?'

'They want to know about a refugee boat. The thing is, they were in contact with the boat by phone, then they weren't, and they'd like to know what happened.'

Vasilios feigned nonchalance, 'Alright,' he said, 'we passed a refugee boat, we just went on.'

The Mayor, wise in the ways of the world, at once saw the picture. 'They saw you. You got rid of the witnesses didn't you? Fuck me. I thought you were just taking a boat out to do whatever business you had out there, I didn't expect you to commit a fucking massacre.'

'Nothing to do with us,' said Vasilios angrily, 'they saw us and they died – did you expect us to pick them up? Fuck me with a crucifix, I can't be expected to patrol the seas picking up the scum of Asia. Why the hell does it matter?'

'You're right,' said the Mayor, thinking the right policy now was to quieten Vasilios down, not make him so angry that communication was impossible, 'it doesn't matter if there are no more questions, no one else shows an interest, everyone shuts the fuck up. Why is the Coastguard getting xenie asking about it? When something like this starts to unravel, it can go badly wrong.'

'I'll sort it out, my cousin,' said Vasilios who saw the wisdom of the Mayor's approach.

'You're sure?' he nodded, they gave a firm handshake with no further word.

Later, back in the warehouse where they were working Vasilios called Kostas to him.

'Your xenie friends,' he said, 'have been asking questions about the other night, on the water.' Kostas was taken aback, about to deny that he knew anything about it but Vasilios gave him one of his glowering looks, any response would be superfluous. Kostas nodded his understanding.

'Give them a warning,' Vasilios said quietly.

'But I know them, they know me,' Kostas said.

'That will make it easier for you to get close to them.' Vasilios turned and left him, the conversation was over.

Kostas considered what to do, not happy with this commission. He understood the principle well enough, it was a good idea to exert authority, disobedience could not be tolerated, he wanted to let the xenie know that talking about what they saw would result in real problems. A simple warning with no injury to persons would fit the bill.

Kostas did not consider there was any contradiction between his conviviality with the Café Europa crowd and his destruction of their property. Friendship was one thing, this was business, it had to be done.

He drove to a petrol station, filled the tank of his motorcycle and, without being seen by the garage owner, presented a plastic soft drinks bottle to the nozzle and squirted a few centilitres of petrol into the wide mouth. Late that night he drove round to aunt Aspasia's, left the motor bike outside but did not rouse her. He walked the two miles to Café Europa, dry-mouthed in a night illuminated only by a sliver of moon. He picked a spot from which he could watch the restaurant and the house up the hill. He sat for the time it took to smoke a cigarette to make sure the lights were off in the rooms he knew as windows.

He created a simple, improvised time-delay fuse which (not that Kostas would have known) was developed during the years of dictatorship for clandestine operations against the junta. He opened a matchbox half a centimetre and lit a cigarette. He placed the tip end of the cigarette into the match box with the little brown heads packed close up to it, so when the cigarette burned down it would touch the matches to ignite them in a blaze.

With a definite sense of purpose, moving easily in the warm darkness, Kostas walked across to the jeep in the spot used as a car park, scarcely visible in the slight moonlight. He undid the top of the soft drinks bottle and tipped the contents on the upholstery front and back, threw the bottle in, then placed the fuse in the foot well.

Kostas turned and walked away, making no sound. He moved at the smart pace that his young, strong body would afford him, with the wild hills to his right and the crashing of the sea to his left, towards Aspasia's where he would roll his motorcycle off down the sloping road towards town so he could turn on the ignition at a distance.

Kostas was not a very reflective young man, and he was not constantly allowing his mind to muse over previous and future actions, but he did think on this walk about that business with the boat and the refugees: did that mean he'd killed someone? Because it was a big thing to kill someone, you weren't a man in this world unless you had killed someone, but it all happened so fast...how sure could he be that he had killed one of them, or any of them, and it hadn't been death by their own exertions? He looked boldly out at the Aegean sea beyond the bay. It would be satisfying one day to be able to say with certainty that he had killed someone, to be a man.

Chapter 11

A dull boom rolled out over the bay and the flame, at first as high as a tree, lit up like day the vine veranda of the house and the bougainvillea of the restaurant. Aroused by the noise and light, the students stood like the sheeted dead shocked alive, staring from their balcony on a scene illuminated by the blazing car, not believing what they were seeing.

They saw Hester run from the restaurant building, her dressing gown flapping open, standing at the edge of the car park staring at the blazing jeep. Sven was the first to rush from the house, wearing flip flops on his feet and clad only in boxer shorts, he headed for the restaurant, wrenched the fire extinguisher from the kitchen wall and ran out to the burning vehicle, but by the time she got there the upholstery was ablaze, molten plastic was running down and some of the metal frame was glowing red hot.

He fiddled with the extinguisher's mechanism, bruising his flesh on the handle. His fists clenched and eyes closed as he fired into the seat of the fire, squirting a stream of white foam into the inferno. The car sent up a cloud of grey smoke that forced the almost naked man to back off and the angry fire regained its hold. Flames of orange and black gnawed around the wheel arches and flickered in the radiator, more uncertain flames consumed the upholstery, plastic fittings melted in the furnace and folded in sadly upon themselves. As if in response to Sven's efforts, the fire flared and sizzled as it seized on some particularly flammable fitting.

Sven, a white figure under the stars, illuminated by the leaping flames, continued to battle the fire with a stream of foam, but it was too late, it had already spread to the plastic fuel tank.

Hester ran inside to telephone the fire brigade but didn't have the number and wondered how soon they would get there anyway. While she dithered whether to call the police Anton arrived with the two girls following. Sarah and Anne came running down the hill in shirts and knickers, staring aghast at the scene of destruction. As they watched, the melting fuel tank breached and a trickle of flaming petrol began to emerge in a stream of flame down the slope

'Get the scooters away from it' shouted Hester to Anton and they both struggled with the little machines, rolling them across the uneven ground and up the hill, out of range of the heat and flames. The petrol from the tank, a fiery stream, trickled harmlessly down towards the beach.

Sven was a silhouette against the flames, pouring his jet into the burning wreck. When the can was exhausted he threw it aside and stepped back, just now realising how hot it was.

'Water' shouted Hester, with the girls beginning to fill a cleaning bucket and a large cooking pan in the kitchen sinks. Anton unravelled the garden hose to its fullest extent, to the edge of the car park, and they began relays, filling the bucket and pans from the hose and carrying them slopping across the car park to throw on the burning vehicle.

Water hissed and rose in steam from the red-hot frame, acrid black smoke billowed up from the tyres and plastic fittings. They kept throwing water on the wreck until finally it was smoking and smouldering, smelling of fuel, burnt grease, rubber and plastic.

'What was that? An electrical fault?' said Anne staring into the ugly black pile of burned-out rubber and metal.

'A car can't blow up from a stationary position without help,' said Sven. His white body was smeared with sweat and smuts from burning rubber.

'Arson?'

'Greek fire,' said Anton dreamily, staring transfixed at the blackened mess, '*ignis graecus*, weapon of the ancients.'

Sven was excited, angry and unhappy. He felt he had come into his own, fighting the fire almost naked between the sea and the rocky land, he had become an elemental sprite, but all his efforts had not saved the vehicle. He was angry that anyone should do this to them when they had tried so hard to fit in and to do everything well.

Standing before the charred and smoking mess, they started to think more rationally. Why didn't Hester have the fire service number? But would it have made any difference anyway? 'I'll call our old friends the town police,' she said.

They were together in the early morning, not a confident dawn, but a tremulous and weepy awakening as the sun slowly warmed the mountain behind them and lit up the little red, yellow and blue villas with the toy-box churches and the play castle up the mountain across the bay. Anne was shivering with excitement in the unexpected surge of adrenalin, Anton put his arm around her and she moved in close. Sarah looked to Sven but he was with Hester who had found some soothing ointment to put on his hand and thigh that had been too close to the fire. If he wanted comforting it was not from Sarah. Sven was congratulated by everyone except Anton, who was light on praise in any situation, though he was the one person from whom Sven wanted it. Sven was shocked by the event, from the physical exertion and from the retreat of hope that he saw in the flaming vehicle, the hope of an idyllic lifestyle or that people would behave better in beautiful surroundings. For Sven such beliefs now were crisped, were carbonised, or melted or twisted or burned beyond use and recognition.

The five cleaned up and reassembled at the restaurant. By that time Café Europa had another visit from Captain Papadopoulos. He looked at the wreck and made a clucking noise. His eyes turned to heaven as he noted the centre of the fire, the spot where the matchbox had been, there were even some charred remains of matches that had been scattered by the explosion and the fire-fighting effort.

The cigarette had burned down to the matches that flared and caught the vapour of the fuel that had been previously spilled. Petrol vapour had enveloped the vehicle in an invisible haze so the flare caused an explosion and a fierce fire, loud and dramatic but of no great danger if a vehicle were parked away from buildings and the fire started when no one was around. This was a practical statement that he had seen before. It was a sign. It was, as it were, a deliberate trademark, designed and crafted so those in the know would recognise the cabal of tradesmen whence it came.

'Who does these things on the island?' asked Hester.

Captain Papadopoulos was no fool, but he had a marked preference for a quiet life. 'I can't say,' he said, 'there are a lot of refugees here now, they come from war zones, they can be desperate people. You have one often down here…and then there are the gypsies and the Albanians….'

Hester recognised she was not going to get very far if she relied on the policeman's investigative skills. As usual in these situations, Hester took a breath and quickly assessed what she could get out of it. At least he wasn't saying it was an accident.

'I am sure you are correct, while you are doing your good work investigating the bad people who did this, I will make an insurance claim, so I would be grateful if you give me a crime number and tell me what other paperwork I will need.'

Over at the tables where the students were sitting disconsolately eating breakfast, Freddie turned up, having seen the smoke rising from the top road.

'What happened here then?' he asked.

'We woke and the jeep had been blown up,' Anton explained.

'They are always blowing things up,' said Freddie, 'a couple of years back they blew up the Italian war memorial – strong sense of patriotism, you know.'

'Bet that taught the war dead a lesson,' said Anton.

'How are you all?' Freddie asked.

'OK considering someone tried to kill us,' said Sarah.

'It was a warning,' Freddie said simply. They looked at him as if to ask *how do you know*? 'Trust me, I'm from Catford,' he said, 'if these people wanted you dead, you'd be dead.'

'Very reassuring,' said Sarah.

'But,' said Anton thinking ahead as usual, 'if they killed us there would be one hell of a row – the place would be swarming with police.'

'Reporters,' said Anne

'TV crews,' said Sarah. They envisaged the television news coverage and the banner headlines, 'Students Slain on Greek Island' 'Five Dead in Paradise Massacre' 'Secrets of Murder Island.'

'There'd be questions in parliament,' said Anne.

'Questions in the European Assembly, surely,' said Sven.

'Do they have questions there. I don't think so,' said Sarah.

'Lunches,' Anton declared, 'they will have lunches about our deaths at the European Assembly.'

'Washed down with a nice bottle of Piesporter.'

'Yummy.'

'Don't you take anything seriously?' Sarah said, more in admiration than judgement.

'If being serious would make a difference, I would,' said Anton.

'What do they think we will do?' said Hester, who had returned from talking with the policeman, 'just pack up and go?'

'Maybe they don't think that far ahead,' said Sven, 'to see the consequences of their actions, maybe they just act on instinct, like animals. If something bothers them, they kill it.'

'I don't even know what it's to do with,' said Anton, 'is it drug smuggling or the refugees or the other restaurant owners....?'

Freddie looked contemplative, 'You know how when you were a kid,' he said, 'you used to play happy families and everyone had their own job? Mr Chop the Butcher, Mr Pint the Milkman.'

'Dr Dose the Doctor,' said Anne, glad the conversation was about something she understood, she felt frightened and way out of her depth. Freddie winked at her. 'Well' he said, placing three coasters one on top of the other, 'here they don't. Here Mr Talk the politician, and Mr Blag the burglar and Mr Cash the businessman, they are all in the same happy family.' He held the cardboard coasters together as if he expected applause, 'Please one, you've pleased them all, offend one, you've got a lot of enemies.'

'And the moral of the story is...?' asked Sarah.

'Best not to cross people here,' he said.

'Freddie, how easy is it to get a gun on Doxos?' asked Hester.

'Now there's a girl who's getting serious,' said Freddie. 'Have you ever used a gun?'

'A revolver, on a shooting range in the US.'

'I'll ask someone. It's possible, a lot of weapons come in from Turkey.'

'You don't have to be so discreet about who it's for,' said Hester, 'I want them to know I've got it, and I am prepared to use it.'

'It's the wild west out here isn't it?' said Sarah, 'or maybe the wild east.'

'Well, you're laughing, that's good,' said Freddie, 'the worst thing you can do with these people is to be scared of them. If you take my advice, you'll make a lot of noise, be happy.'

'Right,' said Hester instinctively, 'that sounds like good advice. We need to show we're not afraid. We need to get a lot of people here. Let's have a big night, party time. Who can we invite?'

'Most of the expats are old. Well, older than all of us,' said Anne, realising she might be offending Freddie. 'A few are still working like Jess and Pete, but we don't see many of them out at night, they're tucked up with their cocoa.'

'Let's make them young again,' said Hester, 'let's have a night of oldies.'

'Don't you mean adult orientated rock?' said Freddie, 'Heep and Quo?'

'Er... yeah, stuff like that,' said Sarah.

'Freddie,' said Hester, 'tell all the expats you know, we want them here tonight, if they don't come any other night, we need them just to be here and have a good time. And the supportive Greeks, the ones that don't want to be controlled by these criminal bastards.'

'Anne, can you text the people whose numbers we have, to tell them – invite them over. It's time they showed a bit of solidarity. And make up a group email. Party food, Anton – croquettes, prawns in batter, fishcakes...I'll get Grandma Poppy to make us a big order of cheese and spinach pies. I'll tell her what it's for and then she'll let the world know. And Sarah, get the yacht paints out, let's have a big symbol against the evil eye on the wall on the side of the restaurant, in the O of Europa.'

'Sending the evil back to them?' said Sarah, 'that's deeply spiritual.'

'What are we going to do with the jeep?' Anne asked, in almost a wail as she looked dismayed at the faithful vehicle, 'Have it towed away?'

Hester looked towards the wreck of the jeep, still smouldering in the now brilliant sunlight, 'No, let's put some balloons on it,' she said, 'make it a feature. People will want to see it.'

Freddie went off on his social calls round the island, happy to have some news to pass on. Much of his life was now this whipping round Doxos on his scooter, carrying information from one group to the next, stopping at cafes and markets and private houses, a verbal newspaper picking up messages and sending them on, pollinating gossip, gathering the seed from one location and sowing it in another. Freddie was right about the attitude to adopt: the locals expected Hester and the Café Europa crew to be cowed, to be thinking about leaving the island and abandoning the business, to see them zipping around announcing a new party at the same time news was spread about the arson attack was bemusing.

Other visitors came through the day, including Malik. He fixed the burnt-out carcass of the car with a hypnotised gaze. He looked for an English phrase, but his literature did not supply it. 'More war,' he said simply.

'It's not war it's....vandalism,' said Anne, but Malik did not seem convinced, or really to know what it meant, and Anne was too tired to explain.

He said he had come to see if Anne's enquiries about the missing refugee boat had yielded any results. 'We asked the Coastguard but he couldn't help us,' she said. Malik nodded, he knew what had happened, as well as he needed to. She had delayed telling him they had found the bodies, but when she did, he was not shocked as she had expected he would be, he just nodded and muttered something in Pashto which she assumed was the Muslim equivalent of 'Rest in peace.' Malik had seen enough, he had heard enough stories about death on the journey, to be unsurprised.

He had hoped Anne would take him out, but she was busy with preparations for the evening and was not doing any volunteer work today. They also now had only the two scooters for transport. He had to return to the compound on foot, feeling the foundations of freedom in Europe crumbling as he surrendered himself to the mountain climb. Samir was gone, he knew it as well as he knew anything. He had such hopes for the happy reunion they would enjoy, had replayed it in his mind countless times. Now, he was sure, he would never embrace Samir and make it up to him for having left so suddenly. Malik's only European friends were under attack, the whole dream was darkening.

Jess called round in her rusty blue Ford and walked swearing around the wrecked jeep. 'I'd tell you to fight the bastards,' she said to Hester, 'but I don't want to encourage you to fight and then go off. We're leaving on Saturday, I've got to be back in London next week. You can have this car while we're away, just get us to the airport in it and you can look after it till we're back. It'll tide you over till you get a replacement.' Such gestures of solidarity moved Hester, who had enjoyed little in her life except for the product of her own labours. A loan without expectation of reward was valuable indeed and she hugged the little fat woman with real affection.

Sarah collected the light blue, dark blue and black yacht paints from the outhouse and took them to the outer wall where the sign she had previously painted proclaimed CAFE EUROPA. She filled out the rim of the O, which was already dark blue against white, then put a light blue circle within the O, separated from the fresh dark circle by a white ring of background, then waited for the paint to dry a little before she could put the final black spot of the pupil in the centre.

Smelling the paint and the salty breeze, she tried to call Kostas to tell him their news. It was surprising he had not come by, it was his habit to drop in, as if he were checking on her. She rather liked the unpredictability of his visits, but not when he wasn't visiting at all.

She wanted to tell Kostas she was frightened about

what was happening with their car being blown up and Hester wanting a gun. Kostas knew this island, its dangerous places and its bad men, he was strong, he would protect her. Kostas would know who had attacked the car, or he would be able to find out, he knew everything about Doxos. When he hadn't answered the telephone or her texts, she assumed his phone was out of order or turned off for some reason.

She sat listening to the waves and the screeching cicadas; on the wind she could hear goat bells and, far away, the amplified call of a gypsy truck announcing the sale of carpets, and the raucous noise of a wedding, a cavalcade of cars with music, hooting and firecrackers proceeding around the island. She needed to be more active than this, Sarah was not a girl made for watching paint dry.

She knew what she must do, she had to go and find Kostas and tell him to find out what had happened to their car, who was responsible. She would get to the bottom of this, and that would redeem her in the eyes of the Café Europa crowd. What was a boyfriend *for* except to do things for you?

She did not know exactly where Kostas lived, it was with his family over Kephali way, but he mentioned only his mother, and she not often. Sarah packed up the paints and took one of the scooters, not telling the others where she was going, she did not expect to be long. She chugged along the coast road, feeling the free wind in her hair.

Sarah had neglected to tell her friends at Café Europa that Aspasia was Kostas' aunt. It did not seem relevant, and everyone was related to everyone else on the island anyway. She had hardly spoken to Aspasia but sometimes Kostas had called in to Aspasia's café when they were passing and if not effusive, she had not been unfriendly to Sarah.

When she arrived, Sarah found Aspasia's place did not seem open, perhaps it was too early. The path from the gate had not been swept and had been made slippery with the rotten fruit of the male fig tree squished underfoot on the pathway – overripe and inedible. The café was closed but she could hear Aspasia's voice singing along with a Greek tune on Radio Doxos. She called out and walked through the flyscreen hanging in the open door into the restaurant.

It was dim inside, the curtains were drawn, as if Aspasia was not planning to open today, the main lights were off but there was still the sizzling of insects on the glowing blue light of the exterminator.

Sarah called again and walked behind the bar into the back room that led to the living area where Aspasia was sitting at a dressing table, selecting jewellery from an open box before her in a room smelling of makeup and old perfume. She was dressed formally in a grey silk gown, with a matching shawl over the back of the chair, though it was still early in the day.

'Excuse me, good morning,' said Sarah. Aspasia did not start or look around, as if she had been expecting her. A life of work in brothels and bars had given Aspasia a steely self-control, she liked to think she was ready for anything, particularly the unexpected.

The exchange was conducted entirely in Greek. Sarah spoke respectfully in the polite form to say, 'Excuse me for disturbing you, I am looking for Kostas, do you know where he is? His telephone is not working.' She gave a small, apologetic smile.

Though she bulged around the midriff and upper arms, Aspasia's hands were spare, her fingers long and agile. Her image was reflected in the mirror and two side panels of the old-fashioned dressing table. She turned slowly from the glass where she had been fiddling with an earring and laughed unpleasantly.

'*Tha pau sto gamos tou Kosta se Pantoni,*' she said, 'I am going to Kostas' wedding in Pantoni.' Her red mouth leered wide.

'Wedding?' Sarah repeated, though her Greek was good enough to understand every word Aspasia had said, 'I didn't know.'

'No,' said Aspasia, 'you didn't, did you? There are many things you don't know. You are dirt, you are cheap and miserable.' Sarah felt the insult like a blow to the chest, she could not conceive of a response. Aspasia said as a passing shot, 'Go fuck yourself.'

Sarah, utterly shocked, could think of no response, she backed out of the room and ran through the restaurant, got on the scooter and sped off, as fast as the little machine would go. She thought only of putting the maximum distance between herself and this scene of devastation, she felt enveloped in anger and shame. She turned off the main road and went up, through the gorse bushes. Finally she stopped on a small track just short of a cliff, dismounted and sat facing the sea.

She wept unceasingly for her shame and humiliation. She could not bear the thought of being used, of being the butt of the scorn of that witch Aspasia, of Kostas' duplicity, just letting her find out like that. Her emotions veered between pain and fury as she seethed with resentment. She didn't want to marry Kostas, the thought had never entered her mind, but to be used, publicly, was more than she could bear. How could she live with such a memory? She sat for more than an hour staring at the sea then she knew what she must do. She wiped the tears from her eyes and mounted the scooter, her pretty mouth pursed in determination.

She drove down to the Pantoni parish church with its red dome and chequered courtyard, went though the red and white brick arch of the door to the familiar churchy aroma of old incense and the wax candles in the entrance vestibule on their raked brass stand.

Sarah could hear the loud mumble of the priest and through the window she could see, standing between the pillars of the church, the backs of men in suits, the hair-dos of the women, some cooling themselves with fans. The guests were standing on either side in the body of the church amid the pillars, watched by the flat painted icons of saints with their stereotypical features and blank stares.

Down the centre aisle, flanked by the plump arms of the bridesmaids, she saw the familiar head of Kostas at the front before the altar. The priest with his black robe covered by a white stole stood by his table with a flask of wine and a gem-encrusted Bible by his side.

Kostas and his intended, she in a white dress, full arms and shoulders bare, were both standing with their backs to the congregation, facing the priest. The ring ceremony had been completed and the priest was preparing to place the crowns, white circles of paste diamonds and faux pearls linked by a white ribbon, on the heads of the bride and groom.

Sarah flung open the door and marched up the aisle through the standing congregation. 'What?' she shouted. The men in dark suits, the women with their fragile hair-dos turned towards her in horror, what was this outrage? The priest hesitated and stopped, glaring at the intruder

Kostas was unfamiliar, in a shiny grey suit with a collar and tie, like a dress-up doll. His bride was like the figure on a wedding cake, covered in chiffon and tulle. Kostas looked like a man who had been hit in the face, uncertain what to do in the immediacy of the situation.

Under the dome of the church, before the eyes of the painted saints and the priest holding the crowns, Sarah stopped before him. 'When were you thinking of telling me about this?' she demanded in clear tones of fury, 'How about now? What have you got to say for yourself? You useless piece of dirt. What lies have you got for me now?'

Kostas looked round helplessly, as if he could not believe this was happening, and gave forth a most unmatrimonial oath.

'Get out you whore,' screamed Aspasia, standing at the front, purple faced with rage.

Aspasia had already been angry even before the day began, put out that the bride's family refused to allow the wedding reception to take place at her restaurant, which they felt was an improper place. Now she wanted to assert herself as a matriarch. She felt she had the right to speak out to defend the wedding of her sister's son against this xenie.

'Call me a whore,' Sarah rounded on Aspasia, 'you're the whore around here, you do it for a living,' she shouted, a statement which amused some of the women wedding guests for its forthrightness, such that they helpfully translated the English for their neighbours who did not understand.

The men looked towards the floor. Their collective thought went as follows: 'That Kostas kid has never been good for much....This was woman's business, woman's business indeed. You went along with all this marriage stuff but it wasn't very interesting...The squabbles between families were a bore, only the party at the end was good, there was dancing and a man could really show vigour there, show what a man he was, but all this women screaming business – best not to get involved. It would sort itself out....Do nothing and it will all blow over...' No man felt it would be a tribute to his virility to engage with a mass of hysterical women. Let the priest do that, it was his job, what were they paying him for?

Despite this clearly being an outrage, the congregation was unwilling immediately to hustle her out – the priest and not a few of the guests immediately assumed Sarah was coming to claim her right to marry Kostas because she was pregnant. This would have created a genuine dilemma, for right thinking would have backed her and stopped the wedding, this foreigner would have a prior right to marry the boy, or at least come to some kind of settlement.

The priest, a man in early middle age with a full black beard, knew this was a test. The one person who must not be hysterical was himself. He contained his anger with the thought: this must not happen in my church, but if it does, I'm going to make very sure I do not publicly endorse an improper state.

When Sarah stopped, having run out of breath as well as insults, the priest said to Kostas, 'You. Is this woman with your child?'

'No' said Kostas, 'that's not what she says. She is just jealous I am not marrying her....' He wanted to continue but the priest waved him down.

The priest turned to Sarah. 'You have said what

you want to say, now go,' he said in good English.

Sarah stood aware of the eyes of the congregation, the concentrated hatred of the multitude on her. Indeed it was time to go. Her words failed her, '*va al diabalo*' she said finally, flounced out with the wedding guests howling after her – or some of them, some such as Vasilios just looked sourly upon the scene, waiting for the wedding to resume.

Sarah left, her head up, past the now hissing and jeering wedding guests, nearly knocking over a table of sugared almonds in tulle packets tied with a lilac ribbon by the door. One woman mimed picking up a stone as if to throw at her. Sarah gave her a small smile for the ridiculousness of the gesture, mounted her scooter, kicked off and drove up the old road out of town, out into the hills, exhilarated at her actions but fearful, as if she were going to be attacked, but no one followed her.

Amazed at her own audacity, horrified and chuckling at the event in turns, Sarah went back to her perch overlooking the sea, where she had sat after leaving Aspasia's place. She looked out at the string of islets reaching out, little rocky humps with the water foaming around them. The flocks of birds swooped and changed direction above the scene.

Oh shit, she thought, I've been really, really stupid, going to have to go back to Hester and the crowd, back to Sven, oh no, oh fuck. What will I say to Sven? Everything she had forgotten in her anger came back to her. Oh my god what have I done? she thought, must I leave Doxos? What then? Would any of this get home? Probably not, why should it? What was happening at the old manor house? She didn't even know what day it was; she counted out on her fingers from the last date she remembered clearly.

Oh no – she had forgotten her father's birthday, two days ago. She took her telephone and texted her father happy birthday, with a message from the island of sun and happiness. She felt calmer after that. Well, she said to herself, using a phrase used by her father when disaster struck, at least it wasn't boring.

A lot had happened. This whole period had crushed one crisis into another so her breakup with Sven and coupling with Kostas and the bodies being dragged up from Pixie Hollow and the car exploding in the night and the wedding scene she had just disrupted became one glorious riot of events. At least it wasn't boring.

She was glad, anyway, that she had publicly insulted Aspasia, that was a plus, and the look on Kostas' face was an image she would cherish. Now she had to make what peace she could with Café Europa. She'd probably caused Hester an awful headache with the islanders.

She'd better get back to help with preparations for the party – shit! The party! She'd forgotten all about it. She drove back to Café Europa, parked next to the wrecked vehicle and approached the restaurant, looking sheepish, thinking she would have to tell them what had happened. In fact her exploits had preceded her as Hester and Anne had been communicating about the party across Doxos by phone, email and text, and news had been returning back to them. Sarah was the talk of the island.

Anne was the first to see her, 'Way to go, girl,' she said, explaining they had learned of the wedding event. Anne was a good sort, Sarah thought, and rewarded the small girl with a huge, mischievous grin, but with shoulders hunched, as if against a blow from on high.

'Have I caused a big problem?' she asked Hester, apologetically.

'I wouldn't have put gate-crashing a Greek wedding first on my list of things to do,' answered Hester diplomatically, 'but it shows we're not afraid. The revenge of the xenie, eh?'

'You don't want me to leave the island?'

Hester smiled and shook her head, 'How do you feel?' she asked.

'I feel like I should start smoking again,' said Sarah.

'That's constructive,' said Anton, who had joined them.

'I thought you'd appreciate it.'

'The Greeks love a scene,' Hester said, 'they do shouting and screaming themselves, then things are fine afterwards. I know, my dad's family was like that.'

'So you don't think it's going to make things more difficult for Café Europa?'

'No,' said Hester, 'that's not the way it goes, they will respect us for standing up for ourselves. Being polite and keeping to the rules hasn't helped, the Mayor and his gang are still out to get us. Right, let's get dressed up and put on a show. You're the star, you'd better look good.'

Anton had been cooking row upon row of little delicacies, supplemented by Grandma Poppy's pies; Sven had organised downloads of every big rock song they had ever heard of; Hester and Anne had decorated the restaurant and invited pretty much the whole island so even those who had no intention of coming knew of the attack on Café Europa and their gesture of defiance.

The Café Europa sound system played Pink Floyd and Deep Purple as the evening of this eventful day came upon them with the arrival of the first guests, who watched the sun set and the moon rise and the stars blister the night sky.

Jess and Pete came early, they thought it was a great wheeze, they were 'always good for a scrap,' as Pete said to Hester, but sadly were soon going back to England. Alekos sat with them, and entertained Pete with his explanation that the absence of the Reformation or Renaissance in Greek history had preserved the purity of Greek civilisation.

Some of the expats, though they came, were upset at Café Europa's truculent attitude, thinking it would disturb the equilibrium on the island between the locals and newcomers. Toby and Renate, Richard and Ilva talked among themselves. Richard and Tony always enjoyed a party but they had to cajole their respective partners to get them to come along. Ilva and Renata thought the whole Sarah-wedding thing appalling and they pointedly avoided her and made no pleasant conversation when she was serving them. The Greek way of life was what they had come to the island for; invading a Greek wedding to throw a girlie fit over a boyfriend was so dreadful it did not bear thinking about. For them Greek culture was something traditional and perfect, to be admired at a distance, to show due deference if they were invited to so much as observe it.

Freddie had, as usual, an earthier view, he gave Sarah a friendly hug and said, 'You must have been as welcome there as a fart in a phone box, good for you.' He came with his pretty, quiet Greek wife Maria, who was uninquisitive about the events of Café Europa, or anything else, it seemed.

Gossip among the Greeks, particularly those unrelated to the families involved, was that it was a shame for the young bride, but it was about time someone showed up Kostas for the way boys like him carried on with the foreigners. Not a few Greek girls were secretly rather amused, if sympathetic to the bride about the disruption to the wedding.

Not so many of the local islanders came, but there were some who had not visited before: the solicitor and his wife, the dentist, the owner of a furniture shop who also organised the traditional dance troupe for the island. These were the educated of Doxos, often Athens-educated, the ones Jess called the Olympians. They were people who had resisted the dictatorship, or were the children of those who had done so. They came out of a sense of quiet solidarity, because they knew their presence would be noted. They did not really care about the continuance of the restaurant and if it failed for some business reason it would not raise a flicker, but the criminal families were getting above themselves. If they attacked legitimate businesses, then respectable Doxonians had to stand up and be counted. Such were the quiet gestures that moved island society.

Across the bay, at the best venue on the island, the guests for Kostas' wedding had put the events of the day behind them, why should they allow their celebration to be spoiled by the momentary antics of a foreigner?

At Kostas' wedding party, after the feasting when the bride and groom had danced, guests had come forward to outdo each other in the amounts they pinned to the bride's gown; and the traditional ring dance had taken place; the guests with young children had gone off and the adults were continuing traditional dances, or just sitting round and enjoying being there and nursing their resentments against other family members.

Vasilios leaned over to present his mouth to the ear of his nephew. 'Let's talk,' he said, always an ominous beginning to a conversation with Vasilios, which tended to be somewhat one-sided. They went into a side room overlooking the beach and the sea where kegs, soft drinks and spare glasses were stored. Both were now in shirt sleeves, Kostas had been dancing and his shirt was sticking with sweat to his hirsute back.

When the door was closed Vasilios started quietly, 'You know I asked you to go to the xenie café to give them a warning.' Kostas nodded. 'And the idea that you torch that car was ....?

'Mine,' said Kostas simply, aware that there was no right answer in these circumstances.

'And when I said I wanted you to frighten them a little, you thought that was it, not to have a few words, tell them there are people who could act rough, so it was better to say nothing, do nothing? You thought frighten them meant blow up their car?'

Kostas had, in fact, considered the options, but he had been unwilling to face the Café Europa crowd to give them a verbal warning. His confusion of feelings meant he did not want to mix business with pleasure. Also, he knew as Vasilios did not know, how smart those people were: they would not be frightened and shut up, they would keep asking questions, that was what they did, they couldn't ever just let things be, they had to find out.

'But when we did that job together we blew up the car and shop over in Megalo Limani...' pleaded Kostas.

'Yes,' said Vasilios in low tones, 'and that was

because he hadn't paid the levy on drink he was importing, it was damaging our business. So we had a go at his business and now we understand each other. So what was the point of doing the car?'

'To...frighten them?'

Vasilios seemed to have doubled in size, blocking out the light, his face was contorted with rage, 'well, you frightened them well and good, didn't you?' he shouted, 'terrified aren't they? Fucking running away for their lives aren't they? Hiding under the stones? Why don't you look under the stones for them you wanker?' Kostas looked shamefaced, of all the people on the island, the last one he wanted to disappoint was Vasilios. 'Like turning up at your wedding, that was quiet wasn't it?' he raged, 'and making enough noise to wake the dead over there tonight.' Vasilios flung the window open. Wafting on the wind across the bay came the cymbal clash and the opening bars of Tales of Brave Ulysses, 'Think they've got the message, do you? Fuck me, you've got so much to learn.'

'So you don't want me to do any more?' Kostas said quietly.

'And what was it that you might do?' Vasilios asked, genuinely curious.

'That refugee,' said Kostas, 'the one they call Malik, the one that saw us unload, he was in contact with the boat we saw...out there,'

'Yeah, yeah,' said Vasilios, not wanting to dwell on any mention of the boat.

'I could whack him,' Kostas continued, 'no one would know, refugees go missing all the time...Everyone would think he'd run away. They do it all the time, they move on.'

'That was the plan was it?' said Vasilios, 'And you

didn't think you needed a bit of guidance before you rubbed someone out and put the whole operation in danger? I mean, a big operation, the biggest in my life. Have you any idea how difficult it has been to make this thing work?' He looked away in exasperation, then returned to his pedagogic presentation, 'How easy do you think it is to kill someone? Come on. What were you going to do? Where were you going to put the body?'

'A knife, I suppose, I hadn't thought it through, and throw the body in the sea, then he'd be just like the others.'

'Fucking hell.' Vasilios looked at the ceiling, as if for divine guidance, 'Just you, just you alone?' He blew out air as if indicating the insubstantiability of Kostas, 'you think you're a strong lad, but killing someone's harder than you think. That little prick's just come out of a fucking war, you think he's going to lie down and let you gut him? Because it's got to be first time, you got to disable a man with one blow, 'cos if you don't get him first, then he knows he's fighting for his life and maybe *he's* not in trouble anymore, maybe *you* are.' Vasilios invoked the Almighty and all the saints as Kostas stood with his head bowed, 'a knife, think about it, a knife: the blood all over everywhere. All over you. Throw the body in the sea, and it comes back on that evening's tide, an identifiable body covered in knife wounds. That'd stop everyone from talking, wouldn't it? You're a sad fucking excuse for a man.'

Kostas bit his lip, looking miserable, Vasilios continued, 'you've been fucking about with the xenie and they are...' he searched for the word, 'unpredictable. Stick with your own kind in future. Have some kids, that will quieten you down.'

'So what do you want me to do?' Kostas said quietly.

Vasilios nearly exploded, 'I want you to shut the fuck up, go home, shag your missus, I suppose you're good for that at least. You've done enough. Now do nothing.'

Kostas went off in a bad mood to his new bride and his guests.

Aspasia had already returned to her lair. She sat fuming on the day's events. She could have put on a better party for Kostas than the one she had just left, she could have been the hostess, but the bride's family had objected, as if they were any better than she was. Then she'd been insulted in the church and they had all tittered about it. Sitting at her dressing table taking off her make-up she could hear the music from Café Europa.

Aspasia thought grimly they could make as much noise as they liked, both Vasilios and the Mayor had got it in for them, and they controlled the island. She picked up her phone and called the Mayor, who was not particularly keen on receiving calls from her and certainly did not relish receiving them late at night when he was with his family. 'I've got to take this,' he said, and slipped out to the veranda.

He held the phone to his ear and heard Aspasia ranting about the xenie disturbing the peace of the island. She held the phone up for him to hear what was at that time King Crimson rolling across the bay. He suppressed a laugh and said, 'It's the Greek in her, she's spirited.'

Aspasia spluttered, 'You've got to get rid of her.'

'We'll do it my sweet,' said the Mayor, 'got to go,' and he shut the phone up.

After midnight, when the night was rounded off with Stairway to Heaven, as was only proper for such an event, the team turned off the sound system and cleared the detritus of the party. Sven and Sarah flopped down at a table looking on to the beach, still too excited to sleep. The others went to their rooms and left them to their conversation.

'Sven,' said Sarah, looking resplendent in the moonlight, 'I know I've been stupid and it can't have been easy for you.' That was the nearest Sarah ever got to an apology: if the subject of an anticipated apology was something she had done, it could not be wrong, for she could never be in the wrong, so she was not sorry, but she was certainly sympathetic to the negative outcome of her actions on others. 'I regret I ever met Kostas.'

'I bet he's sorry he ever met you,' smiled Sven.

'Well,' she said, sipping a glass of wine, 'I gave him a wedding to remember, something to talk about in times to come.'

'Weddings are very important in this culture,' said Sven.

'Yes,' she conceded, 'and my relationships are something I think are important. Kostas treated my relationships lightly, so I've done the same to him. So it's a cultural interchange. Let's say we've both learned something. Now we understand each other better.'

'So much for getting on with the natives,' he said. Sven was losing his respect for modern Greek culture in all its manifestations. Perhaps, he realised in the light of the persecution of Café Europa, he ought to be more discriminating. 'Ulysses' men were like that' he said, looking out into the wine-dark sea, 'like

Kostas, headstrong and quick to anger, greedy for booty and women, recklessly taking their own decisions when to submit to leadership would have been wiser, thinking always of short-term personal gain rather than the long-term benefit of all.'

'Yes, I think you've got him worked out,' she said, with genuine respect.

'It is difficult to understand such behaviour back home,' said Sven, 'but here in this landscape, it is easier. I think I finally understand Homer.'

'Isn't education a wonderful thing?' she said, and reflected, 'I thought you'd be appalled at what I did.'

'You were bold, you refused to be humiliated, I admire that. Half of being a great soul is not to do any ignoble thing; the other is not to allow ignoble things to be done to you. I think you passed the test there.'

'You mean you think I've gone native?'

'Perhaps. I admire you for it, you did what you felt was right and you didn't stop to think or be talked out of it. You were true to yourself. You did what you wanted to do at the time, you didn't pretend you didn't want to, or swallow the insult.'

Once Sarah used to love looking at the blond hairs on his strong, sinewy arms; then at one time, after she had gone with Kostas, she couldn't stand the sight of him; now she didn't feel desire or resentment but was just comfortable with Sven.

Out of nowhere, across their glasses on the table, with the sea sucking at its pebbles beside them, Sven said, 'my family was involved in supplying the Nazis with war materials,' Sarah looked quizzically at him, 'I've never said anything.'

'Since it all happened forty years before you were born,' she said, 'the effect of saying anything would have been….'

'Yeah. Limited as to its outcome. It's not that I could have changed anything, but I never even said anything, to my grandfather, the one who just died, he was primarily responsible. I should have said something, not just gone along as if it had never happened and I didn't care.'

'When did you find out?'

'I pretty much always knew. It's no secret in Sweden. I suppose I started to care when I was about sixteen.'

Sven had always wanted to know what she was thinking, as if knowing everything would give him peace. Now he didn't really care what she was thinking. In fact Sarah was thinking of how she did not quite comprehend basing your actions today on your revulsion at the behaviour of people in the past, but she was pleased to be let off the hook for her infidelities because Sven was contemplating his family's war history.

They walked up to the Wendy House, she wanted him to put out his hand to take hers but he did not, and they went to their respective rooms. Sven was thinking he loved Anton, and how nothing he could do eased the pain of that, how everything was trundling into disaster because he, Sven, was weak and unworthy.

Chapter 12

The next morning in his office the Mayor casually asked Alekos who had been at the Café Europa party the previous night. He listened to the names with a quiet thoughtfulness and made no comment. There were people with whom he did not want to argue on that list.

Alekos and Theophilus were able to assure the Mayor with perfect honesty that they had nothing to do with the attack on the Café Europa jeep, though they were unused to candour and felt obliged to leave the suspicion that they might have been, or that they knew who did. The Mayor knew it was most likely to have been Vasilios's crowd, but he had to appear ignorant before Alekos and Theophilus who, of course, knew that the Mayor probably knew who had attacked the vehicle, but also knew that he would not be sharing any information with them.

'I didn't think it would go this far,' said Alekos. The Mayor looked at him with disdain, but the more they mused, the less comfortable the whole thing seemed. However, none was willing to back down in front of the others and be the first to call a halt to it. All contemplated their fallback positions, if it became an embarrassment. Alekos remembered he always had reservations about the scheme; the Mayor recalled he was assured by Theophilus and Alekos that it would work. Theophilus reassured himself that he was just obeying the orders of the Mayor. Still, the business at hand was what to do next about Café Europa.

'So how do you prosecute over this food hygiene thing?' The Mayor asked Theophilus, smartly moving the imperative for action from himself to the little man.

His functionary effortlessly batted this back, 'I guess you send Papadopoulos to arrest her, sir.'

'I've spoken to him,' said the Mayor, 'he says he can take her to the police station to talk about it, but he can't hold her, what charge? Take her to court for breaking what law?' All three men mentally chimed in the unasked but blindingly obvious question: *What's in it for him? Why should Papadopoulos put himself out over this?*

'She can afford her own lawyer,' said Alekos. Relying on his reputation as a man of culture and vision he looked ahead and said, 'Even if she is arrested for not closing down, because she doesn't have the food handling certificate we ask for...she goes to court and then what?'

The Mayor mused on this. The judiciary was not universally sympathetic to him. One of two available judges would oppose a case specifically *because* it came from the Mayor. The other could be cajoled, but then the Mayor would owe him, did he want to become indebted over this issue? These were the cares of state.

'She gets fined?' said Alekos, 'then she'll go to Rhodes to take the exam in Greek, she's not the sort to back down. Then she returns.'

The Mayor could see where this was leading. He had no problem with the creation of enemies, but there had to be some gain if he were going to wield his power, and there wasn't enough in this. He had to be decisive, however, or he lost his authority. He spoke quickly and dismissively.

'Let's just give the order to close, so closing her forcibly is a threat we could carry out at any time, but we don't have to do it. Maybe she will close. We'll see where it gets us. You can go now.'

Theophilus was disappointed, he had an excellent plan to order Café Europa to provide disabled access to the beach, now it wouldn't be needed.

Sarah woke to a hangover and more sunlight, always the brilliant sunlight on whitewashed walls. More sunlight, more sea smell, more sound of distant goat bells. Sometimes in these days Sarah yearned for the warm beer smell of the student union bar and, through the open doors, the green grass of Sussex highlighted against the red brick, all glowing in the northern light. It was somewhere where people didn't blow up your car or lie to you about getting married – getting married! For chrissake! I mean, you could lie about how much money you had left or how long your course work took you to do, but to be screwing another girl when you were getting married! For the first time her fury over the situation subsided enough for her to feel merely foolish for having ever trusted Kostas. On the whole, she preferred rage, so she stayed annoyed, and amused at her humiliation of him.

The students had qualms about their situation but were beginning to feel the ebb and flow of island passion. The possibility of a torch-wielding mob marching towards Café Europa, like an image from 1960s horror films, receded from their minds. The islanders were not sharpening sticks at both ends for the display of captured heads; that was not how this was going to be played out. Café Europa was furnishing much-needed gossip for the island, and not all of it negative. They were still having more visitors from among the local Greeks, maybe they were just curious, to see this xenie woman who was standing up for herself and her attractive young helpers.

The students trailed down to breakfast, all still tired after yesterday's long day of excitement that had kept them awake almost twenty-four hours, but eager to see each other and plot the next move. Hester had gone off early to see her solicitor in town.

'If this was an adventure story,' said Anne, 'one of us would find the contraband and get kidnapped by the smugglers and the others would track them down and get the police.'

'Unless, of course, the smugglers are the police,' said Sarah.

'So there's a small flaw in the adventure story scenario, then,' conceded Anne.

Sarah was keen to show off her knowledge of the island, she did know more than any of the others about what went on, she had been deeper into the sheltered recesses of Doxos life. 'Anyway,' she said, 'I don't think we need to track down whatever is being smuggled in. If it was on Vasilios's boat it would end up in his warehouse in Kephali. So what? We're not going to do anything about it.'

'I didn't see our role as the island's enforcers,' said Anton, alert to the dangers of engaging with that aspect of Doxos life. 'Drugs, booze, tobacco? What does it matter to us if there's smuggling?'

'What does a drug warehouse look like?' said Anne.

'It looks like a warehouse, dummy,' said Sarah, 'the same one they use for handling the soft drinks trade.'

'Oh, I suppose it's not all shiny, like a pharmaceutical factory. Maybe we should have a look at it.'

'Maybe we should leave the thinking to the grown-ups,' said Sarah.

'We need,' mused Sven, to use the abilities we have, we have a lot of skills, but we have to know how to deploy them.'

'Skills?' said Anton, 'we are like super-heroes in reverse, we have powers that aren't actually any use. Sven always tells the truth, I am good at general knowledge questions, Anne is truly caring, Hester is Mrs Angry and Sarah, well, Sarah...'

'Shags the locals' said Anne.

'Yeah, OK shags the locals.'

'Steady on, crew,' Sarah said. She was glad her transgression had become a subject of humour rather than resentment, but still felt guilty about her liaison with Kostas, as if she had let the side down, a guilt which made her more truculent, 'Hey it wasn't me that was taking pictures of the smugglers,' she said.

'I wasn't taking pictures, I was just there,' Anne protested, 'keeping Malik company, and he was waiting for a boat that never came.'

'That's alright then,' said Sarah.

The conversation was ended by the arrival of Hester back from the solicitor's in the little blue Ford that Jess and Pete had loaned her. She was wearing a white skirt and green blouse with a white linen jacket, the nearest thing to a business suit anyone wore in this hot climate.

'They've ordered us to close by the end of the month, that's the end of this week,' she said flatly.

'If you don't do it, what happens then?' asked Sven

'Send the heavies in?' said Sarah, trying to envisage what that would entail.

'We've got a real problem here,' said Hester,

'everything I own is in this restaurant, I can't let them take it away.'

'What did the solicitor advise?' asked Sven.

'He said just state my case, with a copy of my hygiene certificate - and leave it to them to make the next move.'

'When is this test in Rhodes?'

'Next month, I'd lose the rest of this season if I stopped everything to take a test; it would ruin me and it wouldn't get them off my back, they'd think of something else. The tourism ministry in Athens said it's up to the local authorities, they can't step in.'

Sven hugged the slim woman, 'You'll make it work,' he said, 'you always do.'

Hester went to brood in her office. She was not so sure she *would* make it work this time. The way it had gone was that the students provided the ideas, Hester provided the nurturing and the willpower. Hester would say, 'I'm not going to stand for it' and they would work out the means of resistance while she brought refreshing cold drinks. Now it was becoming grim, she was tired with the weight of work, of running the business, with the grinding of the constant opposition, dodging the authorities and wondering where the next blow would come from, with the long days and the sleepless nights.

She wanted to fight the bastards. Every instinct she had told her that if you are under attack you fight back, but how? Hester looked out at the little yachts on the sea and the castle-topped mountain on the far side of the bay. Sven was right, she would make it work, but how?

She had increasingly come to rely on Sven as a strong, calm figure in the world of Café Europa. Anton's mind was too intensely focused, Anne was too ditzy, Sarah too idle, but Sven was hard-working, helpful, and no bad thing to look at.

Hester had hoped Greece would be different, but it was part of a pattern in which she had made life-choices which had found her with the employment, the location and the sex partner who would bring her the most misery. She had the unerring ability to enter a crowded room, locate the most inappropriate man and, by the end of the evening, contrive a way to lie under him.

She had not been happy with her men, indeed, she had been unhappy with such regularity it seemed to Hester that she could not have planned misery with greater efficiency. It had been hard work, it had all been her motivation: the moves, the businesses, the ambitious job applications. Occasionally she had supported men who were indifferent students to get to the position at which they would either fail in their studies or, the ones who could pass muster would, equipped with their higher degree, leave her for a more tractable woman.

There was no shortage of men willing to take up the Hester treatment for eighteen months or two years, knowing her steely character would stiffen their backbone, but once the therapy was over, they would use the escape hatch. Not even marriage would keep them, it would merely make their departure more protracted and complicated.

Of the assortment of men she had been allotted, each one had seemed good. They had been withdrawn, examined, carefully nurtured and put to use, and all turned out duds. There was not a single long-staying boyfriend or husband among them; all petered out after short-term application. Now she did not bother. If sex came her way she took it and was grateful or disdainful as the act merited.

Her analysis was fine so far as it went, but as her judgement was the only judgement she had, it was of questionable use in leading to a course of action. Was Sven one of these boy-men, she pondered. He certainly liked to be told what to do. Sven admired her courage and determination, her refusal to be beaten, her criticism of corruption, but did he find her attractive? He was a real friend of Anton's and that pleased her. If he was going spare, maybe they could do something together. She might meet a humiliating rejection from him – he hadn't exactly been flirting either, but he did not seem a man given to flirting at the best of times.

Anne hung back as they went about their tasks. She was upset that Sarah had been spiteful to her, just when she thought they were getting along well again. Anton hadn't helped, either. She looked for reassurance from him. 'Anton,' she said, 'can I ask you something. What did you mean when you said I was a prize?'

Anton sometimes did not say anything, if from experience he felt it would make him seem odd, but he always answered a direct question without evasion; it was one of the things that endeared him to Sven. He said, 'If I am not weird enough for a bit I get to have a real relationship, I get you, a prize for not being weird.'

'So what do you want?' Anne meant what did he want from her, but he misunderstood. 'I more often think of what I don't want and try to avoid it,' he said, 'I try not to be a nerd.'

'I thought nerds were high-earning experts and innovators.'

'Not when they're twenty they're not. I know I'm serious and intellectual, but I don't want to be nerdy.'

'Why not?' her voice was squeaky and pleading.

'I need the sex now, not later when I'm a high-earning expert,' he said absently, not contemplating how important the subject was to her, his mind homing in on a menu.

She was welling up to be upset but could see he was distracted, 'What are you thinking?' she asked him.

'I'm thinking,' he said, 'is it possible to make stifado with fish? Why was it always beef, what proportions should be used, is it to do with the moisture?'

'OK, see you later,' she said, feeling relegated and hoping her quick dismissal of him would be as wounding as his was to her, though in fact he did not notice.

She took the car and went off to her refugees, picking up Malik at the compound gates. He was sometimes the only person she felt at all comfortable with; he didn't fit in, much the same way that she didn't.

To her greeting he said, 'My heart is singularly heavy.' He explained that sealed military lorries had come and taken some people off. Where? Perhaps back to Afghanistan which was now said to be safe, though he suspected it was no different from when he left. Anyway, safety was the least of his concerns, he had his fortune to seek.

'I can't go back,' he said pressing his knuckle to his mouth, looking out of the window at the rocks and brush.

They collected their supplies and Anne looked at her watch and said, 'Let's drive around the island a bit,' Anne just couldn't restrain herself; she wanted a look at that warehouse. She would go and look, just look, and find something out that would help them, that would redeem her. There weren't so many roads in Kephali, maybe she would be able to see something that would help Café Europa, just sniff around a bit.

'Do you have time?' he asked

'Mmm,' she said, 'Sarah's working this morning, I am on tonight.' Malik thought: *there was Sarah, unpunished and unrepentant; this morality they have in Europe is a rum thing*, but he said nothing.

Malik continued his English education. 'What is a cucumber sandwich?' he asked, 'why is it special?' Anne did her best to explain.

Kephali was a spit of land on its way to becoming an archipelago, where the sea and occasional earthquake had worn away at a neck of land, on the other side of which was the head. Kephali, home to a few hundred souls with a semi-independent attitude to the island, as if the head had already broken off from the neck and declared itself an autonomous state.

Crossing the neck with the sea on one side, they drove down a road like any other, with modern whitewashed houses with wrought iron gates, and sometimes brightly coloured plastic children's toys in the forecourts. There was a booth where a man sold cigarettes and ice cream, a closed pizza bar and a general store.

One road was clearly a dead end, the other went up to the left so the little blue car trundled down it. The warehouse, behind a chain link fence, was constructed from aluminium panels with a large shutter at the front that could be raised to let a truck through. There was a Land Rover on the tarmac frontage and Anne jumped as she saw Kostas, smoking a cigarette and fiddling with his red motor bike.

He looked up, saw her, she gave a weak smile and drove on, flushing with embarrassment. She looked to the road ahead, suddenly noticing how hot it was and bursting into a sweat. She hoped for a turning right or left but there was none, it just petered out. It was necessary to make a turn in the road just past the warehouse but she struggled with the gear lever and the clutch in the unfamiliar vehicle and stalled it.

In the rear view mirror she could see, behind her, Kostas walking over the forecourt of the warehouse and up to the car. She wound down the window with its old-fashioned handle. Kostas leaned over with his usual smile a little strained today.

'Hi,' Anne said brightly.

'Having trouble?' he asked.

'Just stalled, I'm not used to this gear box.'

'What are you doing up here?'

'Just driving round the island, to see it all.' Her mouth became busy in her nervousness, 'we thought there's be a point at Kephali to look out to sea but...

'Just houses,' he said, 'no reason for you to be here.'

'Yes, just houses,' she said, 'we found that out, better get back, don't want to keep you from your work.'

'Every time I turn around I see you two,' he said. He looked past Anne at her small passenger, 'You,' he said to Malik, 'you are lucky to be alive.'

'Nice to see you too old chap,' said Malik, knowing he was in no immediate danger.

Anne drove off, feeling guilty that she has put Malik in harm's way, it wasn't necessary for her to go up there, she had been stupid. She drove as fast as possible back to the compound, swiftly wound up her business there and said goodbye to Malik.

Kostas watched Anne and Malik drive off, walked past his motorcycle and went straight into the warehouse. Inside one corner sheets of polythene hung from the aluminium ceiling rafters. Within the polythene bubble, with the patience of craftsmen, a couple of men were working on trestle tables clearing up the plastic packaging that had covered the consignment pulled out of the water by the Spirit of the Island crew. This job was nearly at an end.

Kostas found Vasilios in his office, 'Boss, I've just seen something,' he said. It was rarely that Kostas could command Vasilios's full attention. Now Vasilios looked into his dark eyes as Kostas told him the same foreigner and the same refugee that he had seen at the quay had just been seen outside. Vasilios's quick mind pictured the xenie hanging about when the Spirit of the Island docked, the Mayor telling him xenie had visited the Coastguard, now xenie around his warehouse.

'Time for a clear message,' said Vasilios quietly, 'I'm going to try something.'

'Let me get rid of him, that little Asian,' Kostas said, 'if we did anything to the girl, there would be too much fuss. She will go home soon anyway. But he's not someone anyone would miss. It would be like killing their dog, they would take notice, no one else would care.'

'I like your thinking,' said Vasilios, 'but don't do anything, I'll make a call.' Kostas went to speak but he said, 'I'll deal with it.'

Kostas went morosely outside to his lookout post. He brooded over his resentments: he held Malik responsible for giving away his affair with Sarah, which he connected with Sarah's making a scene at his wedding, something she surely wouldn't have done if she still had a boyfriend. Plus, the little pup was always around, as if under his feet, he didn't just stay in the compound like the others, where no one needed to think about them at all. Kostas also wanted an education, wanted the skills, to know how to make someone disappear, and he could practise on this one. He had a hankering for certainty over his engagement with mortality: he wanted to be *sure* he had killed someone.

Back at Café Europa, Anton had been told by Anne to pay more attention to Sven. The previous night in bed she had said she was worried about Sven, 'he's not funny anymore.'

Anton had commented that Sven wasn't always a bundle of laughs but that was not what Anne had meant, 'He's not finding things amusing,' she said.

'Is that how you tell, how you know someone's not in their right mind?' Anton had said, always eager to learn new facts.

So this morning found Anton pleasing Sven by asking him to join him while he prepared the vegetables on the wide table in the kitchen smelling of cooked garlic, olive oil and oregano. Anne was right. When Sven was away from the passion of the fight he felt as if his mind settled into dull anomie, there didn't seem any point in anything; even his work on his dissertation had lost its savour.

'All this stuff, this country,' Sven said, in inexact phrasing for him, 'where is it going, what's going to make it better?'

'They get tired, start persecuting someone else, perhaps?' Anton was taking the cores from a pile of fresh green peppers and slicing up the flesh into juicy strips that he threw in a stainless-steel colander.

'I don't mean just with us, with Café Europa, but this country, the corruption, the bad debts, the lack of planning...'

'Free trade,' said Anton blankly, aware of the inadequacy of his response, 'competition within a country gives you better quality services, and the improving influence of contact with other countries...people with more sophisticated practices coming to visit or trade, teach everyone how to do things better...'

'Bullshit,' said Sven, surprising Anton as he rarely swore. 'My family's lesson in free trade came when they sold steel to the Nazis so they could process it in slave labour camps and make bombs to drop on Britain. They took advantage of the steel shortage and sold in a buying market, very good business, a triumph of the entrepreneurial spirit. So Sweden stayed a successful democracy. Don't think we had much positive influence on the clients, though, for all our sophistication and tolerance. I don't know how I have lived in my family, with the lies of it all.' Anton looked at him, willing him to continue, 'My grandfather, the one who died, he was pro-Nazi, supported *Nysvenska Rörelsen*, New Sweden, they wanted to end Swedish neutrality.'

'And not in a good way'

'No. Though he was young then, he was in charge of our steelworks during the war.'

'How did your family cope with that,' asked Anton, putting down his knife, 'in the end, after it was obvious they'd backed the wrong side?'

'My family was full of lies and justifications – Sweden was the richest country in Europe after the war, so they were pleased they had got strong enough to help other countries in reconstruction.'

'So helping the Nazis was justified because it gave an opportunity for later altruism? Sweet.'

'Does it make a difference to you,' asked Sven, 'thinking about European history, being partly Jewish?'

'Not at all,' said Anton, for whom present being was all-important, drowning out any influence from background inheritance, 'my father was Jewish but he didn't practise anything...except the saxophone, and that didn't have much of a message...except for true believers. I'm not even circumcised.'

'Why not?' Sven said, enjoying a conversation that put the focus on his friend's penis.

'My father couldn't care less about religion and my mother wouldn't have seen a spiritual value in genital mutilation, New Age hippie though she was, she would probably have prized the idea of a cock ring more.'

'But she didn't go down that route either?'

'I don't think she could focus on one thing for long enough...' but Anton was uncomfortable with personal revelation, and moved the conversation back, saying, 'Sven, you should not blame people for what their ancestors did. Or we'd all be saying sorry about slavery forever and the Romans would have to beg forgiveness for the rape of the Sabine women – picturesque, I suppose. Even the Germans have stopped saying sorry now. I don't think the Austrians ever were very sorry....anyway, almost all the people who did those things are dead now. Let their guilt die with them. I think you can give yourself a break.'

'We still have the money,' said Sven, as if pleading, 'It's not national responsibility I am thinking of but personal, what should I do? The wealth we have, that allows me to live the way I do now, my trust fund, came from that tainted source.'

'I'd say it's long since been recycled and renewed. Maybe when you get your inheritance you can give it away – or some of it, but do something final, it shouldn't be your responsibility for the rest of your life. Feel guilty for things you've done yourself – or will do.'

'That's good advice. You always give good advice.'

'I just say the logically obvious thing.'

'Not everyone does.'

Sven was moving closer to Anton as if to hug him but Anne appeared in the door. As she entered the restaurant Anne felt as if she was returning to safety from a world of danger. She confided her fears for Malik's future in the Greek asylum system, without mentioning she had been foolish enough to go up to Kephali. The day's evils were sufficient for her, without making a display of her guilt. She slipped in beside Anton and began to help him cut and slice.

Vasilios called the Mayor that afternoon but he was unreceptive, their business was settled, Vasilios couldn't be calling him up for favours every week.

After a few pleasantries Vasilios said, 'That refugee kid that's hanging around with the xenie, you know who I mean?'

'Yes, I've seen him,' said the Mayor, who had in fact been brooding over the Café Europa crowd, and wishing they would all go away. Nothing connected to them seemed to be conducive to the easy life in office to which he aspired.

'Can you get rid of him? Are there ways you can get him off the island?' Vasilios said lightly.

'What interests you about him?' the Mayor started doodling a skull and crossbones on his jotter.

'He saw us, saw us coming back on the boat, after we had picked up the merchandise that we had gone out for. And he's been seen near where we work, with one of the xenie.'

The Mayor was very quick on the uptake, particularly where the possibility of embarrassment or shame was concerned. He turned his pencil around and rubbed out the sketch. 'I don't know anything about any boat,' he said, 'and if I started getting involved with the refugees that would attract more attention, not less. People would start saying why am I interested in one of them in particular? There's something else you need to know: Frontex, the EU border people are coming here on an inquiry about refugee boats: where they come from, who's funding them, about how we treat them, boats lost at sea... They'll be sure to be asking questions round the refugee camp.'

Vasilios sucked his teeth and said nothing. They both knew they didn't want outside officials investigating what happened that night; soon they'd get round to asking the little refugee kid, who knows where that would end?

'We're in this together, I don't get in the way of business,' the Mayor said.

'As if you could,' said Vasilios.

'Hear me out, cousin,' said the Mayor, 'I don't get involved because everything runs well, it's got to keep running well. No fuss.'

Vasilios was irritated because to admit all had not been smooth was to admit a failure and Vasilios was not practised at such admissions. He ended the conversation in a bad humour.

At the end of the day when the others were leaving, Vasilios called Kostas to him.

'I think it's time I showed you how to make people go away, efficiently and quietly,' Kostas sat and leaned forward attentively. Vasilios began, 'A knife's good, no noise, but much too messy. You can shoot, but you have to carry the gun around with you, not so easy in summer – where do you put it, in your jeans? Plus, a gun's valuable you don't want to throw it away, and if the law gets hold of the gun, they can link it to maybe several different shootings, maybe ones you had nothing to do with. Then you could be in trouble.' Kostas absorbed this information, his handsome face showing keen attention. 'Here's your weapon of choice,' said Vasilios, producing a length of fishing wire with a handle at each end, 'the garrotte. It's quick, if you've got the element of surprise; easy to handle for a strong lad if you don't mind getting close; quiet if you use it right; easy to make, easy to carry; easy to use, easy to dispose of.' He put the makeshift weapon on the desk and Kostas picked it up, testing its tensile strength. It was a hangover from the days of the Greek civil war when those who had political differences fought them out and those who had old scores to settle did so under the guise of politics. The knuckle duster, the stabbing knife and the garrotte were instruments of the civil war that continued into the civil peace that followed.

Vasilios taught Kostas to study the movements of his subject, to catch him unawares in a quiet place, to conceal and transport the body for disposal. 'You don't want to go hiding the body in a cave, some idiot climbing around will find it. If there's big building work, your body can go in there and get some concrete in on top, no one will find that, but you probably have to let someone else in on it, someone to let you on site, tell you when the cement's wet. The best way is this: body weighted down, dropped in the sea, doesn't even have to be too far out, then the fishes do the job for you.'

Kostas grinned, he loved to learn. He felt proud he had an uncle who so dutifully showed him the ways of the world.

Hester was sorting out the morning's takings. She and the students got together around one of the long tables and contemplated their doom. Tomorrow they had to close or face the worst the island could offer.

'So who could make it different? Who knows what all this was about?' asked Anton, ever eager to comprehend.

'The Mayor, probably,' said Sven 'that's his job, keeping an eye on things.'

'And I thought it was making sure the drains work and filling potholes in the roads,' said Anne.

'Have you seen the state of the drains here?' said Sarah in mock amazement, 'the Mayor hasn't been preoccupied with the drains recently. He's been busy lining his pockets with EU money.'

'Do share,' invited Hester, pouring herself a coffee. They turned their heads towards Sarah in expectation like an array of satellite dishes.

Sarah was eager to reintegrate herself into the Café Europa circle, and to demonstrate how helpful the knowledge gained with Kostas could be. She wanted her relationship with Kostas to be an asset to them, not an embarrassment. 'Kostas thought the Mayor an idiot because he has taken so much money from the airport project that he is going to get caught.'

'Kostas thought the embezzlement was wrong?' asked Anton.

'Er...not so much,' said Sarah, 'He thinks the Mayor was stupid for almost getting caught. The German contractors nearly pulled out last month because they weren't being paid.

'So there's a big hole in the finances, that doesn't surprise me,' said Sven.

'Everyone suspected something like that,' said Hester.

Sarah enjoyed being a positive centre of attention again. She said, 'The Mayor calls himself father of the island – the joke is that he takes it literally, given the number of illegitimate kids he's got.'

'So he's open to that sort of thing? That's interesting to know,' said Hester.

'Knowledge is power' said Anton.

'I think he's shagging Aspasia,' Sarah said. In fact she did not think it, she knew it, but she was nervous of revealing too much of what she had learned from Kostas in case she would be accused of previously withholding it from the team, and that would impede her rehabilitation.

'That would certainly explain a lot,' said Hester, 'though I thought Aspasia's days of harlotry were at an end. I would have thought the moving parts would have been worn out by now.'

'Gross!' said Sarah, glad to be back in the swing of things.

'I've been thinking,' said Hester, 'The work we have been doing to the house and café, the way we haven't let them push us around, even Sarah's escapade at the wedding – even though it wasn't exactly the counter-strike I had been thinking of, it shows we've got balls. Now we have to be proactive, as the corporate motivational speakers put it. We've got to take the initiative.'

'That's inspirational,' said Sven 'but our problem is not presentation, we're not trying to sell a product. Look, we think they are smuggling, maybe dope, we know the mayor has been corrupt over the airport development, a boat load of refugees went missing in mysterious circumstances: how does any of that help Café Europa?'

'They've got a lot to hide haven't they?' said Anne. Sarah nodded, she too had learned the locals' love of subterfuge. For all their expressive Mediterranean manners, they liked their secrets.

'From whom?' said Hester, 'the Greek authorities are either in it with them or are looking the other way. There aren't enough of us foreigners to make a difference, and the expats that are here are all too unconcerned, they came here for an easy life. We need reinforcements.

'We need a powerful ally,' said Sven, 'someone who would shake out their dark corners.'

'At one time,' said Anton, 'in one of the sieges by the Ottomans, all the Knights of St John in Doxos castle were dead, except one. He was just eighteen, but he defended the castle against the Turks by dressing women and children in the armour of dead defenders. He kept them moving about on the battlements so the Turks thought the place was well defended and they went home, they didn't push their last assault.'

'And your point is...?' said Sarah.

He turned to her, surprised she had asked the obvious, 'We don't have to have reinforcements. We have to look like we have reinforcements. We have to look as if we've got more fire power than we have.'

'Like....?' said Anne.

'We need a government inspector, from the European Union, or someone who can call one in, to get some light in on Doxos. A credible representative of the real world.'

'Haven't got one of those,' said Sarah.

'We can make one,' said Anton, 'They know who we are, but they don't know who we are connected to, they don't know our families. Families are a big deal here. We're students but we could be related to someone powerful. We are only thinking about ourselves, what we bring to the party. They see us as members of a family.'

'A minister, a European commissioner?' said Anne

'It's too easy to check up on someone that important,' mused Anton, 'they'd be able to tell it was a fake. Just a civil servant or a member of parliament is enough.'

'Sven, didn't you say you have the same name as a Swedish MP?' Sarah said, 'people in Sweden ask if you are related to him...'

'Yes, they do that, though I am not,' said Sven who could see where this was leading.

'But you could be...' she pressed

'But I am not.'

'Come on,' said Sarah, 'for team Café Europa, for us....'

Sven shook his head as if upset that he should even be thought of, 'I can't pretend to be something I am not, I can't lie,' he said. He seemed so emphatic, the assertion of identity so clearly aimed at her, that Sarah raised her hands to show she had ceased resistance.

A little later they dispersed, uncertain of the future. Sarah and Anton went off and Anne started sorting out the tables for the evening. Hester, now alone at the table with Sven, tried another way. 'We've been getting this wrong,' she said, 'we've been playing it straight with them: tiling the toilet when they said they wanted it, paying the IKA tax, assuming we'd have to go to Rhodes to qualify for a food handling certificate. That's not what they do. They bribe and they lie, we have to work on deception. We shouldn't be countering their lies with the truth, or with efficiency, what we need is better lies.'

'I see what you are saying,' said Sven, 'but don't ask me to lie, to be something I'm not.'

Hester looked sideways at him and with a smile said, 'You've got to fake it to make it,' but he was not charmed by such cynical humour challenging a core ingredient of his personality. She turned the full allure of her eyes on him, a gaze no man, once in her ambit, had been able to resist. 'I'd really thank you for doing this for me, I'd consider it a real favour, she put her hand on his arm just above the wrist, 'I'd do anything for you.' She glanced down, as if only just realising the meaning of what she had said.

Sven looked back, not wanting to catch her eyes but looking slightly over her shoulder at the castle across the bay. 'Thank you, Hester,' he said, 'I like you, I admire your courage, your resistance, but I can't, I can't do what you want. I have to go now. No, thank you but no...'

And he went up the hill to his single room in the Wendy House.

'That didn't go so well,' said Hester to Anne who had reappeared from her tasks as Sven went off, 'my seductive powers have met their match, my desirability quotient has obviously gone down.'

'Don't take it to heart,' said Anne, then, wanting to

say something reassuring, 'wrong sibling... probably.'

'You what?'

'Sven's got a thing about Anton, haven't you seen the way he looks at him?'

Hester began staring intently at Anne. 'Yes, I suppose I have,' she said, 'but I didn't think anything of it, Sven was with Sarah so I didn't consider.... So that's why he always wanted to talk to me about Anton, I suppose I should have guessed. Do you think if Anton tried? Sven might comply?'

Anne giggled, 'I think he'd have more chance than you...or me,' she added, not wanting to suggest the inferiority of Hester's charms.

'Let's ask him,' Hester said, 'ask Anton to persuade Sven to help. It was Anton's idea after all.'

'I'll ask,' said Anne. She was still feeling guilty about Malik, that the Afghan's contact with them had not been entirely to his benefit and had probably endangered him. She had been musing on Kostas' words, 'You are lucky to be alive,' that on the surface were comforting but sounded like a threat. She wanted to ask for a reciprocal favour from Hester but knew this was not the right time.

Hester called into the kitchen for Anton to join them. Anne explained their thinking, 'Your plan for someone with family connections to shake up the authorities here, it's a good idea, but Sven's all we've got to make it work, it's got to be an unknown factor. They know everything there is to know about Sarah, down to her shoe size; they know a bit about you and Hester's family; I haven't got the...gravitas. They all know too much about Britain anyway, but Sweden is far enough to be exotic, no one would have the language to do more than a cursory check, and Sven looks the part...Do you think you could talk Sven into being our representative from the real world?'

Anton looked to Hester, as he did when he was uncertain of a response. She nodded, 'Anne's on to something, would you persuade him?'

'I could see us getting into the metaphysics of morals with asking him to play a part,' said Anton, 'I could try but I don't see why he should listen to me.'

'Because he...he cares about you.'

'What?' he said, not appreciating the meaning.

'You mean you really haven't noticed the way he looks at you?'

'Hmm, I just thought he was concentrating particularly closely on what I had to say.' So Anton wandered up the hill to the Wendy House where he found Sven in his room with the door wide open, sitting on a low chair reading a book with a cover showing a contemplative warrior leaning on his sword.

Anton sat on the bed and with his usual lack of guile said, 'I am an emissary from the world of plotters.' Sven nodded, 'They want you to pay the part of a well-connected Swede.'

'What do *you* want?'

'I want you to do it as well.'

Sven looked down at his book, 'I've been reading about the heroes of old.'

'Ulysses was hardly Mr Truthful, and he won the war.'

'Those men in their boats and their camps on the shore...do you ever feel; the need for purely masculine contact, Anton?'

'What like the D.H.Lawrence thing, nude wrestling? Now there's a contact sport. It'd be Greek at least.'

'That would be an idea but it wasn't what I was

thinking of...'

'Sven I'll do what you like. If there was anything I could do, tell me. I know I'm asking you a difficult favour.'

Sven was not sure if he was approaching the end of his life, there seemed a geometry about decline and depression these past weeks, where the only thing that was really worth staying alive for was Anton's company. This was, he felt, his last chance, if he told the truth about nothing else or never said another thing, he must speak now.

He let the living stream flow, 'I need to be truthful: I love you, I don't know what I am doing, I think about you all the time, I don't feel I can live without you...' The trite phrases that Anton remembered from light fiction spilled out of his friend's mouth, bursting out as if from a broken dam. Sven sank in a fluid movement onto the floor, so he was kneeling in front of Anton. He hunched his shoulders and buried his head in his hands, sobbing silently.

Oh no, thought Anton, *here's another time I'm alone with someone and I don't know what to do.* Anton did not understand homosexuality, it was one of those areas, like religion and anti-Semitism that he could know about, he could see the objective evidence for it, but couldn't see himself in it, couldn't see the reason for it, the value of it, the joy in it. An anti-Semitic homosexual, on his knees in prayer would be the embodiment of an enigma for Anton. He could go part of the way: he supposed that in a situation where there were no women, men might obtain the required orgasm by penetrating each other, but the thought of wanting to do it, to do it in preference to sex with girls, when girls were ready and willing, was foreign to him. So he did not accept or reject Sven's glances, they simply did not translate into anything approaching real choices. But here he was, being presented with a situation. Anton therefore did nothing, waiting for another cue from Sven.

Eventually Sven looked up. Anton nodded, waiting for his friend to speak. 'Did you know?' Sven said.

'No,' he said, 'I just like to be unsurprised. What would you like me to do?'

It was an epiphany, Anton framed in the light bouncing off the courtyard walls and through the open door, if ever there was a time for the truth this was it. *So what would you like me to do?* he had asked.

Sven knelt up and fixed Anton with his full gaze. 'I want you to fuck me,' he said. 'I love you, I want you to do it with me. I want you to fuck me. I want to see how it feels like.' His grammar was wavering, a sure sign of emotional distress in Sven. 'I want you to come into me, to know what it feels like to have sex with you. Love me, love me like you'd do it to a girl. Bugger me.'

'Not something I've done before,' said Anton, 'I didn't do that stuff when I was young, I was too busy studying, finding things out.' Anton did not like to dwell on his lack of close relationships with other boys, it was too suggestive of difference. 'If you don't do it then you lose the experience forever. You are unlikely to start shagging boys at forty, and it would probably be considered pervy if you did start then.' Here was an offer of an experience he had no reason for rejecting, except that it didn't particularly excite him. If he did it, however, he would please Sven and help Hester, and satisfy basic curiosity.

'Will you, with me then?' Sven said.

'Yes, I suppose so,' said Anton, thinking: *how difficult can it be? No more than entering a girl.*

'Do you want to?'

'You're my friend, and I want to make you happy, and it's an experience I haven't had before, and I know I'd regret it if I didn't seize the moment, so let's do it.' Dry mouthed in the hot afternoon, he led the way, 'Let's get naked, we'll see what we can do.'

They removed their few clothes showing the contrast between Anton's dark-haired body and Sven's blond nudeness. Sven embraced him, the Swedish boy's head was light from the sudden realisation of his dreams.

Anton was shorter than Sven and his penis not so long. It was surprisingly easy to get an erection, considering he hadn't been aroused by men before. Sven lay on his side on the bed. Anton thought it advisable to think about the entry rather than Sven's penis that had risen up like a classical column.

Anton chose not to look closely at the light hairs and the pink flesh, treating it as if he were entering a woman, he rubbed lubricant on, excited by an unexpected sexual charge.

'I'm going to come in you.'

'Come on, do it.'

Sven felt the entry as a searing pain that he resisted but desired at the same time. He experienced the unfamiliar feeling of a solid object inside him. He pressed down on it, to take the discomfort all in one movement and then rest with it suspended wholly with an excruciating pain that repelled and delighted. Taking Anton in and pressing down he drew him as deep as possible. All of his being was concentrated on that stiff thing inside him. For once in his life he was not contemplating the future or brooding on the past but was seizing the immediate need. It was not what coupling with Anton would lead to, but what it *was* that enthralled Sven. He needed to be invaded, penetrated, needed to have his body filled, the very thought of fluid shooting into his body cavity thrilled him. What a crazy desire, he thought, but how *right* it felt, to have Anton inside him.

Anton, unused to the male anatomy, did not know what to do with his hands and just kept them on Sven's haunches, exerting pressure to pull him in.

He fucked gently for a time, looking at Sven's glistening back. 'You alright, not too painful?' he asked.

'Do it like you do to Anne, come in me like you do it to her,' said Sven.

'OK' said Anton, surprised at how aroused he was at the forbiddenness of the exercise rather than its erotic content, and thrust determinedly to ejaculate in three surges.

'How was it for you?' he said, uncoupling.

'It was....different,' Sven said, laying his head down with a smile of deep satisfaction.

Anton gave him a hug. 'You're my friend, I hope I've given you what you wanted, did you enjoy it?'

'Yes, I didn't want to die without doing it,' he said.

'I don't want you dying at all,' said Anton, 'tomorrow, let's save Café Europa.'

Sven turned and embraced him and said 'Yes,' his naked body bathed in the sun and the erotic experience.

'Sorry, I've got to go,' Anton said, dressing, 'there's a restaurant to run, I've got to get back in the kitchen.

He returned to Café Europa and told Hester that Sven was with them, with no details, then joined Anne who had been dealing with a table of customers. Only now did it occur to him that she might have an opinion on what had just happened, that she might like to have taken into account.

'So how did you persuade Sven to renounce the Cult of Truth?'

'It was just a matter of pressing the right buttons,' said Anton, washing his hands.

'So what was it that made him do it?' she asked.

'He wanted me to shag him' he said.

She paused, 'I'm thinking he probably put it more delicately than that,' she said.

'Er...not much.'

Rather than reacting with outrage, Anne said, 'I always thought there was something like that about his relationship with you. Now, how could I tell?'

'I don't know, how could you tell? If you work it out, let me know,' said Anton, 'because I certainly don't. I thought he was just a friend.'

'So he'll help us if you go to bed with him?'

'It wasn't so explicit as that but...yes that's about it. That's what he wanted. He wanted a fuck.'

'So...you agreed?' She was swept with the realisation that the event had already taken place. 'So, what exactly did you do together?'

'Nothing that you and I haven't done,' he said, wondering if he should enumerate the things two men could do with their sexual equipment, but thought better of it. Anne looked down and even began to blush, something Anton found endearing, and he held her. He was just about to explain that Sven had wanted to be fucked the way Anton fucked Anne but thought better of it, for a reason he could not fathom, he somehow knew that would be the wrong thing to say. Instead he said, 'He was unhappy, it was what he wanted, so I did it.'

'Was it...just the once?' she said softly.

'I didn't have any more in me,' he said.

'I didn't mean that,' she said, 'I meant are you going to do it again, is it now part of your relationship with him?'

'Oh no, we haven't done a contract,' Anton said, 'I should hope not, I wasn't thinking of moving in with him and downloading some Judy Garland.'

She laughed 'Did you want to do it?'

'I've never done it before, and I haven't wanted to, but was an experience, so, yes, I liked to try it out.'

Anton's obvious lack of desire or emotional engagement made Anne feel the exercise was more acceptable. 'Please don't let this change anything, Anton,' she said.

'Why should it change anything?' he asked, in genuine surprise.

Anne looked at him with her head to one side as if literally seeing him in a different light. Some customers appeared and she had to get back to work.

Later, during a break, she sought out Sarah, finding her on a towel on the beach. Considering that Sarah had a stake in the matter, Anne told her about Anton and Sven. Sarah rolled her eyes in comic amazement. 'People do the funniest things,' she said, 'For Anton to give up his man cherry, wow...I don't know about Sven, whether he'd done it before, maybe they were both homo-virgins, quite sweet, really.'

'But,' Anne said, 'do you mind?'

Sarah was thoughtful for a moment, 'Yes,' she said, 'I suppose I do, but I haven't got much of a platform for complaint...you know, people in glass houses and all that....and I don't think I've got a right to, Sven and me aren't exactly together at the moment. I suppose it makes me feel a bit weird, but I'm not jealous like I would be if it was a girl. It might even make things better, Sexual Healing, one of my parents' favourite songs.'

'I think mine would have gone with Lead Kindly Light,' said Anne.

'Don't *you* mind?' asked Sarah, gathering up her towel and sun cream, 'I think you've got more right to than I have, you're in a relationship.'

'Anton treats the whole thing so lightly. He doesn't care, so why should I?'

'I suppose I think if I have any future at all with Sven,' said Sarah, 'he has the right to do something with someone else, after me and Kostas. I'm not so self-centred I couldn't see that. I just thought it would be a girl, I didn't think it would be boy-on-boy action but, you know, I'm the YouPorn generation – what the hell?'

'YouPorn - you mean you've grown up with different kinds of sex...'

'Yeah, and I'm not frightened of it, or even fascinated by it, it's just there like food and drink. There are things I won't eat, but I don't care if someone else chooses them, I'll have something else off the menu. I've tried most drinks once, but I stick to wine. I'm just not going to get hung up about what people do sexually.'

'I suppose travel broadens the mind,' said Anne, 'it's certainly broadened mine,' and returned to her tables.

Sven stayed in his room that evening, enjoying the satisfaction of a desire fulfilled. That night he dreamed of Gunnar the great warrior, dead and seated in his burial mound, laughing in the moonlight and singing songs.

Chapter 13

The next bright morning, now not too hot nor too cold, Grandma Poppy was taking her weekly shopping walk on the coast road round to Zeste, past the familiar smell of the kuri plants and wild flowers.

As she passed Aspasia's place the patroness, who was brushing leaves off her tables, took the opportunity to address the old woman on a subject that had been irritating her for some time. After the usual greetings, 'how are you – good, and you – me too – bravo,' Aspasia said, 'these foreigners: why are you so friendly with them? All this visiting them and greetings, how are you should have nothing to do with them.'

'They buy my pastries,' said Grandma Poppy, 'I have to speak to them.'

'You should not sell to them, you should care for your neighbours,' said Aspasia, 'you are unGreek to put foreigners first.'

'The foreigners *are* my neighbours, and they have been kind to me. They buy from me. When did you ever give me work, Aspasia?'

'You put yourself outside the affections of good Doxonians. I will give you no more help,' Aspasia said as she slapped her hands twice, crossways in a gesture of finality.

'So what help have you given me?' rejoined the old woman, 'how you going to give me less help? You going to take away help I've already got?

'You are not a Doxonian,' she said.

'I have never set foot off the island,' said Grandma, 'I have not been to Piraeus as you have.'

'I will have no more to do with you,' said Aspasia.

'Good, I don't even want you at my funeral.'

'I won't come.'

'Don't be so sure I'll die first,' the old lady said, though she was eighty if a day, and went off to her shopping, to tell everyone she saw along the way and in the grocers about her altercation with Aspasia.

Aspasia was full of rage, that an old peasant woman should answer her back. She, Aspasia, a property owner who had the Mayor of the island as her confidante. What was happening when people no longer knew their place? She called the Mayor to see when she would have the satisfaction of seeing Café Europa closed down. Over in the town hall, the Mayor looked at the display, saw who it was, and turned his phone off.

In Café Europa, Hester and Sven were preparing to go to town. Hester was dressing, finally settling on a blue blouse and white skirt, both of which could reveal, as she practised in the mirror, just enough to be agreeable but not vulgar. She made up under Anne's tutelage. 'You need more hints than statements,' the girl said, sitting in Hester's bathroom with her, 'bit of highlighter here, no foundation if you are out in daylight, the light's too bright here for that...' Hester had asked for advice on her appearance, not that she was in great need of it, but she wanted to engage everyone in the plan.

Over at the house Sarah was coaching Sven, 'The secret of a good lie is that you believe in it at the time,' she said, 'you don't question it or the other person will too...Try a small lie first, one that is obvious...tell me you are a champion diver.'

'I was almost on the Olympic team in 2008,'

'That's great, now tell me another one.'

'No, that is true.'

'Well tell me something that isn't.'

Sven looked blank.

'We all have to start with small lies,' Sarah said patiently, 'we teach children about little abstract concepts like fairies and Santa Claus so that they can accept the big ones like justice and fidelity.'

'I didn't know that's why we did that.'

'You have much to learn, O warrior of the north.'

She had Sven try to convince her that the table-top was wooden, not marble. She coached him, 'Don't look them in the eye when you are lying, that's what people do who are trying to convince you they are honest. So no wide-eyed expressions of honesty or pushed body language. You have to give them the information to process into their own reality. Take them on a journey, repeatedly seek affirmation of what is correct at each stage so it is hard for them to question because they have bought into it.'

'This is an art form, isn't it?' said Sven.

'Props are good,' she said brightly, 'show them something to back up the lie, you know, like the conman who shows you his bus pass pretending he's come to read the gas meter, then the person who is being lied to is engaged, has contributed something to it, now they believe in it too.

'Where did you learn to do all this?' he asked.

'They teach it to us at girl school.'

She left Sven to practise on his own.

Anne walked back up to the house, but was restless, unable to settle in her room. She had wanted to help Malik, had wanted to be a friend to him, instead she had led him into danger. When Anne heard Sarah leaving the house she went down to the little courtyard to speak to Sven.

He was staring into space, going through his exercises in lying, *'I am an atomic physicist, I am a government inspector, I am a large blue bunny rabbit...'*

Since having sex with Anton, Sven had felt squeamish about Anne, perhaps guilty, certainly awkward. He felt as if he should say something to indicate it was no reflection on her that he had had sex with her boyfriend, but there were no applications of tact that would suit this particular situation. He could not imagine that she did not know; Anton had no personal reservations, it was one of the things Sven found attractive about him.

She noticed the lines of strain around his mouth, this was not an easy day for him. 'I wanted to talk to you,' she said. He stiffened. 'About Malik,' she said. He was immediately relieved it wasn't about Anton. 'I'm worried about him, I think they'll just bundle him in a lorry and take him back to Afghanistan. His brother was killed by the Taliban, he's frightened that the same would happen to him.'

'I understand that, but how can I help?' Sven asked.

'Can you raise it with the Mayor? I want you to ask him to let Malik leave the island?'

'You don't make things easy, do you? I can promise to ask, I can't promise to get a positive result,' said Sven diplomatically, but glad Anne wanted a favour, it was something he could do in recompense. 'The Mayor may say all these issues of refugees are out of his hands.'

'I do just want to you to ask, then I will have tried,

I feel responsible.'

It might have been the feast day of the goddess Até when the others gathered to send Hester and Sven on their mission. With Sven also in blue, in a white shirt and powder-blue trousers, they had unintentionally matched their outfits with each other and to the colour of the vehicle. 'We will combine our various powers into an unstoppable machine,' she said, as they climbed into the car. Far from being ground down, Hester seemed to thrive on the conflict, Sven admired her for that and she knew it. She wondered if going through this shared operation of subterfuge would endear her to him...but she let the thought go, she had other things to do.

Sven was as nervous as if he were going into battle. He almost asked Hester to stop the car so he could throw up on the way, but gritted his teeth and went on. The spirit of Até the Great Deluder flew beside them on the road ranging around the island and up to the old town.

In the more temperate weather of the end of the summer the Mayor was in his shirt sleeves with the air conditioner off when they arrived to see him. They could hear the fishwife selling her wares from the back of a truck in the square outside through the open window. Hester noticed the nicotine-stained wooden panels from a more refined era and the harsh strip lighting installed in the 1980s as a concession to modernity.

The Mayor had asked Alekos to be present in case he needed translation, though the Mayor's English was good and Hester could cope in Greek. The Mayor shook their hands, he was about Sven's height but broader and almost twice his age. He took in Hester's height and figure without staring, but she noticed. He welcomed them to sit around the conference table.

'So glad to be able to meet the leader of this wonderful island at last,' she said, 'I wanted to make sure there was no doubt that the council had received a copy of my food safety certificate, at the highest level; and a letter from my solicitor explaining that we fulfil all reasonable requirements.'

'Thank you,' said the Mayor, not looking at the documents.

'I was hoping you would be able to help us, we would like to be treated in the same way as any other local businesses.'

The Mayor shrugged, 'All are treated the same, all are.'

Hester smiled indulgently, his brown eyes met her blue gaze. 'There seems to be a very high level of regulation on Doxos.'

The Mayor held his hands open, 'There is always more regulation, it is because of the European Union, always there are more rules.'

Hester argued that the island was better off only lightly regulated. The quality of island life should be preserved, people came to Doxos because it was different from everywhere else, not because it was the same. The Mayor saw value in this. Soon she was running out of things to say, with Sven having not yet contributed.

Hester went on as best she could, fearing she would exhaust her material and her time with the Mayor without Sven's input. Then he said simply, and looking at no one in particular, 'My uncle is a member of the Swedish parliament, I could ask him how things are done in other European Union countries, I am sure he would give good advice.'

The Mayor and Alekos slowly turned to Sven.

'Please tell us more,' said the Mayor.

Sven looked nonchalant, as if surprised they were so interested. He continued, 'He is Jan Ygeman, he has been in parliament many years,'

'That's the Riksdag,' said Alekos, pleased he could contribute from his store of knowledge.

'Yes, that's right,' said Sven, 'Uncle Jan was very interested in European affairs. He was one of the people recommending Swedish entry in 1995.'

'What is his name again,' said Alekos, 'I must look him up, we are honoured to have someone from such a distinguished family on the island.'

'The same as mine, my father's brother, Ygeman.' Alekos paused with his pen over the paper, straining at the unfamiliar consonants. Sven pulled out his wallet and gave Alekos his driving licence with the blue twelve-starred flag on it and his own name, Sven Ygeman, with a little picture of him looking severe. 'That's the spelling,' he said.

'Well it would be a pleasure to meet him if he ever visited the island, do let me know,' said the Mayor.

Hester crossed her legs so as to favour the Mayor, leaned over so her blouse fell open a little and looked in his eyes. He luxuriated in the exotic allure of this slim foreigner, who didn't have the pear-shape of a Mediterranean woman; she had small breasts, not melons, and not distended by childbirth. That was a point: down below – was she shaved or natural, he wondered, stroking his chin. Hester was at least ten years younger than he, and that appealed to his vanity; a younger woman without children: almost as good as a virgin.

Hester too appraised physical attributes. The Mayor had a belly but he was a big man and carried it well, he was handsome in a swarthy sort of way. He was pretty much in control of himself, didn't need to be told what to do, so not the sort of man she normally went for; and that was good.

They were about to leave and Sven said to the Mayor, 'Sir, one last thing, we have taken an interest in the welfare of one of the refugees.'

'I don't know why *we* have problems with these people,' said the Mayor, 'It wasn't Greece that invaded the Middle East…'

'Not this time,' said Sven with amusement, 'but if you think of Alexander the Great…' The Mayor waved his hand with a smile, he did not want to wade into areas where he was immediately out of his depth. 'Anyway it's a refugee called Malik, we have got to know him, his brother was killed by the Taliban in Afghanistan, is it possible to send him away, out of the island?'

The Mayor paid attention, it was the second time Malik had been mentioned to him in a week. 'If a member of his family has been killed and he fears for his life he has a case for asylum, we will give him leave to appeal his deportation order, he can go to Athens for that. Not a problem. I'll give the order to let him go, but you must pay his passage and see him on the ferry, I don't want refugees hanging round the island.'

'Agreed, and very much appreciated, sir,' said Sven

They had risen to leave and Alekos was chatting with Sven while he showed him out. Hester turned her eyes on the Mayor, standing fractionally closer than propriety would have demanded for a business meeting. Her eyes stared into his, a gaze no man had been able to resist, at least in the short term. 'I'd really appreciate you making things easier for us here,' she said, and put her hand on his arm just above the wrist, 'I should like you to visit, to see the work we have been doing. Café Europa is a credit to the island. Come tomorrow in the afternoon, my brother and his friends will be off swimming.'

'Yes,' he said, noting her perfume for the first time, 'I will come, thank you for asking.'

Hester nodded to Theophilus as she walked past his tiny office at the entrance of the town hall.

'I didn't know you were going to start talking about Malik,' she said as soon as they were outside.

'I didn't know you were going to seduce the Mayor,' said Sven.

'I have to keep him on side,' she said, 'not just now, but in the future. Also, I have a thing for decent, compliant men, and they've all let me down. This time, I thought, maybe I'll go for someone who starts out sleazy, then there'll be no disappointments.'

'Isn't this giving in to the enemy?' said Sven.

Hester looked contemplative, 'No, this is not so much a defeat, more a mutually beneficial alliance between previously warring partners.'

'I presume he's married,' said Sven.

'Yes, I was too once, and that never stopped anyone screwing my husbands,' she said, and pressed on the accelerator.

They returned to Café Europa, and a welcome so warm they might have successfully negotiated an EU treaty.

The Mayor looked out to the square and watched Hester's slim arse as she returned to the car. Alekos connected to the internet on a computer in a corner of the office. He looked up the Riksdag on this less than state-of-the-art machine; there in the list of members was Jan Ygeman, Social Democrat, born

1954.

'Of course, it could still be a scam,' said Alekos, 'they might have no connection to this man, I've never heard Sven speak of him.'

'I've thought of that,' said the Mayor, who was well versed in the guiles of the world and thought it possible they were bluffing. But they had come to him with friendship looking for a favour; they had not come threatening with bared teeth. He was gaining nothing by harassing a thriving business, he had already decided it would be too much trouble to take them to court. Yet if they felt they were being persecuted, in their resentment they just might start looking for an EU official to complain to. Not that he had anything to hide, but sometimes the situation was a little messy and did not bear too much outside examination. Staying friends with these xenie would be more advantageous in the long term; the Mayor pondered what he could get out of it.

'They want to be left alone, and they'll leave us alone – sounds like a good Greek trade-off to me,' the Mayor said, presenting this as the solution of considered statesmanship. 'I will go and visit her, take a look at this business.'

The damage they could do was potentially great, and the boons they wanted were few. The only thing in the way was Aspasia and he was thinking of retiring her: a mistress who is too demanding is no better than a wife. Also he'd hardly had any foreign women at all, if you didn't count Bulgarian whores. You saw all those foreign women around the island on beaches, on scooters and in cafes, with almost nothing on, swimming gear or shorts and bikini tops, and he wasn't getting any of it. Boys like Kostas were always in there. That wasn't fair, that just wasn't right. *Afto then einai sosto.* He was the Mayor, after all, some of that foreign pussy should be *his* pussy.

Back to business. He sped off to the new airport to celebrate completion of the penultimate phase. The building was now recognisable, with a control tower and departure lounge all complete except for the electrical wiring and fittings. The Mayor had invited the German contractors in and presented a cheque with all the pomp his office could muster. Now they were toasting each other on site with their hard hats and fluorescent jackets. The Mayor had one of his own with DIMARXOS in Cyrillic lettering on the back. He said a few words of fraternity, the Germans applauded politely, the islanders more vigorously.

The Mayor had invited Vasilios and a few other island notables. As the event wound down he leaned his head down towards Vasilios in a quiet corner, in a gesture that he wanted a word. 'That little refugee you mentioned,' he said, 'the one who had been hanging around with the xenie, I did as you said, I'm getting rid of him, sending him off to Athens.'

'Why thanks for that,' said Vasilios, 'I thought you said it couldn't be done.'

'Let's say an opening occurred, a favour, and I remembered your request. I will sort out the xenie, don't worry about them.'

'I wasn't worried,' Vasilios said flatly

'You know what I mean, cousin,' he said, but there was nothing in it for him to trade words with Vasilios. 'That Hester's a good sort, she doesn't want any trouble.'

'Yeah, that's what my friend Freddie says, fine by me. No problem.'

As they spoke, up on the hill Kostas was toying

with his garrotte, twisting it one way and another. It was a long wait, but he was there early enough, he knew Malik always went out on Tuesdays, sometime in the morning. Kostas was a professional, some things take time, like fishing. He may have had his faults, but he was not impatient.

His green truck stood on the lower track, it was part of the plan – finish the man off, then move the body quickly down the slope and into the back of the truck, cover it with canvas, get it away. There's got to be no sign of anything: no screams, no struggle, no blood, the body goes in the back of the truck. Simple.

In the compound Malik was busy collecting money and orders to go shopping. He was called into the office where the head guard, who liked the unshaven look, sat drinking coffee from tiny cups and smoking cigarettes. 'You have friends Mr Malik,' he said from behind a formica desk covered with buff folders and flimsy white paper forms, 'this is a release, it cancels the deportation order on you. You can go to Athens to appeal your rejection for asylum. You have missed the ferry today, you can stay here tonight. Tomorrow, you go.'

Malik received like a benediction the release paper and the leave to appeal the decision not to grant him asylum, which he did not know had been made. Now he had some new Greek papers; a white field of freedom opened up before him. He ran out to the compound to share his news.

Down the track Kostas stood breathing into the fir trees, going over and over again in his mind the steps of the execution. He had taken the care of a

325

craftsman over his positioning. There were not many places on the path where there was enough cover to shield him while his quarry passed, while also giving a view of the victim's approach. Kostas had carefully studied the mountain road, marked out the terrain, had practised his moves with an imaginary enemy. He would let him pass, then leap out, with the garrotte around his neck pulled as tightly as two strong arms could pull, no time to scream, no voice to shout out. Then drag him down the hill to the waiting vehicle, in the back before anyone could see, back to the warehouse and through the doors, take the body to the small jetty behind, just enough space for a tiny boat where weights and ropes were already waiting in preparation, to take the body out after midnight and drop it in the sea. Simple.

Malik left the office. He wanted to get away, to see the Café Europa crowd and to do his shopping, but after he told one person he was leaving then everyone seemed to know and they all wanted to talk to him to ask him for help or wish him luck or just to be part of the excitement, it was half an hour before he got away. He walked the path up and over the mountain, thinking he was doing it for the last time.

Kostas saw the little dot that was Malik on the track below. The refugee would follow the road snaking around and up to where Kostas stood among the trees. Now it was just a matter of waiting, his hands were comfortable on the garrotte's handles his face set in determination, it was just patience, slow breathing and self-control. Now he could hear the footsteps of the little Afghan approaching in the beaten earth of the track.

Malik quickened his pace, once even the minutes had stretched here on Doxos, the hours had gone on forever, now he wanted to pack as much as he could into the decreasing amount of available time here. He smartened pace to approach the turn in the road where the foliage grew dense for a time and gave a welcome cover from the sun. A sound rang out on the quiet path, a telephone – up here?

Malik looked up, turned the corner and saw Kostas, with a look of shocked surprise on his face. Malik nodded and hurried on. Kostas acted as if he had just been standing there waiting for a parade to pass or a sporting event to begin. He tried to still his palpitating heart and lifted the phone. Fuck! Why hadn't he turned it off? 'Yeah boss,' he said. 'No, not done yet. Call it off? OK, I'll call it off, I'm coming back to Kephali. See you.' Kostas stood there in his animal dismay at missing a kill. Still in shock, he went back to the van, fingering his redundant garrotte like a string of worry beads. As calm passed over him he realised he had been sweating with tension. In a way, it was a relief, really, not having to do all that stuff. What the hell? He had showed he was prepared to, that was man enough.

Oblivious that he had been in any danger, Malik walked on over the hill and down to Café Europa, to hug Sven and share his joy with his friends. They arranged to see him off tomorrow, and Sven booked his passage.

Finally Malik, alone with Anne, looked down the coast road towards Zeste, 'Got to tootle off, for the last time,' he said, 'buy these things for my customers, got to take care of business.'

'Customers?' Anne said, 'Those things you buy, phone cards, cigarettes, nappies...I thought you did it as a favour for the other refugees.'

'Yes,' said Malik, 'it is a favour, but it is also a business, they give me a little for helping them, easing the wheels of commerce, so to speak...'

'Oh, I see,' said Anne, who had thought her voluntary endeavours were matched by Malik's voluntarily going shopping for his co-detainees. It had not occurred to her that he was making a profit on every transaction.

'Can we go shopping now?' he asked.

'Not today,' she said, 'I have to work,' though this was not true, Sarah was on tables today. Anne had developed a distaste for acting as Malik's driver.

'No problem, I will walk round to Zeste,' he said, 'cheery-bye.'

She watched him walking along the coast road, not sure what she felt any more, and returned to the house.

Sven was on a break, talking to Anton at the front of the building, under the vines, now growing heavy with grapes.

'You've done well,' Anton said.

'I finally think I understand how things are around here,' he said, 'It is not that they lie but they have a different concept of the truth, the truth is what seems is best for them at that particular time, the idea of an objective truth that is the same for everyone is foreign to them. I don't know that I did well. Good, bad, well, not well – we are all trying to tease meaning out of the random accidents of our lives,' Sven said.

'If this is what lying does for your mental state, we'd better go back to the old Sven.'

'Don't mock me, Anton. You know it is said that life is a comedy for those who think and a tragedy for those who feel.'

'So I had better go on thinking,' said Anton, 'if I want to keep getting the laughs in. The alternative is less fun. Life has to go on.'

'Not everyone's life, how does it matter if I am not alive?'

Anton had the glimmerings of understanding here, and though he had no one to prompt him on what to do or say, he put his hand on Sven's shoulder, 'I don't want you to die,' he said, 'I want you to promise me you are not going to die, I'll be there for you.'

'Do you love me?' Sven asked.

'Yes, I love you man,' he said, hugging him briefly. Anton had developed empathy, perhaps at the level of a cat rather than a dog, but it was still there. Sven basked in the comfort of the lie; he had a reason to live.

Anne was watching from the upstairs window, catching the murmur of affectionate words.

'Tell me,' Anton said, 'why do you like me so much?'

'Because you are so different,' Sven said, 'so unusual.'

Anton smiled and nodded. It was time to get away. This was not what he had Sven for. Anton felt knowledge: creeping up on him, then leaping out from behind a curtain was the realisation that Sven was becoming one of the train-crash girlfriends.

Sven went off to the restaurant to get some work done, and Anton joined Anne upstairs in their room where she was folding up clothes. She looked across at him, and said what had been troubling her, 'What did Sven want, that seemed very intense?'

'Oh, he was talking about topping himself, wanted me to tell him I loved him.'

'Did you tell him?'

'Yes, of course. I didn't want a dead Swede on my hands,' Anton realised this was probably not the most sensitive remark he could make in the circumstances and said, 'If you'd been there, I am sure we would have handled it better.'

She was silent, then said, 'You going with Sven, the sex, where does it leave us?' Anton and Anne had not made love since his sexual encounter with Sven. Anne wasn't fastidious about these things, but somehow felt it had contaminated their relationship.

'It leaves us where we were before – I haven't plighted my troth, it was a one-afternoon stand. It motivated Sven to make the plan work. It was the right thing to do.'

'Do you love me?' she persisted, 'You never say it to *me*.'

The question for Anton was whether what he had with Anne was love. What independent test was there? Could he measure it against someone else's love, someone that he knew to be in love, and determine whether its PH balance was within the defined parameters? Where did you find this gold standard for love? The best evidence was that before trusted witnesses, at marriage ceremonies people in their right minds swore they loved each other and yet in half of these cases they would later divorce, making a somewhat less public declaration that they did not love each other, and in many of the unions those that did stay together were unfaithful or abusive. So where was the validity of the love declaration? What did it measure? If it could not be verified even under such open conditions, maybe it did not exist, maybe it was a self-delusion.

Anton judged it probably not exactly the right time to share these thoughts with Anne, but instead said, 'Actions speak louder than words – do excuse the cliché – I'll show you how I love you.'

He summoned the gift of erotic fluency to remove the few clothes she had on, lay her naked on the bed, face down and lifted her light brown hair to kiss the nape of her neck, he went over her body kissing the places which normally saw little affection: the back of her armpits, the crooks of her knees, the backs of her toes, the place where the curve of her pert bum met her upper thighs,. He rolled her over, delighted as always at the speed at which she melted under him.

Afterwards, they lay glistening in the sunlight. He said, 'I need to find a place to live next term, shall we move in together, would you like that?'

She snuggled close to him, 'What would you like?' she asked.

'I'd like that,' he said, 'can we have an ordinary life?'

'Yes,' she laughed showing her dimples, and ordinary was revealed in all its loveliness, 'we can have an ordinary life.'

If there was deception in their relationship, there was also a loving accommodation, if it was less than perfect, not a triumphal pageant of love, it was also not a train-crash.

On the afternoon of the following day the students gathered to see Malik off on his way to register with the Athens Police and make an appeal. There was little trade at Café Europa by this time in the season and Hester was expecting a gentleman caller in the form of the Mayor, so she wanted them out.

Sven and Sarah went on a scooter, to leave room in the car for Malik. They all arrived at the refugee compound, for the first time for everyone except Anne. Sven was shocked at how bare and miserable it was, at the rusting wire bars on the windows and the clusters of scrawny brown bodies.

'The Middle East is one big war zone,' said Sven, 'you can't help them all.'

'I helped one,' said Anne, 'one more than if I hadn't bothered.'

Sven had got Malik a ticket and gave him some money which Malik would accept only as a loan; Anne told Sven he had more than done his bit to ease the refugee crisis. Anne was still glowing with the happiness of her secure future with Anton when they all went with Malik down to the harbour. The shopping business troubled Anne, but she was also nursing another thought: Malik had not caused problems, the problems were there already, but telling Sven about Sarah, getting Anne herself to go down to Agios Nicholas that night, those were complications that Malik contributed. She took him to Kephali and that was her mistake, one that she would like to forget, and in that exercise of forgetting, too, his permanent absence was desirable. Anne was glad, in a way, that she had those experiences, for their educational value, but she did not want to be led into any more of them. Malik could make his own way.

When he emerged from the compound to the envious cheers of his compatriots, Anne noticed how he was so clearly better nourished and better dressed than they were. He was chattering happily as they drove to the ferry port, the wide, deep harbour beloved of the Phoenicians, the Romans, the Crusaders, the Turks, the Italians, the Nazis and finally the Greeks and their European Union partners.

They sat around the plastic tables eating kebab and chips and giving their little traveller words of encouragement. When the ferry appeared at the mouth of the harbour the others stayed back at the table to let Anne go forward with Malik to the jostling crowd.

'You are the first girl I have ever been friends with,' he said. She smiled, there wasn't an obvious answer to that. 'I have your telephone number, for when I get to England,' he continued.

'No,' she said without thinking, '...that's just a phone I bought in Greece because it's cheaper.' Immediately she realised she had left herself open to giving him her permanent, English number or refusing to do so. There was so much Anne had to learn about the world of deception. She hesitated, giving boys her telephone number was a big thing in her world. Malik too felt that – he had never asked a girl for her telephone number before. For Anne caring for refugees, even individual ones, was very different from having a telephone number relationship with them. It was her own number, only for special friends. Malik was part of the holiday. In her mind he belonged with the island, she didn't want him turning up on her doorstep in Biggleswade – or even in Brighton, especially since she would now be living with Anton. She had helped Malik on his way, that was her contribution. Her life was her own. She did not proffer a number, and he did not ask.

'I wanted to give you something,' she said, and tried to hand him a pink fifty Euro note, a large sum for her, representing many hours of work.

He smiled, motioning her to keep it, 'I am an Afghan,' he said, 'I work for money, I am not a beggar.'

'You weren't begging, you didn't ask, it is a present, please take it,' she said.

'No, thank you,' said Malik. She had wondered about this parting, whether she should lean over to kiss him on the cheek as she would any other friend, ones with whom she had shared far less than with Malik. He pre-empted this by extending his hand to shake, itself a gesture of some intimacy for him.

'Toodle-pip,' he said, 'I will never forget you.'

'Goodbye, good luck,' she said, and watched him board the ferry along with the crowds of Greeks and foreigners, the motor-cycles, back packs, cases and trucks.

Anne felt guilty, but also relieved at his departure, the moral basis of their relationship had been established: the chasm between their cultures was too great. No amount of good feeling between them was going to change that. Anne backed off as the seamen started to release the cables for the ferry, and fell into the arms of Anton who had come up to wave with the others.

'Malik will be fine,' he said, 'he's got the right combination of talents.'

'What?' she said.

'He's young and strong, but so are most of the immigrants. He's also good-humoured and adaptable. That means he can survive anywhere. It's like the plants, the one that will go on to procreate is the one that's pretty so it is attractive to bees, but also tough, so it is able to withstand a hard winter. Just being pretty or strong or being on good ground won't help. Both looking good *and* being resistant to cold and you'll pass your genes on.'

'Is that the way you see it,' Anne said, amused,

'scattering people across the continent like scattering seed on the ground, like in the parable?'

'Yes, I think there'll be lots of little Maliks in Europe in the future.'

'Just as well,' said Sarah, who had joined them. 'We need them to do the work we don't want to do.'

The steel door of the loading area slammed up shut, the ferry sounded its mournful hoot. Standing at the rail above the huge ferry doors, looking at his friends in the harbour, Malik was sad at the parting, sad to leave Doxos and Café Europa, sad at his awkward last moments with Anne. But with his irrepressible good humour, he reasoned that affairs of the heart often went awry, they did for Bertie Wooster and for Bingo Little with a host of nubile women. With this thought, the healing balm of literature did its work. He stood on the deck of the ferry, watching the island of Doxos recede as he, Malik, sailed on to a merry morrow. In Europe he would have a car and a house, and he would go on making stories.

There was a sense of finality about the departure of the little Afghan. It was happening at the end of the summer, the end of the university vacation, the end of the battle for Café Europa. Sarah slipped her arm around Sven's back as they watched the ferry plough on in a foamy streak until it was so far out it could no longer be distinguished from the sea. They walked back to the scooter while Anton and Anne went in the car, they were all off to the quiet western part of the island for a picnic, back on the long slide to happiness.

'Do you mind it that Anton and I have been ...affectionate towards each other?' Sven asked, when they were alone.

'Is *that* what you call it,' Sarah said, 'not gross indecency between males or the crime that can't be mentioned among Christians or...'

He stopped her, laughing, saying, 'No, none of those things. Just an expression of friendship.'

'Yes, I guess I've had that kind of friend,' she said.

'It's natural to express feelings that way.'

'You're going to tell me about the Trobriand islanders and the bonobo monkeys aren't you?' she said.

'You've got it,' he said.

'I like it that you are so predictable, I can see a bonobo monkey incident coming from a mile off. Look, Sven, I don't need the anthropology. I thought if there was going to be a future for us at all, you would have to go with someone, to even it up, so to speak.'

Sven had not in fact thought of there being a future for himself and Sarah, but he went along with this harmless line of reasoning. She looked directly at him, 'Sven, I want us to make up,' she said, 'I don't want to spend my last night on Doxos alone. Will you come in with me?'

He said slowly, 'I can't have the trust in you that I'd like, but I admire you. You are not truthful, but you have other qualities.'

'Maybe I don't want the truth,' she said, 'maybe I want stories we both believe in.' He was silent, absorbing this, 'Do you mind so much, ' she said, 'about not trusting me?'

'No not at all,' he said.

'Is that true?'

'No,' he said, 'I'm lying,' and they laughed and embraced like an old couple who understood without speaking, taking what tenderness they could, irrespective of motive. Maybe it was not a relationship that was going to endure, but at least they wouldn't be alone that night, and that was something. Today was a day to be writ in the annals of deeds that did not take place. Today was the day on which Malik was not assassinated; and Sven did not fulfil his existential destiny and commit suicide – not now, anyway, not on Doxos. Far away the European Union Referendum Bill passed its third reading, but none of the students were aware or commented on it.

The Mayor's blue Mercedes swept down from the town, through Agios Nicholas along the coast road to Zeste and on toward Café Europa. The Mayor had hoped to drive on past Aspasia's place but she happened to be outside her restaurant, delighted to see him making an impromptu visit. She welcomed him, literally opening her arms.

She was all smiles as he stopped, but he left the engine running. He got out of the car and said, 'No, my sweet, just passing.'

'Where are you going?' she asked, full of cruel realisation. There was only one place he could go on that road in that direction.

'I am going to see Hester, and her restaurant,' he said. Aspasia began a low hissing like a cat, 'I want to see for myself,' he said.

'What do you want to see? Didn't you order it to be closed?'

'It's not so simple, my sweet.' Of late the Mayor had noticed Aspasia's skin a little too sagging, wrinkles a little too deep, caught a sight of the weary looks she tried to conceal. 'There are regulations we have to keep to now, the government, the EU, everyone has a say now…'

'You cannot visit, you must close the place down,' she said. He shook his head as if regretfully.

'I know you fixed the deck to beat the Coastguard,' she spat.

'You what?' he asked, turning on her.

'I'll tell the Coastguard you fixed the game against him,' she said.

The Mayor did not take kindly to being threatened by anyone, and certainly not someone of Aspasia's social standing. His body stiffened and he said quietly. 'You understand, I know everyone's weakness, it is my job. My weakness is I am too generous, I want to give to people all the time. I have to guard against this. Your weakness is greed, which is why I am saying to you now: I will do nothing more for you. Whatever you have, you will want more. Do your worst. By the way, the Coastguard hasn't paid a cent, I let him off the whole debt. So what are you going to tell him? That he didn't have to pay what he hasn't had to pay? Do your worst, but remember, it was your establishment, if you knew cheating was taking place, you were responsible, got me?'

'It was my place,' shouted Aspasia, 'but you did it.'

'Yes, we used your place and you were paid for your work. I assumed you had a gambling licence, if you did not, you have committed an offence, you will have to pay a fine.' She gestured as if to spit, now both her stance and her face were showing her age. She was not a courtesan, even an ageing one – now she was a vindictive old woman. The Mayor got back into the cool car that was humming, waiting for him, and took off, shaking his head as if in sorrow.

Aspasia wept with rage, torn between murderous anger and the overwhelming sense that the only thing left was to beg, she must crawl on the ground pleading for him to take her back; but pride stiffened her figure: Aspasia had faced worse setbacks than this. She went back inside and paced about, making barely human sounds of fury. In a moment of relative calm she decided to storm out across there and make a scene, to surprise them, but what was the surprise? She knew what they would be doing, her misery was complete, and she abandoned herself to tears.

Hester took the Mayor's hand as soon as he arrived, and he held her round the waist as she showed him the restaurant and they ran through the necessary formalities of courtship, 'This is a lovely place...you have done so much work here...a tribute to the island.'

She took him upstairs. He walked behind her enjoying her slender body that was to him exotic, like a model, not like these mothers he'd been having. Hester put effort into pleasing him and he was satisfyingly enthusiastic. She noted his penis was not large, considering he was a big man, but he was eminently virile, hard and eager.

The Mayor sighed deeply with the satisfaction of entering a new woman. She raised her legs and inhaled as she felt his weight dominating her. She could get to like this.

'You must come and see me again,' she said, afterwards.

'Yes, I will come,' he said, 'and sometimes I will bring friends, we will play cards, in the winter when times are hard for restaurants, it's good business.'

She paused. 'Don't take that work away from Aspasia,' said Hester. 'Let her be your host for that, I'll look after the xenie who are staying on the island.'

'You are very generous,' the Mayor said, 'she has

not been your friend.'

'I know. I just don't want to take away my enemy's livelihood.'

'You are smart, that is the Greek in you,' he said, and they fell to talking about her parentage and where she had grown up.

He left and drove slowly round the island, waving benignly to friends as he passed. For the Mayor things were looking up – phase two of the airport finished, this foreign woman falling into his hand like ripe fruit. There was the big hole in the council's finances that would be found out, but not before the next election, and if he won that, he'd have years to sort it out.

He did not know how he was going to get through the next year, the next inspection, the next set of records, but something would turn up, he would trust to his loyal friends, to his supporters on the island to whom he had been so generous. He would trust to the form of the outside authorities – that they would be no more efficient in the future than they had been in the past. Tomorrow might be a day of reckoning, but today definitely was a day for good food, wine and companionship. Anyway, he could always bid for another big EU project, and he could pay off the airport with money from the new venture; there lay before him a future of endless opportunities.

It would not do him any harm at all to form a bond with a xenie woman, there were a lot of them now, and they looked as if they were here to stay. Being a successful leader meant ensuring his position of power not only now, but for tomorrow. This Hester was resourceful and well connected. She was in touch with all the other xenie, it would be a good idea to have them on his side, he must send out Alekos to make sure they were all eligible to vote. Democracy, he mused, is a wonderful thing, a great Greek invention.

Out at the warehouse in Kephali, with the sound of the sea in its diurnal washing at the same neck of land, Vasilios called Kostas into the office to give him his cut.

'Look, this is yours,' he said to Kostas, handing him a fat packet of money. Kostas reached out and Vasilios pulled it back, loosely dividing the bundle of notes. 'Here's half of it,' he said. 'You're going to give that to the xenie woman to say sorry. Don't even think about arguing, just do it.'

Very early the next morning Kostas parked a mile distant from Café Europa and clambered down the rocks to the beach, forgoing a cigarette to breathe the pure air, walking along the slippery rocks, with the seagulls settling to eat fresh sea debris then rising in a flapping flock at his approach.

In a way he was sorry he had not killed anyone, not directly, but he had been prepared to do so and that was enough. If he ever had to tell anyone, he could tell it as if he *had* done it, and that was as good. Anyway, killing or not killing, what did it matter really? It wasn't killing people that made a man, thought Kostas with newfound maturity, it was being calm, strong and steady like Vasilios, that was being a man. Kostas smarted from Vasilios's harsh lessons, but he knew he was right.

This morning he wanted to avoid the approach he had made before when he had gone overland, so he made his way carefully along the rocks. Eventually they gave way to pebbles, then to sand and the small stretch of the Café Europa beach. He walked through the tables and left the brown bag of notes he carried, holding it down with an empty retsina bottle he found there.

Sarah left Sven sleeping and went out on the balcony to greet the Doxos morning for the last time. Looking out to the beach she saw Kostas, the unmistakeable curly head and broad shoulders that she had adored. She wondered if she should run down and speak to him, but what for? And what was he leaving there? She just watched as he made his way back down the beach.

Kostas nodded to himself, didn't look up but walked away, now he pulled out his cigarettes from his pocket and slipped out a thin lighter from the packet, lit one and made his way back to the bike. He had, he felt, been through a lot for very little, but he was still there, still in the game. Summer would soon be over, there would be the period of exhaustion after the island closed down, then Christmas when life would brighten briefly. Then the winds and rain and everyone would sit indoors in thick woollen clothes until the firecrackers and feasting of Easter; and then would come another summer season. He had learned a lesson, he thought ruefully: in future he would not tell the foreign girls anything about island business.

The four students packed into the little car with their luggage and presents: jars of island honey, tins of olive oil, quarter-litre bottles of ouzo wrapped in Greek newspapers and bunches of the now ripe grapes, sweet produce of the Wendy House vine.

'It's been a hard year for you, sis,' said Anton, hugging Hester.

She had tears in her eyes, 'I have never felt so alive as when I was fighting these bastards with you,' she said, 'You are all welcome any time.'

She watched them roll along the coast road. After Agios Nicholas they would circle round and up to the airport. Freddie would drive her over to pick up the car later. Freddie's pretty wife Maria had been engaged to help Hester in the Café Europa kitchen. In future Hester would sleep with a gun in a bedside drawer, but she never felt the need to produce it.

There were high winds on their exit and the tiny plane was shaking, but they plunged on into the sky, flying back to the hard lands of the winter, saying goodbye to the island of the goddess Até who hurts all, and perfects all; goodbye to the Byzantine babble of words, the crusty food cooked in oil, the sharp, young wine, the impenetrably complex motives of the Doxonians.

They came down in Athens with a bump. There was the visible recovery of sophistication as they entered the marble halls of the airport and saw the businessmen with briefcases, the back-packers with their loads, the society ladies with their handbags made from the skins of exotic species.

The four flopped down in chairs to await the boarding call. Sven looked longingly at Anton. The object of his devotion had seen that sort of dumb adoration before: Anton thought he would not be seeing so much of Sven in the future.

'Our revels now are ended,' Anne said, 'and that was quite an experience. I suppose whatever doesn't kill you will make you stronger.'

'Says who?' asked Sarah.

'Says Nietzsche,' said Sven.

'He had syphilis, who's asking him for health advice?' said Anton.

Sven said, 'Europe: where everyone gets what they

want.'

'What? Lied to and buggered?' said Sarah merrily.

'Maybe it's just where everyone gets what they deserve,' said Anton. 'Well, we are all in one piece, ready for another adventure.'

'Anton you are classic,' said Sarah. 'Where are you, Anne?'

Sarah cast a hand in front of the small girl's pensive face. 'I was thinking,' Anne said, 'if they really had lunches to commemorate our deaths at the European Parliament...'

'Yeah?'

'What would have been on the menu?'

Notes

The migration of nationals from the north to the south of the European Union has been variously documented, generally by those who wished to retire there. The younger expatriate experience in Greece has been noted in This Way to Paradise: Dancing on the Tables by Willard Manus (Lycabettus Press, 1998) and in Vignettes of Modern Greece by Melissa Orme-Marmarelis (Cosmos Publishing 2004), both have been helpful in writing this book.

The massive and perilous migration from the East to Europe has left precious little record. I have found: Mohammed's Journey: A Refugee Diary by Anthony Robinson and Annemarie Young (Frances Lincoln, 2009) useful in attempting to come to terms with it. The best series of accounts is Embracing the Infidel: Stories of Muslim Migrants on the Journey West by Behzad Yaghmaian (Delacourte Press 2005). Also of value in the context of this book has been 'The Truth May be Bitter But it Must be Told': The Situation of Refugees in the Aegean and the Practices of the Greek Coast Guard (Pro Asyl, 2007).

The everyday contact with refugees that the Croydon-based charity Nightwatch has given me has been invaluable as has work with the Leros Solidarity Network.

In this book official business has been recounted as accurately as possible in keeping with a fictional work. I have ignored the role of the port police and have divided their functions between the coastguard and the town police with, it is hoped, no offence to overall veracity.

For specific research queries I gratefully thank the following, though all errors are my own: the sea Barry Faulkener; food hygiene Shayne Coulter; Greek language Eva Pylas; Swedish language Marie-Louise Ek; gambling Victoria Coren; refugees Anne Tsakyriou and Mo Ball; boats Sue Gibson; the text Bevis Hillier; structure Claire Luckham; conversation Francesca Peschier; dissimulation Zoë Russell-Stretten. Professional advice came from Diana Tyler and Fiona Barrows; the cover illustration was by Rupert Sutton and cover design assisted by Ian Lynch. General support, love and encouragement, as always, came from Julie Peakman.